The Legend of Swell Branch

- A NOVEL -

By
JR Collins

Produced by:
Dancing Rabbits Publishing

No part of this book may be reproduced or transmitted in any form or by any means, graphic, electronic, or mechanical, including photocopying, recording, taping, or by any informational storage retrieval system or by hand, without prior permission in writing from the publisher – Dancing Rabbits Publishing, LLC.
Legend of Swell Branch © 2020 all rights reserved by Joe R. Collins

www.jrcollinsauthor.com

This is a work of fiction. All of the characters, organizations and events portrayed in this novel are either products of the author's imagination or used fictitiously.

Book Cover designed by S. Johnson Gore.

Published in the United States of America.

– Author's Notes and Acknowledgements –

The simple phrase of "thank you" can have meaning as deep as the sea or as shallow as a dry creek bed. The folks I thank for this book need to know that I am most sincere in my appreciation. I give the glory to God for anything I write. Why He has given me the desire is yet to be known. Selfishly, it is my enjoyment of "spinning a yarn" that has led to my first four novels. This one being the first of a series I am calling, "The Longhunter Series." I look forward to the coming adventures as much as the characters I've created, maybe even more so. Take some time and sit a while. Read my story. You might just find yourself lost in the big woods at dusk or watching Old Man Sun rise from the tallest ridge of the great Southern Appalachian Mountains at dawn. Wherever you land while reading this book, I pray you will find it most intriguing. Take care and enjoy!

A special thanks to Mr. Tom Coleman III, Director, Savannah Theatre. Your insight was a breath of fresh air at a time when this author needed it. Structure is so important and your intellect is amazing. Take care my friend! I look forward to the next one!!

My most gracious appreciation goes out to my editor, Mrs. Colleen Harper. Thank you for being courageous enough to stand firm when it took a firm stand to make me see the light. Your grasp of my character's personalities and their dialect was inspiring and pivotal. Thank you for your patience and your talent.

A big shout out to Alex Collins Photography for the headshots. You are an amazing young man with a keen eye. Your talent shows through the work you do. Stay the trail and follow your dreams, Son, it will be interesting to see where God takes you.

Finally, and most gratefully, I want to thank the talented Mr. Andrew Knez Jr., for allowing me to use the digital image of his painting, "The Rifleman." It is a perfect fit for this story. His paintings are so amazing and lifelike. I hope to use some of the others as this series progresses. Thank you again, sir. It was sincerely special to me when you gave us permission to use it!

Now folks, after sixteen months of work, "The Legend of Swell Branch" is ready. Read slow at first to catch the dialect. I pray you have a wonderful experience. Until we meet again, God bless you and keep you… and thank you most kindly for your support!!!

Contents

Chapter 1: A Seasoned Warrior 9
Chapter 2: Unexpected Visitors 17
Chapter 3: My Savvy Sister 30
Chapter 4: A Trail for Mary 45
Chapter 5: We Make Our Escape 55
Chapter 6: A Time of Healing 68
Chapter 7: My First Killin' fer Purpose 78
Chapter 8: "Thou Shalt Not Steal" 89
Chapter 9: Blue Dove, the Healer 102
Chapter 10: A Way Home for the Dead 115
Chapter 11: Sky Watcher 127
Chapter 12: A Stranger in the House 141
Chapter 13: Bible Told Times 154
Chapter 14: A Trail to Henri's 167
Chapter 15: Calvary, My Secret Place in the Woods 178
Chapter 16: Mourning Comes 189
Chapter 17: My Mourning Time Ends 200
Chapter 18: The Bear Hair Sandy Gang 209
Chapter 19: Life Begins Without Dad 221

Chapter 20:	A Trail North Begins	230
Chapter 21:	A Need for Justice	240
Chapter 22:	Our Second Day on the North Trail	251
Chapter 23:	Rogues Come to Call	262
Chapter 24:	To Feel Death Close	272
Chapter 25:	A Cherokee Doctorin' Hospital	282
Chapter 26:	We Leave for Home, fer a Time	290
Chapter 27:	The North Trail Tavern	300
Chapter 28:	To Set a Maiden Free, the Rope	312
Chapter 29:	Justice for Gideon Swift and Sure	325
Chapter 30:	Home to Long Shot	339

The Longhunter Series

Book One

The Legend of Swell Branch

CHAPTER 1

A Seasoned Warrior

A war between the Federal government and the Confederacy of the South was nothing more than a worry the year I was born. The year of our Lord, 1849. At that time in history, one could not have imagined the great horror our young nation would commit upon itself a dozen or so years later. Those livin' in the South called it "The War of Northern Aggression." Those of history refer to it as "The Civil War." Well, I can tell ye, I never took no stock in their way 'a thinkin'. I seen the fightin' first-hand on numerous occasions, much closer than I ever should 'a been, really, me bein' so young and all. Some encounters I had was purely because of my curious nature, I suppose; but others, most likely, from the stubbornness I inherited through my ancestors. Got caught up in skirmishes more'n once because of bad fortune. I can testify, there ain't nothin' civil about war... nor the killin' it demands.

My family name is Whelan (Whay-lan). My Christian name was give to me by my granddad as Buach (Boo-ock), out 'a respect to the Old Country where my ancestors come from. It's an ancient Irish name which means "victor" or "conqueror," dependin' on what part 'a the country a body hails from. Most all I know'd called me "Boo." The Cherokee called me "Lone Eagle," after a time. I liked that name. It fit the way I come to live.

My folks and me lived on a big, long flat place called Long Shot Ridge. It laid just shy of the big ridges south, way back in the deep woods of the Southern Appalachian Mountains. Sat a ways above a little town called Swell Branch. Not far from where the Cherokee, the ones who survived the government forced removal by President Andrew Jackson, had found safe enough to gather and live. My father, Francis, kept a small farm on Long Shot. He grow'd enough to provide for me and my older siblings, all our stock. It was just the five of us livin' there bein' me, my sister Mary, two brothers, and Dad. Mom weren't with us when we moved to Long Shot. She'd gone to be with Jesus when I was little. I remember her goin'. First time I'd felt pure sadness. Her passin' made Dad cry, and even though I was little, I remember the pain I felt when I seen him cry… and for the reason what made him cry. It felt like a bad cut a body gets sometimes. The sting no different, just on the inside, where your soul lives. It was a rainy day, the day we buried her, cold.

All my folks was Christian. Lived a spirit filled life. Believed the Bible as truth. Know'd Christ was killed, then brought back to the livin' by God Himself to defeat death. We all believed in the power of His blood. Depended on Him for our take. Most mountain folk we called friends or neighbors believed in the power of the Blood same as us. Trusted in Holy Spirit for guidance. Depended on Him constant for that guidance… we lived in the wilderness.

I know some doubt His guidin', but if a body don't believe Holy Spirit can communicate with ye, they never met my grandma Dew. She talked to Him a right smart. Claimed He spoke back. I believed He did.

Grandma Dew could be plumb scary in her spiritual doin's. She'd often speak words from a language few ever hear. None know'd what them words meant when she'd speak 'em, but ever once in a while, Holy Spirit would reveal to a chosen the meaning of what she'd said. It was spine chillin' when the Lord's messages was made clear. She could be full on spooky durin' those times.

My kind, as most in the mountains, for sure the Indians, understood livin' in the spirit world. Lived life by its rules constant. Died by 'em on occasion. Many I know'd had visions. Natural among Appalachian folk. We never thought no different of a body if he or she come claimin' they'd had a vision. Most of us know'd how it felt to have one. Kind 'a like a dream when it come to you, but not really.

One could tell the difference in a sent vision from Holy Spirit and a simple dream what could be tainted by the evil one. Weren't hard to discern, if your heart was right. Now, visions didn't happen all that often, mind you, but they did happen. Most times the "dreams" would come as a warning, but other times for matters of the heart. A body is wise to pay mind to them kind 'a spiritual doin's when they come... and they will come.

Dad read the Good Book to us every day 'fore Momma died. Didn't read it as much after her passin', but out 'a respect for her, when I got older, I held strong to the Word fer purpose. Mary did, too. We had to commence readin' it on our own, though, 'cause Dad quit readin' to us after a time. I missed his readin's. Sometimes, if he was at our place to visit, it would be a friend of ours what read to us... a colored man folks called Uncle Silas. Claimed he was the only colored Confederate a body would ever meet. I understood how he could claim that, even though it was illegal for slaves to be Confederates by Southern law. How it was then, was the why of it.

Toward the end of the war, General Sherman tore the South's heart out on his march to the sea. While doing so, he let his troops destroy and pillage in whatever way they saw fit. Didn't matter who they had to kill, rape, torture, or take from to accomplish their chore. Total destruction of the South bein' their determined desire. They near achieved it. Some would say they did, as they scoured from place to place in their pillagin', leavin' destruction every place they found.

Uncle Silas, and others of his values, was forced to fight 'em when they come to the farm him and his lived on. He loved the plantation owner and his family, wanted to help 'em escape, but unfortunately, all but Silas and the other slaves was killed. At the end of his days, I heard him say he was proud to have claimed life ending blood from more'n one Yankee soldier what come to the farm that day, for sure since they was the particular ones what killed the owner whose farm he'd lived on all his natural put together. They killed the man's wife and daughters, too, while he and Uncle Silas, along with all the other slaves on the plantation, was made to watch. Them soldiers let Uncle Silas go as they left out. They didn't know he'd killed some 'a their own. Had they gained that knowledge, they'd a slayed him, too, right after guttin' and hangin' the farm owner.

Once the war ended, Uncle Silas headed for the deepest parts of the mountains to "answer the call of the Lord." He claimed that call was to go deep into the backwoods and preach the Gospel to any he could find. Outlaw settlers, renegade Indians, bandits hidin' from the law, common settlers stayin' away from folks at large, and runaways, lots 'a runaways. Them was the kind what lived where he traveled.

He become a circuit ridin' preacher of sort. Rode a fine stallion he called Zion. Claimed it was give to him by the owner of the plantation he'd lived on. Only problem with that claim was… it held a U.S. brand on its rump. He kept that covered most times with his sleepin' truck, but I'd seen it in the barn when he'd take the saddle off. I never questioned him over it. Weren't none 'a my business. It was a strong horse. Could ride all day and all night, if needed. I allowed Uncle Silas picked him because of that strength. It was clear to me he hadn't walked away from the plantation that terrible day on his own legs. I was sure he had four under him, and maybe four followin' on a lead, when he left… just after dark.

Uncle Silas would make it by our farm ever so often to "rest up from the weight of all the folks' sin I've been quarrelin' with," he'd say. Sometimes stayin' many days while doin' his restin' up. I liked it when he come. He'd tell us tales for hours concernin' his travels through the backwoods, the curious folk he'd meet. We'd sit out by the fire pit 'til late of a night listenin' to his tales, smokin' our pipes, warmin' ourselves, sippin' hot brandy, watchin' the skies for falling stars, listenin' to the far away songs of the wolves as they night hunted the big ridges south. Old Man Moon laid full. It was a good time fer 'em to hunt.

Dad liked Silas comin'. He'd help out around the place fer his keep. Most handy when it come to workin' a farm. Raised to it from a pup. He held proper in his faith, too. Laid strong in the Spirit, founded in what he allowed was a divine calling by God Himself. He never married or carried on with the lady folk, that I know'd about. It seem to me he took the Apostle Paul at his word on the doin's 'tween man and woman.

    Uncle Silas was faithful in his preachin'. Faithful like nobody you'll ever meet. Wouldn't speak one word of a sermon 'til he felt it "called of the Lord." That could be troublesome on folks' patience when he'd preach the yearly time of revival held every fall to give thanks. Some years we'd be waitin' four, maybe five days 'fore he'd finally feel the call and take off declarin' for the Lord. Oh, but them sermons was powerful. Went on for hours most times, for sure if Grandma Dew was there, praisin' the Lord in spirit with him. Why, I've seen Uncle Silas pass plumb out while shoutin' so hard at revival his lungs give out 'a air. He was dedicated to his callin'. I respected him a sight fer what he did. I couldn't 'a done it. I'd just as soon kilt many of the folks he held compassion for, outlaws like they was, and fer what they'd done, but, he weren't like me in his anger. No, he'd pray for folks what done wrong to him. Bein' that way was strange to me, fer I'd seen him on his knees for hours askin' favor from God for the soul of a certain person what'd been evil to him or others. Many times he'd fast for days while prayin' in the spirit for where to go search out lost souls. God don't make 'em like him no more. He could whoop you, too. Strong, and tough, like a pine knot. I'd seen him bend a mule shoe straight with his bare hands, usin' no heat. I liked that side of him. That side was more like me, bein' he claimed to be a soldier for the South, which was strange for a freed slave. I allowed due to his word that he'd shot his share 'a Federals. I was proud 'a that. He was my friend. I crossed paths with him out in the mountains many times. He was good to share a camp with.

    My older brothers fought in the war. Enlisted when the thing first started. Both took rifle wounds early on, dyin' 'fore the end of the first year 'a fightin'. Dad never got over that. Weakened him a sight. Me and Mary hurt deep, too. We loved our brothers. They was good to both of us all the time. Looked after her as a younger sister and as woman of the house. Taught me how to hunt, how to fish, and most importantly fer the times what come, how to fight. They were good men.

I was big and strong when I become old enough to be called a man. Bigger than both my brothers was when they went to war. I could near whoop 'em together at the time they left to go sign up. Their teachings carried me through many fights after the war's end. Fights where I could 'a been kilt, or worse, had they not looked out fer me durin' my growin' up years. I loved my brothers. Hated fer 'em to be took, but I did exactly what they would 'a done when the fight come to Swell Branch. I just wish they could 'a been there with me.

It was ex-Yankee soldiers what brought the fight. They homesteaded our farm on Long Shot while me and Mary was away. Four different families turns out. They'd come to figure the spoils of the South belonged to any and all from the North what felt like comin' down and takin' it. Many others what come felt the same. That thinkin' would bring 'em great trouble from those what didn't agree with it, and I was one of a few that would bring 'em that trouble. I made my mind, after seein' their intentions, that I'd not tolerate the evil what was comin'. I aimed to see our farm returned to its rightful living owners, too - my sister and me.

Fightin' for one's home and family, or fightin' for one's country, those are two separate things that can be locked together like rattlesnakes quarrelin' in matin' season. Hard to tell one from the other durin' the struggle. Clear as creek water in a drought once the end comes. The prize taken by the winner. From that forced reaping of Southern spoils, come the trouble I fought against for many years. Reconstruction they called it. Destruction and damnation was what I lived through. The new did come, it just took a long, bloody while.

A soldier has no choice in war. His is to kill or be killed. I wished that thinkin' would 'a stayed on the battlefield to die with the surrender, but it didn't. Southerners like me saw their share 'a fightin' and killin' for years after the war ended. The settling of postwar ways in the South required much conflict. This I grew to understand while livin' through it all. I learned to appreciate Uncle Silas' patience to duty and faith, by respecting the effort it took to stay in one's faith with all the wrong that was happening across the South in 1868. You could see how his need for God made him the man he'd become after the war. I had the same faith. Used it to keep the fear 'a death away. That made me a dangerous man to those who tried to wrong me or mine, for sure when the evil got to comin' down from the North in full.

The old timers could tell ye when meetin' a body whether that person was God fearin' or not. Uncle Silas could tell ye as well. I figured it fer spiritual. They'd read folks right off by how one carried themselves, by the words they spoke, their actions of respect. I was a God fearin' man throughout my whole put together. Let Holy Spirit guide me through the many struggles I faced, fightin' for those I felt obliged. The South come to be a most dangerous place after the war. Weren't no law that people could depend on. Folks had to fend for themselves. I did my best to help with that, considerin' the families I lived among. Many had suffered loss of both their men and their properties. After losin' my family to the fightin', both durin' the war and after, settlin' with heathens never bothered me. Folks said I got good at it. I didn't mind obligin' the call, when there was a circumstance to be made right. Kind 'a seemed natural with all the hate I run on. That hate, I come to learn and folks need to know, could be a weakness, if allowed to fester. I kept my hate tempered best I could.

The overall South was devasted once the war ended. All the killin' had taken a lot 'a men that called the Southern States home. Left a right smart 'a farms vulnerable to the taking. Fortunately, when the takers come for our place, my sister Mary was in Atlanta visiting our Aunt Catherine, my momma's sister, who lived there. Aunt Catherine was like a mother to me and Mary after Momma's passin'. She was special to us. I was fortunate in that I'd gone with my Cherokee friends, huntin' late winter hog meat on the big ridges south. We both survived the takin' of our place by not bein' there when the ex-Yankee soldiers come to do their thievin'. The problem was, and this made it much worse than losin' a home, Dad was there when they come... alone... and I know'd, no I feared, how he'd respond to the threat. That give me worry.

I guess all the loss and destruction changed me inside. Made me what I become, a seasoned warrior. My war commencin' the morning I come back to find strangers livin' on our farm. That kind 'a takin' was something I could not tolerate - I would not tolerate, for sure in the land I called home. Returning from a hunt to find our farm took sent me down a trail I'd not leave 'til it all settled out years later. The death of my family and the takin' of our place seen to that. I didn't feel it as revenge, no, I considered it honor, a return in sorts, of a kind. We'd worked long and hard makin' a home on Long Shot, and I meant to live out my days there, however many or few those turned out to be.

The Legend of Swell Branch

CHAPTER 2

Unexpected Visitors

The air was cool the morning I come home from hog huntin' with my Cherokee friends... to find our farm took. I had my mule, Gus, followin' on a lead. I always kept his lead in my left hand when out on trail, leavin' my right free for usin'. The right bein' my primary arm. All my travelin', campin' and huntin' truck was strapped to Gus' back with a braided leather cord what run across the top of the pack, then down under his belly. The tie bein' to his right side. Layin' bound on top 'a that was the meat of four whole hogs I was bringin' back. One full grow'd boar for sausage and three shoats fer fry meat. Me and my Cherokee friends was havin' us a prosperous time huntin' all the hogs we'd found recent. They was feedin' the winter on top of the big ridges to the south and east. I'd loaded my young mule with near all he could tote for the trail home, but he seemed to understand it was necessary. There was a danger of him fallin', bein' packed heavy like he was, so I decided to take a trail out to the main road. Use it to get back home on. Travelin' the main road would help the mule with his burden and make us better time, but it was more dangerous than the back trails.

All four hogs had been cleaned, washed, and the meat cuts took from the bone. That helped about the dead meat weight pushin' down on Gus, strainin' his back and legs. I'd gone ahead and sliced it into strips after takin' it from the bone. It was ready for washin' and hangin' in the smokehouse. Once it was hung, we'd let it cure for several days over constant smoke. Dad was home waitin' fer me.

We'd worked up our smokin' wood winter 'fore last, so he'd have that ready. Seasoned air-dried hickory made smoked meat taste best. Dried white oak was good, or maybe dogwood, but hickory was best for sure. Apple tree wood weren't bad, but we only ever cut but a precious few 'a them. We all liked apples.

Me and Gus' trail back to Long Shot had been slower than I'd figured it for, when first leavin' out from camp with the Cherokee that mornin'. We'd not made it as far down the trail as I'd wanted when I first noticed the afternoon changin' on toward evening. Gus was havin' to watch every step, seemed like. That'd slowed our trail some, but us and ours needed the meat, so I didn't mind takin' the time he needed. It was better leadin' him a little slower than riskin' him fallin' from leadin' him like I would on a normal trail. He could easily break a leg while totin' as heavy 'a load as he was carryin'. That would not do. I'd be without a mule, then, and mountain folk depended on their stock. I depended on Gus. Couldn't make it without him, or one like him for replacement.

The main valley road weren't no more'n a wide trail covered in leaves. There was sign a right smart of folks'd been usin' it recent. That had become common. Our way 'a life in the mountains was changing with the coming of the horde. I doubted it would ever go back to bein' the way it was when I was raised. Shame, that. It was the best way to live, mountain life… peaceful, and free.

I know'd it was risky takin' the main road, for concern I might run into bandits, but I was tryin' to make up for the slow time Gus was havin'. It was good for him, too, 'cause the walk was easier on the main road. Less chance 'a him stumblin' or fallin'. The back trails was steep in a lot 'a places. Risky for a heavy loaded mule to be travelin'. Risky for common folk to be usin'.

I was wantin' to get home 'fore dark in the worst way, and I was tired, so I felt a need to hurry. Gus was tired, too. I had to respect that. I hurt for some 'a Mary's home cookin'. I had to watch that pull didn't make me careless in handlin' Gus, but jerky and dried fruit get tiresome after livin' on it for several days. I was ready for some belly fillin' food, then a good swig or two from a jug 'a Dad's hard cider. Apple bein' my favorite. 'Company that with a good smoke and a warm fire, and, oh… my… goodness. Heaven come down for a mountain man like me.

It all got to soundin' so good in my head that I lost my thoughts to day dreamin'. I come to realize, after not movin' fer a minute, that me and Gus had stopped plumb still in the middle of the road. My face to the sky. My eyes closed. I could near taste the home cookin' I was longin' for. Could all but scent the sweetness of fresh baked buttermilk biscuits and sweet cake, so strong to the senses it made 'a body's mouth water. The comfort of an inside bed was gonna feel good, too, after sleepin' on the ground for several nights. Hard to beat a good feather stuffed bed for sleepin'. Had to be filled and stuffed proper, though, or you'd wake with your back hurtin' somethin' terrible.

The off trail from the main road to home was through the woods. Not as much danger to watch out for as the main road typically held. It was our personal trail. Dad and my brothers built it when I was just a pup. It ended at the edge of the woods what circled our log home, barns, pasture, and cornfields. If ever we seen anybody on that trail, we know'd they was either lost, or comin' to see us, good or bad, dependin'.

Dad cleared our homeplace so that our log home sat on a small rise to the south end of all he'd cleared. That made it so you could see a long ways to the east and to the north. A body didn't have that view west and south. Them directions laid in behind our place. That's where the steep was that ended Long Shot Ridge. The biggest of the mountains was on south 'a that.

Dad cleared the land circlin' our farm so he could keep our growin' fields up closer to the house. That made it easier to protect from critters and thieves. Only problem we ever had, other than the bad folks what got mixed in with them comin' from the North, was water. If rain held off for any length 'a time through spring, summer, or early fall, it put our crops in danger of dryin' up. We had a dug well, but it only provided enough water for our livin' essentials, and maybe the family garden up close to the house for a short time, if needed. That well never made enough water to save our field crops when the dry times come. Weren't dug fer it.

No, to save our fields of corn, it took a much bigger chore than simply goin' out to the house well and raisin' a bucket 'a fresh, cool water for drinkin' or washin'. Field crops required barrels of water to survive durin' a drought. Only way to provide that much water was to wagon it up from the closest source, Tiny Creek, and that flow was near a half-mile away, downhill. That made it uphill all the way back, and it had to be done 'fore daylight or Old Man Sun would drink it all dry as the day aged. Still, despite how hard it was on us and the stock, we did it. We had to, or lose our stores for not. If we didn't get the water to the fields, nothin' would grow. If the field corn didn't make through the growin' season, then the stock would most likely starve through the winter. We didn't have the fields to grow much hay. We'd make some each year, but not near enough to keep our stock alive durin' the cold time. A man and his family couldn't clear the amount 'a woods it takes to make enough stayin' hay to feed a common farm's stock for a winter. Corn growin' took a lot less ground fer what made, so folks in the mountains took to depending on corn to keep their stock from starvin', their jugs full. Only problem was, the corn had to be ground for feed. That was a whole other chore itself. Had to haul it all the way to Swell Branch for the gristmill there to grind it for us, but like totin' the water uphill durin' a drought, it had to be done.

Mountain folk couldn't make it without plowin' critters and travelin' critters like oxen, mules, and horses. Their lives depended on 'em for plantin' and harvestin' and travelin'. Had to have 'em fer goin' to market for sure. Survival in the Appalachian frontier was a vicious cycle mountain people understood and lived by. It was terrible hard work movin' all the water to keep our field crops from burnin' up, but neither us, nor the stock, ever went hungry. Dad always saw we had food. He allowed it was Holy Spirit what provided. He just did the earth work.

I'm not sure where the name Tiny Creek come from, 'cause it weren't no little creek at all. It was a good-sized flow with some big swimmin' holes formed by boulders what looked to be rolled down the valley and bunched up in different places. We'd swim in them holes when it got hot and a body needed coolin' down. Near all the

Cherokee lived south and east of Tiny Creek, 'cause to the south laid the big, steep ridges what protected the tribe from behind. There was a couple Cherokee who stayed around the village of Swell Branch a lot. Worked with the town folk for keep doin' different jobs like huntin' meat, tendin' stock, helpin' at the sawmill or gristmill, or doin' such as folks needed. I always figured 'em for tribal spies. A few more was spread out in the woods not far away keepin' small farms, but the bulk of the tribe lived south 'a Tiny Creek in what we all simply called "The Settlement." They felt safe in the solitude of where they'd found to live after the removal. Common travelers didn't wander as far back in the woods as Swell Branch, for sure Tiny Creek, 'cause it was even farther south.

 Another thing that helped keep the Cherokee stay hid was that the mountains in behind The Settlement laid mule face steep, makin' it difficult to walk over for men and animals. Weren't no trouble movin' along the tops, but the steeps off the sides was plumb dangerous to about anything with legs, 'cept them what was made for it like deer, cats, bears, wolves, and hogs. Them big ridges with their steep sides kept the Indians safe, for the most part. They had their share 'a troubles on occasion, but mostly folks just left 'em be whenever they learned of 'em. Dangerous to your person not to, really, 'cause they was a bait of 'em livin' back in there. They seen to each other, too. You angered one, you angered 'em all. That could be bad fer a body's well bein'.

 Swell Branch was too far from anything of value except privacy, so few come there lookin', that is, 'til the Northerners commenced trailin' south. Our little corner of the world weren't much for outside folks to desire. Didn't offer nothin' to make 'em wanna travel that far from the main road. Most folks comin' near to our part of the mountains weren't even aware that Swell Branch existed, 'til they found it. Hunters, mostly, some prospectors, a few settlers, woodsmen, the lot of 'em. They all respected the Cherokee's privacy and kept The Settlement secret when comin' to knowledge of it. I was happy fer that. We'd all come to know the place as home.

 The Cherokee know'd that's how it'd be when they started hidin' out there after all their troubles of 1838. The land south 'a

Tiny Creek was perfect for 'em. Many Cherokee found Tiny Creek by bein' guided by the Great Spirit through visions. They was a bait 'a Indians what lived back in there, too, but they stayed hid. More'n a body would figure for 'til you went there and seen it. I know'd several of 'em. My family lived in with 'em for many moons. Understand, we didn't really live with 'em, just in with 'em. Indian folk never trusted settlers complete after the removal. They tolerated us, but I don't think but a few ever become real friends with any settler folk much… except for those like me and my family, who the Indians learned was trustworthy, over time. My dad built that trust. I was actually trained by their tribe as a full warrior while we stayed with 'em followin' Momma's death. Honored among their ranks after I made manhood.

 I was trailin' home like usual, thinkin' all was good, when I stopped on a hill not far from our farm. There was an old white oak tree there we used as a lookout. Dad had fashioned footstep holes so a body could climb up about a third 'a the way to the top. From there, you could see the whole of our farm. We all made it a habit of stoppin' to climb that tree when comin' home from bein' gone. Standin' up in it was handy fer givin' the place a once over 'fore possibly walkin' in on a bad circumstance, or to catch a warning if trouble had come to a family member what needed help. One could never know what might 'a happened while they'd been gone. It's always better to be safe.

 I weren't familiar with the wagons I was seein' out in front of our barn. Nor the strange stock penned in our corral. Times had got dangerous around Swell Branch, with all the strangers trailin' through the mountains. A body needed to be careful. It was wise to guard your person constant when travelin' the local trails. Weren't uncommon to run into bad folk while usin' them trails, or as I'd just learned, for a body to come home to strangers on their property. I sat and watched for awhile. Evening was on us 'fore any come from the house. I watched for Dad.

 I know'd the wagons I was lookin' at. They was the Northern built kind like I'd seen durin' the war, but I didn't recognize any of the folks movin' about the place. Look to be they was doin' the late evening chores, and there was heavy cookstove smoke commencin' to draw out from the stone chimney of the cook room. It laid to the north side 'a the house. That was strange, fer Dad wouldn't need a fire that big to cook for just himself, and... why would these folks be doin' the late evening chores? We didn't need help with chores... unless Dad weren't able to do 'em, for whatever reason. My heart stopped for a beat or two when that thought come to me.

I watched hard all the ones I could see for a time, but Dad never come in sight. My soul sank as I got down from the tree to start figurin' what might 'a happened? Who them strangers was? Weren't like him not to help with the chores if folks was doin' 'em. Could be he was sick, but none I seen looked like the neighbors that would 'a come to his help if'n he was. No, looked to be strangers. Most likely from the North, judging from their wagons. I weren't likin' what I was feelin', what I was thinkin'. My blood got to heatin' while studyin' on it all. Strangers didn't need to be on our place like these was. Looked like they was livin' there. My spirit commenced to screamin' at me. It was tellin' me somethin' bad had come.

A heavy concern come on me after realizin' things weren't sittin' like they should 'a been when I got back, or at least like I expected 'em to be. Where was my father? Why hadn't I seen him durin' the time I'd been watchin'? Why weren't he out with the others? Who was cookin'? I had questions that needed answers; since it was lookin' like we might 'a been moved in on by homesteaders. Stood to reason they would be the ones what held the answers to my questions. That thinkin' got my anger to stirrin'.

A lot 'a mountain folk had been took from by folks trailin' to the South fer profit, both legal and illegal. Made me reach for my long knife when the realizin' of who these was come to mind, but I reasoned it was not the proper time to respond to 'em. It would be wise to stay calm. Scout out what was happenin'. Gather information. After my scoutin', I'd go talk to the strangers 'fore any settlin' that might need doin' was thought over. I'd learn for myself exactly what they had in mind by bein' on our place. It was important to know how many fightin' folks was there, too, 'fore I commenced to gettin' our farm shed 'a their presence.

I had no hankerin' for killin', but if this bunch had hurt my dad while tryin' to take our farm, my feelings would change quick. I'd never killed no folks before, not even durin' the war with what fightin' I'd got caught up in on the edges, but I weren't feared of the prospect. I would have no shortage of killin' desire, if what I was feelin' about the things I was seein' come true. Weren't nobody gonna homestead our place while I had breath in my body. We had papers provin' Dad bought where we lived on Long Shot. Paid for it with gold coin before the war ever started. Owned it fair and square from purchase. Signed by the man who first bought it after the Indians was moved out. It was all legal. Dad did not owe one dollar on Long Shot to nobody. No law could take it from us. The owner, what got it original, thought they might be gold somewhere about, but after findin' they weren't, he sold it to Dad for a lot less than he'd bought it for. It was a great place to grow up, and it was gonna be a great place for my family to live and die, too. I was gonna see to these folks if they was tryin' to move in and live. That would not do.

I decided to approach the strangers on the clever. Using caution like I'd learned from the Cherokee. I would stop by as one just passin' through, or a friend of the family. A traveler, maybe, lookin' for a meal like I might 'a got there before when passin' through. I had my keep about me, like I'd been out on a longhunter's trail. They shouldn't be too suspicious of my stoppin' in for a visit, or maybe a meal. I was dressed in my homespun and skins for travelin'. My possibles pouch slung under my left arm from over my right shoulder. All my campin' truck was packed on Gus, includin' my long rifle and two short guns. I'd leave him tied out in the woods so they'd not see him, then just go on in like I was familiar with the place. I would fetch my bedroll from my pack and sling it over my shoulder to look the part of a travelin' longhunter. I figured it best to have my rifle with me, but I didn't feel I should bring either short gun. Too threatenin' to my purpose fer bein' there.

The strangers didn't need to know who I was 'til I allowed the time was right, then I'd let 'em know, if what they was doin' called for it. For all I know'd at the time, this could be friends of my dad's just come for a visit. He was well known. Had a lot 'a friends I never know'd about 'til I'd meet 'em one day. Maybe that was what was happenin'? I didn't feel it in my spirit as bein' like that, but I had hope.

I worried for my dad. I'd watched from the white oak for a time and never saw him. I didn't see Mary or her horse, neither, that was good. I grew anxious, as fear worked its way up my back. Not fear of the takers I was lookin' at, no, they scared me little. I was feared for my family. Hopefully, Mary weren't back yet. She'd planned to stay with Aunt Catherine in Atlanta most of the winter. That was good, but I know'd the time for her return was near. If our farm had been took, she didn't need to be near the ones what took it. She was most pretty. Any available bucks would for sure notice her. That could be dangerous for them, 'cause Mary could defend herself, same as me. She carried a couple sharp little knives my brothers had made for her. She know'd how to use 'em, too. They'd seen to it. Teachin' her how to defend her person. I'd been with her when she'd used what my brothers had taught her. Both her blades had draw'd blood from such deservin' folk as she didn't want gettin' too close. A body had to be careful of mountain women. They was tough like boot leather, but soft as a pillow when feelin' compassion for loved ones and family. Most could shoot, too. Mary weren't no different. She was mountain to the core. Raised to it by Dad, just like me. She held favor with our Cherokee friends as well. That's why it shocked the folks of Swell Branch when she moved off to Atlanta to marry a storekeep kind 'a man from the North. That was something I never expected. She claimed that way 'a life made her happy. I was proud for her if it did. I couldn't 'a done it.

My first instinct, when reachin' the edge of the woods what surrounded our farm late that afternoon fer scoutin' purposes, was to go straight in. Introduce myself to the two men I seen splittin' firewood outside our woodshed, but concern for caution got the better of me, so I didn't. I eased back south, away from our farm, fetchin' Gus, and makin' a cold camp for the night not far off our home trail. I wanted to be able to see Mary if she happened to come by on her way home. I was hopin' to not see her, but she was due home anytime. That had become a fear for me. I'd come to realize it could be that evening as well as any other.

The night's camp would be a good time to pray. Study on the things I should ask the strangers when first meetin' 'em next mornin'. I would allow myself a small enough fire to light my pipe a few times. That would be a comfort. They'd not sense that little make 'a smoke. Sometimes it's the little things that are most pleasurable.

As the night aged, I come to realize truth. I would need to be ready to hold back any urge for revenge if the men said to my face things what seemed provokin'. For sure, if they was Federal soldiers. No different than the ones what'd been causin' folks trouble of late. I was only one, and even though I was strong, with size over many, I was still only one. They in total was eleven, that I'd seen. Two full grow'd men, three good-sized boys lookin' to be in age from about ten up to maybe fourteen, four grow'd women, and two girls - one maiden, one younger. That's all the folks I'd seen for sure. Could be more I'd not seen. That was something I'd need to pay mind for. My camp was gonna be a long one this night. Sleep would come late, if it come at all. My thinkin' was full.

The thoughts in my mind swarmed like mad hornets over a broke nest, as I lay in my bedroll tryin' to find sleep. I'd scraped up a thick pile 'a forest floor mast to sleep on for comfort. The rich, sweet scent so strong I near couldn't breathe. My dad's whereabouts, and the condition he was in, laid foremost in my thinkin'. I was near positive Mary was still with Aunt Catherine, so I weren't all that worried over her, but Dad would not like folks comin' in on him like these have. That was a strong worry, 'cause if they weren't friends, he'd most likely fight 'em. That could end up bad for him. These looked to be stout men, from what I'd seen while watchin' 'em do the evening chores. Dad was still weak in spirit from my brothers gettin' killed. His mourning had lasted for many moons. I got near sick with thinkin' on where he might be. What little sleep I got was a long time comin'.

Morning broke slow. I waited long as I could 'fore strappin' on my braided waist belt what held my long knife, then shoulderin' my Springfield rifle for the walk to our farm. I wore the handle of my knife forward, layin' over my left hip where it was easy to get at with my right hand, which was my main fightin' hand. I carried another knife, too. It's sheath held on by a tightly braided leather cord that strung from the braided belt in front at my right hip, then across my right shoulder, tyin' on to the belt again in back at my left hip. This sheath held a knife that, over time, become my favorite. No matter if carryin' it laced to my back or over my hip.

The blade weren't as long as a common long knife most folks carried for huntin' and skinnin', but it was long a plenty. Most never know'd I could use my left hand near same as my right, which come in handy for me many times over my life's walk. I kept the handle of my special knife just behind my left side with the blade run up my back a little. Handle turned down. A simple flip with my left thumb, to loose a small leather loop, and the blade would fall free to do its master's will in a short second. I worked hard for a long time, learnin' how to draw that knife fast. I could have it at a body's throat 'fore they ever know'd I was movin' my arm. Saved my hide a couple times when fightin' close up. The handle fit my hand perfect, too. It was gifted to me by an old Cherokee woman who'd lost her husband to mad sickness. She said the knife was special. Give to him by a knifemaker from the old times. The one who forged it claimed the blade was watched over by a spirit sent from the Great Creator. Claimed he seen the spirit come into it durin' its makin'. After carryin' it for over forty years, I come to believe that was true.

I was done waitin' to go check on my dad, our farm. Old Man Sun had been up for some time, so I decided to go on to the house and introduce myself in proper fashion to those what was there. I had no mind as to what was gonna happen. This was my first action since the war had ended several months earlier. We'd been hearin' about bad North folks comin' in, 'causin' trouble to a good many who lived closer into civilization, but out where we was, we'd had no call for fightin'… that is, 'til I went to meet our visitors that morning. I guess you could say the fight come to Swell Branch as I walked up to meet those, I'd suddenly come to realize from all I could see, was tryin' to homestead our place. That sudden knowledge punched me in the gut hard, but I never flinched as I walked on. This was turnin' bad.

The two men I'd watched the evening before met me just inside the front gate beside our herb and pepper garden. They was holdin' Yankee carbine calvary rifles, gripped by the handle in their right hands, the front stock layin' in the crook of their left elbows, shined like they'd just been oiled. It was clear to me, and any other soul from the South, that these men was ex-Federal fightin' men. They wore soldier blue pants with stripes down the side, leather boots and belt with the shiny buckle, and them funny little hats all soldiers from the North wore. Didn't keep the sun off your neck fer nothin'. Worthless, far as I was concerned. Their scent was different than Southern folk, too. That scent was strong comin' from them men's person. I had to hold steady my anger after comin' to know for sure who these was. I felt rage start risin' up my back, headin' for my shoulders, as everything settled in my mind. It burned hot as it crawled up my neck then down my arms. I near reached for my special knife when I felt that. My soul's desire to end these men where they stood, but I stayed calm. Almost friendly, really. That prob'ly saved my life.

Then something happened that near made my knees buckle. Made me draw in air on the quiet. I come close to losin' all the control I had over my doin's seein' it. In that one quick second, our little meeting turned dangerous for all that was there. Mad suddenly made my blood turn red hot. My fist clinched so hard I felt knuckles pop. Could feel my fingernails diggin' into palm meat. I could not believe what I was seein'. I hadn't allowed for this. Mary come walkin' from the house. Her face bruised. Her bottom lip swollen and split on the right side. Her ridin' skirt torn. Blood dried thick what'd leaked from just above her right eye and mouth, with some of her long hair, what was matted up hangin' about her face, mixed in with it. Seein' her hurt was more'n I could stand. I would kill whoever did that to her, and I figured I was standin' in amongst 'em, but I had to stay calm. I forced myself to stay calm. Took all I had, but I know'd these men would shoot me and Mary both if they figured out who we was. Then, if we was dead, they'd be nobody left to lay claim to the place. They could homestead it free and clear. Near legal they'd call it. I weren't gonna let that happen. I would see this made right.

I couldn't let my bein' mad at seein' Mary show. My warrior training would help with that.

She come on out the front door and across the porch to the front edge without doin' one thing to make them folks figure she know'd me, or me her. She had good sense about her person when danger was near. Dad had taught her well. It was a shock to find out she was there. The look on what I could see of her paled face, cold. She'd been through a tough time, that was obvious. I still didn't see Dad. Maybe Mary know'd where he was. Somehow, I would need to talk to her, if she could talk. The right side of her face was in a bad way. Her head lay droopin' to that side. Her hair dirty and matted. I hurt from how she looked.

THE LEGEND OF SWELL BRANCH

CHAPTER 3

MY SAVVY SISTER

Mary was hurtin'. That was obvious. Had her arms crossed tight around her middle like she was holdin' in pain. They'd most likely kicked her while she was down, or maybe punched her. She stood slumpin' from the waist at the edge of the porch like it was too painful to stand straight. Her hair matted, hangin' wild about her head. Looked to be she'd used it to wipe the blood from her eye and mouth, way it was matted. From what I could see of her face, she weren't lettin' on at all that she even know'd what day it was. Just kind 'a starin' down at the porch boards. I could hardly see the left side of her face under all the matted-up hair coverin' it, but I could see the right side. It was bruised and swollen. The right corner of her mouth looked to 'a been leakin' blood not too long 'fore I'd got there. Her right eye was swole plumb shut. A purple knot in the upper eyelid what looked like a ripe cherry ready for plucking. I felt a deep hurt for her standin' there on weak legs, kind 'a wobblin'. Like she was ready to fall over. Pitiful lookin' for her, strong as I know'd her to be.

Then, of a sudden, without a bit 'a warning, her body took a spasm what seemed to go through her whole being, jerkin' her up straight-back stiff. She moaned out loud when that happened, then throw'd her head back far as she could like she was tryin' to stretch out her front. Her arms went to flailin' toward Heaven while her legs did a kind 'a wobbly dance without her feet movin'. She was a sight. Then, just as quick, she went right back to bein' slumped over again. Her arms crossed over her middle same as they was before the spasm. Everybody had turned to look at her, includin' me. I realized then, that's why she'd done it. Get the folks' attention so I could look closer at her person without the takers knowin'. She'd done that fer purpose. It come to me then, she needed me to see her.

Without the strangers knowin' I was payin' mind, I stared harder at her with concern. I seen her left eye lookin' out at me kind 'a hateful 'tween two tangles of matted hair. I come near to lettin' out a semblance of knowin', when I realized she recognized me. That would not 'a done. The ol' boy in front of me would 'a for sure seen that I know'd Mary then. He'd acted accordingly without hesitation. I willed myself to keep my mind. I never reacted, that he saw.

The look her eye was holdin' made me think she was scared, but I know'd that weren't right. She feared little. I started to wonder if her mind was bruised from the beating she'd got, 'cause 'a the way she was lookin' at me with her one good eye. That maybe they'd hurt her that bad, but no, that weren't it. After a second or two of us starin' at each other, I caught the slightest of winks from her left eye. The left corner of her mouth broke into a sickly little grin that she made sure only I could see. I loved my sister.

My soul jumped when I first picked up on her lookin' at me. She'd made sure nobody saw but me, as was her intent. She seen I saw her grinnin', too, as was her intent. My steadiness returned. I was proud to see she weren't hurt as bad as she looked. Her communicatin' like that let me know she was playin' 'possum with the ignorant takers. Goin' on like they'd hurt her worse than they had. I would pay mind to her goin' on's for more 'a them signals, while prayin' the takers didn't catch on that we know'd one another.

These happenin's me and Mary was caught up in had a most uncomfortable feel to 'em for me. No folks, 'cept for Dad, seen to what I'd been doin' for the last couple years. I lived free like the Cherokee. Only time I was required to lot out, was the time our farm would need my hand. Dad know'd he could depend on me for work - be it spring plantin', fall harvest, any preparin' of the ground, or farm work in-between. I know'd what to do and when to do it, and I did it. I could be depended on. Dad know'd that. Weren't never a need to be told what to do by nobody, be it farmin' or livin'. At least, that's how I lived once I got old enough to be responsible for my own doin's. I for sure weren't gonna take no commands from the likes 'a them thieves what'd took my home.

Still, and it worried me a sight, they had a hold on me 'cause 'a Mary. I weren't likin' it none, but they did. I made my mind, as I walked toward our farm that morning, not to forget one thing that happened durin' my visit, or anything I learned while in their company. As I got to speakin', I seen a couple of our good layin' hens was missin' from the pen. I would remember that, too, when it come time to settle things proper.

"Good morning, friend," I said, as the biggest of the two men stopped me, center the trail what led to our house. The barrel of his rifle laid solid in the crook of his left arm. His right hand held to the walnut butt stock handle. There was purpose to him holdin' it like that. If needed, he could slap me upside the head with the cold steel of its barrel 'fore I ever seen it comin'. I'd been taught to recognize that danger. I know'd trained soldiers fought in them kind 'a ways. I'd need to be watchful for any other tricks he might set himself for… his mate, too, what'd slipped over beside me. I could still see him from the corner of my right eye. He had his carbine in the crook of his left arm as well, but I never took my stare from the man in front, nor he me. He was the leader. He's the one I needed to be talkin' to. Weren't hard to cipher that.

"I am not your friend, boy," he kind 'a growled back while studyin' me hard. "Tell us your purpose, mountain man. You come here for a reason? Lost your way? Searchin' for a meal, maybe? You look mighty pale. Ain't eat in a while? Or… could be… you're returning from somewhere Indians go. You look like you might know some Indians. Oh! I know! A journey to the "spirit world," maybe? That's what Indians do, right? Yeah, that's it!" finishin' them words with a big grin 'fore startin' back in on me.

"Well, I'll be. Now ain't that something. 'Cept for the color of your skin, I believe you could be just that, Indian. You got the hair and all! Is that it, huh, boy? You been traveling in the "spirit world" recent? Running with Indians while doing all them heathen spiritual things?" Both takers turned to each other, laughin' out hard. That made his mate commence to coughin' all nasty like. Sounded so bad I looked to see if he was blowin' blood out from his mouth or nose. Made him seem sickly to me. I began seein' in my mind ways to end his sufferin'. Out 'a compassion, of course.

"Or, on the sly," the big one kept on, "have you come here to claim this place as bein' yours? Like this girl did a couple days ago?" he asked, while turnin' toward Mary, then back to me. Him sayin' that was a shock to my reckoning. Near caught me by surprise. "We had to teach her a thing or two about respecting her elders. She tried to cut my friend Walter here with her hid little knives. We found 'em, both of 'em. She won't cut no more with them knives." He smiled all nasty at me.

Mary and I caught eyes, best we could, after he said those things about her tryin' to cut one of 'em. The weak little smile still showin' in the left corner of her mouth. I felt, as much as saw, a slight wobble of her head back and forth, while she made sure to keep her good eye locked with mine. That told me right off not to try anything with this bunch. She'd been with 'em for a time. She know'd what was goin' on, I didn't. I allowed it wise to pay mind to her newfound wisdom.

Looked to me they'd hurt her some. That was obvious. Slapped her around a little, maybe. I doubted they'd forced her with all the women folk and kids there. She weren't full-on herself for sure, no, but she weren't as weak as she was makin' the takers think. That was good. Might be able to use that to help free her later on.

I needed to be smart, or me and Mary both would end up bein' held by these I was comin' to hate so. I backed up a step from the big one. Rested my rifle's butt on the ground at my feet. Crossed my left forearm over the end of the barrel, restin' it there so that my right arm could lay on top as I settled my legs fer standin'. I could easily grab my long knife from that position. The look on the big one's face told me he'd picked up on my intentions as I took my stance and looked back at him. I spoke as calm as I could when answerin' his stupid questions, which I didn't answer right off, they irritated me so. We stared at one another for a short minute 'fore I spoke back to him. I had to hold back calmly what I really wanted to say.

"You folks ain't from around here, are ye?" I asked, clearly but still calmly. "I can hear from how you say your words that y'all are from up north. Am I right? Most likely finished up soldierin' when the war ended. Decided to come south for profit like so many others you know, or have heard of… yes? Tell me true, old man. Am I right?"

"That's none of your concern," he said, kind 'a mean like while studyin' me a little tighter. "I'm gonna ask you one more time. What is it you want here? Me and Walter got work to do. Your visit is interrupting our morning. Time's wasting standing here jabberin' on with you. Say what you need and move on, or we'll have to move you on. Hear? Boy?" He finished sayin' all that as a heavy anger wrinkled the place between his eyes. I saw no fear there. He would see none in mine.

"No reason to get riled, newcomer. I mean you no threat. Just stopped by to see my ol' buddy Francis. He's the one what owned this farm last I was through here. I try and get by ever now and again to catch up. I ain't been by in a while, with all that's been goin' on with you folks from the North." I stared him a minute 'fore speakin' on. Me sayin' that raised his blood. "That's what I was wantin'. Just stoppin' by fer a visit."

Me and him stared each other hard after what I'd said to him. Gettin' tired of all that starin', I turned my head slightly to lock eyes with Walter, as I'd just come to meet him. I nodded slightly 'fore lookin' back to the big one to continue our conversin'.

"Is he here? My friend Francis? I was hoping he would be. I mean no disrespect to you and yours, but I need to speak with him. I got news he'll be wantin' to share over a jug. I live some ten miles north, down closer to the river. Me and my dad keep a farm there. He sent word as well. Him and Francis are friends from years back, but Dad can't travel this far no more. The night air is hard on him when campin'. I hope I ain't trailed all this way fer him not to be here. Have you seen him since y'all been visiting? If he was here when y'all come, did he say anything about goin' out on trail? Gone huntin', maybe? If so, is he due back soon? I could wait a couple days if you think he might be back 'fore too long. I ain't in no hurry."

"I do not know this Francis. Nobody was here when we came. We searched all around. Place seemed abandoned. Didn't look like anybody had been living here for some time, but then this girl wanders in. Claims this place as hers. Told us her pappy bought it years ago, but she's got no proof. Can't find no proof about the place. So, who would know? You, boy?" He changed his look to a more curious kind 'a wonderin' look as he finished speakin'.

I know'd that as a possible danger look. I'd seen one like it before. I would needs be extra careful and not move to fight back with that carbine handy like it was. I watched him close as he commenced speakin' again. His look changed to mad.

"You wouldn't be claiming likewise yourself, now would you? One thing we need to be clear on - we are not visiting here on this farm. We aim to homestead. We're gonna live here," he said, while him and Walter both leveled their rifles at my chest on the quick.

Them guns got my attention, as my blood rose 'bout as high as it could from hearin' their true intentions. I had to stay calm on the outside, no matter how hot I was on the inside. They was homesteaders. Their aim was to take our home. My previous notions had been correct. That told me what'd most likely happened to my father. They couldn't homestead with him in the way. He'd not allow it.

"Now boy, say if you know this girl to be the owner of this farm, because we mean to stay here. We like it. Our families like it. What say ye? Tell me now!" he yelled, on the edge of out of control.

I couldn't dare say the things I wanted to say. Couldn't do the things I wanted to do. In my mind, I could see my special knife centered in his chest handle deep. A look of shock on his face, but that weren't gonna be real life fer a time. Them thoughts would get me and Mary dead real fast if I made 'em known. I had to watch my tongue. Be careful how I answered. How I reacted. They was watchin' my face for signs of deceit. I could not flinch in my emotions. That was hard to do at that particular time, bein' they was two heavy bore Spencer carbine rifles pointed at my middle. I did not like the way that felt. Those two guns goin' off together would cut me in two. That'd do Mary no good, but, as it stood, she'd most likely be kilt sometime over the next few days anyhow, if I didn't get her out from bein' their captive 'fore they took to their murderin' chore.

I spoke with a surprising calm I didn't realize I possessed until that day. I would use that calm many times in my life from then on. The Great Spirit has strange ways 'a showin' us things about ourselves when He needs us to know. Folks should pay mind to His voice. Our spirit battle rages constant.

"What? Me? No sir. I got no claim to this place. Like I told you, I live down in the valley near the river. As for her, I been here a few times. I ain't never seen a pretty thing like that runnin' 'round here, or I'd 'a been back more recent. I can honestly tell you that. He must 'a kept her hid if she's his. I know Francis as a widower. Lost his wife a few years ago. If you find any womanly things in there, they's prob'ly hers. It struck him hard, her leavin'. Wouldn't prove that girl yonder one way or the other, so I'd not figure her fer claimin'.

They was a couple boys, but he told me a story 'bout how they was both killed at the first of the war. Never know'd 'a no daughters. He never spoke of any. Far as I ever seen, they was just the three what lived here. Francis and his two sons. That's all I know. I keep my own place north. I like it down on the flats around the river bottoms, not perched up here on these big windy ridges miles from nowhere."

The men both stared me hard. I held solid. I figured they was makin' sure they believed I was speakin' truth about not havin' a claim to the place. They had no call to not believe me, but Mary's claim could be founded. They might 'a believed her. Most likely found some girl stuff around on the inside. I couldn't be sure. That's why I said those things about Momma. I had all my possibles with me. Any I'd left inside could 'a been Dad's easy as they was mine. They weren't anything in there that would connect me to my family that the takers would know. I lived there very little anymore.

The look on their faces said they was believin' me. I took that as a good sign to get gone from there while they kept contemplating what I'd said. I spoke calmly again 'fore they could say anything or ask any more questions I'd have to answer. I did not want either one 'a them gettin' an itchy feelin' in their shootin' finger, lettin' go with one or both 'a them carbines on accident.

"I've bothered y'all enough," I said, as I shouldered my rifle's sling while turnin' to walk east. "Time to be on my way. I wanna stop in to visit some of my Cherokee warrior brothers 'fore leavin' for home. Maybe we'll take us a trip to the "spirit world," hey? You're right, soldier man, I do know me some Indians. Call several of their warriors family," I said with a grin as I kind 'a stopped to look back at the two men. The big one looked almost scared. I kept on.

"You folks do as you will. I got no feelin' for this place. I would like to know where Francis is, though. I believe I'll scout around some. See if I can find where he might 'a left out from here. It ain't rained in a few days. I should be able to locate where he made trail. I'll not pester you folks no more… uh… 'cept for one thing. Now, I ain't tellin' you what to do, and you'll do as you see fit I'm sure, but I believe I'd see to that girl y'all got there. Looks like she's hurtin'. Might need doctorin' attention from the beatin' somebody's give her. You don't want her dyin' on ye. She's prob'ly got folks up in these mountains. They'd not take too kindly to hearin' she'd been killed by the likes 'a y'all. I'll be goin' through to the Cherokee land with the next sun. Want I should take her with me? Leave her with them fer doctorin' purposes? I don't mind. Get her out from your homesteadin' work. They might even buy her for a slave. Now, what say ye? Take me up on my offer to rid you of her?"

"All right now, boy," the big one said, all fed up like. He cocked the hammer on his Spencer. Walter did the same. That cockin' sound speaks a lot 'a words when you hear it up close like I was. "I'm not listening to no more of your talk. We all know this Francis ain't here. I'm telling you the girl is staying. No reason for you to be here any longer. It's time you moved on. Whether we stay here or not, is none of your concern. Like I said before, we got things to do. I will watch for this Francis to return. If he does, we'll make him a fair offer for his farm and holdings. Now, get going. I'm done talking with you boy. Be gone from here." He waved the point of his gun back to the east. Smiled a nasty smile showin' several black teeth. That was disgusting to me.

One thing that got my attention for sure that morning, as the two men come to the front gate to meet me, was that these comin' folks was dirty. It appeared they didn't wash like mountain folk and Cherokee did. We kept ourselves clean so our scent would stay down. These folks show'd filth on their skin and clothes top to bottom. You could see clear it'd been a while since the two I was facin' had washed. Smelled that way, too. Bein' that these was the first Northerners I'd ever met up close to converse with, outside 'a fightin' men, which couldn't help but be dirty, got me to wonderin' if all their kind carried themselves in filth. I hoped that weren't the way, but even with these, their women was nasty. I'd scented 'em when the breeze shifted ever so often while we stood talkin'. Near soured my stomach with their stench. You never come across Cherokee folk or smelled Cherokee women what stunk like them did. Most settler women, neither.

I didn't like none of any I seen that morning. Three women and the two ex-soldiers was all what show'd themselves. Never seen the young ones. I allowed they was hid, 'cause I'd seen a few when lookin' down from the old white oak day before. The older of them kids prob'ly had a rifle rested at my middle from wherever his hidin' place was. Ready to pull the trigger if I made a hint of a wrong move, which I had no plans on doin'.

East was the direction I wanted to go. A quick look to Mary told her I'd be back. I saw the slight smile rise again from the left corner of her mouth as she drooped her head even more to the right. The right side of her face did not work. These would pay for that after a time, but the first thing I had do was free her, and for that, I'd come to realize after talkin' with the takers, I would need some help. It weren't a chore one should do alone. The risk to Mary would be much less with two of us going. Still, she had to be got out. If I had no help, then what would be would be.

I know'd just where to get the help I would need. A Cherokee friend I'd not hesitate to call on. His name was Henri. A body I'd trusted with my life many times throughout our days. A man I'd know'd since I was a young boy. He weren't a man then, but he'd grow'd. He was family, in consideration. His granddad and my granddad was the best of friends. His dad got killed durin' the Indian

Removal fightin' for his family. Give his life for his loved ones. That sacrifice let Henri escape into the mountains with some of his kin without bein' found out. Many that escaped with him had long since moved on leavin' the mountains for the west, but Henri loved his home. Stayed in the Appalachian Mountains where his heart was. I was proud he did. Me and him had become closer than most family over the last few years.

His place weren't far to the east. He would help me, if he was home. If not, then just me, Gus, and Holy Spirit would make it work. Through life or death, one way or the other, Mary would be free soon… of that, I had no doubt. I hoped, without much thought, to take the big one out as well. I never liked bein' called "boy." I would tell him so, when the time come I could.

As I was turnin' to leave, I seen one of the womenfolk grab Mary by the arm, shovin' her hard back into the house. I heard my sister grunt as she hit the plank floor on the inside of our log home. *Even their women was mean,* I remember thinkin'. Could be it was one 'a them what'd hurt her original. The thought come to me that I may have to settle with some of the womenfolk as well. That bothered me little as I walked away. To me, they was all the takin' kind 'a folk. That made 'em enemies to me and those they took from. I would treat 'em as such.

I had no reserve about killin' any one 'a them women for bein' hateful to Mary… for sure, if theirs had a hand in sending Dad to be with the ancestors. That thought struck me hard. I had to sit for a minute after I got into the woods 'a ways. Pray to Holy Spirit for comfort. I loved my father.

***

To say I had a good friend in Henri, would not give proper justice to just how good a friend, and how good a person, he was. His mother had named him Henri, after his father, who was a member of the French military. This French soldier had abandoned Henri's full blood Cherokee mother on orders from his commander to return home. The Turtle Clan took watch over him and his mother after the soldier never come back. The warriors raised Henri from the time he was a pup. Through visions the elders had many times over the years, the call of his spirit was set. Through their wisdom in understanding those visions, they taught him all the old Cherokee traditions. They taught him plants for healin' sickness, ailments, and wound care. Showed him how to fight proper for defense or for killin'. Under their holy fold, he learned religious ceremonies that tendered the ancestors for guidance. I never took to hearin' from the ancestors, but the Cherokee did. I'd been around Henri when he'd talk to 'em. Made a body uncomfortable what didn't know what was happening. Some 'a their kind 'a religion could get plumb spooky with all the paintin' up and outfits they'd wear, most likely caused by the things they would drink or smoke or eat. Some 'a their visions was created, yes, but others natural. There was a difference in the two, for sure. The elders could discern that difference. You couldn't fool them with a fake vision. They'd get mad if you tried. Could cost you your life if they felt it was evil spirits tryin' to leave messages in false visions. Messin' around in the spirit world without knowin' what you're doin' is most dangerous. Ignorance is dangerous as a whole around Indians.

All that may not make sense to those what lived outside the mountains, but Indians have a different connection to the spirit world than most folks. Somehow, through that connection, they understood about Henri. The spirit world wanted him guided toward the kind 'a warrior he needed to turn out to be, so they raised him accordingly. Marked him as such. The visions showed the elders which warrior should prepare him for certain aspects of his life's journey. They did a good job with his upbringing, trained him whole just like the spirits had guided. Only problem was, and it was a big problem for the tribe, he didn't cotton to it full on. He come to be the most respected warrior in all the tribe, but as that, had absolutely the least to do with it as any warrior there once becoming an adult. After he passed to manhood, where he could make his own mind, he moved to a cave he'd found a few miles east of The Settlement. He'd had to dig it out some to make it big enough to stay in. Later, he added a three-room log home in front of it with a huge fireplace right in the middle. Had a circle hearth all the way around it. I loved that fireplace.

Henri was a prized servant to the Cherokee, and to any what lived in the mountains, if he trusted you. He was different than most warriors in that he was able to calmly harness his anger through his spirit, same as his fears, for strength, when needed. You'd not know which you was bein' sided with 'til he made it known to your person. All that make up to his soul made his life unusual among the Cherokee, and they treated him as such. Me and Mary was his friends, as far as he had any friends. He stayed in the mountains to himself mostly, hid. The tribe was so concerned for him they pestered him if they know'd where he was. They felt he belonged to them and theirs after the raisin' he'd been given. They saw his life as a kind 'a gift from them to the spirit world, but he wanted nothin' to do with it. His spirit only cared for freedom. They kind 'a held that against him in certain ways but commenced to leavin' him be. They welcomed him to the main camp anytime he wanted to visit.

Henri taught me much. Helped me when I needed, as I did fer him. I believed all my growin' up years they weren't nothin' he couldn't do. His courage had roots deep in his bein'. That makes for a hard way to live when right and wrong draw you to their call. He was someone like you'd only meet once in life, and he was my mountain brother, thank God. I would not want him as an enemy. I tried more'n once to let him know how grateful I was for his friendship, by tellin' him I praised the Lord we was mates, but he never understood what it meant to praise the Lord. The Holy Trinity held little stock to him. The Frenchman soldier, who had promised to return for his wife and child, never come back fer 'em, so Henri was raised Cherokee in his beliefs. His mother remained as a member of the Turtle Clan after he moved out from under the hold of the tribe. Henri still took care of her. Provided all her needs. Protected their clan, too, just from the outside lookin' in. Him and his was some of the best folks I ever met.

He was older than me by about ten years, but he weren't near big as me. Kind 'a small, really, compared to most. He was stronger than you'd figure for, though, given his size. Kept a disposition about him one could feel you'd not wanna stir up, strange as that sounds. His spirit connected him to the world from the inside out. Beat all I ever seen when he'd tell what was gonna happen 'fore it ever happened. He would do that often. His spirit would show him things. Saved our hides a few times, I know that. The Cherokee called him a spirit talker, 'cause he was deeply connected, and communicated with, all they seen as spiritual. They believed everything was hooked together between the real world and the spirit world. I believed that was so.

His life's trail was a special thing the Cherokee understood and respected. Most folks never recognized it for what it was, 'til they got to know him. Unfortunately, as I understood his mind, his spirit weren't connected to the Peace Child. I prayed for him many times each moon about that. I believed only a divine touch would change him. I know'd that could happen, if he'd allow it, so I kept my faith when travelin' in his world. Some of his spirit friends didn't like me, bein' who they was and all.

He was a fierce warrior. He'd fought many soldiers, both North and South, for comin' into what the runaways from both armies had started calling "The Place Forgotten." This was the land that lay east and south of Tiny Creek. It was the land where the Cherokee that was able escaped to during the years of the forced removal. Me and Henri had become friends not long after Dad settled us on Long Shot Ridge. I was just a boy. He was like an older brother to me, then. Good friends with my brothers as well. Held a hard place in his heart over them gettin' killed in what he called a senseless struggle. He lived alone at the base of White Rock Mountain. His spirit was just too deep to live among common tribe folk, his thoughts too troublin' for their conversations. Those things led in part to him seekin' freedom away from the constant watchful eyes of the elders.

His home weren't too far from the main village south 'a Tiny Creek. A battle-hardened warrior who kept to himself except in times of need, he allowed his callin' in life made him wander away from folks. He didn't trust the majority of the settlers he met and very few Indians of any tribe. Me and Mary was two of few exceptions he'd let visit or stay over. He trusted us. We was close. Me and him spent a lot 'a time together after them from the North commenced to settlin' about. His fight was my fight. My fight was his fight. He was soon to prove that to me.

It was early afternoon when me and Gus got to Henri's place. Good fortune was smilin' on me, and Mary, as he was there in the yard, skinnin' rabbits he'd collected from his snares that mornin'. He must 'a had half a dozen good-sized ones already skinned, and at least that many left to start, when he called me out for slippin' up behind him. I know'd they weren't no way I'd get close to him, even with leavin' Gus tied a ways behind, but I liked tryin'. Some said his spirit could feel the vibration in the air as a body moved in close. I did not doubt that.

"Why you and Gus slipping up on me, Boo?" he asked, without ever turnin' his head, holdin' steady to his meat skinnin'. I actually thought I'd got up close without him knowin', but I hadn't. Not many could. I never did. "You smell funny. You been gone for hog meat. Been up on the big ridges recent. You got at least three. That right, Boo? Or more? Gus packing heavy back where you left him tied? Trade you some of this morning's snare caught rabbit for some 'a that ham meat. Been a time since I've had some skillet fried ham meat. What say ye, brother?" he asked, as he turned to walk toward me, wipin' his hands on his buckskin britches.

We locked forearms in our common way 'a greetin', then he hugged me hard 'fore backin' away to stare up at me near eye to eye. He favored huggin' as a way 'a greetin'. That way he could connect to a body's spirit through touch. If you held spiritual talents, he would feel 'em, then know how to treat you accordingly. He never failed to look you close while starin' deep into your eyes when first meetin' you, or likewise if he'd not seen you in a while. He would "read" you spiritually. I know'd what he was doin' when he did that, whether he know'd I know'd or not, I could feel him doin' it. He had a pull for readin' folks. I promise you he did.

"What is wrong my friend? I can see the worry in your eyes. A lot of bad things have been happening here of recent. I hope nothing has happened to you or yours. How is Francis... and Mary? Are they with you? Come, we will sit. Smoke. Then we will talk. Some brandy, maybe? For the blood."

"That sounds good for a later time, Henri, but for now, I've come over a matter that may mean life or death for some we love. Let's sit, so you can listen close and think. You are not gonna like what it is I will tell you. It concerns our farm, Mary, and something I can hardly think on… my father may be gone to where the ancestors live. I believe he might 'a been murdered."

THE LEGEND OF SWELL BRANCH

CHAPTER 4

A TRAIL FOR MARY

My mind was being forced to consider something I weren't wantin' to think on as fact. I had a burnin' question that kept steppin' up to the front 'a my thinkin'. The answer laid the same each time my mind responded. It repeated to me over and over what I know'd deep inside. Dad would not tolerate folks movin' in and takin' over our home the way these had. That's just somethin' he'd not allow. He'd die fightin', 'fore lettin' outlaw homesteaders take our farm. We all know'd that. None of us would 'a done no different. That's why it felt in my soul that he was most likely gone.

To my way 'a hearin', when first talkin' to Henri that afternoon, it weren't me sayin' them words about what I'd found when returnin' home from hog huntin'. Didn't feel like me sayin' them words about Dad maybe bein' dead. Kind 'a seemed like somebody else was speakin' fer me. That I was just a listener. 'Cept, strangely, I could feel the words vibratin' in my chest. Hear 'em in my ears. I tasted the dry bitterness of sudden figured truth what sticks to the back of your throat when that truth is finally realized. My heart sunk to the bottom of my bein' as the understanding of it all hit me. From that understanding, Holy Spirit commenced to tellin' me I should accept how things might be. That made my insides moan. I prayed from my soul he'd only been run off, not kilt. I reasoned that Mary might know. I would have to wait for answers.

"I pray the words you say cannot be true, my friend," Henri said softly with much feeling, "but those are words from one who would not say them, if he did not think they might be so. My soul is troubled for you, Buach. My spirit burns, Brother. Speak what it is you have come to tell me. Take your time. This is hard for you. I have seen it. I feel it. I understand."

"Homesteaders have took our place, Henri. Ex-soldiers from the North. I believe they might 'a killed Dad," I said right back, not hesitatin'. Starin' him eye to eye. "You are right my friend. I have been hog huntin', and when I returned, I found families of ex-Federal soldiers done took to livin' on our farm. I seen 'em from the white oak on the rise to the south. You know the one. I watched for a while. Dad never come in sight. I went down to the front gate this morning. The two soldiers come out. Dad did not, so I made like I was there to visit. Acted like I needed to see Dad. Francis, I called him. That felt like a lie when I said it, Henri. Made me feel cowardly. Like I was hidin' behind that lie. They allowed they'd not seen him. That nobody was around when they come, but he was there when I left days before. He'd told me nothin' about plans to leave while I was gone. His mind was to help me with the cleanin' and smokin' of the meat I'd be bringin' back, so I know he was there waitin' on me when them heathens come. 'Sides, we always leave a horseshoe hung on a nail out by the barn door if we ever leave without havin' told anybody. That signal let the rest of the family know we was okay but had left for a spell and would return shortly. Leavin' a pole axe layin' flat on the back porch meant they was trouble about and whoever left the axe had gone for help. Their plans was to return soon. We have other signs he would 'a left, too, had he gone somewhere without me or Mary knowin', but Dad left no signs that I could see from the front gate. Nothin' tellin' me he'd left or that he was hidin' out nearby. I'm sure he was there when they come, Henri. He had to be. Everything in my heart tells me bad has happened to him. My soul is weak. My spirit is growin' weaker. I don't understand this.

Also, and I know little of how this has come to be, but Mary is there. She come out from the house while I was talkin' to the soldier men. She's been beaten. They said she come a couple days back. Allowed she claimed the place as hers when she come but could give no proof. Unfortunately, as far as I know, only Dad knows where he keeps his papers. She tried to fight 'em at some time. They told me about it. Tried to cut 'em with her knives, but she must 'a been weak from their beatings, so they was able to take 'em from her. I believe they mean to kill her for claimin' ownership. Might be they already have. If she still lives, we'll need to get her out from their hold come daylight. They laid on about me claimin' to own the place when I went there this morning, but I denied any claim. Acted like I didn't know Mary. That hurt me deep. I will see to 'em for beatin' her like they have, Henri. I promise you I will."

"Ah, as will I, my friend, but first we need to free her. We must be careful to not let them know we are there. If they realize we've come, they will know the reason. They will want to kill us all to cover the evil they are trying to do. We must consider our way with that in mind. I believe Mary will be expecting us to come. I figure she'll be awake, waiting. Did you see any dogs? How about their stock? Were they jumpy when you went earlier today? Do you think they will give us away if they scent us coming near? As you know, the back trail lays in behind the barn near the corrals. If we use that trail, we will walk right by their mules to get to the house. If they are the jumpy kind, they could give us away. Think it through, Boo. We must be careful. These are men who are used to the ways of war. They will not be easy to get by. What say ye, warrior? What does your spirit tell you?"

"I allow the same, Henri. We must free her. I don't know about the stock. I weren't near 'em. I come in on the main trail. I saw no dogs. I do know they'll want to do away with her and her claimin', when the time is right. I figure them bucks will have their way with her, too, once out 'a sight of their women. Be just like 'em to do that 'fore ending her life. I can't think on it. Her bein' in their capture is near more'n I can stand, what with the wonderin' of what might 'a happened to Dad. Come on, Henri. Let's just go kill 'em all right now. Get this done. What say ye, Brother?" I started turnin' to leave. He grabbed my arm, spinnin' me back around to face him.

"Whoa now, Brother," he said, still holdin' my arm tight. Any other man would 'a been on the ground with a broke nose fer grabbin' me like that, but not Henri. I didn't even think to act against him. My spirit stayed calm.

"That's your mad talking, Boo. Don't listen to it. Calm your thoughts. Make yourself see reason. Remember your warrior training. These are full on U.S. Government trained army soldiers we're fixin' to try and save Mary from. They ain't your common settler. These are trained killers who've most likely practiced their trade on many 'a Southern soldier over the last few years. These are two that survived the fighting they surely saw. Death does not scare them. Killing is not something they fret over, for sure if it's Southern folk like us. Two more notches like me and you on their rifle stock won't worry them. We gotta outsmart these foolish takers. Use our wits, then make no mistakes when we move, or Mary is likely to get killed right along with you and me. We can't risk being careless. Let us go into the house. Sit the hearth. Cook some rabbit over the flames. Eat a bite, then we'll smoke us up a plan to free our sister, find Francis. We must consider this thing for the whole, or we might all end up with the ancestors before they are ready for us. Let us pray to the Great Creator for guidance. I trust we will find it."

We spitted two rabbits each over the fire inside. His fireplace was big. Sat right in the middle of his log home. Had a round hearth circlin' the fire that was so big you could sit facin' the fire with your feet restin' on the inside of the hearth same as if we was outside sittin' by the main fire pit. A draft hole and chimney built from creek rock laid through the roof. It worked perfect for pullin' out the smoke. Most folks' fireplaces was big what lived in the mountains, but not as big as Henri's. He got that from livin' Indian.

Fireplaces was purposeful for folks' survival who lived in the mountains. Kept 'em alive in lots 'a ways. Many in the backwoods around where I lived still cooked over open fire. Cherokee for sure. I liked it. The fire's heat and smoke made the flavor of whatever meat or stew a body was cookin' taste better than about any other way 'a cookin', 'cept maybe skillet fried ham or steak. Of course, some things was better cooked in a store-bought woodstove, too, like cornbread, biscuits, and sweet cake, but you could do some proper fixin' with open flame cookin'. It took practice to not burn your meat 'fore it cooked good on the inside when usin' open flame cookin', but I'd learned how to cook that way just fine. Roasted many critters when out on trail, or when out on a walk where you'd hunt fer what you ate. I could make a tasty fruit cobbler over open flame, too. Peach bein' my favorite.

Now, goin' for a walk in Indian speak, ain't like goin' for a walk around a town or out on the farm like settlers would do. No, most times goin' for a walk in the mountains like Indians did it, meant a body was out wanderin' the woods for spiritual reasons. Many trailed for days just livin' off the land. Sleepin' out in the open. Prayin' constant to Holy Spirit, as mountain settlers believed, not the same for most Indians, for the desire or need that drove them to go on their walk in the first place. Often them trails lasted for a few days or more. You'd not take no food with ye, neither. Simply harvest it along the way, if you meant to eat. Cook it in camp of 'a night for supper or fast the whole time to 'company your prayin'. Water was plentiful with streams all over, so that weren't a worry. Going for a walk Indian style was a way to get close to the Great Spirit. Live off what He provided to all folks. I went several times a year. "God walks" I called 'em. I just trailed where He guided. Helped a bait 'a folks by His call. Miracles for some, really, them walks of faith.

"I'm troubled over not seein' Dad, Henri," I said, as we sat the hearth, warmin' after eatin'. Smokin' our pipes. Our bellies full 'a tasty, roasted rabbit. "I tell you there is a hurt on the inside like a hole's been shot through me with dull point. I know he'd not allow our place to be took. He would fight. You know that. Them takers would 'a learned that, too, after meetin' him. Tell me straight what it is you feel about what we're walkin' into, Henri. What do you sense? What thoughts come to you that will help us plan our trail to fetch Mary? My spirit is weighed down from a heavy load 'a worry. I am becoming confused in my thoughts. I know your spirit speaks. Tell me, friend. Say the words I fear to hear. Tell me my father's fate. My soul senses the ancestors are crying. You know the truth. I know you do. I will listen to your words. My mind is out 'a balance with my soul. Help me, dear friend."

"Your spirit is growing wise with your learning, Buach, and… I'm sorry… I sense your notions could be founded," Henri said, as he stared me back eye to eye. "I believe Francis to be in a bad way, just as you, yes. I hold only a small hope that he has not gone to be with the ancestors," he finished, as he paused to look away and take a long pull on his white oak pipe. The smoke smelled sweet mixed with that from the fireplace.

"The spirit world is a dark place, Boo. Full of deceptions for the mind," he started again, "but I think these takers have wronged our loved one. I hear the cries of his soul. I sense his confusion. It seems to come from the darkness. I can feel the cold that surrounds him. That is so. I regret, dear friend, these are the thoughts to consider when planning what we should do about getting Mary out from her circumstance. I believe her freedom to be our main intention. It is possible, and these are the words I don't want to say to you, that we are no longer able to help our father. I am deeply sorry, Boo. Please, take your time to pray. Find your strength to move on these that have done so terrible a thing as to have taken your home and family. I will have no mercy. Your God's Will may allow you the same. I pray that it does."

"My God doesn't like what I'm feelin' about these that have taken my home, Henri… maybe my father's life. I have no mercy throughout my whole put together for any that are there but Mary. Let us rest. I need to settle my spirit. Take some time to figure a good trail that will rid us of the evil that has come. I want back all there is to get, Henri. Then, if we find my father has been made to cross over, I will take from them as they have taken from us. After this, I will ask forgiveness from "my" God, as you say. It will be in His hands. Me and mine will be justified. I must do this or die in the effort, Henri. I aim to have this squared. I want my home back."

"We will work this through, Boo. These folks will not have Mary past tomorrow, then we will return to take back your home. Now let us rest as you have said. Fix our thoughts to be about Mary. I hope they've done no more to hurt her. I know she is a tough woman. She will stay strong 'til we get there. I believe this. That will help us in our efforts to free her."

Those was the last words I remember him sayin' as I moved to the nearest bed to stretch out and get comfortable. That made thinkin' easier. It never come to me durin' supper that I was so tired, but when Henri raised me a couple hours 'fore daylight, I was shocked to know I'd been sleepin' for a little over seven hours. I must 'a needed it, 'cause I felt better than I had in a while. My vision no longer clouded from hurt, hate, and anger. A calm had come to me durin' my rest that I know'd was purely spiritual. I had confidence Holy Spirit was on me. Through that, I know'd all would be as it should be. Dad always told me that the Good Lord tends his hand when livin' and dyin' come to folks, so my spirit put it all up to Him. If I had to kill any we was goin' up against to get my sister out from danger, then so be it. I had no worry over the work. That gives a body comfort in the worst of struggles. With them thoughts clear in my head, I know'd just what we was gonna do. My blood got up when I commenced to tellin' Henri how I thought we should handle gettin' Mary out. We sat the hearth sippin' steamin' hot cups of black coffee. He brewed a good coffee. Mixed some sweet root into it for flavor. I liked it a sight. It give a body calm.

"Henri, that rest has cleared my mind. My spirit is calm. Listen close to what I'm thinkin'. Mary is at the front of my worry. Her life is most important to me right now. That is why I feel we should do as our Cherokee warrior brothers would do. How they would act to help Mary. The takers are most likely keepin' her in the house so they can watch over her in comfort. Keepin' her in the barn would mean they'd have to go out and stay with her in the cold. They ain't gonna do that. 'Sides, I saw 'em throw her back inside as I was leavin'. I feel confident she is in the house. We won't waste time checkin' the barn 'til we've been through the house and not found her. We will slip ourselves inside the house 'fore morning light hits good. Take Mary out while they sleep. Fortunately, and this is why I believe this is a good way, Dad changed the latchstrings to store-bought doorknobs a while back. We are not dependent on the latchstring bein' out to get in, and, this is the secret, them doorknobs ain't got no locks. The only thing there is the hickory bar used to block the door from the inside in case of attacks, and I don't believe they will have that up. It's for protection from intruders. These Yankees feel safe I'm sure. No need to block out intruders. 'Sides, havin' that heavy beam in its inside braces makes it hard to go to the privy durin' the night. They wouldn't have that neither, lazy as they are. They seem spoiled in their thinkin'.

So, knowin' how our doors work, I think you should enter through the back," I said, as we still sat the hearth, our coffee near gone. "Me through the front. We must move smooth and quiet like the mountain cat. Find where Mary is bedded down, then get her out without wakin' a soul. Hopefully, all will be asleep. If any wake, we will protect her. No human must hear us 'til we want 'em to. I have no fear over these folk, even if they do wake. They are not mountain bred as we. I laugh inside when I think what a surprise it will be for the big one, when once he feels a cold steel edge at his throat. My long knife will end him. You should bring your sharpest knives, Henri. We may need to fight our way out if things turn sour. I know there are women and children among those in our house, but I will see these thieves come to justice, whatever that justice may be. I will spare all that want to be spared except for two. You do as your spirit leads. What say ye, friend? It is your soul, it is your life, we risk for us and ours. Speak reason if you sense it, please. I would expect nothin' different from you."

"I believe same as you, Boo. We should go in before Old Man Sun wakes. It may be that Mary can't walk from being hurt. Could be they got her tied to something. Could be she needs help to move in the dark, since her eye has been hurt the way you say. Might be hard for her to see clear. Yes, if there are no locks, we should slip in. Lead her out. That will be the best for Mary. Best for all, I believe. We can get her in close to our person. Keep her close until we are out and gone. We know the house. We can move quietly. They will never know we are there. I think this is a good plan you feel, Boo. The back door will work just fine for me. We should go. It will be light soon. Even lazy soldiers will be up with Old Man Sun. The farm chores demand it."

We said no more words that amounted to anything. Maybe some chitchat type talkin'. I don't recall. I had a lot on my mind. I took a minute to lift up a silent prayer to Holy Spirit for courage, good judgment, and safe keepin'. Once done, I checked both my knives, makin' sure they was tied secure to my braided mid-belt. I toted my rifle but left my short guns at Henri's. They was hard to run with. My rifle could be strapped over my neck and across my shoulder. Easy for carryin' when trottin'. My special knife was just where it should be. Wouldn't be nothin' to have that thing in my left hand within' a second of needin' it. I hoped that would be quick enough, if the need did come. In a fight, things move fast. You gotta be ready. Your life depends on you thinkin' clear about what folks around you are doin'. One of 'em might be tryin' to kill you. It was important to your bein' to recognize that before it happened.

We left Henri's not long after he'd rousted me from sleepin'. Old Man Moon was shinin' enough for us to see the outline of our chosen trail. That little bit 'a light would allow us to use the warrior's trot. That would help us make good time.

I'd relieved poor Gus of his meat carryin' burden the day before, not long after makin' it to Henri's. I weren't gonna be concerned over him. That would help me keep my mind clear. He'd carried that meat 'bout as long as he could. I felt for him. He was a good mule. Never let me down once in his whole put together. I left him in the corral along with Henri's stock. He'd earned some fresh oats and rest. I'd collect him back after our rescuin' chore was complete. I didn't like leavin' him alone at Henri's. They was thieves what slipped around in the woods lookin' for valuables they could steal to sell for gold coin. Me and Henri had met a few. The Cherokee made sure them bad folks was took care of, if and when any were ever found out. After a time, the common word among the outlaws, bad settlers, and rogue Indians was to stay away from Swell Branch. Mostly 'cause 'a me and Henri and them we know'd. True warriors of the Cherokee.

Henri's eyes, bein' Indian, was better in the dark, so he led our way. We'd need to hurry to get to our farm with time to spare for coolin' down and catchin' our breath. It was difficult for a body to stay silent and sneak up on folks while breathin' hard from travelin'. Them kind 'a noises could wake folks from sleepin'. Not natural like other things you hear durin' the night.

Usin' the warrior's trot, we made it well within' the time we needed. The smells I was pickin' up from our farm, as we squatted on the edge of the clearin' that surrounded our place, was most familiar.

A sweet scent of the coming spring had eased down durin' the night. Smelled kind 'a like syrup frothin' up from boilin'. You could feel the coolness of the air surrounding your person. Taste it when you breathed in. That honey sweetness laid over all makin' me wish for some fresh garden vegetables. It'd been a long winter. I was ready for some recent grow'd greens, onions, and Ir'sh taters. Wouldn't be long 'til I'd need to be droppin' some 'a them taters fer growin'. We depended on 'em as a big part of our winter stores. I thought about that as we cooled down. Gus was good with a plow. He made straight rows when a body worked him proper. Straight rows turned out better plants. Easier to tend.

In the dark, waitin' to sneak into my own home, I thought 'a Dad and how I was most often with him when noticin' the scents of spring around our farm. Them smells usually come around plantin' time. Barn stink was mixed in with it all. Only one common to farm life would sense that or appreciate it fer what it was. That really brought Dad to mind. Made the hurt I was hidin' start risin'. I had to fight it back down.

Studyin' on it all while waitin' in the dark got my back up. This was my home that'd been took. Everything around me was makin' sure I know'd that. I made my mind it was gonna stay my home, too. My spirit ached to get the evil folks out and gone no matter what that looked like, and I wanted Mary back safe. A simple glance over to Henri told me he was ready. I know'd I was ready. The time for makin' things right was on us. A simple nod in my direction sent us on our way. The fate of our plan, and those in the house, would soon be rendered.

The Legend of Swell Branch

Chapter 5

We Make Our Escape

A gentle rain got to fallin' as we began easin' our way down the back trail toward our log home. I covered the action on my rifle with the possibles pouch I'd been totin' for my recent hog hunt. I had several of them pouches. Used one or the other dependin' on the trail I was takin'. Coverin' the workings would keep the cap and powder dry for firin'. Henri did the same. It was a habit woods folks learned when they first started totin' their rifles. Bein' mindful like that could mean the difference between eatin' and not eatin'. Paid a body to be cautious.

All looked to be as it should be the closer we got to the house. It was still that early morning light just as dark begins its fade to dawn. Made it hard to tell what things was for sure, unless they was up close to your person. The misty rain was pesterin' but shouldn't cause no problems. I'd noticed more chickens was gone from the coop as we passed by on the back trail. Layin' hens, too. I figured these folks lacked the common knowledge to recognize layin' hens from cookin' chickens. That made me mad. I liked eggs mixed in with my morning meal, not unlike most everybody else I know'd what lived in the mountains. If these ignorant folk kept eatin' our layin' chickens, we weren't gonna have any left to make eatin' eggs. That was gonna be a problem once we'd finished the recoverin' of our farm. It made me wonder if they know'd how to hunt. I felt I'd need to explain things more clearly once the fight ended. Fortunately, the Cherokee liked eggs, same as me. I could trade with some 'a them for more layin' hens later on. Good ones, too. Still, it made me mad for havin' to bother with it. Everybody know'd you don't eat your layin' hens 'til they was done with their life's work 'a makin' decent eatin' eggs, and we had some good layin' hens we'd had fer a spell. After their egg makin' life was up, they went to the dumplings for Sunday dinner. That was just common doin's among farmin' folk.

"All looks as it should, Henri," I whispered toward his right ear while turnin' my face in his direction. We crouched to listen a minute some twenty paces shy of the east porch. He never took his eyes off the house while I spoke.

"I don't see any folks movin'. Don't hear any movin' noises. I'll go ease in the front door. Leave it open just a touch. We should take Mary out that way 'cause off the front porch is the shortest distance to the woods. You make your way to the back but give me your rifle first. Won't need 'em inside. They're liable to cause noise. Wake folks up. I'll leave 'em both leaned to the left side of the front door goin' out. Yours will be the first one standin', mine the second. Havin' 'em leaned up there will make for easy grabbin' as we're leavin'. Once you're inside, check both the back sleepin' rooms for Mary. If you find her, bring her to the front room. If you don't find her, move on through the cook room toward the center of the house. I'll meet you by the stairs what lead to the loft. That's where she'll most likely be if she ain't on the main floor. If I ain't there when you get there, wait for me at the bottom step. I'll do the same for you. We'll go up together. I figure they's folks sleepin' on the main room floors. I'll needs check 'em all for Mary 'fore I can come to ye. That will take a little time to do proper. I hope that's where she'll be. If I find her, I will come get you. If not, we will have to move quick 'fore Old Man Sun wakes full. Stay sharp, Henri. Killin' is near. I can feel it. My spirit is troubled."

"As is mine," he said, without ever takin' his eyes off the house. "I believe these will not surrender your home to us, Boo, once we have taken Mary. I feel they are willing to die trying to keep what they believe should be theirs. At least, from how I understand it…" He turned to look at me before finishin' his words, "they should be."

Thieving from folks what live in the backwoods of Southern Appalachia can get you killed, for sure after the war, for sure when the wrong folks had been took from. Me and mine was the wrong folks to be took from. These takers, and many to come, did not understand how mountain born peoples live. We would show them soon. Time was moving. Old Man Sun was coming. Henri finished, sayin', "Let us get this done, Boo. Let us go get our sister," he said, while handin' me his rifle. Once he was sure I had a good hold on it, he turned to commence his slippin' toward the back door. The rain had let off, leavin' the ground wet, quiet. Weren't but a second, and he was out 'a sight, silent as a mountain cat. Alone come on me quick, it was time for me to move.

The look on his face, as he turned to leave, was one I'd seen him hold many times. It give me worry. Caught my attention. That look told me his spirit had turned. Vengeance and hate had commenced to runnin' thick through his blood. He cared a sight for my family. Him and my dad was close, not as tight as me and Henri had become, but Henri loved my family. The way he looked when leavin' me for the back door was near like spirit possession the way I seen it. I never wanted to be on the gettin' end of his vengefulness. He was a dangerous man to those he felt deservin'. I'd witnessed it many different times.

With all that said, we moved toward the house. Me to the front. Henri to the back. I quietly leaned our rifles against the logs to the right side of the front door facin'. My left hand quiverin' as it eased toward the white glass doorknob. Dad got those at market in Atlanta a couple years before. Mary had wanted 'em. My hand weren't shakin' from fear, but more from anger what laid shallow under the hurt I was hidin', mixed in with the chill of the rain. The knob never offered to squeak as I gently turned it counterclockwise. Dad's craftmanship was amazing. The heavy oak door, which he'd set to perfect balance for swingin' in, opened easily with the push of a finger. More importantly, it opened quietly as it swung in freely. Once I slipped inside, I moved to my right, squattin' against the logs of the west wall, listenin' close to everything around me. I needed time for my eyes to adjust to what little light there was inside.

The door still open but a touch. Cool air flowin' in. My breathing steadied. My eyes settled. All was silent. It come to me that I'd made it inside without wakin' a soul. I was ready to commence searchin' for my sister. I was eager to find her, then get her out from the heathens what'd hurt her.

I could hear breathin' off to my right and d'rectly in front from where I was squatted, but I couldn't see nobody because of the dark. I wondered... *was Henri in, yet?* The fireplace was on the west wall, but it only held a small pile of overnight coals. They was mostly covered in gray ash. No flames was present to shed light to the room. Nobody'd got up durin' the night to put more wood on. That was curious to me. It was cool enough to need some heat. I reasoned these folks must be lazy. Most thieves I ever met was. That's why they was thieves. "Too sorry to work fer their keep," as folks would say.

I wondered for Henri again, so I let out a soft dove call. An even softer dove call returned from the back of the house. That told me he was in. He would now be searchin' for Mary as well. I kept my place, not wanting to move 'til I could make out who all was sleeping on the floor around me. It seemed I was near on top 'a folks. I could feel that from listenin' to 'em breathe. I would needs be most careful. Not wake any layin' close. I decided to settle a minute more where I was squatted. Let a little more morning light come in. I worried over that some. Waitin' made things more risky. Brought us closer to the time folks would be wakin' natural. Still, it'd be best if I could see just a bit better 'fore I got to slippin' around. I allowed Henri was prob'ly doin' the same. Some light would help about not steppin' on nobody or bumpin' into nothin'. Those kind 'a sounds would wake all that was in the house at that time 'a day. We didn't want that. My aim was to locate Mary. Wake her on the quiet, then slip her out 'fore any know'd we was there. I'd come back, after we got her safe, for the settling of my family's affairs.

Weren't long at all 'fore there was enough light comin' through the front windows that I could began to see faint shadows of things takin' shape. It was a shock to me, even though I know'd they was near, when I come to realize what I was lookin' at. Bodies - *bodies* layin' about on the main room floor. More than I'd seen from the white oak. Old Man Sun was far from bein' seen yet, but his light was givin' form to the things in our main room. The humps layin' about.

Most of the sleepin' bodies I was lookin' at was small. A couple looked to be older. I know'd in a second who they belonged to. That was not what I was hopin' for. I had no notions for killin' the young ones. The women? Maybe. The men? For sure. The kids? NO! Without question. NO! I'd need to keep 'em quiet, though, if I did roust 'em. I had to think a minute 'fore actin'. No kids was to be harmed. Weren't their fault for what the parents was tryin' to do. I had it in mind to end those thievin' dads 'a theirs, though. They'd not like them doin's. Most likely turn me into their lifelong enemy. I didn't care. I figured what was gonna happen would teach 'em a little right from wrong, and stealin' what's owned by someone else for keeps is wrong.

Fortunately, the Great Spirit teaches us things in life that we must know for His purpose and our well-being. Unfortunately for these young ones, those teachings are not always pleasant. Many times, for sure in my life, those lessons can be most uncomfortable. Terribly painful when livin' through the circumstance what'd been allowed. It looked as though it had become their time in life to learn, and this lesson was gonna hurt. The deep kind 'a hurt one feels way down in their soul. I could not help that. Pain comes when people wrong others for purpose. That's just the way.

I made my mind on how to proceed in my hunt for Mary. I could see the bodies sleepin' on our main room floor well enough to walk among 'em real quiet like. Movin' silent in my own home would make no more sound than a fox slippin' through the woods, considerin' the footskins I was wearin'. That would help about not wakin' the little ones. Leavin' our rifles on the porch helped a sight with that, too. I didn't like being without mine, but inside the house it was more of a burden when tryin' to slip around quiet, and each soul had to be checked. I wanted to know for sure if Mary was sleepin' in the main room or not. I doubted she was, and of course, after lookin' at all of 'em there, I learned she weren't. I looked into every face and not one was her. All was young. None seemed older than about twelve. The two bigger bodies was older boys. Seven sleepers, all total. I for sure hadn't seen that many kids while lookin' down from the old white oak.

I moved on to the stairs what led to the small sleeping loft. Henri was there waitin' on me. He'd checked the back rooms where Dad and my brothers slept. Two men and their women was sleepin' in there. Most likely the big one and Walter. Why would they not be? They allowed they owned the place. They should get the best sleepin' rooms. We moved together to the top of the stairs. There we found her. She was not alone. We quietly moved in close to get a better look at her predicament. It was bad for her.

In the loft, there were two feather beds. One against each wall with a space in between. Oak planks laid for the floor. I slept on one bed. Mary the other. For the time bein', they was full 'a strangers. Looked to be a couple grow'd folks to each, maybe more. It was hard to tell with the light bein' how it was. Mary weren't in no bed. She was bein' made to lay on the bare floor between the two beds. Her right side flat to the oak floorboards. Her face toward the stairs. When I first seen her, I couldn't tell if she was awake lookin' at us, or asleep. It kind 'a looked possible she was dead. Hands bound behind her back. Feet tied at the ankles. The hurt side of her face hid in all the matted hair they'd not let her brush. Her left eye was showin', but I couldn't tell if it was open or not. A small rope was noosed around her neck. That rope was tied to the leg of her bed. Hers sat against the west wall, mine to the east. I figured the ones in her bed for her keepers.

They'd bound her up good. She weren't gettin' free without some help. From what little I could make out, she looked no different than when I'd seen her previous the morning before. I was hopin' they'd not beat her more once I'd left. She'd been hurt enough from the first beatin's. Light was beginnin' to slip through the upstairs window. Made things easier to see. That meant the sleepin' folks would be wakin' soon. We needed to get Mary out 'fore that happened.

Upon closer study, the folks in our beds looked to be grow'd women. That concerned me a sight 'cause I'd not seen that many adult women from the rise, nor had I seen 'em at my morning visit - kids, neither. That give proof to my thinkin'. I'd not been allowed to see all that was there fer purpose. That brought a pound 'a worry to my mind. Just how many was they in all? Had I not seen all the men, either? Was there more ex-soldiers about the place? I turned my face to Henri. He moved the right side of his face in closer to me. I whispered direct into his ear, speakin' slow and clear. So quiet he could barely hear my words, but clear enough so he heard me. I could feel our lives was gonna depend on him hearin' me. He would know that.

"Henri, there's more women folk and kids here than I accounted for yesterday. More than I saw when I visited. We must be careful. More women could mean more men. You move in between the two beds to the other side 'a Mary. Keep these from making noise if they wake. I will come in behind you, get Mary loose. You must watch the sleepers close for us. I will need to pay mind to Mary as I cut the lead from her neck. If you see any of the four waking, signal me. Once I'm done freein' her, I will lift her to my shoulder and stand. You will know then it's time to leave. I will only cut the lead. No need to free her hands and feet as yet. Once I've got her lifted, we will make our way straight to the front door. You first, then us. Do not worry over makin' noise or wakin' anybody once we have her. Move with speed. Let's get her out to safety fast as we can 'fore they rise. They don't know we're here. It will take them some time to wake once they hear us. I believe in that little bit 'a time we can get her loose, snatch her up, and get her out without one soul here hardly wakin' at all. At least not 'til we're done and gone. What say ye, Brother? Nod if you agree."

His slight nod was all the yes we needed to commence. Without hesitatin', he moved between the beds to the far side of where Mary laid. I draw'd my short knife, then slipped in behind him while squattin' down close to her. I still couldn't tell if she was asleep and alive... or dead, even up close like I was. I heard no breathing. She felt cold as I put my hand over her mouth to keep her from hollerin' out, if by chance she woke enough to realize there was a knife bein' put to her neck. I prayed she was still among the living as I eased the cold steel blade between her neck meat and the leather binding what was holdin' her. A simple twist and pull of the sharp edge let me feel it had done its chore. Soon as I felt that, I lifted her like a sack 'a potatoes over my right shoulder. Lockin' her down tight with my right arm. Oh, she smelled terrible. The blood on her ridin' dress was soured. They hadn't let her bathe nor had they washed her. I know'd she hated bein' like that. She was always clean and proper when out among folks. Never would she be seen out so filthy. I felt for her.

The slight grunt I heard as I stood liftin' her over my shoulder was a good sign. She was alive, but she'd woke. That meant the sleepin' folks would be awake soon, if she had any strength left. She'd see to it. Be wakin' 'em with her threats she would, once she woke good. I know'd her well enough to know her temper. It was an Irish temper, and she could pitch a hissy fit with the best of 'em. She'd not like bein' carried out all hog tied like I was plannin', neither.

I looked to Henri as I stood, after gettin' Mary laid solid over my shoulder. I wanted to let him know it was time to go, but I couldn't. He'd done gone. I allowed he'd seen me lift Mary and went ahead and started for the front door thinkin' I'd be followin'. I weren't... I couldn't... 'cause standin' where he was supposed to be standin' was the biggest, meanest, most hateful lookin', ugliest woman I'd ever seen, holdin' the nastiest look a body'd ever wanna see. She was starin' straight at me. Dressed in full nightclothes. It was hard for me to know, just by lookin' her in the face, if she was a man or a woman at first. She had a kind 'a beard workin' around her mouth, but I took her for woman bein' she was outfitted in women's sleepin' clothes. The look scrunchin' her face let me know she didn't want me there. Her teeth was showin'. She only had two. Looked like dog's fangs. I feared she might try and rip my throat out with those things.

I could hear the others was beginning to roust up, too, but I stayed focused on the one in front of me. This could get bad if all the women in the loft was as big and nasty as the one I was facin'. Where was Henri? What in the world was I gonna do? My primary fightin' arm was full 'a Mary. I couldn't fight with it without droppin' her, and I for sure weren't gonna do that. I'd just got her, and I meant for her to be goin' to safety, and this woman was not gonna stop that. My left arm went by instinct to the handle of my special knife strapped in the middle of my back. I was gonna open this woman up if she come at me one step… and she did. I commenced to defendin' myself.

The look holdin' that woman's face as she lunged at me and Mary made me think she might be the actual bride of Satan hisself, if ever there was such a thing. She was hideous. I'd never before in my life seen as mean 'a lookin' woman as her, and I'd seen some bad ones. Weren't hard to read from her look. She meant to do as much harm as possible to my person. I was still tryin' to figure out if I was gonna have to draw my special knife to stop her or turn and try to run carryin' Mary, when of a sudden, Henri's right fist come out 'a nowhere sendin' that ugly woman flyin' backwards. She hadn't got more'n a half step my way 'til he laid her out cold. She landed hard on them what was sleepin' in my bed. My left hand released the handle of my special knife. My trouble from her had been ended, at least for the time. She weren't that mean lookin' laid out like she was, after Henri busted her in the side of her head.

It was good she'd been took out, but it was also bad fer us. The scream one 'a them women let out, after bein' landed on by the big, ugly one, had to 'a woke the whole of the house. It for sure told me Mary was awake, 'cause she commenced to screamin' out threats of her own loud as any there. Her hollerin' would for sure wake the house. I know'd when I woke her, she'd be wantin' vengeance on these what'd hurt her once she seen who it was totin' her out. I couldn't blame her for that. My spirit was feelin' the same.

One thing was clear, if we didn't get movin', me and Henri was gonna have to fight our way out. How much of a fight we might get was gonna depend on how fast we left the loft and who we might run into 'fore gettin' to the front door. The second woman in the bed, where the ugly one landed, commenced to hollerin' like a mad hen scoldin' her chicks. Warnin' everybody within ear shot we was there and what we was doin'. Oh, she could holler loud. Mary hollered right back at her. It was pure chaos by the time we got turned toward the stairs. Me and Henri took a quick glance at each other 'fore startin' our run toward the front door. Him in front. Me followin' with Mary over my shoulder, kickin' and screamin' for all she was worth. It was hard to hold her. She was cussin' them women at the top 'a her lungs with all the strength she could muster, floppin' front to back like a fish out 'a water. It was good she was alive, but I was wantin' her to calm down a mite. She was makin' it hard fer me to carry her. Hard to get to the front door.

I smiled as we went. I figured no less from my sister. She could be a wild mountain cat when she wanted. I had no doubt she'd a tried to kill every woman in there if I'd 'a let her down, and oh, she was wantin' down. She got to hollerin' at me 'cause I hadn't cut her hands and feet free so she could fight them women. Make 'em pay for the way they'd treated her. Turned out, I was right in my earlier thinkin' about them women bein' the ones what'd hurt her. From what she was hollerin', it was them what'd treated her so bad. If I'd 'a had one of my short guns, I'd 'a shot one of 'em in the face fer spite… the big, ugly one, most likely.

I kept headin' toward freedom with Mary over my shoulder. Listenin' to her ever-worsening threats at the women we was leavin' behind. Also at me for not lettin' her down so she could, "kill 'em all." I come to realize, as I topped the stairs headin' down, that our path would be through the young ones sleepin' on the floor in the main room. I hated that was fixin' to happen. They'd most likely be awake from all the hollerin' above 'em. As my feet hit the floorboards at the bottom of the stairs, I prayed none did anything stupid like try and get in mine and Henri's way. I turned for the door. I was not of good fortune in my concerns. What looked like the oldest of the boys stood to try and stop mine and Mary's escape after Henri had passed him by headin' for the outside. I figured after he'd seen Henri go out, that he allowed his dad would expect him to front me fer slowin' down purposes or stop us cold by gettin' us to trip and fall. That weren't gonna happen. I could not stop. I would not stop. That would mean death to at least me and Mary, then most likely Henri too, if I did.

These was takers. Me and my kind owed 'em nothin'. I cared fer 'em little. The boy gettin' in my way weren't gonna be a problem. Without breakin' stride, I lifted my right foot for my next runnin' step, sinkin' it deep into his middle, knockin' him flat against the wood floor. I heard the air jump from his lungs as he fell straight in my path. My foot caught up in his middle. I could do nothin' about it. It was impossible for me not to step on him hard as I left the house. It was bad fortune for him, that he ended up square under where I needed my foot to go so me and Mary wouldn't be the ones flat out on the floor. Poor fortune fer him.

I grabbed my rifle with my left hand as I cleared the front door, holdin' Mary over my shoulder with my right. Her kickin' and floppin' and hollerin' all she could at them what was in the house. Mad all in her bein'. I remember thinkin' it was gonna take us a long time to calm her down once we got her to Henri's. He had some stuff what helped with that, but it would still take a while. She was mad, hurt, and tired. Tired finally won for us.

As I only hit the middle step what sided our front porch, makin' our gettin' away run for the woods, my heart recollected how soft the boy's gut had felt as my foot sank deep into his middle. I actually felt the oak floor through his person with the sole of my footskin. I realized then that my foot had landed in him, more than on him. That would hurt the young'un more'n I meant too, but I could not help that. My thought was to follow close to Henri while gettin' Mary to freedom any way I could. The boy should 'a never tried to stop me. That show'd strong courage on his part, even though it would cost him dearly. I always hated that.

We'd made it out the front door, grabbin' our rifles as we went, but we weren't in the clear. I could hear the men was up and movin' as I jumped from the front porch step, runnin' for all I was worth straight toward the woods. Doin' all I was able to keep Mary on my shoulder. I could hear one of 'em, I figured it for the big one I'd met at the gate the day before, shoutin' orders. They was bad orders for us.

"Man your weapons, men! Man your weapons! They've got the girl! Shoot to kill! Shoot to kill! I want all three dead before they get to the woods. Load and fire. Load and fire. Move! Move! Move! They're gaining freedom! They must not get away! Fire! Fire! Fire! Don't let them make the woods. Shoot straight, men! Hurry up now. Fire at will! Fire! Fire! Keep firing!"

I heard at least four different guns go off several different times while we was makin' our escape. All come from different shootin' directions. Lead bullets from the rifled barrels of their carbines spun by us like mad bees buzzin'. That's a sound you never wanna hear up close to your person. Gettin' shot at while we was runnin' made the woods seem a long ways away. Made me feel I was movin' in fresh plowed ground. I was prayin' the whole time they didn't hit Mary. She was screamin' hate and death like a crazy woman. Weren't feared one bit. Oh, but she was hatin' them takers fer what they'd done.

At any second, I figured to feel hot lead tear through my person. Not unlike many of the animals I'd killed for food. Blowin' my insides apart while breakin' bone, muscle, and vitals. Sendin' me face first into the forest floor mast. I dreaded the slammin' meat slappin' thud and the hot sting of what I could sense was my comin' death by one 'a them spinnin' lead hornets they was sendin' after us. These was soldiers. I know'd that. Trained to shoot and kill folks runnin' away like we was. I know'd that, too. It come to me, while we was gettin' away all we could, that God was the only protection I had against their skills. That didn't help a sight while bein' shot at, but it helped some, 'cause I know'd many that had a walk with the Lord, but they'd got shot dead just like any non-believin' folk did. Bein' a believer in Jesus didn't make you bulletproof, but it did give you a place in eternity with God if the bullet did kill you.

I felt I was barely movin', even though I was runnin' with all I had. In my mind, that made me an easy target, which made it worse in my confidence about not gettin' hit. I did not feel they would miss us, but by the time we'd made it to the woods, got stopped behind some big oaks, they had, or at least I thought they had. Henri proved me wrong. One of the lead bullets had cut the top of his left leg in the back, just below his hip. Didn't seem to be more'n a bad, kind 'a deep cut with burnt edges, but it made us know just how close we'd come to gettin' our killin'. Henri would have a hard time sittin' for a spell. Several moons for sure. I hated that fer him. I felt responsible, but we'd made it. Mary was free. We were alive. That was something I weren't sure would happen when makin' the plans to go in and get her earlier in the morning. I know'd it was divine fortune we'd made it out with just a flesh wound to any of us. No doubt Holy Spirit was lookin' out fer us. Henri's wound would smart for a few days, but as long as it didn't fester, he'd be back in the fight 'fore long.

It didn't go unnoticed, by me, that Dad was nowhere in the house. That would only mean one thing… my feelings must be right… Dad was gone. These takers had killed him. I know'd it. Them folks had no idea the hell I was gonna bring down on 'em startin' in a couple days. I would have vengeance fer Dad's killin'. I would have our place back, too. It would be no other way. I was gonna see to it, if I had to end every last one of 'em that was taintin' up my home.

CHAPTER 6

A TIME OF HEALING

Mary tolerated bein' slung across my shoulder for a long while, 'til the bouncin' from us runnin' got to hurtin' more'n she could stand. We was a half mile or more from our farm toward Henri's 'fore she made it known. I'd carried her 'bout all I was able anyhow. I let her down for a short minute. Cut her bindings so she could walk, but she couldn't walk. Her legs was too wobbly to make any time. She had to ride my back for another half mile 'fore me and Henri felt safe stoppin' again. I never sensed them takers trailin' us, and we never heard no followin' noises from our back trail durin' the times we stopped to listen. Still, just to make sure they weren't comin', Henri would drop back ever so often to watch for a spell. He never seen any of 'em followin'. Caution was always wise when usin' the mountain trails, for sure if you're travelin' any distance.

Mary was strong, but she'd stood the pain 'a me totin' her long as she could. She know'd it best to put ground between us and them fast as possible, so she held off makin' us stop long as she could. She was something else, when it come to considerin' a young woman doin' the things she could do. It felt safe stoppin' where we had. It was a good place for an overnight short camp. Give Mary 'til mornin' for restin', gettin' her legs back.

After searchin' fer a bit, me and Henri settled on a kind 'a flat holler laid full 'a ivies just above a small, freshwater branch. It was a quiet branch flowin' quick, with the sweetest water I think I ever tasted in the mountains. I would go there many times in my life just for the water. That was a gift from the Great Creator as I saw it. Like a good ramp patch what produced every spring.

The holler was a short ways off the main trail, but it would hide us and our camp smoke from anybody passin'. Henri went on ahead to fetch back Gus. Me and him both allowed it was best for Mary to ride. Her legs was spent, bein' tied like they was fer all them nights. Him goin' on ahead was good, too, 'cause his wound needed seein' to. He had medicines and homespun rags for bandages at his home. Hard cider fer doctorin' with, so goin' on to get Gus would allow him to settle his wound some. He'd not be back to camp 'fore morning. I allowed there was a chance he might need more'n what he had at his place to see to that wound, once I seen it good. It was deeper than I'd first thought. I could see it prob'ly hurt like hell's fire, had to, but he made not one sound or grimace that would let a body know he was painin'. He had uncommon strength when holdin' to his spiritual nature. Made it home walkin' that evening. It was the next day his wound commenced to givin' him trouble.

His bein' gone from camp fer the night was good for me. I needed to sit with Mary fer a spell in private. Speak family concerns. Talk to her about all she know'd of the happenin's at our farm over the last few days. I was mighty curious about the whereabouts of Dad. I felt in my spirit I already know'd the truth, but I still needed to hear it for certain. If I didn't find out for sure, I'd keep up hope for something that could never be, if it was. A person needed time to mourn full, too, without any doubt to the fact of what happened to their loved one. Knowin' the truth would allow me to move on... in time.

I would miss him a sight over the coming moons, if my suspicions proved true. My heart would ache near to death. Weren't no doubtin' that. The mourning of my brothers give proof to the hurt I know'd was comin' to me and Mary, if Dad was indeed gone. The fullness of it all would hit her now that she'd made freedom. I know'd how that was gonna feel. Oh, I wanted him to be alive.

I went to where Mary was resting. She looked asleep, and some cleaner than earlier. What water was runnin' in the branch let her wash some. She was still in need of fresh clothes and a long, hot, soakin' bath. I'd come to notice, in the short time I'd been tryin' to figure females, that they liked soakin' in the tub. They'd do it for any reason. Flowers picked fresh and brought in made 'em happy, too. Payin' mind to their person when they prettied up on preachin' Sundays meant a lot to 'em as well. Sometimes I'd wonder things about 'em I shouldn't... but couldn't help. Like... what it would be like to slide in beside one of 'em 'bout my age soakin' in the tub. Soak right up next to her for comfort. My skin next to her skin. Any one of 'em I ever touched for meetin' hugs or on accident was soft, but I'd never touched one for feelin' purposes. Them was nice thoughts to have, most likely sinful, but nice. Not near as hateful as the thoughts I lived with every day, since the war ended.

She'd chose a nice place to bed down for a while. Laid flat to the ground at the base of an old growth ivy bush. It's family standin' thick all around. She'd double folded Henri's winter quilt to lay on, one end turned back for a pillow, of sorts. He'd left her his sleepin' truck 'fore he headed out earlier. We most always carried a rolled up sleepin' quilt and bed roll when out on trail without a mule. Kept it bound with a small braided leather cord while carryin' it looped across our shoulder. The two ends of the cord tied under the arm opposite the side we carried our possibles pouch on. Carried it that 'a way to let a body step out of it quick if they needed. He'd be home 'fore dark, didn't need his bedroll, no, he'd be home, sleepin' in his own bed for the night, under his regular quilts. That sounded good to me. I hadn't done much inside sleepin' in a while.

She was layin' flat to her back with her face to the sky. Her hands crossed over her middle. Her head uphill from her feet. I could see the bruises on her wrist from the bindings she'd been tied with. You could hear the little branch what give us our drinkin' and cleanin' water, but just barely. It weren't good to camp close to runnin' water. The splashin' caused too much noise. Made it hard to hear if bad folks got to slippin' in durin' the night. Woods folk know'd to camp far enough away from streams so a body could hear danger if it come, man or critter. That was just common thought among my folk.

"Mary... Mary... wake, Mary," I whispered softly as I sat down cross-legged to the left side of her head, of course. I know'd a whisper was all that was usually needed to wake her. "We need to talk, Mary... Mary... wake, Mary, roust up, I need to know about Dad. Please, Mary. Tell me what you know. Don't keep it from me, be it bad or good. You're hearin' me, Sister. I know you're listenin'. Don't act like you ain't. You know I know you are. You always do. Tell me, Mary. Are we the last of our family? Has Dad moved on to be with Momma and the brothers? I will wait for you to answer. Take your time. I'm in no hurry, really."

It was a while 'fore she answered. I allowed she was asleep and might not 'a heard me after a bit. I was gettin' ready to poke her with something, make her wake, but then she spoke, if only but a whisper. Her one good eye never opening.

"I love you... Buach," she whispered soft. I had to lean my right ear toward her to hear. "Hate it that I do, I must tell you true. Proper you should know. Brother... stay yourself... the truth for you... it is as you have said... we are the last... our father is gone." She never looked at me while she spoke. I weren't sure she could.

My heart screamed out hearin' the truth. A bright light exploded behind my eyes. A ringing went through my ears that pierced my thoughts like light to darkness. Rage blew through my body like a dam bustin' loose, 'fore the sadness of him dyin' tore my heart out. It hit me hard. Like a deep sinkin' fist to the gut. My father was gone. I'd not see him again on Mother Earth. That thought was near too much fer me.

The words sounded strange as she spoke a little louder. Her mouth and jaw had to hurt when tryin' to talk. Whisperin' was most likely easier on her, but her blood had got up, tellin' me those things. Her mad was comin' on. She calmed herself enough to speak.

"The man... you spoke to yesterday... bragged to me... he killed Dad," she opened her left eye, turnin' her head to look square at me. "He... cut... Dad's... throat, Boo. Buried him... not sure where," she said, as her strength left her. She could talk no more. "I'm sorry... Boo... I must rest."

She settled herself after sayin' that. Her face turned back to the sky as her left eye closed. It weren't hard to see she was give out. She was hurtin' in her body, too. A single tear rolled from the corner of her left eye. Her heart was broke, same as mine. I took her hand and held it for a time. Nobody know'd but us.

There it was then. In my spirit, I'd been feelin' it was so. I just had to hear for certain. My dad was gone. He'd been made to move on. His soul had left to be with Jesus across the Great River, where most all our ancestors lived. I would never see him alive again, in my world, but I know'd I'd see him again when I crossed over. The Blood of Jesus give me that right, out 'a mercy and grace. It made me sad to realize he would not be helpin' me smoke the meat I'd just brought back from my hunt with the Cherokee. I'd been lookin' forward to spending that time with him. Tellin' him stories of our hunt. It was a good hunt. He would 'a wanted to hear all about it.

His way 'a livin' always made whatever you was doin' enjoyable, in some way or another. My dad loved life. His soul took the sadness sickness after Momma died. He never got over it whole, but he got all out 'a life that he could without her. Her passin' changed him. No doubtin' that, but he was always kind to me and Mary. Loved us like Momma would 'a wanted him, too. Never said nothin' to me after I took to livin' Indian most all the time. He gave our upbringing a foundation. I would not have that assurance from him anymore. Losin' that was painful. Caused a deep hole in my bein'. It give me comfort knowin' him and Momma was finally together, forever. My soul commenced to cryin' after the realness of all I'd learned hit me later in the night… it still cries.

Mary never woke again 'til morning. I figured she'd not slept much recent, bein' she was among hostile folk the last few days. She was still kind 'a dazed and confused as she come to the morning fire to warm. I poured her a hot tin 'a black morning coffee. She would need more rest to 'company some fresh food 'fore gainin' her strength back full. All her body parts seemed to be workin' except her right eye. It was still swollen. You couldn't see the eye at all, but the purple knot had gone down a right smart. She admitted her morning call produced some blood, but she expected that. She told me about it there at the fire. Said the big man had kicked her in the gut for askin' about Dad. It'd been hurtin' ever since. I would remind him of that soon. She allowed the women was mean to her as well, more so than the men, really.

I waited 'til she woke good 'fore commencin' our conversation from the previous evening. I weren't goin' back to the farm 'til I know'd all I could about what and who these takers was. I needed to store my emotions for a short time. Like a warrior preparin' for battle, I would move all my hurt to the back 'a my thinkin'. I made my mind to mourn Dad after we'd seen to riddin' our place of its recently obtained varmints. I would not let his passin' bother me for a time. How soon that time come to an end would be known when it was known. Mournin' a close loss is a difficult thing to work through.

"I'm sorry for what has happened to you, Sister. Life has come on you hard for this last little while. I am glad we got you out safe. We will pray later. Thank Holy Spirit fer lookin' after us, and for the well-being of the young one I stepped on leavin' our house. You should stay at Henri's for the next few days. Take some time to heal. That way you can be looked after. I believe that would be best for you. I will be there as well. At least, some of the time. Considerin' what I know you're gonna tell me, I believe I have a chore to finish 'fore settlin' in to mourn Dad. Tell me true, Mary. Don't hide anything from me. Tell me about how you found the place when you got back from Aunt Catherine's. I need for you to tell me all you know about these takers. I know you hurt in spirit and in body, your mouth is sore, but I have to know the truth so I can figure how to get our farm back without gettin' my killin'. Make things right for Dad. It's come time to settle with these evil ones from the North. Think clearly as you speak about all that has happened. Take your time. I will get revenge on these that have done this to us, Mary. Do not doubt what I say."

Her speakin' was slow. Her mouth just couldn't work like it should. Thankfully, nothing in her face was broken. Her right eye was in question, but it looked to be healin'. At least some of the swelling had gone down. I felt for her, as tears leaked out from both her eyes, just not as many from the swollen one. We both took a cross-legged seat on the ground. It took a few minutes 'fore she could talk to me. I smoked while we waited. I heard the deep pain we were both feelin' when her words finally did come. I said a little prayer for her on the quiet. She never heard it. It was hard for her to say all the words normal talk made, but she said plenty for understandin'.

"Confused when I came home, Boo. I saw folks, none I knew. I asked for Dad. None would tell me where he was. I rode my horse into the barn to dismount. My world went black. I heard, felt, fist of big man from behind as foot touched ground. When I woke, I was layin' on front porch floor. Couldn't see from right eye. Hands tied behind. Feet tied together. Corner of my mouth stinging. His fist split both my lips to my teeth. Hurts a sight. Pains to talk. They didn't tell me about Dad, so I asked when I woke. Big one said for me not to worry over him. I should worry that I didn't end up like him. I asked again, he kicked me in the gut. Sent a shooting pain through body. He got down in my face, while I was curled up on the ground, bragged about what he'd done. Tied Dad to pole in barn. Dad fussing over them being there. They got tired of him hollering. Cut his throat… to shut him up. He died… in the barn. They buried him. Never said where. Sorry, Brother."

She continued slowly, with much effort. A quiet whisper the best she could do, "As for all that are here as takers, six women and one maiden, eight young ones, four middle-aged, four soldiers. Two men went to hunt. All have guns, bullets, knives, and short guns. Getting into Dad's hard cider. Start drinking, men and women, after supper. Drink on 'til they're asleep. Kids, too. Terrible bunch to be with. I wish you'd send them away, Brother. I want to go home. Take a bath in our tub. Sleep in my bed. Make it happen, Boo. See justice done for Dad. Get our farm back. I'm sorry I have not the strength, perhaps tomorrow, stronger. I must rest now."

She went back to her restin' place on wobbly legs to lay down. I went to be alone in the woods, but not so far that I couldn't keep an ear on our camp. I needed to seek wisdom from Holy Spirit. Smoke things over. I built a small warmin' fire. Commenced to packin' my pipe with some air-dried Indian tobacco. My prayer took only a short while to converse. Weren't much time required when prayin' like I was prayin'. I didn't really know how to ask God for forgiveness of killin', when I ain't even done killin', yet. I left it for Him. I had all I could figure on at the present time.

After prayin' some, I sat for a spell just thinkin' about the matters I was facin'. I did receive some comfort rememberin' my dad was no longer sad for my momma. I thanked Holy Spirit for the thought. When I returned to camp, Henri was back. I could see right off something weren't right. He was laid out belly down on the ground atop a folded quilt, with another rolled up under his middle. His bare backside to the sky. Layin' like that made his naked behind look like the fat end of a new egg pointin' straight up. It would 'a been something to laugh at if it weren't kind 'a serious. Mary was bent over him, tendin' to what looked like just what it was. A small trough cut through his left behind cheek just above his leg. Mary was cleanin' it out and puttin' on some salve lookin' stuff he'd brought back from his place, along with a small poke of supplies. He was not in too good 'a shape. The wound had begun to fester. Fever was comin' on him. He was sayin' things that didn't make any sense. That would keep him from helpin' me for a few days, at least 'til he got clear headed again. I decided I'd use his healin' time to scout out our farm. Might be best to let things lay for a time, then move on in for justice once he healed, but I weren't comfortable with that thinkin'. I longed to make things right and I was fightin' the sadness that kept easin' into my mind, my spirit. I weren't sure how long I could hold it back. I couldn't believe Dad was gone. I felt so empty inside.

"Henri, my friend," I said, as I leaned down to look him in the face. His eyes was hollow. "How you feelin'? You don't look so good. You know who I am? You know whose tendin' to you? Do you need anything? I know the world seems kind 'a upside down to you right now, but you'll be up straight 'fore you know it. Can you hear me, Henri?"

He opened his eyes when he heard me, noddin' slightly, but sayin' not a word. I don't think he know'd me from any common outlaw that might 'a walked up. Fever was catchin' hold to his mind, and it'd come on him fast. We would have to stay close to him for the next day or so. It would take that long for the medicines he'd brought back for Mary to start workin' good. He must 'a know'd by the time he got home that fever was comin' for a visit. He'd brought back the quilts and doctorin' supplies so we could tend to him. Our short camp had turned into a long camp. That was just the way things worked out sometimes in the mountains. I never minded sleepin' out in the woods, but inside comfort was nice, too.

"Mary, how do you feel?" I asked, as I moved to sit by Henri. "You look tired. I will be here through the night, maybe you can get some sleep while I am here, fer I will not be here when Old Man Sun brings his light to this camp in the morning. You must care for Henri while I'm gone. Will you be able to do that?"

She stopped tendin' to Henri to look over at me, and said, "I feel stronger, but I can feel the weakness, too. I believe you are right. A good sleep will help me feel much stronger. Tomorrow, you go and do what you must do. Wake me before you leave. Come back before dark if you are able, if not, come when you can. We will be fine. Henri explained how to use all the wound mixes he brought back. I pray he will be better in two or three suns. We will go to his place and wait for you, if you are not back here before he is strong enough to travel. Do not worry over me. You've done enough of that lately. Leave here with a clear mind, Boo. All will be good when you return."

I slept like a dead oak log durin' the night. Not risin' but twice to check on Henri. Havin' Mary back safe was a relief to one 'a my main concerns. Henri slept like a log his own self. Them medicines he'd brought back was potent. He know'd different plants, herbs, and roots, that when you mix certain parts of this or that together, could make you feel better. Much better most of the time. Learned it from the Cherokee. Kept a whole store of glass jars with all different kinds 'a mixes for different ailments and uses. He kept 'em in the cave part of his home where it stayed cool year 'round. I'd seen him drop a huge black bear with a root poison he'd made for the tips of his blowgun darts. Seen him shoot folks as well. He favored his blowgun. That bear didn't go twenty paces after Henri stuck it in the rump. We eat on that thing for several days. The hide made a great bear blanket. Weren't no killin' holes in it.

Come morning, I was gone from camp. I never woke Mary. Weren't no reason to disturb her sleepin'. Henri was fine. Still sleepin' when I left a couple hours 'fore daylight. I wanted to get to the old white oak on the rise above our farm 'fore Old Man Sun rose. I had my knives, rifle, and short gun. I'd packed a possibles pouch with enough essentials for a week. Didn't think I'd be gone that long, but it was best to be prepared when goin' out on a trail like I was makin'… and I didn't think it wise to run low on powder and shot. You'd not want to overpack, but you had to have what you had to have. I was most likely goin' to a fight. I packed the weapons I would need. I was still tryin' to settle with that as I climbed the white oak and got comfortable. Old Man Sun was soon to rise.

CHAPTER 7

My First Killin' fer Purpose

My watch from the white oak show'd me much that morning. I finally seen them other soldiers Mary'd told me was there. They weren't no different than the two I'd talked to out at the gate, maybe some younger. Most likely family, or family of friends. It made me sick watchin' 'em live life on our farm. The feelin' of strangers livin' natural in our home pushed me to all I could stand. I was intent on seein' to their thievin' sooner rather than later, Henri or no Henri.

Mad went full up my back when I seen the big one come from the house not long after daylight. I felt my fist clinch. My back muscles jerk tight. He looked some different movin' along than the last time I'd seen him. His shoulders was slumped. His head hangin' low. Didn't seem like the herd bull I'd dealt with a couple days before. Look to me like he might be sick or hurt in some way. He come out the back door, then went back in several times as I watched from the rise. The last time he went in, he didn't come back out for a spell.

I did not expect what happened a bit later that morning. I know'd when I thought about it, the night we got Mary free, that the boy could die from me steppin' on him. Only after I watched the family come from our log home carryin' his body for burial, did I realize the full extent of the tragedy. That boy had died, and I'd killed him.

It was an accident. It weren't planned, but I'd ended his life when I stepped on him. The sickness from realizin' what I'd done near made me black out cold. I had to catch hold with my whole body to keep from fallin' off my perch in the old white oak. It was a sickness like I'd never felt. I'd took life, innocent life. That just weren't the way. I know'd killin' fer right would enter my walk one day, but I'd never imagined killin' an innocent. A body could never be ready for how I was feelin'. The hurt inside was pure agony fer that young 'un. I had to force myself to stay focused on the happenin's of everything else I was dealin' with. Yes, that boy was dead, and that was an awful thing. Yes, Dad was dead, and that was an awful thing. Yes, the big one killed him. Yes, he'd be made to pay justice fer doin' it, but they was takers livin' in my home. That changed the rules.

From the slouching I'd seen earlier, I allowed he might be the father of the boy. Did that make it fair in the eyes of justice? Was justice done for my dad? No, how could it be? Dad had been murdered by the big man. That boy's killin' weren't fer purpose. Death happened in the mountains, for sure when happenings one was involved in was outside the law. Common thing, that. Weren't nobody's fault a lot 'a times. Accidents happen in dangerous places. I would let it settle there.

I stayed the old oak watchin' 'til way up in the morning. Them folks dug a shallow hole in our family cemetery to bury the boy. Never took the time to fashion him a proper coffin, which they didn't even need to do. Dad had some pine boxes made up for family, standin' on end in the barn. Most homesteads did. It was important to get bodies in the ground not too long after dyin'. Havin' some burial boxes made up 'fore death ever happened helped with that.

They at least wrapped him in an old quilt 'fore tossin' him into his cold grave hole. One of the women fell to her knees when the first spade 'a dirt hit the quilt from the big one fillin' the hole back in. It was sad to watch. Made me figure Northern folk didn't care for their loved ones the way Southern folk did. They could 'a used a coffin, just chose not to. That left the grave where nighttime varmints could get at the body. Foolish and disrespectful, way I seen it.

Learnin' all I could about my new enemy got my legs to crampin' hard from sittin' way too long in the white oak, watchin'. I had to come down a little 'fore dinner to stretch 'em out. I'd seen all I needed anyhow. I trailed back east a ways, after my legs got their feelin' back, wantin' to find a place for an overnight camp. I had some thinkin' to do. Prayin', too. I was now a killer, of sort, and I needed to study on that a while. Come to season with it. I hadn't meant to kill that boy. Figured they might be some purposeful killin' since they was outlaws to be settled with, but I never figured fer innocents. It weren't murder straight out, like what they'd done to my dad, but a body had lost its life… and I'd took it. That didn't set well in my soul. It bothered me a sight. I hoped the killin' what was comin' didn't feel so terrible. I was comfortable thinkin' it wouldn't. A price was to be paid for what they'd done to Dad, to our place. I'd see to it. I just regretted the boy got mixed up in our freein' Mary.

I made a small warming fire after gettin' settled into camp. What little jerky I was able to get down give me sustenance, but I was of no mind for eatin'. I sat cross-legged by the fire thinkin' on the things I was aimin' to do. The settling I longed for. The father I wanted back. Death had tampered with my appetite. I could feel my body needed food, but my mind couldn't settle on eatin' it. That boy dyin' was a bother. I couldn't move on from it in my mind. That was dangerous fer me. My soul was holdin' guilt. I had to try and make the worry get gone to rid myself of any distraction thinkin' on it could cause. That kind 'a distraction could get me killed in a second when fightin' folks like I was fixin' to confront. It was messin' up my thinkin' on how to plan my settlin' of their doin's. I bowed my head while speakin' a slow prayer to Holy Spirit for understandin'. After finishin' up my talkin' to the Lord, I packed a pipe bowl full 'a air dried Indian tobacco, fetchin' a splinter from the fire to light it with. That'd calm me some while I listened for the voice I know'd would come.

Weren't but a little while 'fore my waitin' was over. I heard Holy Spirit's voice in my heart clear as an owl hootin' on a dark night. The thoughts He give me changed my whole reasonin' 'bout how I felt over all the wrong what'd been done. Brought me back to the real of what was happenin' to me and my family. I know'd in my soul the word was from Him, too, 'cause He made me to remember just how things was, and whose fault it all had come to be. It weren't fair that them evil folk was able to bury their dead. Got to pray over 'em for their goodbyes... we did not. Accordin' to Mary, Dad was butchered like a hog and tossed into the cold ground without one family member bein' there. That was unacceptable to me.

I cared little of the death of that boy after Holy Spirit brought that thinkin' back to my mind. I still hated it'd happened to him, but I cared little that I'd done it. I felt in my soul that Holy Spirit wanted me to move on. Have a clear mind, so I did. That would make the coming confrontation much more dangerous to them outlaws. I felt good about that.

As I stretched out long ways on my sleepin' quilt beside the fire, all my thinkin' turned to Dad. Bein' careful not to stare into the small flames, I let my thoughts wander. The scents and sounds of the night filled my spirit with a fullness and comfort only the mountains can wrap a body in. A connection one must live to understand. A cool, soft breeze brought the strange sense of a calm one can only feel when layin' flat on your back at the bottom of a valley while bein' surrounded by the huge ridges of the Southern Appalachian Mountains. That peace allowed me to stay myself inside my soul. The things Mary told me these takers had done began to fill my mind. My anger got to burnin' for vengeance. I wanted to charge in while drawin' both my knives. Go full bore into them folks killin' all I could, worryin' over the rest as they come, but I know'd I'd not be able to do that. Actin' foolish would get me killed. That'd do Mary no good.

I studied on the things I was facin', 'bout takin' our farm back, justice for Dad, settlin' for Mary, 'til way up in the night. At some point I dozed off. Moon hollerin' ki'yotes woke me after a time. They was close. Not sure how long I'd been asleep. Not sure that it mattered. What did matter, though, was that I'd come to a decision as to my responsibility concernin' the effort it was gonna take to make things right. It was my farm. It was my task to get it back. I couldn't ask nobody else to get hurt tendin' to my business. Henri'd near got his killin' when we went for Mary. That was his blood that was draw'd from my call. They shot to kill, but, fortunately for us, failed in the deed. I would not miss. I wanted my home back. I was aimin' to have it. These ones from the North did not belong there. They would be gone soon, or dead. It mattered not to me. I just wanted 'em off our place.

I slept in some next morning. Daylight was showin' over the big ridges to the east when I woke. I chewed some jerky for my morning meal. Figured it best that I eat a bite 'fore startin' out to sit in the white oak again. I felt it wise to watch the happenings around our place for a second morning. Make sure all was as I thought it would be. I had in mind to let 'em know I was around come the afternoon. My fight was beginning.

Even though I'd settled with the death of that boy in my mind, I still felt I needed to say my apologies to his spirit in person. I'd not wanted to hurt none 'a the little ones. He should 'a stayed the floor where he was sleepin'. Not tried to interfere. His life was not worth the cost of what might 'a been.

I allowed it was safe enough to ease myself into our family burial ground not long after midday. I figured them lazy takers to be restin' after dinner, 'fore goin' back to workin' their afternoon chores about our place. The boy's grave was freshly humped where all the dirt wouldn't fit back in. Some 'cause 'a the boy's dead body. The rest from it bein' a full moon night the day it was dug. I bowed my head while sinkin' to one knee thinkin' the things I wanted his spirit to know. Starin' hard into the fresh dug earth hopin' the young one would come to know my heart. I never felt he heard me, but like how long I'd slept earlier, it didn't really matter to me. If he heard me, he heard me. It was good with me if he didn't, 'cause at the bottom of my bein', I found no care for him. I should 'a felt more, bein' Christian and all… but I didn't. My dad was dead on account 'a him and his tryin' to steal our place. That truth burned hot into my desire to send these away.

As I rose to leave the boy's grave, I saw something that was off. It was only a faint catch of the eye, but it draw'd me like a bad spirit to a killin'. The ground next to the boy's grave was different than it should 'a been. It was of a color and mix that kind 'a matched the fill dirt from the new grave. It should 'a been a place covered in old leaves and hardened dirt, cause we hadn't buried any of our family in a while, but it weren't. The old ground had been disturbed and kind 'a covered back over with the old leaves and such to hide a fresh dig, but I could see the dirt mix bein' down low like I was while prayin'. It was near the same mix 'a dirt as what the new dig looked like. That couldn't be, seein' how they was only one grave present. At least, only one fresh from that day.

I bent a little closer from the waist to try and figure why the dirts looked the same. It come on me hard after studyin' over it fer a minute. The only way that could be was if the ground next to the new grave had been turned same as the dirt what filled in the boy's grave. That thinkin' took me to my knees. From there, I could see what I didn't wanna see. Obvious as lightnin' strikin' close. Laid out right in front of me was the outline of a not so fresh dig, but fresh enough to know it was a recent dig. I know'd what it was right off when I seen it. I'd found where they buried Dad. My soul commenced to cryin'. I could not move.

I weren't sure how long he'd been dead 'cause I didn't know how many days the takers had actually been there. I figured they'd killed him when they first come, but however long that was, it'd been long enough for the humped-up dirt in the center to settle. That would 'a took a few days for sure. Dirt on a grave settlin' that quick meant only one thing to me, they hadn't buried Dad in box, neither. Them sorry takers hadn't buried either body in a pine box. They had to 'a seen the built boxes standin' in the corner of the barn. The diggin' tools was right next to 'em. Once I got our farm back, I would needs tend to that. Dad's body needed to be moved to a box. I weren't sure I was gonna worry over the boy. Depended on the critters. None had bothered Dad's grave, yet, that I seen, but it would take a while fer 'em to find him. If that was same for the boy's grave when I come back to re-bury Dad, I'd leave him where and how he laid.

I've tried to put into words the way I felt when it come to me there was a recent grave next to the boy's. I wanted to dig up whatever was in there, but I didn't want to, neither. The not wantin' to won out for the time. I planned to ask the big one if this other hole held my dad's body. No doubtin' it did, but I wanted him to tell me. I meant for it to be the last words he ever spoke.

I was shakin' some from realizin' what I was lookin' at. It took me a while to rise off my knees and back to my feet. My legs wiggled like a new foal tryin' to learn to walk. My whole bein' was racked. My senses full. Still, I had to make myself move. It weren't safe bein' out in the open, weak as I was. I know'd the takers was gonna want blood over losin' their loved one, and the blood they'd be wantin' was mine. They'd take it quick if they found me standin' over Dad's grave struggin' like I was. It didn't matter to them that burial ground was considered by most folk, what lived in the mountains, to be sacred ground. No killin' was allowed among the dead. That just weren't right. Mountain folk believed spirit haints would haunt you if you disrespected the dead where they slept. I believed the same, but if one 'a them takers come on me while I stood among our dead, I'd defend myself - haints or no haints. The ancestors would just have to understand.

I laid in camp all afternoon studyin' on how I was gonna present myself to the takers. I thought to just shoot the big one from a little ways off and fight 'em that way, but that seemed cowardly to me. Weren't proper justice, neither. Nor did it satisfy my need for vengeance. They'd beat and abused Mary. Killed Dad in a most hurtful and disrespectful way. Why would I give them the ease of a lead ball through the heart? No, I had some things I wanted to say to the big one 'fore he went away. I was gonna make sure he know'd just how much hurt him and his had caused, and that what he'd done to my folks had cost him his life. He deserved it. I didn't even want his hateful ol' body to rot anywhere near our place. I'd burn it, or worse, if they left without it after his killin', which I figured they would.

I slept some while thinkin' on the coming confrontation. I'd been able to hide the hurt deep down in my bein' of coming to know for sure Dad was gone. It would hit me hard later on, but for the time, I had to keep my thinkin' clear. I was facin' my own death, if I made the slightest slip up with these soldiers. They was trained to kill folks when they wanted, but I meant to have a settlin' with 'em anyhow. There was a good chance I could be kilt, yes. Weren't no guarantees on how this thing was gonna end. That's a worrisome thought when havin' to deal with men who was common with killin'.

I woke a couple hours short 'a dark, with a fullness from my rest... my spirit surprisingly calm. It'd come time to let these tryin' to homestead our farm know they weren't welcome on Long Shot Ridge. Never had been. Not sure who'd be left to leave out when the fight was done, 'cause I was gonna kill all it would take to get shed of 'em, for sure the ones responsible for murderin' Dad. Maybe I'd even end that mean woman what beat Mary, too. It's wrong to hurt folks for purpose, and I'd see they understood how I felt about that.

I stripped off my shirt and made my way to the small branch I'd camped near. The scent of the woods strong as evening was closin'. I said my prayer while lettin' the sound of the little creek take my cares to the Great Spirit. I dipped my hands into the flow, fetchin' enough water to pour over my head and down my back. I felt the coolness of it on my bare skin as it ran. Felt the cleansing as it left my body and fell to Mother Earth. Holy Spirit was hearin' my prayer. My spirit felt His answer. It was a good answer. I would not be killed in this fight. I would have my way. I would get our farm back. I was confident of it. That give me a power I'd not known just the night before. Like the Ark of the Covenant going on before the Israelites, my given courage would lead me through. Holy Spirit was with me. My soul felt Him. Justice would soon be on its way for Dad.

My plan was to slip into the barn and wait for whoever come to tend the stock that evening. I would make myself known' to that one. Tell 'em I wanted them and theirs gone. I hoped it would be the big one. I'd like to be done with him. Surprise would be in my favor. I would use that. There were too many for me to fight at one time. I needed to even out the odds 'fore takin' on the big one, if he weren't the one what come to the barn to feed. Of course, he weren't. Our fight would have to wait.

Walter didn't know how to act when he come face-to-face with me in the barn that evening, just before dark. He was aimin' to feed their stock our oats. The look on his face was one of true surprise that he'd found me where I was. He let out one of his sick coughs 'fore makin' his last purposeful movement on earth. A reach with his right hand to try and grab his short gun brought him his end. I can't blame him. I figure I'd 'a done the same thing. Instincts on his part what it was. He'd prob'ly done that a hundred times in the war. It was instinct on my part, too. I never hesitated once I seen him goin' for his gun, closin' the ground 'tween me and him on the quick. The next thing he felt was the sharp point of my long knife, edge up, sliding smooth into his middle. I missed his main vitals for purpose, not wantin' him to die right off. Me and him needed to talk a bit 'fore he went to be judged by his maker. He looked me in the eye as his knees went weak. I held him up with my blade. Slicin' up on his insides as he slumped his full weight. He was strugglin' for air.

"I know what your thinkin', soldier man," I said while drawin' him in closer with my long knife, starin' him eye-to-eye. I tilted the blade up just a bit makin' him feel it. That opened the lung worse makin' him struggle harder for air. I felt good about that as his warm blood run down from my blade to the handle of the long knife, coverin' the fingers of my right hand. His breath smelled of blood, hard cider, and old tobacco. Near made me wretch. Most likely some 'a Dad's best brew and rolled burley. I turned the knife a little more when that thought hit me. He grunted as I moved my face closer to his left ear, without touchin' him, to speak.

"You're wonderin', Walter, now just who is it that has ended my life? Maybe you want to know why? Well, let's see here, just if you ain't figured it out, yet, I own this place, boy. Me and that pretty girl y'all been beatin' on the last few days. I come back from a hunt. Found y'all had took over our farm. That's why you're dyin' here, stuck to my knife like a gigged frog. That and…" I moved in closer so's he'd hear me and understand for certain, "you rats killed my dad." I twisted my long knife again as I finished sayin' that. He moaned.

His eyes got big as I tilted my knife even more, cuttin' his lung even deeper, then slicin' his heart. I give it another twist while slowly slidin' it out lettin' the blood flow. Walter wobbled on spent legs fer a short second. He spoke what little more he could while pressin' at the wound I'd made with both his hands. Blood leakin' out through his fingers.

"I had… nothing… to do… with… killin'. Stuart, he… done it. Forgive… me… boy," Walter said, as he settled to his knees on the barn floor. I kicked him over flat so's I could talk to him face on as he died.

"My name is Buach, heathen, not boy, and them's words you need to save for your Creator." I squatted down beside him. Blood leakin' through his fingers every time his heart would beat, "'cause you're fixin' to meet Him. Stuart, he must be the man I talked to out by the gate when I come the other morning?" Walter nodded what he could. "That's who he is, huh? I figured him for doin' the murderin' deed, like you say, but you had a hand in it, Walter. You could 'a stopped it, but you didn't. Now look at ye. Look what the thievin' life has cost ye… your life. Was it worth it… boy? Would you do it all over again?… Yeah, I believe you would."

"Do not… kill… my…" Walter never finished what he meant to say, as he'd run out 'a air and had no strength to draw in more. I could kind 'a figure what he was meanin'. Begging for his family most likely. That took a goodness I didn't think these kind from the North had. That part of him mattered little, now that the settlin' had begun.

I made no plans to hurt his family, or any of their families, really, as I sat the fire in my camp that night thinkin' about what I'd done to Walter. I hoped once I settled with this Stuart, that the others would leave. I'd drug Walter out to the privy and put him inside, then made my way back to camp. I'd sat him up like he was there to answer the call but fell asleep in the effort. That'd get a rise out 'a them takers when they went for their morning callin'. They'd be out lookin' fer me once they seen Walter had been kilt, and they'd find me. I'd left an easy enough trail to follow back to my camp, then on south the next morning for about a mile. I figured them to find me not long after they got to lookin'. I'd be ready. Made my mind, while studyin' on things durin' the night, to bring 'em to my ground for the fight. I grow'd up in the woods around our place. I know'd every inch of every mountaintop and holler. They would pay when they followed my trail. I felt good about that, too.

I would respect Walter's dyin' wish. Gettin' the fightin' folk away from the women and kids for the settlin' would help with that, unless one 'a them huntin' me was his son. I would not honor his request, then. Killin' was bound to happen from the first footprint these heathens put on our place. Weren't no doubtin' that. I felt nothing for killin' Walter. It hurt much more knowin' I'd ended the life of the young one who was an innocent. He'd paid the price for his family's stealin', while the others hadn't. I would remind the big one of that as well. As far as I was concerned, this Stuart's fate was sealed.

The Legend of Swell Branch

CHAPTER 8

"Thou Shalt Not Steal"

I could smell their stock 'fore I ever heard 'em. Heard 'em 'fore I ever saw 'em. It was kind 'a spooky when I finally seen 'em actual, ridin' their soldier horses while lookin' for me. Looked to be near all they'd been give to fight the South with was on them horses, 'cept I didn't hear nor see no sabres. I wondered fer that. Maybe they was smart enough to know they made noise that would give 'em away in the woods, or maybe not. Them comin' loaded full like they was, told me they didn't respect my threat as an enemy much, or they'd be slippin' along on foot all quiet like. Hopin' to find me 'fore I found them. Folks movin' through the woods like they was weren't natural to the forest like me and mine, or critters. Strange lookin' when you'd see 'em.

They was followin' the sign I'd left fer 'em. That was good. It was a back trail what led toward the north end of Long Shot. I wanted 'em to find me. Anybody with a little sign readin' talent could see where I'd left out from the privy evening prior, after leavin' Walter fer 'em to find. Weren't nothin' mountain wise or savvy about 'em ridin' them horses while travelin' a back trail lookin' fer me. The mountains had become a dangerous place fer any, for the times, considerin' me bein' there or not. Outlaws from the North was rangin' constant, lookin' to take what they could find. They'd take from their own, too, I come to learn.

A body couldn't be an easier target in the woods than when they're travelin' the small trails while ridin' up high on a horse. Main trails weren't much of a worry. Folks rode those with little threat, but a body had to be careful ridin' stock on the back trails. I'd ride Gus a right smart, but only on common travels or when usin' the main road. I usually walked him with a lead on the off trails, lessin' I was in a hurry. It was obvious these rogues weren't in no hurry. They was just lazy. Amblin' along like they was near asleep. Backs kind 'a slouched. Heads up enough to see. Eyes searchin' the woods. Arms crossed over their saddle horns. They didn't seem to be payin' much mind, just kind 'a watchin' as they went. The one in front doin' the sign readin'. Them followin' me would be bad for 'em real soon. I was gonna see to it.

I stayed the ground to confront the takers. More cover to hide in. Gus was still at Henri's, so I had no worry over him, but I wondered for Henri's leg, if it was healin'. He'd be mad I didn't wait fer him to confront the takers, but I allowed he'd suffered enough. Most likely gonna suffer more 'fore his wound healed complete. Turned out it was dangerously deep. Knowin' that, I made my mind to go ahead and see to the takers and not worry my friend over helpin' me. He'd already helped 'a plenty. After studyin' on it overnight, I come to see that gettin' my farm back by myself weren't gonna be all that big a problem, if I worked it right. A plan come to mind. It weren't no vision, but I felt comfortable with it just the same.

I weren't expectin' 'em to be mounted when I picked out my watchin' place 'fore daylight, but here they come, steady as a deep creek flowin', a few hours after daylight. Stuart bringin' up the rear as the trail started up a little rise. I was sittin' to the east side 'a that rise. The sun at my back. My Springfield pointed down trail at 'em. They followed one behind the other in a short line. Every muscle I had knotted at the sight 'a Stuart when I first spotted him at the rear of his bunch. His head was hangin' same as it was last I'd seen him. I allowed the hurt of death was still smartin' him inside. I felt fer him over that, but it give me comfort knowin' I was fixin' to end his sufferin'. He'd not have to worry over his recent loss much longer. My thinkin' was to send him where his son was real soon, or maybe not, considerin' his soul's reward. Thinkin' that made me feel like I was doin' him a favor. I didn't wanna do him any favors, but I couldn't help it. Justice was to be served. He was gonna die fer killin' my dad, even if it cost me my life.

These men was followin' my trail with the single desire of ending me. If they caught me, they'd torture me for killin' one 'a their own, then lay me low. They'd done killed Dad. Since I'd returned the favor by leavin' Walter in the privy, they'd know I know'd they'd murdered Dad. That was a settlin' thought as I draw'd a fine bead on the one leadin' the bunch, but I weren't gonna shoot him off his horse without givin' him a chance to make things right. Cold killin' for vengeance weren't justice. Seemed cowardly to me. That's what men like the ones I was facin' would do. I weren't like them. I didn't wanna be like them. I would honor them as people. Give 'em a fair warning. A favor they'd not hesitate to take from me, if I was the one who'd done wrong.

I was hid good as could be and still be able to shoot toward where they was. I'd been waitin' on 'em behind a big poplar tree some thirty paces off the trail. The tree was on the steep at a place where the trail turned to climb a small rise. I picked a spot above where they trailed to address 'em. I'd made my mind to shoot the first two, if provoked. The one in front bein' my first target. I wanted the big one to be alone when me and him had our little talk.

The words I chose gettin' 'em to stop might not 'a been the exact thing I should 'a said. I was kind 'a new at assaultin' folks, but it worked out well enough. They stopped when they heard me. I wanted 'em to know it was me they was trailin'. I wanted 'em to know it was me confrontin' 'em. The son of the one they'd murdered. Owner of the farm they'd took.

It was my intent to even out the odds a bit. Three on one, when dealin' with men like I was lookin' at, was too one-sided, considerin' their fightin' history and the lack of mine. I needed to slim down the threat to my person a little. At the distance I was, I would not miss if they forced me to shoot. I was gonna give 'em a choice to leave out, takin' their families with 'em, or die. Either way, I aimed to get our farm back for me and Mary. If they had any smarts at all, they'd take the trail home to where they'd come from real quick like. I doubted they had that kind 'a reason to their bein's, so I settled the butt of my

Springfield into the meat of my shoulder nice and solid. That thing give you a kick when it went off. Not hard and quick like a smaller rifle, but smooth and solid like the walnut stock it was made from. The half-inch wide piece 'a lead it throw'd out did some nasty work when it struck meat and bone. You could hit things a long ways off with it, too.

"That's far as y'all need to be goin', takers - home stealers," I said, speakin' loud as I needed fer any of 'em to hear me. They stopped where they was, kind 'a shocked lookin', while raisin' their lazy heads to look toward where my voice had come from. "Anyone 'a y'all moves one finger, I'll shoot that 'un off the horse he's stole. I ain't makin' fun, neither. I got a fine bead with my Springfield on one of ye. Try me and see if I ain't speakin' truth." My words got the big one to raise his head full. His face turned to mean when he figured out it was me talkin' at 'em. I kept on explainin'.

"I ain't gonna tolerate the takin' of my home… nor am I gonna let pass the murder of my dad. Justice is to be paid. Now listen close. I want the two 'a y'all in the front to get gone. I'm givin' you a chance to fetch your families and leave. The big one in the back there, Stuart, the murderer, he'll be stayin' here with me. We gonna have us a little talk. Y'all hearin' me? Understand what I'm tellin' you?"

They stood their ground, starin' in my direction. None moved to spite me. Never made one effort toward leavin'. None said a word back in reply, neither. I thought maybe they didn't hear me good. I started sayin' it again, louder.

"Did y'all not hear me? Let me say it all once more. Maybe a little louder this time. I'm tellin' you two in the front to turn around. Go back and pack all your truck. Get yourselves and your families gone from my home. This is my only warning. Out 'a mercy, I'm gonna give y'all one chance to leave without harm, 'cause 'a my good nature I suppose… but if you leave here alive, and ain't gone from our place by midday tomorrow, I'll see to your leavin' personal. The big one in the back there, that… boy, like I said, stays where he's at, or I'll just shoot him now." I cocked the hammer back on my Springfield. It needed to be ready to fire.

I'd waited about cockin' my rifle 'til the time was right. The cockin' sound was loud, like it should 'a been, but they never flinched when they heard it. I thought they might, but I should 'a know'd they wouldn't. I was hopin' to spook 'em some. I allowed the Springfield was fixin' to speak fer me more direct.

"Hey, y'all deef? Am I makin' myself clear? Say if I am," I hollered even louder.

I know'd they weren't no way they was gonna do what I told 'em. I was simply stoakin' their flame. They sat their horses a minute. Looked like they was thinkin', when of a sudden, the front two commenced to turnin' their right shoulders over in front of their left sides to look back at Stuart. He didn't look at 'em. His gaze was straight at me. It was obvious he'd figured out which tree my voice was comin' out from behind. His look was hard as cold steel. I could see he was lookin' right through the big poplar to where I was now squatted on my knees aimin' my rifle down at them. He know'd where I was. Prob'ly could see a little of me. I looked for him to lunge his horse straight off the trail and up at me, but he never moved. Sat his horse like the hurt man he was. I'd killed his boy. I'd killed his soldier brother. Now I was gonna kill more. His spirit could sense it. War fightin' made him know that not all who walked into an ambush like the one I'd set fer them would walk away. He didn't know who I'd shoot first, but he show'd no fear. Like it hadn't come to him yet that he'd been caught out in the open by his worst enemy. His look was that of die or kill. I allowed it would be death. Holy Spirit had brought me to mind. I had no fear.

The bead of my Springfield was closest to the first man in line as they turned back to Stuart. Seemed like they might be tryin' to figure out what to do next, maybe. I felt more than know'd they was more to what they was doin' in them saddles than conversin' with their leader. Didn't seem they was doin' much talkin'. He never looked at them. Their movements didn't seem right for such an action as talkin'. Weren't proper motion for just bein' curious, or simply discussin' their predicament. They weren't no need to turn full like they did unless they was up to somethin'. I picked up on that 'cause my senses was workin' full on. Different than I'd ever felt before. It come to me right then, them movin' like they did was nothin' more than a way to hide their real intent. When that thought brought the truth of what was happenin' to mind, I centered my rifle's bead on the first man in line. I'm sure glad I did, 'cause no sooner had I centered my aim, than they both whipped back around fast to their right, openin' their centers to my rifle. Both of 'em's right hands full 'a Colt .44's. I heard 'em both cock as they was swingin' toward me. Stuart never moved. Just kept starin' right at me.

    I guess I weren't hid as good as I should 'a been, 'cause both them lead balls thudded the tree square in front 'a where I was squatted in back. They'd a both hit me had it not been for the tree. I was havin' to aim back at 'em from its side. That made my right shoulder and part of my head stick out in the open some. That let 'em know where I was. Give 'em a target. Weren't much of a target, but I figure they seen me well enough, way their shots hit so close. I had no choice but to be exposed a bit. I had to aim, so I was somewhat out from behind the tree. I would remember how them chunks 'a lead sounded when they hit together like they did that morning, then later on when thinkin' on all the happenings over a smoke. Give me a chill rememberin' how hard they hit. The vibration I felt come through to my side.

    I could see the Springfield's bead was surrounded by the dirty homespun shirt of the first rider as I looked down the length of its .58 caliber barrel. The heavy gun exploded against my shoulder as I pulled back on its steel trigger after findin' that bead. I saw the first rider's arms go out straight as he buckled in the middle. His Colt still clutched hard in his right fist. The lead ball I'd sent blowed him clean out 'a his saddle, landin' him square on his rump with a grunt. The grunt caused by all his air comin' out through the hole I'd punched through his center. I could see he laid flat to his back on the forest floor as I was leavin' out from behind the big poplar. His arms straight out to his sides. I'd just killed my second man for purpose. It bothered me none. I cared little. These folks had murdered my dad and was tryin' to end me. I was glad they was gone.

    Once I'd fired on them heathens, I made to get clean 'a where I'd shot from. As I headed south from the poplar, I seen all three horses was empty of their riders. The one I'd shot layin' flat his back on the ground. Blood stainin' his soldier shirt full across the front of his chest. The other two takers nowhere to be seen.

    I reloaded my Springfield on the run, landin' myself behind a big log some fifty paces away from where their horses stood riderless. It come to me that they was now on foot in my world, lookin' to kill me. That made me smile. Only God could save 'em 'fore they ever got back on them ponies.

    Everything was quiet as I lay behind the oak log… watchin'… listenin'. My rifle reloaded full. I had it laid across the soft, rotting bark of the old oak, pointed back toward their horses. Not being sure where the thieves had gone, I was watchin' close. These men wore heavy soldier boots with hard soles. I'd noticed that soon as I seen 'em comin' down the trail. It was important in a seek and find kind 'a fight in the mountains, that a body knows what foot coverings their enemy is wearin'. Everything makes its own sound in the woods. I would hear these men way 'fore they ever got close to me. That give me confidence to move around and search. I'd wore my lace up footskins like I always did. I could move quiet as a snake slidin'.

    The mast on the forest floor was dry. Crackly when walked on. We'd not had a lot 'a rain around Swell Branch that spring. The fell leaves from the fall season previous had rotted enough to be mingled in among the older mixin's what covered the ground. Cherokee could walk quiet in that kind 'a coverin'. I could walk quiet in that kind 'a coverin', but them soldier men could not. Weren't possible in the boots they was wearin'. It give me some concern thinkin' they might take 'em off. Try to slip around in their sock feet, but that would do them no good. They still didn't know how to move to stay quiet. I thought to listen out for that. Didn't figure 'em smart enough to think 'a doin' it, but it paid a body to be mindful when folks was out to kill 'em.

    I allowed they hadn't gone too far from where their fellow soldier lay dead, so I should hear 'em movin' when they come lookin'. I know'd they'd wanna find me. Most likely search long as it took. I was certain 'a that. No matter to me, we had all day if need be. I was in no hurry. These men was no better than mice trapped by the local stud cat, and they didn't even know it. The cat just needed time to find 'em.

When I left out south from where I'd first shot the front taker, I didn't go far. There was a thick bunch of old growth ivy not more'n twenty paces on to the east from the poplar tree I'd chose to watch from 'fore daylight. I'd spotted an old log layin' long ways around the side of the hill amongst that ivy, not long after a body could see good. My idea was to go there to hide if I shot any of 'em. I'd settle in behind it to listen, watch. So after I fired, that's what I did.

After a few minutes there watchin' and listenin', I'd seen nor heard nothin'. My breathin' had settled. I could hear full on. I decided it was time to go find 'em. I had the advantage bein' in the woods where we was. I'd grow'd up there. I know'd every holler, ridge top, rock face, and stream within all directions for a long way. I figured it smart to use that to my benefit. These mice would not escape. I said a little prayer for their souls 'fore I left out from the ivies. I hoped the best fer 'em… once they was facin' their Maker.

After studyin' on what I should do, my thinkin' led me back to the trail I was watchin' when the evil ones come. They most likely took to lookin' for me once they jumped their horses to go 'a foot. I would look to track 'em from where they'd left them horses. Odds was they split up once they left for cover.

Once I made it out to the trail from the ivies, I seen their horses was still where they'd left 'em. The soldier I'd shot layin' there with 'em. Them was good horses to stay put like that. I'd use 'em to take the bodies back home after I was done with my settlin', but them mean women weren't gettin' 'em back. I was gonna give one of the mares to Henri. His pick. Keep the stallion Stuart rode and the other mare for myself. Henri had earned one for helpin' me rescue Mary. He'd appreciate havin' it, too. That also mattered when givin' a gift of thanks. Respect was expected when dealin' with Indians. Mountain folk as well. We allowed it proper.

Their horses stood solid as I walked up to 'em. Two mares in front, the stallion in back. Thinkin' on what'd happened, I realized the horse in front never quivered when I shot the soldier off its back. These was battle hardened horses. They had no fear 'a guns, loud noises, or burnt powder. They'd been wallerin' in them things for a while. Used to the sounds and smells of war and killin'. It was horrible times in the South. They know'd just like folks did, blood weren't a natural smell they was supposed to be comfortable with. They should 'a run off, but they didn't. They was good horses. Trained for soldiers… or warriors.

Both the leather gun boots on the back two horses was empty, but oh, the front mare still had its Spencer carbine tucked away nice and snug in its boot. I'd seen Federal soldiers near the end of the war that carried them carbines. I'd never held one. Stood amazed lookin' at it in its home. I wanted to take it out and run my hands over it, but I reasoned there would be time for that later. I had to answer to the one what was sneakin' up behind me 'fore I could claim their truck as mine. I know'd it was a soldier man. I could hear the heavy crunch of his boots layin' on the dried leaves. He was still a ways off. I wondered if it was Stuart.

I'd slipped up by lettin' him get in too close without knowin' he was there. That was careless of me as a warrior. I was fortunate the mistake hadn't cost me my life, yet. I'd let myself get distracted. Lost the feel of my surroundings. My senses had gotten too focused on one single thing. Made me forget to listen out proper to the world around me. I'd let one of 'em get in close while admiring their truck. That was foolish, careless.

I eased around the rump of the first horse to the far side from where the crunchin' noises was gettin' louder. They was slow movin' crunches, but steady, for sure not Indian or critter. I was confident it was one of the soldiers comin' back to the horses. Prob'ly figured me, or one like me, might snatch 'em while they was gone lookin' for the one what shot their friend. I crouched low, hidin' behind the horse while makin' my way toward a big hemlock with low hangin' branches not twenty paces away from where the horses stood. I slipped in under them branches and sat down without makin' a single noise that I could hear. Them horses never moved. I was sure proud they didn't. Had they jumped scared, I'd 'a been give away and most likely shot, close as the soldier man had got 'fore I was hid good. I praised Holy Spirt for bringin' me back to hear death 'fore it come to call.

I found a way to sit comfortable among all the limbs right quick, bracin' the Springfield over my knee. My back rested solid against the huge base of the big, beautiful tree. I love the mountain hemlock. They are a most spiritual tree. The one I'd found shelter under was a gift as I saw it. I got quiet. The slippin' noises was comin' on steady. I'd made it without bein' found out. I would learn from the careless thing I did and pay mind when next I confronted outlaws. I'd use the knowledge I gained that day many times throughout my life. Saved my hide a couple times that I can remember.

I recognized the cap soon as I seen it. Them funny little soldier caps had a look all to their own. It was movin' slow above the saddle of the middle horse, growin' 'til there was a head below it. I draw'd a bead on the nose of that head preparin' to pull the Springfield's trigger, but my spirit felt it wrong. I lowered my rifle to watch. I could always shoot him if needs be.

He slipped his carbine into its boot, then laid his arms across the center of his saddle. Took his cap off, hangin' it over the saddle horn. He run his right hand through his hair a couple times then laid his arm back over the saddle to settle with his left arm. His words was good to hear as he kind 'a looked up to the sky 'fore talkin'. He spoke loud so I'd hear.

"I know you can hear me, Buach. Yes, we know your name. Saw it in your family's bible. You need to know for the future, I never hurt Mary. Stuart and his women did all that. No man shamed her, neither. Stuart wanted to, but his wives warned him of it. They didn't like her. He's the one who killed your pa, too, Buach. Me and Billy, the one you shot over there, never had a hand in that. Now my friend is dead. You killed him. I should settle with you over his death, but for me, there has been enough killing. Speak, so I know you hear me Buach Whelan. I got more to say that you need to know."

I near shot him when he mentioned my dad. Called him "pa." That weren't no name for a father. For sure not one like I had. It was good to know Mary had not been violated other than some hurt to her flesh. Her spirit would be full on her wedding day. I was proud for that. One lucky buck would have her as his wife 'fore long. She was too special not to draw attention. I answered him out 'a respect. Spoke softer than I should 'a 'cause I didn't want him to know exactly where I was sittin'. His carbine was easy fer him to get at where it rested in the boot.

"I hear you, outlaw. I wanna shoot you just like I did your friend. From where I stand, I could take your head clean off your shoulders, so if you wanna live, don't make a move I will take as threatenin'. You and your friends come here to kill me. Don't lie and say you didn't. Accordin' to the laws we live by here in the mountains, I can kill you now with justification. I'm more dangerous than y'all give me credit for, soldier man. That's an insult to me. I could 'a shot you earlier, 'fore you ever know'd I was around, but I didn't. I give you fair warning. Give you a chance to turn around and head out, but you didn't. I bet y'all didn't give my dad a chance, huh? Billy's death is on y'all. Easy pickin's is all you rats is after, so I'm showin' you my place ain't easy pickin's. Y'all chose this fight. Now I will end it. Make peace with your Maker, boy. I'm gonna end you like your friend there in about ten seconds. You'd best get busy. You want things square in your soul when I send you to the Pearly Gates." I cocked my rifle again. That time it got his attention.

"NO!" he shouted, raising both hands to the sky, but still standin' behind his horse. His head was a small target from where I sat, but I'd have no trouble centerin' it with what rest I had on my knee. "Listen, Buach! Don't fire on me. We are leaving. I don't want any more of my friends killed. I don't want any of my family killed. I don't wanna die. Stuart is my uncle. He and his family will most likely try and stay. I will not. Me and him and Billy got close durin' the war. He talked us into coming south with him to homestead. It was not my intention, or Billy's, to take anybody's home, but when we got here, Stuart and his wives had already settled in a few days earlier. We didn't know about him killing your dad until a day or two after coming here. I swear to you this is the truth. That's why I'm taking mine and Billy's family and we're going away. You'll never see us again. Your farm is yours to keep. I am speakin' truth to you, Buach. Give me a chance and I will show you. One day, that's all, and we will be gone. I will leave you here to settle with my uncle. I have no peace that he will make it home alive. His wives will want justice, as they will see it, but I will take them and his kids with me if they so desire. Is this agreeable to you, Buach? Let us go. None with me had anything to do with your loss. I promise you I am speaking truth. Please believe me. As proof to you that we mean you no more harm, I will tell you where Stuart is. That's as fair as I can be right now."

It was a few minutes 'fore I answered him. His arms had laid back down across his saddle. I almost shot him for lowerin' his arms. I wanted him to be speakin' truth. I didn't wanna hurt him or his if they didn't have blood on 'em from killin' my dad. Still, him and his could 'a done something about Stuart and his wives. Again, they'd chose wrong. If they found out Dad was killed by their uncle when they come to gain a place to live, then they should 'a done what was right and moved on. Dad always said, "the company you keep means a right smart when survival is concerned." He was right about that. Billy would be alive if they'd done what was right. The two 'a them should 'a hung ol' Stuart fer murder way I seen it. That's what mountain folk would 'a done.

"Yeah? You'd give family up to keep your life? See, that's where you Northerners and us Southerners is different. We might settle with family among our own clans, but we'd never give up family to the likes 'a you and yours. That being said, tell me where he is, and I will think about lettin' you live. Does that sound fair to you… boy?"

"No, but I'll take it to show you good faith, as it is. He went south to circle around behind where he figured you to be. I was to go east then come back from the north. If you saw, I came from the east. I've changed my mind on what we should do. I hope you believe me, Buach. I have given you the whereabouts of my uncle. His blood will be on my hands, but I cherish my family more than I do his thievin' hide. What I've come to understand is… he's evil. I am leaving now. Do not shoot me." He moved to get Billy's horse. That weren't gonna happen.

"No, no, soldier man. Don't touch that mare 'a Billy's, nor the stallion of Stuart's, neither. You can leave, I'll not shoot you, but you'll haul Billy back on your own horse. Lead or ride with him, it matters not to me, but leave the other two. I got a use fer 'em. Which reminds me, as a show of good faith, you can slip your carbine into the boot on Stuart's horse 'fore you leave out. I know it ain't good to leave a man in the woods without a rifle, but you'll make do with that Army Colt you got there. You can have Billy's, too. I don't want 'em. Now, them's my offers. Take 'em or die. Your choice."

He never said no more words. I watched close as he simply pulled his carbine from the boot on his horse and toted it back to the stallion droppin' it in the leather boot strapped to Stuart's saddle. He then went back and loaded up his friend's body onto his own horse, commenced to leadin' it back north toward our place. I believed he'd do just as he said. I weren't sure Stuart's wives would go with him or let him take their kids, but it was better than them stayin' and bein' orphaned. He know'd that.

I eased out from under the limbs of the hemlock I'd took cover in after the soldier had left with his friend. I know'd right where ol' Stuart would come off the mountain tryin' to get in behind me. All around us was steep and thick off the end of Long Shot. They weren't but one holler he'd find long enough or open enough to move back low. If his nephew was tellin' the truth, I'd be waiting to welcome him.

My dad's killin' come to mind, as I headed off to meet Stuart. The hurt tryin' to rise up from my inner bein'. I'd fought hard to keep it hid from my thinkin'. It come to me that I needed to keep focused on what I was staked to at the time. My life depended on it.

CHAPTER 9

BLUE DOVE, THE HEALER

It was a good thing I didn't wait on Henri to confront the takers. I learned from Mary what'd happened after all of us come together on Long Shot days later. Henri'd been took by fever the evening after I left to go to take back our farm. Mary had to lead him home on Gus the following morning. He could still walk some when they got to his place, but shortly after, he couldn't walk no more. Fever took him over. She struggled to get him in the bed after he'd got so weak. His dead weight near too much fer her to move. She was hurtin', too, but she was the only one there to take care of him, so she got her back up and fought through. That was on me. Still, it was important to get our home back quick as possible. The longer them takers stayed, the harder it would be to get shed of 'em. Mary know'd that.

She sat with him durin' the night, then all the next day, as he thrashed around 'a top his bed quilts, hollerin' out things Mary did and didn't understand. The little cane seated chair she sat on uncomfortable at best, but it was all there was to sit on other than the floor. The little chair was one of only three indoor chairs Henri owned. He'd made 'em from oak and river cane, which was common for mountain folk. All straight-backed with curved wood slats for the backrest, the seat softened river cane from close by, no armrest. He didn't need many inside chairs. Spent most of his time outside, even if folks was there to visit, he'd visit with 'em out on the porches. They was several rockers spread around he'd made fer folks to take comfort in. They was all cane seated and cane backed with carved armrests.

I'd helped him with those. Dad taught me how to craft a few useful things durin' my growin' up years on Long Shot. I was gonna miss workin' with him, learning from him… it of a sudden become hard to swallow. That happened every time I slipped up and let his passin' come to mind.

Mary had been tryin' to wake Henri since shortly after daylight the third day they was back. She'd had no luck. Infection had took hold deep in his wound. Fightin' that infection was puttin' him out of his mind. Mary said he told her things she could never repeat for fear the Cherokee elders might come to quiet her. Tribal stuff he never would 'a spoke in front 'a nobody, for sure a settler. When I found out later that Henri had got so bad off, it give proof to my understanding of what Holy Spirit wanted me to do regardin' the task of takin' back our farm. My decision to face the takers by myself seemed justified, once I found out what'd happened to Henri. He would not 'a been able to help me for days, considerin' he made it through the infection alive and in one piece. That was too long for me to have them Yankees livin' on our farm. Too long for my spirit to hold in the hurt for Dad's passin'. I needed to mourn proper.

Henri caused a fuss, fightin' fever most all the time they'd been back. Mary stayed by his side much as she could. Tradin' one cane seated chair for the other one of two, as her backside required it. Somebody had to sit close. Keep him from fallin' to the oak planks what laid the floor. By circumstance, she was all there was for that chore, but she accepted it as his friend would.

Mary said she felt for him. He was burnin' with fever. His body had jerked constant most of the afternoon. As she told it, "seemed like he was gettin' hit by things I couldn't see, but clearly he was feeling." She'd had to stand clear of his thrashings. Couldn't get too close fer gettin' hit or grabbed. Sweat run off the sides of his bare top in trickles, like easy runnin' rain down a glass windowpane. She'd had no luck tryin' to get him to drink water the few times he was in and out 'a wakin'. He was just too weak and dazed to swallow. All the jerkin' around his body was doin' had him sufferin'. She also know'd the seriousness of his infection was slowly movin' him toward the death trail, but what could she do? Her body was tired. She was tired. He was gettin' worse.

Mary felt helpless sittin' there watchin' Henri. She could smell the infection. She'd used hard cider to clean the wound, takin' a couple swigs for herself, but the gash was turnin' more than the cider could fight. Weren't nothin' she could do 'cept change the bandage for a fresh one, put on the medicines Henri had told her to use, but they didn't seem to be helping. There was no more mixin's at Henri's place for fightin' infection other than what she was usin'. He had a lot of mixes for different things, but none to fight infection like his body was havin' to face. He needed something stronger. After a while, she thought he'd took some kind 'a dyin' fit he got so bad. Knowin' him to be deeply spiritual like I did, that was understandable. I figured him holding a fever would let dark spirits come into his mind more than he'd normally allow. For sure, more than most folks could 'a tolerated. No tellin' what he was seein' when the worst of the fever come on him.

Mary sat worryin' fer Henri, not knowin' what to do to help him, but he scared her as well. She didn't come to understand the Cherokee full on 'til after Dad was killed, even though we'd grow'd up around 'em 'bout all our lives. She prayed to Holy Spirit for wisdom to understand how to help Henri. He was listenin'.

"Henri?" Mary said kind 'a loud, as she grabbed the top of his right shoulder with her left hand, his right wrist and forearm she braced down with her right. She needed to hold him somewhat still while speakin' to him. She hoped he'd be able to listen. Leanin' in close to his right ear, she felt as much as smelled, the hot, sourin' stink of infection. It laid heavy around Henri's person. She'd not been expectin' that. First time the rotting stink had smelled that strong. If she'd had any food that day, she'd 'a lost it on poor ol' Henri. No matter. He'd 'a not noticed.

"Can you hear me, Henri?" she managed to speak. "It's me, Mary. Boo's sister, daughter of Francis. Speak to me, if you can." She had to turn her head for some fresher air. Swallowin' hard, she turned back to him, "Hear me, Henri. I need you to wake up and listen. Can you hear me, Henri? You have to drink some water. Henri! You need water. I know you can hear me, Henri. Reach deep. Find the strength. You need water!"

Mary kept tryin' to wake him. Nothing, he was out. He could not wake from his tremors. The way he was jerkin' about, she allowed he should 'a woke, but he didn't.

After a time of trying, she finally come to accept that she weren't gonna get him awake. He was bad off. The infection was havin' its way with his body. Threatening his life. He'd lost control. Lost his purpose. She know'd, if she didn't get him some healin' help soon, the hurt leg would have to come off at the waist. That would not be good. She'd seen wounded soldiers, hurt from fightin' the war, die of the same thing at the hospital in Atlanta. She'd go there on occasion to nurse the wounded with Aunt Catherine. From what she'd seen, most didn't live when they lost a leg that high up. Bled to death once the surgery was done, if not durin'. She felt the only thing she could do was get him to the Cherokee. Yes, that's what she felt she must do. They'd know what it would take to save him, his leg. All she had to do was wake him, load him onto Gus, then walk the two miles to where the Cherokee had homesteaded south 'a Tiny Creek, all before the infection got any worse. She prayed for the strength to get it done, then trusted Holy Spirit to deliver. He did not let her down.

Come morning, her sore body didn't wanna do all it took to move Henri, but she was all there was to do it. Knowin' his life depended on gettin' him moved, and that it had to be done by her alone, she managed it. Mostly by draggin' him easy like from the bed and down the stairs then all the way to the edge of the back porch. The floor of the porch was near as high as a common grow'd man was tall, so by movin' Gus up real close to the edge, she was able to kind 'a roll Henri onto Gus' back crossways bellydown. He'd ride to the Cherokee across the mule's back. His wound facin' up. Old Man Sun helped with infected places. Mary know'd that from doctorin' with Aunt Catherine.

It was a struggle, but she'd done it. Maybe Henri had woke some and helped her. I doubted it, but maybe. Somehow, by divine miracle or not, by dark of the fourth day I was away, she'd got Henri to the Cherokee. They saw to him straight away, her too. She never saw him again for five days. When she did see him, he was walkin' fine on both legs. His wound showin' full to the air. Closed up where it weren't leakin' no more. The infection healed whole. To her, it was a miracle. It made her curious as to how they healed him so well in that little bit 'a time. She thought to ask about it 'fore she left. Might be it could help folks she would tend to one day.

They honored her for savin' Henri, for her courage and strength and sacrifice, by makin' her a full member of the tribe. That meant something in mountain speak. Local folks weren't honored like that much, and when one was, it was a special happening. Required a big comin' together to celebrate. Henri was important to the Cherokee tribe. The way they seen it, if Mary was chosen by the spirits to bring Henri to them for healin', then the spirits must hold favor with her. It would disrespect the ancestors if they turned her away, so they welcomed her like one 'a their own. She'd never sink roots with her new family, though, which she loved, 'cause her heart lay south.

The Cherokee's ability to use the plants of the forest for healin' was known to all that lived in the mountains. Everybody that show'd respect to the tribe was allowed to come for healin'. They actually had a hospital-like lodge where folks went for doctorin'. I'd seen 'em get people better that was near layin' in the grave from wounds or sickness or what have ye. A couple of the elder women know'd how to use near every plant what grow'd in the mountains, 'cept the big trees, and some 'a them had to shed a little bark on occasion for mixes the healers used. Many trees have medicine in their barks that had to be boiled or chewed out. A body can't chew the outside bark on older trees, but the inside bark of several different big trees helped a sight with sores, cuts, and pains. I know'd it was Holy Spirit what guided Mary to take Henri to the Cherokee. That give me confidence in his gettin' healed up. 'Sides, if a person didn't take somebody like Henri, who was important to the tribe, to seek their help, they'd end up offended. You didn't want Cherokee warriors offended at anything you did. They took such things most personal.

It was fortunate that it was Henri she was bringin' to seek healing. Most of the Cherokee didn't know Mary like they did me and Dad. She stayed with Aunt Catherine a lot. They didn't see her like they did us. Had it been just a common somebody bringing in a common somebody, and her bein' unattended, the Cherokee might 'a took her slave or married her off to one of the warriors what needed a woman, be she extra or primary. Them comin' to know her to be Dad's daughter and my sister kept her safe. She know'd to tell 'em that when she went there. The Cherokee, as a whole, weren't all that friendly to outsiders like they was before the Indian Removal, for sure to most settler folk they didn't know.

It amazed Mary just how many Cherokee had come to live in The Settlement. She'd not been there for many moons. It was obvious to her that more had come since she was there last. She did a rough count as she walked Gus through the heart of the Cherokee homestead. The camp itself was over a half mile long extending through the bottom of a huge valley the Indians called "Valley of Life," in the English. She believed there to be more'n a thousand Cherokee livin' there. Not counting the small clans spread out on the north side of the tallest mountains to the south, the White Rock Mountains. The main big top laid east of Tiny Creek and Swell Branch. She saw small log homes and barns, two critter corrals, single row plows, well houses, spring houses, smoke houses, woodsheds, wagons, and stock all along the main road near to the center of The Settlement. Most laid off in the woods a ways. Once there, you had to enter a fort like structure to pass on south or go a mile or more out 'a your way to bypass it. Of course, warriors watched all those trails.

Logs standin' side by side on end made a huge camp for The Settlement, maybe two hundred paces end-to-end and a hundred side-to-side. I'd been there many times over the last couple years, while Mary had been spending a lot 'a time with Aunt Catherine in Atlanta. She liked it in Atlanta. I liked going to visit, but I'd not live in no city, nowhere. Couldn't, I'd end up in touble fer assaultin' folks. First bandit what bumped up ag'in me fer purpose would send me to the hangman's lair for killin'. I could not live packed that tight to the mix 'a folks what called Atlanta home. The nearest neighbors we had to Swell Branch, what didn't live there, was over five miles. That was just near too close for my comfort. I allowed I'd wander some when times settled down and folks started movin' closer... if times ever settled down. Weren't no doubtin' folks would eventually get closer. I hoped I was across the Great River with the ancestors when that happened.

Of all the healers and medicine folk the Cherokee had, none was sought after more than the one they called Blue Dove. She weren't old by any description. Most likely younger than Henri, but it was his good fortune that she was there the night Mary brought him to the main Cherokee camp for healin'. I'd say she saved his life.

She was passin' through on her way home from seein' about some sick Cherokee what lived to the east. Her and her bunch needed a place for the night and the main camp was it. The whole of the Cherokee welcomed her. She was special to all the Cherokee people. Every Indian in the mountains know'd about her healin' ways. Respected her talents. Her clan was charged by the tribe to keep her safe. They'd not let her travel alone. Protected her constant when she was at home or travelin'. It was by Henri's good fortune she'd decided to stay at The Settlement that night. She made her mind to tend to him after he come, he was bad off.

Indians believe in the Great Creator. The Maker of all things. I called Him God, or Great Spirit, some Cherokee seen it same as me. I believe He aligned the two souls of Henri and Blue Dove to come together that evening. Nobody I know'd would 'a thought no different. Henri needed the best doctorin' he could get to keep his leg, his life, and she was it. I always believed, and still do, that the spirit world is connected to the human world. Many times I lived as one guided by the spirit world… Holy Spirit bein' my foundation. All things I did come through Him. It's foolish to live life without His guidance, dangerous where I grow'd up. I've never been certain why He chose me fer service, but He did. I never had no problems with it. I figure He could 'a done better if He'd 'a wanted.

Henri sat the main fire pit in the center of The Settlement, enjoyin' a pipe full of some fresh dried Cherokee tobacco. The flavor strong to his taste. He was thinkin' about all that'd happened before he'd took the fever. Wondered for me. Had I gone to get my farm back without him? Most likely, yes. He was still weak. Not strong enough to fight for sure, but he felt he needed to be with me. I could 'a used his help. I won't deny that, but his fate was sealed when that bullet ripped his leg open. He know'd, with as much time had passed, the settlin' chore was most likely complete. I would be alive or dead or worse. He thought to ask about my whereabouts, but sleep changed his trail. It would be hours 'fore he woke again. His thoughts weren't about me when he did, neither. I could not blame him for that.

***

The holler I was waitin' on Stuart in was long top to bottom, kind 'a wide in places. I'd been there many times. It was a good place to hunt. The ridges off its sides weren't too steep. Easy to climb when stalkin'. It laid more shallow than most common hollers. I liked huntin' it 'cause it was grow'd full 'a big white oaks. There was a few poplar, white pine, and maple mixed about, but mostly it was big ol' white oaks. I was sittin' behind one 'a them big trees, watchin' back west toward the trail. It stood at the bottom of the holler, which was the north end. The whole of the holler was uphill from me to the south. Weren't far from where I'd first seen the takers earlier in the morning.

The trail comin' down from the tops held to the east side of a small branch what'd found the bottom of the holler years earlier. Long leaf ivy grow'd in places along its edges. It weren't a big branch. A small contributor that eventually helped feed Tiny Creek to the north. Still, it was big enough that the noise of its water runnin' over rocks, uncovered ages before, made it hard for a body to hear. I'd need to be clear 'a that noise to hear Stuart comin', if he come.

In my mind, there was question as to whether or not Stuart would be travelin' the trail down. He could 'a got turned around up on them big tops and gone off the wrong side. Weren't hard to do. Happened to me a couple times. 'Bout all the folks I know'd, that traveled the big tops, had done it. Common when it's hard to see the sun for all the leaves overhead, or if clouds move in and get to hangin' low over the tops while you're up there, or if dark comes on ye. I figured he'd be along, though. The leaves weren't growin' out yet, the weather was clear, and it was early in the day. Directions should be easy enough to find. I allowed maybe even an outlaw like him would manage it.

One of us was gonna die when he come. Thinkin' that felt strange, but it was justice for my dad. I'd already killed two fer their murderin' act. Killin' them hadn't bothered me hardly at all. Killin' Stuart was gonna actually bring me comfort. I looked forward to takin' his body back to his mean ol' wife who'd beat Mary. I hated it for his kids, if he had any more, 'cause they was innocent in all that was happening. Life was kind 'a tough on some mountain folks' kids. Many died at birth or later from sickness or injury. Some got stole for slaves or profit. Some for wives. Most families know'd one clan or another what'd been took from. It was a horrid thing to lose a child to such. The few times it'd happened recent around Swell Branch, the takers was caught and hung. Cherokee were the best trackers in the mountains. You'd not get shed 'a them when they got on your trail. Word spreads quick along the outlaw trails about that kind 'a vengeance.

Rogue Indians and slave traders weren't uncommon to the mountains, but most with any smarts stayed clear 'a the Cherokee. Mountain folk what lived near 'em, too. It was known amongst the thieves, what roamed the mountains, to stay clear 'a Tiny Creek. Swell Branch was the closest settlement to Tiny Creek. Profitable to the Indians for trade goods and obtaining settler goods. The tribe watched over it as well. I was proud for that. Give me comfort knowin' the Cherokee looked after our folks.

I prayed as I sat. I weren't twenty paces from where the trail passed. I'd crossed the branch. Moved east on the trail gettin' me shed of all the branch noise, then found my sittin' place. It was important to make sure Stuart know'd exactly why, and how, justice had come to call. I had things to say I wanted him to think on as he went to be with the ancestors. I needed him to understand what him and his bunch had done to my family. My blood got up thinkin' on what we'd say to one another. A conversation I'd just come to realize would be happening soon. I'd figured correctly. Heavy boots was coming down the holler, and he was most likely in 'em. I hoped he was enjoyin' his last few minutes on Mother Earth, 'cause I sure was.

I was eager to get on with our comin' together, so without thinkin' a whole lot about it, I stood and walked the twenty paces to where the trail lay. Took a stance in the center of it. My Springfield laid across the crook of my left arm. The stock held tight in my right. Thumb on the hammer. I wanted to be ready if he went for his gun when first seein' me. I was thankful his mate had told me his plan about tryin' to get in behind me, but I'd 'a found him after a while, anyhow. It had simply become a matter of sooner rather than later. I silently thanked God for the gift as Stuart rounded a big old white oak what sided the trail in a short bend. He froze when he seen me standin' square not ten paces away. His breath comin' hard. The look on his face that of shock, weakness, and desperation. He bent from the waist puttin' his hands on his knees to brace himself. He looked like he was gonna fall out. Something was wrong with him. I watched close, figurin' he'd come up whole soon enough. Most likely a short gun in his hand. Similar to what his friends had done from their horses when tryin' to shoot me. I kept watchin' close for any of his possible treachery.

He stood erect to face me again, his face a grayish white. I wondered if the walk up the mountain then back down had done something to him. He seemed in a bad way. Like he needed to sit 'fore he fell out. I decided to not say anything for a minute, just watch. I paid mind to him not havin' his carbine. A short gun was in its holster. The gun's handle covered in a leather flap he'd not unhooked while stalkin' me. What was goin' on? I leveled my rifle, near shootin' him as he jerked hard to his right, then fell over. I kept watchin' as he crawled back to the big oak, then rolled over on his back, kind 'a leanin' back against the tree. His shoulders propped against a big root what stuck up from the ground covered in bark right at the base of the tree. His arms laid out on the ground to his sides, his head up lookin' at me. He weren't movin' hardly at all. Only what it took to draw a breath ever few seconds or move his eyes some. Looked to be he was dyin'. I moved up closer so we could talk normal, not have to holler. It didn't look like he could talk at all. I almost felt fer him... but my Bible teachin' had become weak in my spirit since findin' out Dad was gone, so I didn't.

"You don't look too good, Mr. Stuart. You feelin' all right?" I said, as I squatted down in front of him. "I'm just askin' to be polite. Don't start thinkin' I really care, boy... just curious is all. Don't wanna catch what might be pullin' you down, if you got the sickness or whatnot."

I held the barrel of my rifle level to his face, cockin' the hammer back to get his attention. He never seemed to pay it any mind, just laid there, starin' at me. Up close like I was, I could see he was sick or hurt or something. Weren't no blood leakin' out no place that I could see. Weren't none in the short drag trail he'd left gettin' back to the big white oak to lean back on. Sweat was pourin' off his head and face and down his front. His soldier shirt top was soaked in it. His mouth and lips were white and dry. I allowed he must be dry on the inside. That made me understand he most likely weren't gonna be with me long, without me even raisin' a hand to him.

"Something happen to you while you was up high lookin' fer me... boy? You fall and hit your head? Snake bite? That it? You get hit by a rattler movin' through the rocks up there? Huh? No, not likely snake bite. Kind 'a early for that I reckon. For sure up high where you was. What is it then? You gonna tell ol' Boo? Can you talk? Point if you can't talk, but like I said, I ain't gonna do nothin' to help ye. You killed my dad. That's a darkness in my soul that will never again hold light. All because of you. All because of your greed and sorry'ness. Die if you will. Save me the trouble, 'cause that's why I'm here... you know, boy... to settle up for my dad. You took his life, now I will see to yours, if I need to. The ol' Death Angel may already be tendin' to that chore. Seems like I can feel him. You got any last words or wants 'fore you go, either by His hand or mine? Say if you do. I will try and honor 'em, if I choose. I owe you nothing."

"Here," he said, as he raised his right arm, bendin' it at the elbow to point at his chest. It flopped back out flat on the ground to never move again. "Pain... sick... hit me... hard... up on top. Lost... my... breath. Yes... I killed... your... pa... took... farm. You...

killed... my boy. No more... kill. Please... forgive... me. Family... please... don't kill... don't kill... my family. Please... have... mercy. They... will leave. Give them... chance... please. What I... did... wrong. They didn't... please don't... kill..."

His eyes got to turnin' dull as he tried to say that last word. Then they closed real slow as his head eased back against the bark of the big oak. He never finished that last word 'fore his talkin' stopped and his mouth fell open. What little air he had in his lungs let out. A strange gurglin' sound come from his throat. Like he was full 'a water or maybe like he'd just drunk a jug 'a cool buttermilk but hadn't swallowed it full. I'd never heard such a sound as that. It was a dark noise, like what it sounds like for life to leave a body. I didn't wanna ever hear that dyin' sound again. Sounded worse than a bear dyin'.

Them was his last words. He was gone, but unfortunately for me, not by my hand. I hadn't had my revenge. Hadn't got to say all the things I wanted him to hear as he died. That didn't seem right compared to the sufferin' I was fixin' to face when I finally got to mourn Dad's death. He'd mourned his son. Dealt with his hurt. He died without sufferin' the way I wanted him to. It just weren't fair. He'd murdered my dad. Took our farm. Now God took him 'fore I could make him feel the hurt I'd felt, and was gonna feel... or... did He? Holy Spirit got to speakin' to me.

Stuart had lost a son because of his greed and ignorance. That was on him. He'd lost his life, leavin' his family to care for themselves. That was on him. They was now without a place to stay. Most likely have to go back north without his help. All that was on him. His family had abandoned him. Betrayed him in the end. That was on him. I'd killed his mate because of things he'd done. That was on him. After studyin' on all that for a minute, I come to the thinkin' that maybe he did suffer a right smart. It weren't by my hand that he'd died, but maybe we was square in our dealings? I would smoke on it all later. Settle it in my mind once and for all, then I'd mourn Dad. For the time bein', I felt to honor Stuart's dyin' wishes best I could. I would try and give his family mercy. Not sure his mean ol' wife would take it, after me bringin' him home dead, but offer it I would.

The pain of death can kill. The pain of losin' a child to anything is worse than that of death. Hell on earth to those who endure it. My pain was a strong hurt. His pain was strong as well. I saw it in his eyes 'fore he died. I believed I'd just witnessed a broken heart cause death. More loss from the evil he'd brought to my home, to the South.

I allowed there'd been enough death, dyin'. A settlement had been reached, of sorts. I hoped they'd be no more killin' while I took our place back. I planned on doin' all I could to prevent it. The ones I'd wanted vengeance on was now settled with. The way I saw it, no one else needs be hurt, but I intended to be sleepin' in my own bed come mornin'… whatever it took to make that happen.

The Legend of Swell Branch

CHAPTER 10

A Way Home for the Dead

Stuart was a big man. Much bigger than Billy, who I'd shot off his own horse earlier. The weight of the big man's body was more'n I cared to sling across either of the horses. That, and it would be way more handlin' of ol' Stuart's person than I'd feel comfortable with. I'd need help to load him proper, but they weren't no help. That left me with the problem of gettin' his body back to his family. They wouldn't want him left for the wood's critters. 'Sides, I needed 'em to see I hadn't shot nor stabbed nor beat him to death… that I was innocent of his dyin'.

There was a lead rope hangin' coiled at the back 'a Stuart's saddle, tied on by a couple thin leather straps. Seein' that sparked a notion that weren't real polite to the dead, but it would do to get his body back. I figured to use that rope to set up a drag, decidin' against a travois to save time, so that's what I did.

I made a slip loop out 'a the coiled rope. Slid it over Stuart's feet, then up his body to catch under his arms, pullin' it tight. I used the spare of the loop to bind his hands across his chest and his head to the lead. I didn't want his head floppin' around gettin' caught on trees, saplings, big rocks, logs, or whatnot. Wouldn't do fer him to be drug back to his clan without it. I didn't want his body comin' loose on the drag, neither. Cinchin' him like I did would keep him from slippin' loose.

After pullin' Stuart's body up close as I dared to the back of the stallion, I tied the other end of the lead to the saddle horn, draw'd my long knife, cuttin' the bridle reins from the stallion's bit, stuffin' 'em in the saddle bag what laid over the stallion's rump. Grabbin' him by the bridle's face strap, I turned him back down the trail they'd come in on. Once I had the horse, and Stuart, headed in the right direction, I used my hat to kind 'a slap the stallion's backside, sendin' him off at a walk. Stuart's heels draggin' the ground, his head toward the stallion's rear. I noticed he had a dark look to him as he was bein' drug off. It was strange how black his face had got. I remember thinkin', as I kept watchin', it didn't seem no different, that horse draggin' ol' Stuart or draggin' fresh kilt game meat. Be it hog, bear, or the critters we raised to butcher. He was dead. Couldn't feel nothin'. Weren't gonna matter to him how he got back to his family. I figured it fittin' for the murderer he was, gettin' drug by a rope in the end.

I stood and watched 'til the horse got to goin' good. Bouncin' ol' Stuart off the roots and rocks that lay exposed in the trail here and there. The stallion would know to follow the trail home by scent. I'd told him to get on back. Trained horses like him know'd what they was supposed to do when told to get back. I weren't worried over him gettin' lost. Outlaw might find 'em, but I doubted it. The trail we was on had been made by me and my bunch. It was a back trail I'd purposefully led them outlaws to. Only folks in our clan and some Indians used it. Connected the Cherokee Settlement to Tiny Creek. My clan had also made one that connected the ridges behind Swell Branch to Tiny Creek and another from Swell Branch to the Cherokee Settlement. Of course, there was spur trails built all over. Them was mostly family or clan trails leadin' from homesteads to main trails. I was concerned there might be some Cherokee, if they crossed trails with the horses, might take my newfound property, but I'd find out who they was if that happened. They would not get by with takin' from me.

The mare turned her head back watchin' the stallion fer a short minute. Figurin' out she was bein' left behind, she turned and commenced followin'. I stopped it as it come by me. Cut both reins from its bridle, stuffin' 'em inside Billy's saddlebags. Slapped her rump with my hat, makin' her kind 'a trot off to catch up. It was near back with the stallion and Stuart as I turned to head south.

I'd catch up later. I was gonna backtrack ol' Stuart 'til I found his Spencer carbine. He had to 'a left it on his trail to find me. It weren't on his horse. Neither of the soldiers had it. I'd made the lone soldier leave without takin' his or Billy's. I meant to trail Stuart 'til I found it. That would give me three all total. I'd catch up to the horses by cuttin' over Sawtooth ridge. Should make it home 'bout the same time as ol' Stuart would be "draggin'" in.

I wondered at how his folks was gonna feel, him bein' drug near a mile through the woods. He'd be looking rough by the time that horse got him back to Long Shot. I cared none. They'd most likely blame me for him dyin'. I didn't care about that, neither. I know'd I had no hand in it. Holy Spirit know'd I didn't have a hand in it. The Bible says it's appointed unto man once to die, then the judgment. I figured it for his time. Fortunate, and unfortunate, for me, really. Not sure it was gonna be good for him, judgin' from his fruits.

I shouldered my Springfield over my head and took off followin' Stuart's trail up the mountain. Weren't long 'til I found the carbine. It was just off the top leaned against a good-sized dogwood. That big 'a dogwood was rare in the mountains. Dogwoods don't grow too big. They get old, just not that big around at the stump. They grow short, too. Old timers would tell you they're cursed. They allowed that dogwood was the stock used to build the cross Jesus died on. So, them trees is cursed to never again grow big enough for such a purpose... it could not be used for crucifyin' folks. I know my kind believed that.

Looked to be Stuart just sat a rock next to the dogwood for a minute, restin'. Leaned his rifle against its base to empty his hands. Prob'ly got to feelin' his death while sittin' there, stood, and just walked on. Forgettin', or not carin', he'd left it behind. No tellin' how long it would 'a stayed leaned up there if I hadn't found it. He was a ways off the trail for some reason. His path was clear from how he was walkin'. That's why I was able to follow right where he'd been. That helped in findin' it.

The gun was loaded. I checked the chamber and rear stock to see. The Spencer carbine has a round chamber bored out of its back stock what held a loadin' tube. Inside that tube was a spring. The bored chamber held seven pre-made loads, cartridges. Stuart left six inside the stock and one in the barrel ready to fire. I'd never fired a spring loadin' repeatin' carbine before. I know'd how, I'd just never shot one. I thought to shoot Stuart's 'fore I got too close to home.

These guns you breached open with a lever what hung underneath the front part of the back stock, forward of the rifle's grip. The lever was hinged inside the gun's action above and in front of the trigger. The fore part of the lever, below where it was hinged in the action, formed a curve to guard the trigger from bein' hit accidental. Unlocking and removing the metal spring loadin' tube from the rifle's butt plate allowed seven loads to be slid into the back stock. Once they was in place, the tube was put back in and locked. The spring inside the tube was then loaded as the cartridges slid inside the tube what held the spring as the tube was pushed back in. When you pulled the hammer back and worked the lever, if there'd been a recent firing, the spent casing would be throw'd out. Once the old casing was gone and the action ready, the spring inside the rear tube would push another load into the chamber of the barrel. That load took the spent cartridge's place and the gun was ready to fire. Didn't take but a couple seconds. A simple repeating mechanism, really, once Mr. Spencer got it figured out of course. It was the preferred rifle near the end of the war, that and the Spencer rifle.

The loads was called "cartridges." The lead bullet, in .52 caliber, was pressed tight into the open end of a small brass cylinder casing using a pressin' machine of some sort. The black powder was put inside the casing before the pressin' was done. The end of the casing was about the same size as the lead bullet, only slightly bigger. When the bullet was forced into the brass casing under pressure, it sealed the casing airtight. This made a sealed finish where the powder could burn once ignited. The .52 caliber cartridge would fire when the trigger was pulled, letting the hammer fall on a small steel pin that struck the rim or back edge of the brass cartridge. That strike to the rim caused a spark inside the casing what lit the powder. The powder then exploded inside the casing, makin' the gun fire the lead bullet down its barrel. The casing was left to eject when the lever was operated. It was all simple in process, really. Much simpler than my Springfield cap and ball musket. The barrels weren't long like my Springfield, though. That made 'em less accurate at long ranges, but out to about 75 paces, a body could depend on it. I hardly ever harvested game outside that range, and if I did, I had my Springfield which was good for shootin' a long ways.

I'd have to find a supply for cartridges, but I felt fortunate to have laid claim to the three carbines I'd took possession of. I figured I might could trade for cartridges with the Indians, when they had 'em. They'd been able to set up a secret trade route to the lands north of where we lived without anybody botherin' 'em. The U.S. Government had mostly started leavin' the Indians be, livin' in belief that they'd got 'em all out from the mountains. Mountain folk laughed at that thinkin'. We all know'd they was a bait 'a Cherokee left in the mountains after the removal. Stands to reason for sure, way they was.

I made a lot 'a gold coin tradin' that route north, but it was a dangerous trail. It was wise to travel with others when makin' a trade run to places north. I always traveled with my Cherokee clan for safety. Still had a couple bad times durin' the years. Had to fight to keep our goods more'n once. I met my first real ship sailin' pirate on that trail. He was bad as they come. The Indians didn't trust him. They sent him and his away in the end.

There is an obvious reason why Sawtooth Ridge is called by its name. The top run of the ridge, which was all a body could travel 'cause the sides was mule face steep, laid like the teeth on a handsaw. Four little tops pokin' up covered in ivy, rocks, and dead trees. Durin' the cold time, it looked like the devil hisself had breathed on it, killin' all the big trees. Hardly anybody went there 'cept for me and my family. It weren't a half mile east of our farm. There was a cave at the base of the closest knob of the four to our place. I spent many nights in that cave. It was big inside. Had water close by. On certain occasions, the Cherokee would use it for special happenings. You didn't wanna be there when they was usin' it for such. Indians can get a little spirit crazy at times. Guided by the ancestors, they could be dangerous for anybody not of the tribe, if their minds got confused by visions.

I know'd an old Cherokee hermit what lived there for a time. Indians considered him touched. Left him be. He weren't the boldest Indian I ever met, but he had wisdom, when he could speak it. Lived in a small, one room log cabin he'd built himself. Couldn't stand to be near folks of any color, gender, or age, but it was the strangest of things, critters would walk right up to him, if they needed him. I'd seen it. He liked brandy, too. Dad would keep him stocked. Said it helped him keep the spirits away. We called him A'kern, or Acorn, 'cause the shape of his head looked like the nuts red oaks drop in the fall, acorns. Big on top and small at the chin. He was strong as a full grow'd bear, too, and he did not like to be confronted. He favored me. I'd took him in one night to my camp, tended to him after he'd got hurt in a fight. Fed him up for a couple days, then I woke the third morning and he was gone. Left without sayin' a word 'a thanks or showin' any gratitude. Next morning after the day he'd left, I was breakin' camp when he come with a gift. It was a smokin' pipe made from the heart of a tight grained piece 'a white oak. Perfect balance in my fingers when I smoked it. Fit easy into my tobacco pouch. He'd made it personal. Carved a face into the front of the bowl that looked like an eagle. He had to 'a stayed at it all night to 'a got it done by that next morning. It become one of my favorite possessions. Smoked smooth… like swallerin' warm honey. It heard most all my prayers for many years. He told me the eagle had come to him in a dream he had for me. That the eagle was special to me. He disappeared after a few years. Dad said they never found him.

    I'd cleared the last of the four points on Sawtooth Ridge headin' fer home, then climbed the white oak watch tree on the rise above our farm in less time than it took for the horses to get Stuart back. I made myself comfortable to watch, but after a time of not seein' or hearin' 'em, I allowed they weren't comin'. Something had to be wrong. I'd not seen no folks, neither. I climbed down from the white oak, makin' my way east around our farm to the trail the horses would 'a been comin' in on. I had to work my way back east fer a while to find 'em. I couldn't believe it when I did, but there stood the stallion, alone, center the trail. Stuart still there on the drag lead. The mare and all her truck gone, includin' Billy's carbine and cartridges.

The stallion stood like he'd been told to stay. Nothin' on him had been touched. The lead still tied to Stuart. That told me who'd done it - Indians. Most likely outlaw rogues. I figured it out once I read the sign they'd left.

That horse stayed standin' where the mare had been took from. That was easy to see from all the sign I found out around him. It was obvious the thieves weren't feared 'a leavin' sign. That told me they was fearless. Made 'em dangerous to my thinkin'. It was clear where they'd met up with Stuart bein' drug on the trail. They had mules. Three of 'em all total. Probably feared the stallion, bein' he was draggin' a dead man, so they left him be, but since the mare weren't part 'a what was bein drug, they weren't feared over her. Seein' her gone made my blood get a little hot. I got angered thinkin' the takers was most likely Cherokee. They know'd better than to bother them horses the way they was trailin'. Know'd they was bound for a place draggin' dead folk like they was. Most likely bein' watched over by the ancestors. Know'd it best if they left it all be, but they didn't. Greed got a hold of 'em. The mare, her saddle, gun, and all of Billy's possibles would fetch gold coin from buyers what traded north. That told me the takers was most likely rogues. Cherokee trail bandits from the sign they'd left. Many young ones, with hard feelings against anybody that weren't Cherokee, had left the tribe and took to stealin' for their keep. It was as much revenge for them as it was profit. Most all Indians had hard feelings against any white man. That caused problems for a lot 'a folks in the mountains, but them disturbin' that procession for Stuart was most disrespectful. I would talk with them about it once I found 'em, and I would find 'em.

I spent a few minutes studyin' the sign around where the stallion stood. Confirmed it was Cherokee, at least they wore Cherokee footskins. That's why the stallion stood untouched. Indians feared dead folk they didn't know nothin' about. He was pullin' the dead. No way they'd touch him. That made sense to my understandin'.

Stuart was a sight. Had I not know'd it was him, I wouldn't 'a know'd it was him. The drag had been rough on his person. Most of his face was gone. All his hair. The hide from the back of his head hung in pieces to the sides. Been torn off as he was drug over rough places. His homespun shirt and Army issue britches was ripped to shreds. His belt gone. It was a good thing he couldn't feel nothin'.

Another hat slap to the stallion's rump sent the horse on to finish his chore. All hadn't turned out just as I'd planned it, but Stuart was fixin' to be with his kin. That's what mattered most right then. Findin' them rogues what took my other carbine and claim would matter soon enough. It was important to me and Mary that I get the rest of the takers gone from our place 'fore seein' to any other problems. Everything in its time.

I fell in behind the stallion as he drug Stuart up a little holler what laid east of our place. The trail cut through it 'fore makin' fer home. I followed on a few paces behind, stoppin' at the edge of the woods while the horse kept goin'. He'd smelled the barn already. I felt his walk quicken near a quarter mile back.

Stayin' shy a few paces from the edge 'a the woods, I hid in next to a big oak tree. I could see mostly the whole farm from one side of the tree or the other, but it was near impossible to be seen by them at the house. The afternoon light was blocked by treetops to the west. I wanted to watch how the women reacted when they seen their beloved bein' brought home like he was. Knowin' how they felt would help me figure how best to go about riddin' our place of their evil. I hoped that once they got him back, they'd just leave. From what the soldier told me he planned to do, Stuart's family should be all that was still there, maybe. I was fixin' to find out. The stallion had just entered the yard.

It was all gettin' heavy on my shoulders. I was startin' to feel the weight of the conflict and killin' now that the big one was no more. Didn't seem right, me havin' to face a man's wives, too. Him bein' dead ought 'a put an end to it all, maybe it had. I'd know soon enough. I was growin' weary of the whole thing. Much more 'tween me and them and I might get fed up enough to just end all the grow'd folk. I didn't want that. They was kids in the bunch. They didn't need to see such as their folks gettin' kilt, them bein' so young and all, but I'd got to the edge of not carin' about that, neither. Still, life is tough enough on young 'uns without them havin' to live with those kind 'a memories. I would use discernment... mercy, if allowed.

She come from the house when the stallion drug Stuart's body to a stop in the backyard of our home. The horse was ready for some oats and a little fresh air, away from the stink he was havin' to pull. To the critters, Stuart was startin' to ripen. Folks couldn't smell it strong, yet, but they would 'fore long. He needed to be gettin' underground soon as somebody could see to it. As I stood by the oak watchin', I got to studyin' over who that chore might fall to as I watched the girl slowly walk toward Stuart. She knelt beside the body and started what looked like a prayer. A soft, chilled rain began to fall as she bowed her head. She never let on like she felt it as the drops got bigger, steadier. I thought to cover the action on my Springfield as the rain got heavier, but it was over my shoulder, already too wet to fire. I paid it no mind as I was carryin' Stuart's carbine, and I was distracted.

No other folks come from the house to be with her. Nobody brought her a cover to keep the rain off. I wondered over that. Weren't no lights on inside, neither. That made me curious. Maybe they all was gone?

As I got to noticin' the lay of the farm closer, it was clear their stock was gone. Dad's mules and horse were all in the pasture behind the barn. It weren't a big pasture - it held a few grasses, but more convenient, a small springhead run constant on the south end for water. I'd never seen it dry up full in all the dry weather we'd ever had. All the wagons and livin' truck it took for the takers to survive was gone. Looked to be that soldier lived up to his word. Seemed most everybody had left out. I was curious as to just who all was still there, if any. For that, I would need to get closer.

I decided to check out the house 'fore havin' a talk with whoever the young lady was. The rain come on a little harder. I remember thinkin' it was nice havin' a carbine when the rain was fallin'. I'd never had that freedom. With a carbine, a body could hunt when it was rainin'. Didn't have to worry over gettin' their powder wet. It was all enclosed in them little brass cartridges what stayed dry inside the gun. The carbine's rounds would fire in wet weather. I was sure proud to have 'em.

I leaned my Springfield beside the front door, choosin' to tote the carbine in with me. Made double sure my knives was as they should be, 'fore easin' into our main room no different than I had when first goin' in to rescue Mary. Crouched low by the west wall, I listened close as I could. I had no mind as to who might be in the house, if anybody. Time before, I had some thought as to who I might be facin', but I had no notion if they was folks there this second time or not. I stayed put 'til I could control my breathin'. Stop the nervous shakes what run up your back when facin' dangerous things unseen. My heart was poundin'. I could feel it all the way through to my spine. It stung between my shoulders when it reached there. I got to thinkin', while calmin' my body down, it might not 'a been too smart me comin' on in without lookin' things over better, but my gut told me all was prob'ly fine, so I'd went on in. Still, I should 'a been a little more cautious. Could 'a been they was layin' a trap for me, sendin' that girl out by herself. Hopin' to make me think she was the only one there. That was careless of me. It was a mistake that could 'a cost me my life, if things had been different, 'cause they know'd I was comin'. I was the only one, other than Mary, that could stop 'em from homesteadin' legal. An ambush on me would 'a ended most 'a their troubles, had they chose to set one up. I should 'a thought on that 'fore I went in. I was fortunate, bein' as careless and foolish as I'd been. I was tired, though, and, I was mostly sure the house was empty 'fore I went in.

It seemed, as I listened, that the girl was the only one there, at least for the present. I eased on through the cook room, slippin' along like a mouse huntin' crumbs, then on out the back door without makin' a noise she could hear. I moved to the edge of the porch near the top of the steps what led down to the yard, the carbine hangin' in my right hand.

She was still kneelin' by ol' Stuart as I took a stance at the edge of the porch next to one of the posts what held up the roof. I allowed she must 'a been close to him, kneelin' for as long as she had in the rain. From the back, she didn't look old enough to be one of his wives. Maybe she was a daughter. I hadn't stood but a short minute 'til I realized I was gonna find out who she was, 'cause she'd just rose and turned to look square at me. I raised the barrel of the carbine with my right hand as we locked eyes. How did she know I was there? I'd made no noise comin' out the back door, but she stared right at me. I could see she'd been cryin'. Could see her eyes was red and swollen, even though the steady rain hid it for the most part. She looked innocent in her grieving. I felt for her, but how'd she know I was there? Even if I had made noise, the rain would 'a made it so she wouldn't 'a heard it. Studyin' on that got me curious.

She stood the rain starin' at me. Arms crossed over her middle. Hair soaked, hangin' curled about her face down past her shoulders. She had on no coat. Her top covered with a white, long sleeved soldier shirt. From her waist hung a tattered cotton skirt that didn't reach the ground. She wore no shoes on her feet. I moved to my right, takin' a seat in the first rocker I come to. The carbine laid across my left arm ready to assault with, if need be. I weren't sure if more folks was around or not. I'd seen too much recent to trust anyone 'cept family and clan, and some 'a them was questionable, fer the times. I nodded my head toward the rocker to my right, makin' her know she could come in out 'a the rain. Sit the rocker next to mine. I hoped we could talk, if she cared to.

It come to mind that she was near my age, as we kept starin' at each other. Her look made my spirit uncomfortable. There was something pullin' about this girl, or rather, young woman, as I'd come to notice through her soakin' wet shirt. I was interested in findin' out what it was, as she slowly moved toward the steps, then up one at a time. Never takin' her eyes off me. Her bare feet, showin' out from under the cotton skirt, gettin' cleaned by the rain with each step she climbed. Once on the porch, she moved to the second rocker down from mine. Her doin' that made it clear she was wary of her circumstance.

That told me something about her nature. She was cautious. I liked that. She was wise to be. I'd not trust me neither, if I was her. As a show of faith, and as a way of showin' her I meant no harm, I leaned forward and set the carbine ag'in the post in front of me what lay closer to her rocker than mine. I didn't need a gun with this young woman, and I was most sure I could get to it 'fore she did, if that kind 'a move come. She'd not be causin' me trouble. I'd become sure they weren't nobody else there to cause me none, neither. The takers had moved on. I was proud of that.

    I could sense she didn't have it in her to fight me right then, but I also sensed she prob'ly could. I seen the hurt she was feelin' in her eyes. Could feel her pain in my spirit. Her heart, or some part of her, was broken. Her father, it seemed to be, was layin' dead out in the yard gettin' rained on. Most of his face missin'. If that was him, we shared a common pain. I could feel a long night comin'. I wanted to trust her, but I dared not.

The Legend of Swell Branch

CHAPTER 11

Sky Watcher

After settlin' straight-backed toward the front of the rocker's seat, she stared me in the eye for what seemed like a full minute. Her body turned toward me what it could with her knees squeezed tight. Her elbows restin' on the tops of her thighs. She was slowly rubbin' her hands one over the other for warmth. Her skin, pale as a morning mist, looked chilled. She had long dark hair, but it weren't straight like the Cherokee. Bein' wet like it was, it held a mess of curls top to bottom. Her eyes was sky blue. She was tall, too, fer a woman, and most beautiful. She had a pull to her bein' I was feelin'. Some women have that.

I found it hard to breathe full on as we kept starin' at one another. Time seemed to stop in the world around us, at least for me it did. It was near more'n I could stand, bein' in such close quarters with her. This stranger that didn't feel like a stranger was doin' something to me. I had to break our stare to breathe proper, but then, with that breath, I caught her scent. Rich and sweet, like that of the woods in late spring. Oh, but she was havin' my attention.

I commenced lookin' her over for hurt places but didn't find any. It was obvious she was cold. I come to notice a slight quiver from inside her shirt. She caught me lookin' her over, but I felt she know'd it was out 'a concern. Her hands was gripped more tightly than before, white showin' in the tips of her fingers, under her nails. I reasoned she was finally reactin' to the cold of the day and the spring rain she'd been soaked with. A cold that was hid from her for a time by the shock and pain of loss. She'd need to get them wet clothes off 'fore long. Change into some dry 'fore she caught her death.

Movin' slowly, she turned her body back to face forward in the rocker lookin' out to Stuart. Almost like she'd forgot he was there. She stayed herself. We still hadn't spoken other than what looks we'd give each other. Grabbin' tight to the armrests with both hands, she commenced to slidin' her person back in the rocker's seat. Stoppin' as she squared herself against the cane strips that formed the rocker's back, leavin' her arms to lay forearm down on the armrests. Leanin' her head back, she closed her eyes. I watched as a tear leaked out from the outside corner of her left eye, then ran down her face to her neck. Leavin' a trail like a tiny little creek bed. Another followed. Maybe a dozen fell total. All of 'em followin' the same trail as the first one, disappearin' one at a time behind the collar of the soldier shirt she was wearin'. She never moved her head or acted like she felt 'em. I looked to her hands. She had pretty hands. Long, slender fingers what laid covered in that fetching pale skin she was blessed with. I seen her hands held some workin' type scars.

Her clothes was soaked and muddy from bein' out in the rain kneelin' beside Stuart. It was obvious, from the tips of her bosom what show'd hard through her thin shirt, now that she was leaned back in her rocker, that she was cold. Without openin' her eyes, she crossed her right leg over her left knee, then laid both arms over her middle for warmth. That left her bare feet exposed to the cold air of the rainy, spring afternoon. Her toes clean from bein' rained on while walkin' up the steps. She stayed like that for a bit, 'fore leanin' her head over to the left toward me slowly opening her red, swollen eyes. She looked straight at me like I'd said something to her. That made me feel strange 'cause I hadn't spoke a word that I know'd of. She'd caught me lookin' at her again, too. She smiled a short little smile as she turned her head back out to where Stuart lay.

The tears had stopped, but sadness show'd strong on her face. Her look one that made me feel she was askin' to be forgiven fer something, but I know'd of nothin' she'd done. First time I'd ever seen her, even though it didn't feel like the first time, strange as that sounds. I didn't understand how, but my soul could feel her spirit's pain. She leaned her head forward and smiled as she looked back to me. It was almost like she was lettin' me know she felt the same. Her spirit was strong. There was a closeness there I was becomin' most comfortable with. Near personal, really.

Takin' her eyes off mine, speakin' to me without words, she stood. Turnin' to her right, she commenced walkin' toward the south end of our porch. We had a braided rope strung tight about head high full across that end of the porch. It was for hangin' out the wash. I raised my head some as she walked away watchin' her close. She was so beautiful I couldn't help but watch.

The rope was strong. Meant for wet clothes to be hung on after they was washed fresh, or as it had just come to mind fer her, and me, after you've been caught out in a late winter rain. My heart got to beatin' a little harder, just considerin' her future actions.

Most folks might not realize, and prob'ly don't know, but it was considered disrespectful to track dirt, ash, water, or fresh mud onto people's clean floors inside their houses. Their planks was sanded smooth with creek sand, but they weren't finished with no kind 'a protector. Wood was just bare wood. You didn't wanna get troublesome things on the planks what made up them floors. It caused a mess that was hard to clean for the folks of the home. Water made stains they couldn't get out. Most everybody know'd to watch for that. It was easy to sweep dry dust and dirt out from houses, but gettin' them other kind 'a things off the floors was a chore. Anything wet would stain. Water and such made a mud when it mixed with what little dirt there might be left over from sweeping. That was a burden to get cleaned up, even when it dried. Wearin' wet, drippin' clothes when you went inside would cause a mess like that. Folks just generally paid mind and didn't track in such what had to be cleaned up. Left their wet and dirty clothes on the outside to wash and dry 'fore takin' 'em in the house.

All homeplaces had clotheslines like ours, common to be seen on porches or out in the yards of homes in the mountains. They were important. Hangin' your fresh wash out in the open to dry helped with keepin' the scent down in your clothes, quilts, and bed linen.

That was important when you lived in the woods. It seemed my visitor might be familiar with this consideration.

She was cold from bein' so wet. She needed dry clothes. I'd been noticin' she was showin' signs of it. She'd kept her mouth closed while sittin' the rocker. We hadn't spoken, but I could see her teeth was chatterin' on the inside like a body eatin' a tiny little ear of corn. Her skin looked cold. Turnin' her back to me when reachin' the rope clothesline, stirrin' my thinkin' even more, she pulled her hands inside the cuffs of the soldier shirt one at a time, never stoppin' to unbutton the front. Slippin' her arms out from each sleeve to the inside, she let 'em hang inside the shirt. From there, she took a quick peek back at me. I hadn't turned my head. I don't know why, I should 'a, but I hadn't. I couldn't. I kind 'a hoped she didn't want me to. She seen I was bein' disrespectful by not lookin' away, but after a second, she grinned a mite and kept on removing the wet soldier shirt. She never said nor motioned fer me to look away, so I kept on watchin'. I could not believe what I was seein'. It was a sight fer a body like me to behold.

After makin' her mind all was okay, she turned her head back away while liftin' up with both her arms. That action slid the wet shirt over her head and completely off her body in one smooth motion. Her bare back showin' full. She turned her head to the left just slightly, enough to see if I was lookin'. I was. Her smile was gone. Replaced by a look I didn't know. Had never seen before on any soul. She still never asked me to turn away.

I didn't mean not to look away. I just didn't think to. I really couldn't think at all. Her bareness was a crippling sight fer me. Made my heart start beatin' harder. I found it confusin' to try and think. I was overcome with strange feelings I'd never felt in all my years of living. A strange pull was comin' from my center. I was not able to look away. She still weren't actin' like she minded me lookin', so I looked on, after a bit, wholly out of desire.

Grabbin' the shirt by the shoulders, she commenced to slingin' the water out. Her arms waved up and down as she shook loose what water she could, then hung it up to dry. She was strong. I could see the outlines of her muscles as she moved. Lean and showin' like the shoulders of a mountain cat as it sneaks up slow on its intended. The small of her back arched perfect. A curved little valley laid just above the top of her bottom, formed by the muscles on either side of her spine. It was a sight more powerful than anything I'd ever seen. I felt stirrin's I was unfamiliar with.

Turnin' back toward me, while crossin' her arms up in front of herself, coverin' her bare breast, we locked eyes again. Starin' at each other for a most pleasant short minute. I was in awe. I'd seen Cherokee women near naked before. That was common among the Indians when the weather was warm, but this settler maiden was more'n I'd prepared myself for. A battle I'd not reckon'd on, 'til it come to me face on. For sure, as I watched her slowly uncross her arms, lowerin' each one to their length by her sides, turnin' her palms out while bowin' her head to profess her comfort. I'd never know'd God to make such an unbelievably beautiful creature. I thanked Him in the silent from my heart for His amazing work standin' before me.

After raisin' her head back up and starin' at me for another wonderful few seconds, her top half bare as a newborn baby, never takin' her eyes of mine, she lifted her hands to finger the cloth string what held up her cotton skirt, slidin' her long, slender thumbs in behind the tie. That made me look away fer not bein' able to stand what I was watchin'. I wanted to scream out for her, but I couldn't. I didn't look away fer long, though. I let my eyes turn back to where she stood. Her beauty was something like I'd most likely never experience again, outside of her. My soul was stirrin'.

Her top was bare... and most beautiful. Her body lean with muscles tight where she needed 'em. Her arms and back strong. I couldn't take my eyes off her. The beauty of her breast caused a stirrin' in me that rocked the very foundation of my person. I felt more than saw the shape of each one as they danced in rhythm to the movements of her undressing. What in the whole put together had just happened? How could a woman, with so much innocence, control the very heart beating in my chest? It was pounding. Oh, I wanted to run grab her tight in my arms, hold her, taste her lips, her neck, her bosom. I wondered if she could feel my longing in her spirit. I figured it show'd in my face.

No sir. No question about it. I know'd what I was lookin' at. A grow'd up young woman ripe for the pickin'. I was feelin' a stirrin' down deep. Feelings I'd never felt before. My legs quivered. They would not move if I'd 'a ordered 'em to. No way I could stand on 'em. Her beauty was makin' me weak. I recognized these new feelings as a danger for me, if I let 'em be, but I didn't care. She could kill me if she wanted. I'd not be able to stop her. I just wanted her, all of her, close. I think she know'd it, too… yeah, of course she did.

I could sense it was comin'. Kind 'a halfway prayed it weren't, but I know'd it was. I thought it might make my heart explode, seein' the rest of her body exposed from sheddin' them wet clothes… it near did.

Without takin' her eyes off mine, her long fingers undid the cloth tie what held up the whole of her skirt. Slowly, she began sliding her thumbs around the length of the string in front to loosen the hold it had on her person… the skirt what covered the lower half of her body… the skirt that was the last piece of covering she had on. I was overcome with what was happening. My longing could hardly wait for the rest of her to appear. I tried to keep my eyes on hers, but her beauty demanded me watch as her nakedness slipped out from under the mud stained cotton skirt. It was more'n I could stand.

I didn't mean to be rude, nor disrespectful, but I figured if she was disrobin' square in front of me, she must not mind me lookin', so I kept at it. Wouldn't 'a mattered if she had 'a minded, I was took. Couldn't 'a looked away if I'd wanted. Why would I? This was a sight rare to a mountain man of my design. I realized, as she continued, that I was fixin' to lay eyes on a sight I'd never seen in my whole put together. I was right.

I understood them wet clothes needed to come off. I understood they needed to be replaced with dry, as a body could catch their death if they wore 'em too long. I understood it was not proper to drip fresh water on the plank floors of the house. She understood all that as well. She was just addin' a little seasonin' to the doin's of it. Maybe as a defense against a possible threat from me? That made sense to my thinkin'. She didn't know me. Had never met me. Whatever the reason, it made me wonder why, and, was that all she was doin'? Gettin' on dry clothes? She'd got my attention full, yes, but I sensed to watch for treachery, even though I was enjoyin' bein' took in by her beauty. I was no fool.

She turned her gaze, and her body, away from me back toward the clothesline. Thumbs layin' to the front of each hip between her pale skin and the tie string of her skirt. With the ease of a snowflake fallin', she straightened both arms makin' the ripples of her wet skirt slide softly over her smooth, rounded bottom. The skirt droppin' down her legs to make a small pile at the top of her feet, as gravity took over from where the length of her arms give out. The build of her body from behind, as she stood there for a moment, was like the beauty one sees in the curve of a rose, smooth, soft to the touch, delicate, but firm.

Lookin' on her natural body was a sight more beautiful than anything I'd ever seen. I had to look away or black out from lack 'a air. My heart had never beat like it was. Never before had I been so affected in my body by the sight of anything I'd encountered, earthly or spiritual. She was most fetching for sure, and her beauty was weakening me deep inside. She'd plumb snagged my full person after showin' me herself in full view. I was at her mercy. Treachery be damned! But, could I trust her? I believed I'd dare to.

Turnin' her head back toward me only slightly, as she stepped out from the skirt pile, she saw me lookin, then saw me look away. After hangin' it on the line next to the soldier shirt, she slowly turned the whole of her body back toward me full on. She seen I weren't lookin' away no more. I couldn't, nor could I help starin'. Her front was completely bare. Her body was completely bare. Oh, her nakedness had a pull to me. I couldn't help my thoughts as I looked upon a sight like I'd never seen. Never dreamed I'd see. The slope of her breast, subtle, leadin' my eyes to the tips I so badly wanted to know. The dark curly patch between the tops of her legs drawin' me to come visit like a fresh opened wildflower teases a honeybee at morning's first light. I sensed she held a sweetness I could only imagine in my thoughts. Oh, she'd wounded me. I had to know this woman, and I needed to know her full. She'd just touched my soul way down deep where it'd never been touched before 'cept in spirit.

I'd never look at a woman of her kind the same again. My life had just changed, and she was the one what did it. I silently thanked her for it.

Her womaness had to 'a let her know I'd been weakened, but it seemed I saw mercy in her eyes. I figured she know'd I couldn't help not lookin' away, me bein' the buck I was and her as pretty as she was. The most beautiful woman I'd ever seen, standin' full on naked in front of me, not mindin' at all that I was lookin'… starin', really… how could she not know? Made me almost wonder if she was real or just a vision… 'til she smiled at me while crossin' her arms back over her front, commencin' a trail toward our back door.

She was a most beautiful creature. I was frozen in time watchin' her. I could not move. There was a power over my heart from her beauty. A feelin' that come to me I couldn't shake. I felt a yearning for this woman, but I didn't know that's what it was 'til later. I'd never had a yearning before. I liked it. I could feel my spirit was doin' what it could to make me understand her. She made me feel different than any woman I'd ever met. I wanted to be with her for a time. Get to know her better. I said a silent prayer for wisdom, as she walked right close to my rocker, headin' for our back door. Her arms still crossed over her front as she moved. I could scent her passion when she slipped by. It laid strong in the damp air after she passed. I turned to watch her from behind. Her backside beautiful, top to bottom. She stopped 'fore goin' in the house, turnin' for a quick peek back at me. She smiled as she had to drop her arm from coverin' her front to open the door. She then disappeared into the dark inside of our home leaving me alone. I was addled.

I couldn't tell from her doin's if she was good, or an evildoer. I was kind 'a dazed. Not thinkin' straight. Truth be told, I was at her mercy. Would be for the next little while. It would take me some time to settle over watchin' her shed them wet clothes. I looked forward to that time of rememberin'.

Her movements was smooth, like one who was natural with where she was. I thought to follow her in as she was disappearin' into our house, but didn't. Couldn't, really, after what I'd just experienced with her. It didn't matter in the end; I'd no sooner thought that than she come back out fully clothed. She was wearin' a fresh full-length homespun dress what looked to be much thicker and warmer than the shirt and skirt hangin' wet at the end of our porch. She carried no weapons under the dress, that I could see, but I weren't sure I could trust my thinkin'. All I saw in my mind's eye under that dress was her. Her beauty still fresh in my thoughts. I couldn't shed the sight of her natural put together. I wanted to see it again, touch her for a time.

I found it odd that the dress was some too big for her. Like it weren't hers. Maybe it weren't. I would remember that. Her feet was still bare. Made me wonder if she had any boots or shoes. Surely, if she had any, she'd be wearin' 'em in this weather. Could be she just didn't take time to put 'em on, bein' nervous over me bein' there… and the death of what I felt was her father. I would worry over her foot coverin's later.

There was a stirrin' in my soul as I was able to stand from the rocker and watch her come from the house. My body finally freed somewhat from her spell. I'd never felt such a pull from a person before. I wanted to know more about her. Had to know more about her. She obliged me by speakin' first, after takin' a seat in her original rocker. I moved to sit in mine. Her voice was fetchin', as she crossed her right leg over her left knee again, her bare feet showin' same as before. Her arms again to the armrests. Hands clinching the fronts, only they didn't look to be squeezin' as tight as earlier.

Seemed she'd calmed herself some, or maybe just warmed up by havin' fresh clothes on, but she'd stopped quiverin'. She leaned her head back. Stared out into the rain at Stuart and his horse. The stallion was now inside the front door of the barn in the dry. Stuart, still tied to the lead, was out in the rain. The stallion was a smart horse. I looked forward to spendin' some time with him.

"I know your name, warrior," she said, in as warm a voice as I'd ever heard. The sound of which was most comforting. Our eyes come together as she began speaking.

"My name is Miriam. My Mohawk name is Sky Watcher. I answer to Miriam, or Sky. I think they got that from the color of my eyes. I am from the North. My father, Gideon, was killed at the end of the war fighting off outlaws who came to his camp near Atlanta to steal his goods. A man named Viktor Soltor and his gang. Mr. Stuart, the one laying out there in the rain, and my father were friends, of sorts… at least as close as Mr. Stuart could be friends to anyone. They traded together, mostly. Mr. Stuart and his wives took me in after Gideon was killed. My mother has been missing for a time. Taken moons back to be sold as a slave. Mr. Stuart said if I came south with him and his family, worked with his wives in their effort to homestead a place, he would help me find my mother, but that's not gonna happen now that he's dead. He could be an evil man at times. Hurt me on several occasions, but his wives are the dangerous ones. Your sister, Mary, found that out when she came here days ago, but you know all this. You have seen their work." She dropped her head to pause a minute breakin' our stare.

She continued speakin' after raising her head. Her thoughts seemed deep as she looked back to me. My heart felt for her. Her look was of confusion and sadness. I wanted to help make things better. "My mother was taken by rogue Seminole in a raid. I learned through the Mohawk that they took her south to sell as a slave. I came with Stuart in hopes of finding where she'd been taken. We have been here but a short time and I've been able to do little in my search. That troubles my spirit. Now the one man I believed could help me lies dead. Tell me, warrior, how is it that Mr. Stuart is being dragged back by his horse? Might you had anything to do with his dying? Say if you did. It matters little to me. I am not sad he is gone. He was good to me, for the most part, but his passing reminds me of how alone I am here, of how much I want my mother. That is why I am sad, Buach. Please don't think I weep for that man laying out there in the rain. My sadness is from a different place than him being dead. My sadness is for my own."

I was right, in a way, me thinkin' she was sad for her father. She was, it's just that Stuart weren't him, and seein' him dead reminded her of the sadness what comes with missin' a close parent. She hurt for her folks, both of 'em. Hoped to find her mother. That was something I would needs smoke over. Maybe I could help with her search, once I was done with the settlin' up of our farm and my time of mourning.

"I had no hand in killin' that evil man," I said, with a little more anger than I meant to. "I wanted to. I meant to. There was no doubt I was gonna try. Why? 'Cause he killed my father. Took my home. I owed him his due, but you know this. I wish I could 'a had the pleasure of sending him to be with the ancestors, but I did not. The Great Spirit took him 'fore I could see justice done. His body got sick from something on the inside. I did bind him up so his horse could bring him back, though. I had no choice for time's sake. He's dead. He didn't feel nothin', unfortunately, 'cause I know my father felt it when Stuart cut his throat to kill him. At least I got to watch him die a somewhat painful death, but that is not true vengeance, considerin'. You are a Northerner. You would not understand my anger. My Cherokee family would understand. They would know how this feels."

"Buach, Gideon bought me from the Mohawk when I was young. I understand how you feel. I know the warrior's mind. I have lived with the Mohawk. They gave me a name. I never knew my birth parents. I was with a small clan who lived in the mountains to the north. Only a few elders and their wives, all old. They found me in the woods next to their camp only a few days after I was born. Somebody left me there for them to find. They raised me like one of their own. I learned their ways. After a few years, most of the clan started dying. I was still just a child. I could take care of myself well enough, but I was young, maybe ten. Too young to cook much, too young to grow the crops needed for our survival, too young to hunt. Before long, it got to where they could no longer provide for themselves, or me. The men had become too old to hunt. Their wives were living their last days. Too weak to plant, tend, and harvest what we needed for food. We lived off the gifts of others. Tending to me, for them, had become something they could no longer do, and I could not care for them properly, either. Living like that became dangerous for us all, so for my well-being, they sold me to the trader, Gideon." She stopped fer a minute, recollectin'. Tears come from her eyes. She stopped cryin' full 'fore she began speakin' again. I felt for her, rememberin' the things she was.

"It was in the beginning of cold time a few years back. I remember that first night I stayed with Gideon. He and his wife had the warmest quilts I'd ever wrapped myself in. I missed my Mohawk family since the moment I left them, but Gideon and his young Cherokee wife gave me a new life, a new start. My clan knew Gideon from many years of trading. Knew he was kind and would take care of me. He was a trader of goods with most all the Indians who used the North Trail for profit. Spent a lot of time with the Mohawk at their main village. Did it for years. I learned the Mohawk ways during those times. They considered me one of their own because of the old ones that found me as a child. Many settlers knew Gideon. I learned their ways as well. He would trade Indian made goods for settler made goods, then sell or trade those back to the Indians. Gideon was wise in his dealings through all those years. Later on, after I'd lived with them a few moons, he and his wife adopted me as their daughter. They were so good to me. I love them very much. I miss them every day."

She had to stop again fer a minute. Tears fillin' her eyes again. It seemed that her parents bein' gone was a terribly painful memory for her. Seemed she still missed 'em somethin' awful even after a few years. That kind 'a hurt proved to me she was speakin' truth about how she felt for Gideon and his wife. I thought of my own family. A knot come up in my throat I could barely swallow back. I would needs mourn soon. After a couple minutes or more, she began again.

"He and his wife, my adopted mother whom I cherish, were good to me. Loved me like their own. Maybe even more than their own. I have brothers and sisters, but I know not where. My mother, as I have told you, is in the South somewhere. She was taken from us during the night off the North Trail. Gideon found out from the Mohawk she was taken for the slave trade. I want to find her... no... I *have* to find her. My spirit cries daily, I miss her so. Yes, warrior. I understand your frustrations about losing your vengeance, but the Great Creator is judge of all. I understand, Buach, I do, for I was raised with the Mohawk, and I've traveled the trade route most of my life. Have been living among all the different tribes along that route for many years. I learned to fight, to shoot, to cook. Gideon allowed me to be who I am.

I went back to live with the Mohawk for a time after he was murdered. They welcomed me to stay as long as I wanted, but I couldn't stay. My spirit was restless for Momma. When I left the North to come south, Stuart, or rather his wives, made me wear settler clothes they didn't wear anymore. I do not like their clothes. I like what you wear, but all I had are gone. They burned my skins and homespun when we left for the South. I hope, now that Mr. Stuart is dead and his evil wives are gone, that maybe I can trade for some new clothes with the Cherokee. Maybe you could help me with that. What say ye, Buach? I have some gold coins Gideon gave me many moons ago."

"You keep your gold, Sky Watcher. I will find you decent coverings. I just want you to promise me I can watch you put 'em on," I said sincerely, with a bit of a grin. She blushed and smiled. I kept on with our conversation.

"Yes, Gideon. I knew this Gideon. Traded with him many times, but I never saw you. How is it that you say you traveled with him, but I never saw you? How can I believe what you say, when I know of whom you speak? Would I not have seen you if you traveled with him constant? I am confused, Mohawk?"

"Yes, Buach. I was there. I would not lie. I did know of you then, your family. You traded settler goods with Gideon. No, you would never have seen me, or my mother. We always stayed the wagon while he made trade. She kept a side-by-side fully loaded in there with us, so if somebody tried to steal from Gideon, she could protect him from the takers. That only happened a couple times. Gideon was good about planning his travels. No, warrior, you would never have seen me when trade took place. I stayed hid with Momma. Gideon always feared somebody would try and steal us, if they saw us. His wife, my mother, was young for a man his age, beautiful as well. Many tried to buy us, but Gideon had a keen spirit. He was a good judge of character when first meeting people. But, you are wrong, Buach. I did meet you along the trail, once. I was young.

Mother was not with us. You traded Gideon a Cherokee made skin pouch for some coffee. Do you remember this, warrior?"

She finished that last bunch 'a words with a not so happy face. Me checkin' her about bein' truthful had got under her skin. Her eyes turned to mine. I thought back to the trade she was talkin' about. I remembered it clear as yesterday. She *was* there. I remembered her after thinkin' on it a minute, but she was young. Had to 'a been toward the end of the war. I guess I was kind 'a young, too, though, but I did remember.

We was out of any provisions, so I'd gone out to search for some. I happened to cross trails with Gideon not far from Swell Branch, but he had little. No provisions hardly at all, 'cept a small bag of coffee beans that was near spoilt. His wagons, mules, and trade goods had most all been took by soldiers from both sides. I was proud to get them beans back then. They tasted fine to me, Dad, and Mary - once we got 'em cleaned off and sun-dried. That would 'a been a while 'fore Gideon was murdered. Killed for his trade goods. I wondered what happened to Miriam when Gideon was killed? Was she there then, too? Did she see it happen? I felt for her. Her life had been hard, but I could tell from the way she handled herself that she'd learned from her trials. The South was a dangerous place to be after the war… for everybody. I was sure proud I'd met this most amazing woman. I'd see to makin' it less dangerous for her, if she'd let me.

The Legend of Swell Branch

CHAPTER 12

A Stranger in the House

As we sat our rockers that afternoon, then on into the evening, we talked of many things. I learned through our conversation that Miriam was without a true home. Had been for a time. The ones what brought her south had cleared out, leavin' her behind to wait for Stuart. Then she and him, or just her, if he hadn't made it, would catch up when they could. That told me them folks didn't care if they ever saw Stuart, or Miriam, again. She prob'ly know'd that, too.

Them wives of his most likely got to blamin' him for all their present-day troubles, prob'ly included her as one of 'em. Easy to charge folks when a body ain't there to defend themselves. She weren't family. They know'd she'd never be a wife. I'd say they come to a mind that Stuart weren't too good as a leader. Got to figurin' they'd not be able to depend on him for proper leadin' durin' troubled times. After all, he'd not been able to protect 'em from a couple crazy mountain folk. The understanding prob'ly come to 'em, how could he be counted on to lead 'em through anything worse, like Indians or outlaws or trail bandits? I reasoned once they commenced to studyin' on all that, and after findin' Walter in the privy, then Billy bein' brought back with a hole through his center, and learnin' I was after Stuart fer murderin' my dad, they'd come to realize it was more'n they could afford to settle for. I'd made it obvious to all that should 'a been takin' notice, I weren't gonna have folks tryin' to homestead our farm. I'd committed killin' to show 'em how serious I took what their evil was causin'. We'd done leveled one 'a them mean women when Henri caught her upside the head with a hard-right fist. I doubted they'd ever been stood up to by the likes of us.

I come to a belief, after a time, that losin' a few of their own had turned out to be a higher cost than them wives was willin' to pay, when considerin' what they'd gained from their troubles. If they lost any more fightin' men, it would become near impossible fer 'em to survive as a bunch 'a women and young'uns wanderin' the new world of the South. A land where able-bodied folks from the North was movin' by the gross. Some with goodly intentions, many with evil intentions. The loss of a child prob'ly figured into 'em leavin', as well. That death comin' to mind brought sickness to my gut. I wondered when that pain would cease… if ever.

Suppertime come on us as we sat the rockers into the early evening. We weren't sayin' much as conversation, just watchin' it rain, rockin', thinkin', occasionally starin' out at Stuart and his horse, peekin' at each other from time to time. My mind turned to the mare and carbine what'd been took from me. I'd get that truck back 'fore long. I was sure on that. Already felt like I might know who took it. If it was the folks I was considerin', might be they didn't know their take was mine.

Hunger got to knawin' at me. Interruptin' my thinkin'. My stomach started makin' empty noises. I seen Sky heard the growlin'. I couldn't remember for sure when last I'd eat, but the pangs was tellin' me it'd been a while. I was thirsty, too. I wondered how long it'd been since she'd took sustenance. I come to realize, bein' in her presence made me forget to think about many things that I thought about common on most evenings. Food, for one. There was chores needed tendin' to, since the previous chore doers had left things a mess, yet, there I sat like a lazy man. Rockin' on the back porch, doin' nothin', 'cept keepin' company with a most unusual creature. She'd got into my thinkin'.

I'd not been in our home recent. Had no idea how the stores was fer food. I know'd she most likely did. Stood to reason she could make supper while I tended to Stuart and the stallion. I thought to say the words to let her know my thinkin', but her voice come out ahead 'a mine, again. I was proud fer that, again. Her mind and mine seemed to work kind 'a the same.

"Buach," she said, while lookin' out to Stuart. The rain had slacked off for a bit. "I am growing hungry… as are you," she said with a grin, while turning to look down at my middle. "It seems proper to at least tend to Stuart for the time being. Get him out of the rain. I will see to his committing once Old Man Sun has driven the rain clouds away. They left me here to do that, if needed, after all. If you will tend to him for the present, I can see to making some supper. They left only a small bit of food for me, but I can make do to get us a meal. What say ye, warrior? I am only trying to be reasonable, as you and I have just met."

"I see it same as you, Miss Miriam. I have no respect for that murderin' pile 'a nothin' layin' out there in the rain, but I've grow'd tired 'a lookin' at it. I'll go fetch him in the barn, see to the stallion. As you said, I am hungry. Makes no mind to me what we eat. Whatever there is will bring comfort. Make do as you can. I'm thankful for the least of what they left us. I expected no different. I'm just glad they're gone from here. I wanted no more killin'.

I will say, though," I kept on after a short pause, "that I'm glad you stayed behind with me." She jerked her eyes toward mine quick as a spider strikin'. We simply stared at each other.

What? What had I just said? With me? Did I say that? Oh, my. I could feel the heat in my head risin' as the blood rushed to my face. I'd never felt so stupid. A feelin' like bein' dizzy come over me. I commenced tryin' to speak my way out 'a the mess I'd just put myself in.

"I mean… I'm glad you're here… yes," I said, breakin' our stare while lookin' back and forth from the floor to her eyes. "Ah… ah… you can… ah… see to Stuart… yes… right, well, I mean… you don't need to see to him… I'll do it… uh, I mean… ah… no… I could do it, yes… uh… wait… or, I can help you… yes… that's right. You are here to take care of Stuart. I can help you, yes… so… ah… yeah… okay. We can see to that later when the rain stops, or maybe tomorrow 'fore we leave out for Henri's… I'd say… maybe."

Oh, I felt the fool of fools as we broke apart to go and tend to our chosen chores. I'd never felt so foolish in my whole put together. I had to get gone from her. I stood right up, went down the steps, then on to the barn. Forgettin' my carbine leanin' up ag'in the post where I was sittin'. Hopefully, I'd not need it. The evil ones had gone. It was fortunate for me the rain had slacked off as it moved on toward dark, or she might 'a got a look at me hangin' up my wet clothes. I figured the rain to come back after a while.

It was mumble speakin'. She grinned at me as I got all flustered, tryin' to tell her I was glad she'd been made to stay. I must 'a sounded like a new schoolboy readin' for the first time in front 'a them what went to school with him. She made me nervous. I thought back on all I'd said as I eased the stallion on deeper into the barn draggin' Stuart's body in out 'a the rain. I untied the draggin' rope from the saddle horn, leavin' him lay, then stripped the horse clean of its saddle and truck, blanket, and bridle. Turned it out to the back pasture to keep 'til I got time to tend to him more. He needed a good rub down and hoof cleanin', but I could see to that 'fore we left out for Henri's next morning. It'd keep 'til then. My thoughts turned to my mare. I should 'a been seein' to her. Knowin' she'd been took got to festerin' in my spirit.

Supper weren't more'n a piece 'a flat bread fried, with most 'a the good meat from some rotting potatoes, onions, and cabbages we'd stored in the root cellar from our previous fall dig. That was the food they'd left her. She'd mixed what little there was together, addin' a scrap 'a fatback she'd found left hangin' on one of our hambones in the smoke shed. The takers had been eatin' off our keep. Them lowlifes eat our stores of meat while tryin' to take our place, now ain't that somethin'. That little fatback made the fry bread taste oh so delicious, once she got it formed up and skillet fried. Hard to make rotten vegetables, fried flour, and ham fat taste good, but she'd done it. We had nothing else. The takers took, or eat, all our hogs, chickens, and goats. Took all our hangin' meat we'd smoked up in the shed for winter keep, too. Fortunately, they'd left our milk cow. She was freshening. Prob'ly why they left her. She was a good cow, as milk cows go, but they weren't much meat on her fer eatin'. We'd had her for a long time. She'd 'a been more trouble to 'em than she'd 'a been worth, takin' her.

So there they'd left us, and because of their thievin', we'd have no food once supper was finished, but oh, that little bit 'a fry bread was good eatin', bein' hungry like I was. I took her bein' able to cook for a blessing, as we sat in silence enjoyin' the fry bread. She'd made a decent meal out 'a what little the Great Spirit had provided for us. I was happy to get it, as was she. Neither of us uttered one word of complainin' about it. I'd go to Henri's come morning. Fetch us some proper meat. Plant food would be hard to find, bein' close to spring like we was. Still, I figured to find some early poke or maybe the leaf tops off some wild turnips or ramps what'd sprung up early. We'd have to make do as we could. I wondered for Mary, for Henri, for Gus. I looked forward to goin' and bein' back with 'em all. I thought to take Sky with me when I went. I was thinkin' maybe Henri had some skins that would fit her.

"I am tired, Buach," she said as she finished her fry bread. She *was* hungry. "I've been sleeping in the loft since we came here, except one night. I was in the bed Stuart's sister fell on the night you and your friend came for Mary. I felt for Mary. Tried to free her the second night she was here, but they caught me. Tied us both overnight to posts on the porch for that. It was cold that night, too, but they gave us no quilts for cover. I am curious as to how you feel about me being here. I was part of the family that tried to take your home, killed your father. I had nothing to do with his murder, just so you know. Didn't find out it had happened until Mary come. I am no longer with them, by my choice, not theirs. I will not be returning to their clan. The wives despise me. I did not understand what was happening here, until I saw how they treated Mary once she arrived. That's when I knew that what they were doing was wrong. I tried to free her, but she was hurt and couldn't move well, so they caught up to us once we made the woods. She will tell you this, so that you know I speak the truth. I am sorry for not being able to get her out from here, Buach, but I did try. Now, I must ask you something that is a serious concern for me. As I told you before, I am without a home. I need a place to live for a while, to get myself started fresh.

I was thinking maybe here, for a time. Tell me, are you willing to let me stay here with you and Mary? I need to try and figure out what my future will look like. I need a place to fast and pray. Seek guidance from Holy Spirit. I could help with the spring planting. I am good in the fields. I could keep the farm while you go to mourn. I know stock and their needs," she paused a minute to let me understand she knew about my need to confront the pain of losin' my dad. "Yes, warrior, I know you will need those days. I can be here to care for the stock while you are gone, if you wish. I will go after a time, but for now, say for the next few moons, may I stay here with you and Mary? That would be proper. Would it not? She and I could be friends. You and I… Buach… we could become friends."

Them last words come with a hard stare I did not want to look away from, so I didn't. Stared her back all I could. She wanted to be friends. She wanted to stay with us for a while. She wanted to help with the spring planting. Was I in a vision? No, a gift from God, the way I seen it. I would discuss it all with Mary when we got to Henri's place, but I know'd she'd not have any worries over it. Most likely be thrilled to have some female company near.

"Yes," was all I could say, once I found my voice to answer with, but it was all that needed to be said for her. No sooner had she heard me agree than she took for the upstairs loft. Most likely to bed down, tired as we was, or to just be alone. She'd done cleaned all there was to clean in the cook room after we'd eat. Weren't but the one skillet she'd cooked the flat bread in. We'd eat straight from that skillet, so there weren't nothin' else to do. That freed her up to leave me sittin' there at the eatin' table. I wanted to talk more about her stayin' with us, but she'd left out kind 'a sudden. I was hopin' there might be more reasons for her leavin' on the quick like she had, other than just bein' tired and wantin' to bed down. I was wonderin' if me bein' near was havin' an influence on her. I know'd her bein' near was havin' a force on me. 'Fore leaving the cook room she turned to speak to me fer a quick minute.

"Oh, I was wondering," she said, turning back to me just as she got to the opening to leave the cook room. "You mentioned Henri a little bit ago, or, going to Henri's, uh, when you were thanking me, yeah, uh, for staying back with you, uh, and, thank you, for that. Thank you for feeling that way. I am glad I stayed back as well. Yes, so, who is Henri, and, do you mean for me to go with you come morning? Just curious, as it is."

"I apologize. I should have explained. Henri is my friend. He lives east of here. I was returning from a hunt when I found your bunch had took over our farm. I left the meat I'd collected at his place then him and me come back to free Mary. We have food there. I was just thinkin' that maybe we should go fetch it early for our morning meal, and yes, it would be nice if you could go with me to help bring it back. What say ye? Can you do this with me, Miriam?"

"Of course. I will be ready at first light from Old Man Sun. Sleep well, Buach. I will see you again in the morning." She turned to leave. I felt alone.

After watchin' her leave the cook room, then studyin' on all that'd happened earlier in the day, I come to the understandin' that me and her was gonna be in close confines for a spell. I felt like I could trust her, but I was wise enough to know I should be cautious for a time. It takes a while to build true trust with folks. As with me, she prob'ly went on to the loft early for need of privacy. Maybe to think on all that'd happened, or to study on her new living arrangements, or maybe just simply to sleep. Could be she was just needin' rest. I know'd I was. I would respect that. Still, those stayin' arrangements would need to be discussed fully once Old Man Sun woke us next morning. I looked forward to that time with her. We could talk as we made trail to Henri's. Fill the time it took us to get there. I said a silent, short prayer to Holy Spirit for Henri after he come to mind. I looked forward to having a long smoke with him. Talk about all I did to get our place back. He would want to hear about every little thing that happened, 'cause all folks' doin's had meaning to him.

I was tired after we eat, but I took some time to wander the house 'fore goin' to bed down in Dad's room. His bed was the best. He'd got it at Market the year before Momma died. Some free colored ladies would come to Atlanta when Market was on in the fall. They'd set up in town and make their goods for a few days. Beds was part 'a their makin's. They'd stuff beds and pillows for sleepin' on. They spun coverings as well. Folks would come from all over to buy from 'em. Cash on the barrelhead bein' their only form 'a trade. Dad bought Momma one 'a their beds for her comfort... did it 'cause he loved her. Wanted her to be most comfortable while gettin' her rest of a night.

They sewed quilts and sheets to fit each bed, too. They also brought homespun rolls of cloth for makin' clothes and washrags and dryin' rags that folks could buy or trade for. Those rolls was highly sought after. Them colored women told me they worked all year-long gettin' enough rolls together to satisfy those who wanted 'em when Market time come. Them women worked up soaps and washin' powders, too. All was fine quality wares. Made with hands what'd been workin' them kind 'a things for many years. A couple of their ladies tooled leather. Others rolled cigars from dried burley tobacco. Dad bought Momma the whole bed set, top to bottom. Cost him two gold pieces for the barrelhead, but he wanted her to have the best. I liked sittin' and watchin' them women make their goods. They'd stuff the sleepin' pads with something made from cotton. Used deer antlers strapped to a stick to get the stuffing where they wanted it. It was amazing to watch. They was kind women, most times. Let folks sit and learn while they worked. You had to be careful of their menfolk, though. They weren't as friendly as the women. That bed he bought her slept good for many years. Dad's great-grandkids even used it for a time, 'fore it give plumb out and a new bed was needed. Them women had a fine hand for craftin'.

Closin' the door to Dad's room, I pulled the latchstring in. I was concerned my houseguest might turn out to be more dangerous for me than I was thinkin' she was, or feelin' she was. I'd finished my walk around inside. Everything seemed to be as it had been 'fore the takers come. I'd look closer, when once I'd slept. My mind would see things more clearly, then. I did see they was truck missin' from the cook room. Made me come to believe that thievin' folk had no self respect, once they commenced to takin' from folks without regard, the ease of it gets in their blood. Comes natural fer 'em after a while.

They take 'cause they profit from it, without having to work for that profit. Most learned by doin' that it was a lot easier to steal for your wants than to work fer 'em. We'd not tolerate that where I come from. Three of the taker's bunch had come up dead on account 'a their thievin'. If you can believe it, after their stealin' ways caused the most painful hurt the Dark Angel holds to come upon 'em, them takers still found mind to swipe our cookin' truck as they left out. A right smart of it, too. I was sure I'd find other things missin' as time went on.

A body would 'a thought they'd learned about the wrongs of stealin' from all the killin' their takin' had caused over the last several days, but sadly, no. You'd think smart folks would reason they should stop their thievin'. No, not them. They should 'a seen it was dangerous to their persons, for sure when takin' from those who'd not be took from, but they just didn't get it. I come to the reasonin', after thinkin' on it later that night while enjoying my seasoned white oak pipe stuffed full 'a tasty air-dried Indian tobacco, that I should 'a shot that last Federal soldier, then we'd still have all the truck they stole when leavin' out. I could 'a put a lead ball right through his head from where I draw'd my rest up under that hemlock tree. I learned from that. I would not make that mistake again.

Mine and Sky's first night together ended as Old Man Sun rose next morning. I could hear shufflin' in the cook room after wakin' enough to listen proper. I allowed it was Sky gettin' fixin's together for what morning meal we could muster. I didn't think there to be much, but then I got to hearin' noises what sounded like a proper breakfast bein' made. For sure, when I heard the stove open and wood get throw'd in. *Why is that?* I got to wonderin'. Fire meant cookin'. We had nothin' to cook, that I know'd about, so why the fire? Then it come to me, them sounds meant Sky must 'a found more food we'd not seen the evening before. Realizin' that got my blood up. I was hungry from lack 'a solid food. I had to see to this right away. My empty belly was most curious as to what was goin' on in our cook room. Could there be real food? I was sure hopin' so.

I jumped from my sleepin', anxious for the smell of breakfast meat fryin'. Started throwin' on my clothes without much thought. The homespun shirt I'd been wearin' for many days fell over my head and shoulders no sooner than I was pullin' up and tyin' my buckskin britches. Followin' that, I sat the bed to lace up my footskins. They reached full up the bottom of my legs, coverin' nearly to my knee. I tied on my braided mid-belt, what held my long knife, then lifted the door latch to free myself from Dad's room. I near ran to the cook room hopin' to find 'a salt cured ham layin' fer slicin' the takers had missed - and Sky had found, but that didn't seem reasonable. We never hid our hams. Left 'em hangin' in the smoke shed. Easy to see for the takin'. They'd a not missed any. *What was it, then?*

I still weren't full awake as I breached the cook room door, but I come full on awake once I did. I seen what was makin' the noises, or rather, that it weren't Sky makin' the noises I'd woke to. A stranger was in her place. I sensed her though, of a sudden, standin' full to my right. She'd moved in kind 'a behind me when she saw our visitor. I felt the fingertips of her left hand grab muscle in the center of my back. She'd come to see what the noises was at near the same time I had. I caught her morning scent. That brought back some strong feelings I'd had aroused the day before. I looked into her eyes fer just a short second. How pleasant she seemed.

I reached to my belt for my short gun, not knowin' for sure who it was I was lookin' at, but found I'd not took time to strap it on, bein' in the hurry I was. I had no notion somebody else would come durin' the night. My hand didn't miss full, though, as the handle of my long knife slid firm into my grip. I draw'd it at the same time the intruder turned quick to look at me. He'd not forgotten to strap on his short gun. His right hand was full of a cocked and loaded Army Colt revolver, most likely in .44 caliber, judging from the size of the hole at the end of the barrel. That I wanted no part of. He could remove most of my head with that thing close as he was. Fortunately for me, and Sky, 'cause she was standin' behind me enough that a bullet goin' through my right side would 'a hit her, he never pulled his trigger. I was sure glad he didn't, 'cause I would 'a been dead had he let go. Sky maybe, too.

The smile what come to Uncle Silas' face, as he uncocked and holstered his short gun, let me know he was just goin' on. Never seriously intended to shoot me actual. I heard Sky let out the deep breath she was holdin' after seein' his smile. Her fingertips released the muscles in my back. She was strong. Her grip was strong. Took me a minute to get my heart back goin' after feelin' the touch of her fingers.

Hearin' the action work on one 'a them Colts, when it's bein' pointed at you up close, gets a body's attention. He told me later that he figured it fer me, what was comin' in on him, even though his back was turned. He'd pulled the Colt just in case he was wrong. Said he'd felt my spirit. I believed him. I know'd he was connected like that. Strong roots to the spirit world. He always said it was a gift from God. That's how folks like him stayed alive when travelin' through dangerous lands to seek out lost souls. Holy Spirit was his foundation, but I'd learned over time that the spirit world can be a treacherous place, if one's mind gets sided with dark thoughts like killin' or destroyin'. Sometimes he did things that made me wonder over his doin's. I know'd his faith run deep, but he was still only a person. No challenge for evil spirits without Holy Spirit protectin' him. Obedience to the called life could sometimes be difficult at best.

He was funnin' with me, drawin' his handgun like he did. Uncle Silas was sneaky like that. Once I gathered back some air in my lungs, I told him how I felt about him near scarin' the life from me. I calmed down when I seen the chunk 'a side meat layin' on the table he'd gone to slicin', and the half dozen turkey eggs layin' beside it. Food he'd brought to share. I allowed it was a little early for turkey eggs, but there they laid. He'd found 'em somewhere. I wanted to hug the old man, but I didn't. He was special, but no man I know'd was that special, 'cept my dad, and he weren't around no more. Still, some decent food was somethin' me and Sky needed, and he'd brung it. I said a silent prayer 'a thanks. I was most appreciative for Holy Spirit's providin'. I'd not be fool enough to think of it any different, neither. It was clear to my thinkin' who'd guided Uncle Silas to us that morning. Who'd show'd him the nest where the turkey eggs lay waitin' fer him so early in the season. Mountain folks understood it for what it was, divine guidance from above. It's just the way, in their world. Faith has power.

Uncle Silas was nothing more, nor nothing less, than Uncle Silas. He had a holy seriousness about him that Grandma Dew called, "as close to John the Baptist as a body could be but mixed with a pinch 'a Peter the Disciple for seasonin'. She was sayin' he was straight up from the Word about sin, and for sure to the body committin' it, but same as Peter, in that he had a temper you did not want sparked at you because of that sin. I loved Uncle Silas, but that didn't mean I cottoned to all his ways. He could be a most difficult holy man, and a most dangerous one. You'd not want him riled over something you'd done against him personal. I'd seen it on different occasions. Blood could get shed from folks he believed deserved it, or required it. Sometimes he'd beat the devil out of 'em what'd been took, near more'n they could stand, but he got the demon's attention.

He'd preach 'em the gospel after gettin' 'em shed of their demons and evil ways. I never doubted his foresight for self-preservation from those what run with demons, neither. He toted no less than two short guns to 'company his long rifle, and I never seen him without his knives. Didn't take but a wrong word from the right person to get 'em pulled on ye, neither, if it come to his mind they was a need fer 'em. Uncle Silas did what he felt Holy Spirit led him to do. Like a good soldier, he never questioned the orders from above. Just carried 'em out best he could. I respected him for that.

Thinkin' about some 'a the things I'd seen him do, or heard of him doin', I wondered at just whose voice he was hearin' sometimes. The spirit world can be a dangerous world. Henri always told me it can be a most confusing place, if one's mind had been weakened somehow. The way Uncle Silas traveled the spirit world constant had to wear him down to nearly nothin' over time. That's why he'd come to our place to rest up a couple times a year. It was always good to see him, but I paid mind to his doin's long as he was with us. A body never knows when evil might strike their person, walkin' where Uncle Silas walked, or Grandma Dew, or others like 'em. Them spirits could hold to you like field burrs. Preachin' folk had to pay mind and pray 'em off 'fore they went to other places to visit. A body bein' tired helped the evil get a foothold on your thinkin'. Uncle Silas was always tired when he show'd up at our place. He most likely brought a bait 'a them demons along with him. Knowin' that was possible made Dad nervous for all of us, but no evil ones ever seemed to 'a come on our clan, that I know'd of for sure. Momma dyin' weren't of no demon. Natural life death comes from the Creator. God holds charge of the soul when livin' and dyin' are in the balance.

Things would be different for a while, since Uncle Silas had come. He'd see to it. Dad bein' gone would not change how he did things. He was a man of God, and when he come for his visits, he let us remember that full on. We'd get no less than one Bible teachin' lesson a day, every day, long as his visit lasted. I looked forward to them stories. Partin' great seas, castin' demons into pigs makin' 'em jump off a cliff, killin' giants with only a sling and some rocks, those stories of faith and bravery stuck with me all my life the way he told 'em. He made you feel like you was right there in the middle of all the action. Sometimes we'd get two stories a day if we begged hard enough, or if he felt the call. He was the same every time he come, too. Never no different, unless he was troubled by spirits, then you'd just leave him be 'til he was ready to converse. Still, I liked it when he come. I was proud he come this time when he did. He could help with all that was happenin' to our family and clan. Pray over us for protection. All would be right on our farm 'fore he left. I was sure of that.

I took a minute, once we'd finished eatin', to lift up another silent prayer 'a thanks for Uncle Silas' comin' to visit at such a proper time. A comfort come over me knowin' he'd be with us for a while. Could watch the place when I was away. That thinkin' give my spirit peace. I know'd then it was time for me to mourn. The hurt that come with findin' out about my dad commenced to movin' forward in my thinkin'. I would needs hurry and get to my special place 'fore it come on me hard. I didn't think I was gonna be able to make it, but somehow, I know'd I had to, 'fore the soul pain broke me in half. Mourning was a much-needed time for spiritual folks like me and mine. It put things back in balance. My world had gotten off center with the murderin' of my dad. I would needs find that center to get things back in their certain order. Holy Spirit would send me comfort, and through that comfort, I'd know my world would be made right. Thank you, Holy One, for mercy.

THE LEGEND OF SWELL BRANCH

CHAPTER 13

BIBLE TOLD TIMES

Henri had healed enough that Blue Dove felt it safe for him to leave and go back home, but only if he agreed to rest for four whole days. She made him promise to drink a different mix of tea on each of the four days. One half the mix in the morning and the other half at night 'fore beddin' down. She made four separate pouches from four different mixes. One pouch for each day. He had to drink the correct mix on the day each was meant to be drunk. If he took one on the wrong day, his wound could get sick again. He'd have to cross the big ridges north to visit Blue Dove's clan for more. That would take several days travel. In that time, his wound could fester past where it could be healed. Blue Dove did not want that, so she marked each pouch of mix carefully.

"Warrior, you have promised me to rest for four days, and to drink your tea each morning and each night," Blue Dove spoke slowly, calmly, as she sat a stool next to where Henri lay in the healin' lodge. He turned his face toward hers. They caught eyes 'fore she spoke again.

"You may go if you say you will do this. Your wound has come to a good place in its journey. These mixes I have prepared for you must be taken on each of the four days that you rest. Do not worry about making yourself rest, if you take these as I tell you, sleep will come. Rest will be welcomed. Each pouch is for its own day. Mix them in hot water and drink. Take it all. Leave none of the mix in the pouches. It is important you remember to do this. If you do not, the evil will return. Do you understand me, Cherokee? You must do as I say, to finish this healing."

Henri laid his cot lookin' her in the eye as she finished her words. She didn't look away. He could see she spoke from a place of concern for him, the one she was seein' to. Henri could feel her spirit. Liked the way that felt. He wanted her to stay. Talk a while. He was sure some conversation would make him feel a sight better. Give him strength. He was thankful for her talents. It would be respectful to tell her face on how much he appreciated the Great Creator blessin' her with 'em. How much he appreciated her usin' 'em to take care of his person, a body what really didn't matter, then she could see he meant his words. That was important to him.

He was comfortable near her, even though she was guarded constant. Could go nowhere by herself, not even the privy. Some of the best warriors from her clan watched her constant. Traveled with her anywhere and everywhere she went. She was important to the tribe as a whole. Keepin' her safe was a big responsibility for those warriors of her clan chosen to do so. A weird thing about it all, the tribe cared near as much for Henri as they did Blue Dove, but he'd have none of what she had to put up with. Henri stood on his own. He had relations with the tribe, yes, helped 'em when he could, yes, but he wanted no part of all their inner workin's or doin's. All he wanted was the freedom of the mountains, and for the time, a way to get to know this most unbelievable woman he'd come to meet. His spirit was troubled by so many questions. He was weak. Her bein' near made him weak. Maybe more so than his healin'.

"I give you my word, Blue Dove," Henri said, kind 'a soft like, still lookin' in her eyes. They were kind eyes. He found it hard to speak full on like normal from the strange feelings he was havin'. Something he could not control was controllin' him. It was worrisome. He struggled to finish his say.

"I will heed your words. I do not want the evil to return. You have worked a mighty healing in me. Thank you. I am grateful. If ever you need me or mine, feel comfortable sending a runner. I will come. I promise. Yours is a debt I can never fully repay. I believe I owe you my life." Their eyes stayed locked. His heart pounded.

"You are more wise than you appear, hurt one," she said with a slight grin, her eyes smiling. "I feel you are telling me the truth. Understand, warrior, it was not I who healed your sickness, but the Creator of all things. The Great Spirit watches over you… Henri," she stopped talkin' when she said his name. Breakin' their stare, she looked down to her lap where her hands lay one on top of the other. "I feel your spirit is strong. I pray you heal complete."

She bent from the waist to lean in closer to him. Their eyes met again as she slightly raised her face to his. She needed to whisper the next thing she had to say. It was personal. She didn't want her warrior guards to hear. The Guard's leader, Big Nose, would not like her whisperin' where he couldn't hear, but she didn't care.

"I would wish, Henri," she whispered softly up close to his right ear, "that you would come to my village for a visit when the leaves begin to fall this season. We need to spend some time together. Learn about one another. Share our beliefs, our spirits. Bring your friend. The big white warrior I see with you in my visions. He is welcome as well," she paused in thought for a bit 'fore finishin'. "The blue-eyed one may come, too, but I will watch that one. Remember these words, warrior. I want you to come visit with me," she got a little closer to his ear near touchin' him with her lips. "Think, wise one. Do you believe it chance that I was here in The Settlement when you came? Hmm? I look forward to your visit."

With all that said, she draw'd away and left Henri layin'. Left him to ponder her words. It was time for her to go home. The place she was required to be by the leaders of the tribe. She'd come to The Settlement ever so often fer doctorin' purposes, but had not planned on bein there the night Henri come. Him needin' her care had been a stoppin' off place for her bunch. Only Holy Spirit could 'a made happen. They both come to know that. Blue Dove was a special woman, spiritually. A spirit filled woman, and Henri had just become the only soul on Mother Earth to understand just how special she'd been made.

It was a spirit world understandin' between them two that no others but their kind could reason for. That's what made it so drawing, so curious to him. He would needs go and see her. Visit with her for a while. Let their thoughts be spoken through the smoke of a private fire. He would take his friend, Buach. Maybe he would know the blue-eyed one Blue Dove was speakin' of. Henri looked forward to meetin' that one, if they were a friend of his brother, Buach… "Lone Eagle," the elders had started callin' him. They would tell him soon.

It'd been days since Mary had brought Henri to the Cherokee Settlement for healin'. Their time there grow'd to over a week 'fore they was able to leave and go back home to Henri's. She wondered for me. Was I there lookin' fer 'em? Was I at Long Shot? Was I even still alive? She know'd me for who I was. Know'd I meant to have our farm back. Know'd I meant to have justice for Dad bein' killed. Know'd that was most important to me fer the time. I'd give up the farm and all we owned on Long Shot Ridge to have him back. Life changed with him goin' on. I changed after losin' my daddy.

She hadn't seen Henri since some Cherokee women gathered him up and took him to Blue Dove quick as they'd breeched the gates of The Settlement. Mary said them women just took him and went straight away, but Mary didn't know where he was goin'. Brought her to worry watchin' 'em haul him away how they did. Way Mary told it, she believed they know'd he was comin'. Like they'd been told to stand guard waitin' fer him. Like they know'd he was sick. Could be so. I would not doubt it if they did. When she finally seen him, he was walkin', but with a brace stick carved to fit under a body's arm. His wound, open to the air through a cut in his leggings, was near healed. There was no more threat from the infection it held when he first come fer help. That amazed Mary. She was taken by how the Cherokee could heal. How they know'd to use certain mountain grow'd plants for whatever ailment they was tendin' to. She wanted to learn more after witnessin' their skills firsthand. Thought maybe she could help folks in other places with the remedies the Cherokee healers used. That stood to reason, her wantin' to know them things. Mary was always thinkin' of others first.

Everybody where I lived understood that the Cherokee was special in their healin' ways, for sure Blue Dove, and a couple others she traveled with. The Indians claimed Great Spirit worked through her, more so than any other healer in the mountains. They believed that as truth, with a strong conviction, too. Obvious to them, from livin' with it as a way 'a life every day. Mary had now seen it with her own eyes. She come to understand the healin' stories she'd been hearin' all her life was true. She was certain before, after Henri took a hard fever, that the infection would mean his death. Outside the Cherokee, many would 'a died with his wound. He near died. Might 'a had if Mary hadn't got him to The Settlement when she did, or if Blue Dove hadn't been there to see to him. Holy Spirit was lookin' out fer Henri. I believe He guided all that had a part in carin' for him. Clear to me, after hearin' Mary tell it later on, His hand was on Henri.

***

Uncle Silas made us a most welcomed breakfast. He'd still not spoke to us as me and Sky took seats at the eatin' table. Kind 'a next to each other but not side by side. He set plates and skillets of food out on the Lazy Susan fer us to serve ourselves from, then took a seat across the table, settin' hisself to pray. My mouth was waterin' smellin' the food. I was ready to eat. He bowed his head only for a second or two, never sayin' a word out loud, then commenced to gettin' food for his plate. We did the same to show respect. Not sure Sky, or me, had calmed complete over facin' a cocked and loaded Army issue Colt .44. Made the quiet we was sittin' in good with me, for the time. I had some things to say, but there seemed to be no need for conversin' while we eat. Uncle Silas hadn't said anything after facin' us down. Just smiled a little, then holstered his Colt and went back to cookin'. That weren't uncommon. He was always quiet when first gettin' to our place for rest. He'd talk more after some sleep. At times, for sure if he was tired, he was a man of few or no words. Most of the time, if he was bein' normal, he had a lot to say. I allowed his spirit could feel our hurting, too. He prob'ly figured it best for us to start talkin' when we was ready. He was keen to those kind 'a feelings. One in touch with the spirit world like he was, and like Henri was, would feel the disturbance around our place, around me, around Sky.

Side meat fried with a touch 'a salt, biscuits, red-eye gravy, turkey eggs, and hot black coffee. It was the best meal I think I ever ate in my life. With all that'd been goin' on, I'd not eat proper for several days. Required me to tighten my belt a couple times recent.

We all ate our fill 'fore I moved over to the cookstove for a smoke. I fetched a straw off the broom to snatch a little pipe lightin' fire with while Sky commenced to cleanin' up. Uncle Silas sat the table, starin' at his coffee. I lit the dried burley I'd packed in my white oak pipe earlier in the afternoon, lettin' my mind wonder on the doin's of the day. It was clear to me we'd need to go to Henri's. Fetch Mary, my truck, our meat, and of course, Gus. I was missin' him. We'd spent so much time together travelin' the woods, he was like a friend. I was concerned for Henri as well. He didn't look good the night 'fore I left to go back to our place fer vengeance.

I had meat at Henri's that needed workin' up from my hunt. It was cold enough for it to keep, although the critters had prob'ly got to it. I hoped it weren't a bunch 'a bears what'd found it. They'd eat most all there was if they come. Still, cats would be worse. They'd wet on all they didn't eat. That would ruin it as food for folks. No gettin' that stink shed 'a your meat, neither. It come to me, that my mourning time would have to wait, again. I was havin' a tough time keepin' the sadness of death from my mind, but I would have to for a while longer. We needed food more'n I needed settlin'.

"Uncle Silas," I said, as I turned from the cookstove to look him face on. He looked up to me from the table. "I am thankful Great Spirit has seen fit to send you to Long Shot, at such a time as we're havin'. It is good that you are here. There are things you need to know. Things that have happened. Things you will not like. It's been a bad time here. The Federals what come sent Dad to be with Momma across the Great River. The same bunch what took our farm. I got it back from 'em yesterday, just so you'll know. Last night was the first night I've stayed here in many days. There is death here, Uncle Silas. Some by my hand, some not, but… you know that, don't you? I figure you got questions. Let me just tell it all 'fore we need to leave for Henri's. You will not like most of what I'm gonna tell you. Just givin' you warning. I'll ask ye to hold your temper about it. My spirit is deeply troubled. I have not yet been able to take the time I need to move on. The time I need to mourn Dad."

I finished my pipe while Sky finished cleanin' up from breakfast. Me and her sat back down at the table with Uncle Silas for our talk. I told 'em both what happened, the way it happened. The hunt I'd come from. What I'd found when I got home. Told about the ex-soldiers that tried to take our farm. Told what happened to all 'a them. Told all I'd done. I wanted Sky to hear it just as much as I wanted Silas to know it. He sat quiet as I spoke. He'd never said a word while cookin' breakfast. Never said a word while we ate. Never said a word while cleanin' up. Never spoke 'til I was full on done tellin' what'd been happenin' the last several days. He was a most insightful man. I respected that about him. His wisdom come from years 'a dealin' with all kinds 'a sinful folk - he'd tell ya we are all sinful folk, accordin' to the Word. Outlaws, renegades, rogues, the lot of us. He'd seen the worst in good people and bad people both. Christian folk and non-Christian folk alike. The best in others. He opened my thinkin' that morning when he finally commenced to speakin'. Confirmed many of the thoughts I'd been studyin' on concernin' what the North folk was bringin' to the South. Trouble, was all, nothin' but trouble, fer most folk.

"These are bad times we're livin' in, Boo, evil times. Bible told times," Uncle Silas said slowly, his eyes fixed on mine. I could see he was tired. Miriam was listenin' close. He'd glance at her ever few words. He'd still not spoken directly to her. I weren't sure he trusted her. He took a long swig from his coffee 'fore goin' on with his speakin'.

"I've seen some things over this last year that has made me most uncomfortable. Dyin' and killin' that weren't necessary, of and by folks I know'd. It's happening in many different parts of the mountains now. The outlaw numbers are growin'. North folk comin' down in abundance. The mountains have protected us 'til now. Kept the bulk of the evil away, but it has become unsafe for common folks to travel the main trails alone. I've had to fight my way out 'a too much of late. Near died twice. Fortunate for my person, Holy Spirit been watchin' our fer me. I've suffered only a few cuts and bruises outside 'a those two near dyin' fights, but I know that will not always be the case at my age, if I keep at it. So knowin' that, I'm thinkin' I might leave the backwoods." He stopped his talkin'. Looked down at the table. It was a short minute 'fore he started back. Quittin' the backwoods was troublin' to him.

"I've come to care little for this travelin' preachin' life," he said while lookin' back up at me. "Coverin' miles upon miles of mountain ridges and hollers gettin' one place to the other as the Spirit directed. Spreadin' the message where they'd have me. Fightin' for my life in places where folks didn't wanna hear what I had to say. No more. I'm over that. I ain't quittin' the Word, mind you, no sir. Holy Spirit ain't lettin' me do that, heh, heh, heh… no, I'm just gonna do it different's all."

His voice rose a little as he finished his words, kind 'a like he was commencin' to preach. I hoped that weren't the case. We needed to be gettin' to Henri's to fetch our meat and bring Mary home. His sermon voice made one feel he could be speakin' a while. It was obvious he was excited by his new callin'.

"No, not gonna do that, just gonna do it different's all. The Lord's voice is clear to my heart. Keep at it, my son. Keep puttin' the Gospel in front 'a them sinners. It's still a call to me, yes, but Holy Spirit is leadin' me down a different trail. He has led me back to Swell Branch. He's led me back for a reason, Mr. Buach Whelan. Hear me now. He revealed to me this reason several moons ago, but I wouldn't have none of it. I didn't believe I was hearin' right, but he corrected me in my believin' by near lettin' me get my killin', twice, 'cause I'm so hard headed I'd reckon. So, like Noah buildin' the Ark, I've been called. I am back to this part 'a the mountains to do the Lord's work. Believe me when I tell you. The truth has come down. Exclaim it from the mountaintops. Let the people know. The Lord is startin' a church in Swell Branch and he's called me to build it. I ain't goin' on with ye, neither. It's gonna be a proper church. A Jesus believin', God fearin', Bible readin', hymn singing church. One where folks can go and be with other folks of a like mind. Christian folk who care to live in peace, as a church family, with other believers that wanna hear the Word of the Lord. Folks who wanna study that Word. Folks who want to mediatate on it through prayer and supplication, listenin' fer Holy Spirit's voice. Learn what God has to say through their hearts. Whoever want, no matter who they be, can come. Don't matter where they call home or where they be from or be they white or black or red or man or woman, boy or girl. North folks comin' down what need the love of the Lord are welcome. Many will be in need of a house to worship in, they will be welcome. We will have a place for all in this church. Same as you and me. It matters not to their souls if they be from the South or the North or lands across the great waters. The devil takes 'em all if they choose to go with him.

Been comin' on a while. God got to tellin' me a time back that I couldn't preach much if I was layin' shot dead somewhere in the heart of these mountains, so I been talkin' to Him about it for a spell. He has showed me the way, His Way, and the means for me to go. I am come to Swell Branch, Tiny Creek, and all the land around to preach the Gospel, Brother Buach, and my sister, uh, just what might your name be, Miss? I've not been properly introduced since we are in such rude company. I am Silas, Uncle Silas, I am called by many. I preach the Gospel of Jesus Christ to any soul that will listen. I will know you and your providence when once we speak. I am a spiritual man, to give you warning. Now tell me, just who do you be?"

Miriam sat, without words for this strange woodsman she'd just met. She could tell right off Uncle Silas weren't like nobody she'd ever know'd. 'Course, she'd not met many Christian preachin' folk, for sure travelin' preachers, and for sure none like Uncle Silas. She'd learn, if she stayed around, that his ways was different than most. Grandma Dew was speakin' truth when she said he was like John the Baptiser, cousin to Jesus, what's talked about in the Gospels. Plumb wild in his ways while livin' in the wilderness, 'cept he didn't wear camel hide nor eat locusts, that I know'd of. I had seen him toss a few snakes around, maybe charm a few revival goin' women folk loose of an extra coin or two, but he eat what was common to most all of us. I know'd of no folk what eat locust. We called 'em hoppers. He did have a healthy black and gray, mostly gray, beard, and I know'd he'd eat his share 'a honey. I was sure 'a that. Most mountain folk had.

Honey was a favorite of the mountain folks food stores, fer them that could get it. Problem was, few had the tolerance to harvest the honey, so they would have to trade for it or buy it with coin. Some, however, did have the skills to get it. Seems like all the Cherokee could fetch it, but it was hard to find common folk that could first find it, then second, be able to go and fetch it. You had to be able to get it out from the hive without muckin' it up. A body had to know what they was doin'. Them stings hurt 'a right smart when a bunch come on ye all at once.

Mary never had a problem with them bees. She could find the honey, good as any. She had a hand fer gettin' it out, too, which was a talent few had. She'd tell ye, them bees never stung her a time in all her years. She'd just say a little prayer, fire up a small poke 'a sage for smoke, then go right in on 'em. Kept us enough that we had it year 'round. Good, raw, fresh honey, from the bees' own natural home out in the woods. I'd eat it straight from the wood bucket we kept it in, but I preferred it in the comb laid out over hot biscuits with a big chunk 'a churned butter meltin' under it. Ain't much better south 'a heaven than a good batch 'a fresh pulled honeycomb. The Cherokee used it in their medicines. Used it for cookin' and eatin', too. Made a tea out of it for their little ones to drink. Kept 'em healthy. Honey was considered a gift from Great Spirit, when bein' considered by the folks I lived around.

"I am called Sky Watcher by the Mohawk, Mr. Silas," Miriam answered back, kind 'a quiet like. Never lookin' up from her hands what lay folded on the table.

"My Christian name is Miriam. I come from the North. Traveled here with a family who were lookin' after me for a time. I am in search of my mother. She was taken and brought south by people who do that sort of thing. The man I came here with, Mr. Stuart, lays dead out in the barn. Not by any's hand, but by the will of Great Spirit. We will see to him this morning." She looked up to stare into Uncle Silas' eyes. She spoke a little louder sounding like she was on the edge 'a mad. "He tried to take this farm. He wanted to homestead it for us a place to live. I had no notion of how evil he could be 'til I realized what he was doing, and what he'd done, here on this place. He was not my father, Mr. Silas. He and his wives took me in after my father was killed." Her sayin' that about wives got Silas' attention. "My mother was taken to be sold into slavery. Stuart was mostly good, but his wives hated me. They were terrible in how they treated me. Their evil made my life most uncomfortable. Mean as blind snakes most all the time. I will not go back with them. I will not go back to that way of life. My hope, from here forward, is to learn where my mother is, then go to her so we can be together. I care about that with all that I have to give. That is who I am, Mr. Silas. No more than that and what you see. Forgive me if I've been disrespectful to you this morning, but I am wary of any I meet these days. Rightfully so, if what you say is true. Thank you for sharing your food with us. I am most grateful."

"Well said, Mohawk," Uncle Silas responded. "I can sense your soul is pure. I hear only truth from your heart. Your spirit is also strong, young one, but you know this, don't you? I respect what you are. I can feel you are good. We will find your mother. Do not worry over that for now. At hand, we must stock up or not eat. There are no provisions here. I figure you know them Federals took all there was, and we just ate all I had, so that leaves us without. We can talk at length in the coming days, Sky Watcher, uh, Miriam. I look forward to those times. For now, let us understand what we must do to find sustenance. Pray the Great Spirit provides."

"He has provided," I responded quick. "We have meat. I must go to Henri's to fetch it along with Mary and my mule, Gus. You remember Gus? We should have plenty to eat when I get back, if the woods critters has left us any. I had to leave it unworked when I come home to find them takers here. Me and Dad was gonna smoke it all up for keepin', but that didn't happen. Won't happen now. I will need Sky to come with me. Help me and Mary get back. I know you are tired, Silas. Stay here and rest. Take Dad's bed. We will be back in a day or so to smoke up the meat. Make yourself at home. What little leftovers they are from the morning will needs last you maybe two days. We will eat at Henri's. I figure you're gonna sleep most all the time we're gone, anyhow, so you'll not need much 'til we get back. It would be good if you did sleep the whole time. You look tired."

He simply bowed his head with a slight nod, then got up and went to Dad's room. Uncle Silas was beat. I'd seen him sleep solid for two whole days when he'd come tired like he was. We'd see him when we got back. I weren't gonna worry over him 'til then.

We saw to Stuart 'fore we left for Henri's, but not in our family plot. I weren't gonna have them evil folk in our family's sacred ground. I'd dig that young 'un what was buried next to Dad 'fore too long, put him in the same place we put Stuart. Even though he was a boy, I still weren't gonna have any 'a that bunch next to my dad… who they murdered. I'd have to see to him as well. His body needed to be in a box.

I led the stallion, draggin' ol' Stuart's remains again, to a place west of our farm that we never used. Miriam followed, walkin' a good ways back. It held a deep, rocky gulley nobody went near. We simply untied the drag rope from the saddle, then kicked the body over the gulley's edge, rope and all. I heard it come to rest somewhere near the bottom. I cared not where. The worms and scavengers would finish the chore from there.

We made trail for Henri's, ridin' double on the stallion after sheddin' ourselves of Stuart. Me in front. Her holdin' on from behind. I liked havin' her arms around me. It was the first time we'd ever got close up and tight like we was. She'd grabbed my back when Uncle Silas surprised us, but that weren't like gettin' squeezed across the middle by her strong arms. I could feel her strength. It was a comfort. Her bein' that close made it hard to breathe, again. Happened whenever she come near. That was something I was gonna need to come square with. It made me weak. That was dangerous for my person.

The soldier saddle was uncomfortable, but I managed. Sky sat the horses' rump behind the saddle, holdin' on to me around my middle, prob'ly more comfortable than I was. Neither of us ever spoke of where we buried Stuart. I never found where they'd put Walter or Billy. Didn't look fer 'em, really, just never run across 'em. I made sure they weren't in our burial ground, so I never worried over 'em after that. Them takers prob'ly left 'em out in the woods some place or another. That'd be something like they'd do. Them two was bad folk, but I'd settled with 'em. They'd never hurt or take from any again. I did not feel bad about that.

The Legend of Swell Branch

CHAPTER 14

A Trail to Henri's

It was a strange feeling, leavin' a man's body to nature like we'd left Stuart's. Didn't seem proper. Still, it was a buryin', good or bad, that's all what mattered to me. Miriam seemed good with it. She'd said a few words over the gulley 'fore we left for Henri's. I saw tears, even though she tried to hide 'em. She felt for this man. I would needs be careful how I referenced him around her. He weren't her dad, no, but he'd obviously made an impression on her in some fashion. I've heard it said they's good in all folks. Must 'a been something good in him or she'd not be hurtin' the way she did. I felt for her, but I could not find the words to speak. That man had killed my father. It weren't in me to hurt fer him, much, for such a bad man as he was. Still, I did hurt some, for all that perish, really. Judgment is the next step. That should scare even the bravest of all men—red, dark, or white.

The gulley was a place we throw'd things we needed to get shed of from around the farm. Wagonloads of rough rock we'd picked up in our fields that was in the way 'a plowin', or stumps we'd dug up while clearin' land that was too big and full 'a dirt to burn, or harvest wagon loads of bad vegetables what got a blight out in the field 'fore their ripenin' come. A body didn't wanna eat them or feed it to their stock for fear 'a sickness, nor did a farmer wanna run the risk of that blight spreadin', so chunkin' 'em in the gulley helped with the worry over that. He'd burn the field then, 'fore turnin' it for spring plantin'.

The worst thing we throw'd in there was bodies. We always did away with our dead stock in that gulley instead of havin' to dig a big hole or burn 'em. It weren't an uncommon thing, them dyin'. Sometimes farmin' stock just died. Many times there'd be no way 'a knowin' why they died, they just died. Old age, sickness, or what have ye. Come out to the barn one morning to get your day goin', and there they'd be, stone cold dead. No hurts to their body or nothin', just dead. Made you figure they'd took some kind 'a sickness or disease. So, like the bad vegetables we'd have to get rid of, it weren't wise for folks to be eatin' off that meat, if the critter was of the eatin' kind. Pitchin' 'em over the edge 'a that deep gulley was a way to keep whatever killed 'em from reachin' other critters. Made it safer for the rest of the farm's stock same as buryin' would, but puttin' 'em in that gulley was so much easier than diggin' big, deep holes, and I hated the smell of their bodies burnin'. That gulley was a gift from the Creator way I seen it.

It was a big problem for a settler when his workin' or travelin' stock would pass. Hurt his way 'a life when a mule, ox, or horse, that they depended on, come up lame or died. For sure if it was all the stock they owned. Settler folks depended on their mules and such for survival. Indians not so much, but settlers and common folk needed 'em.

Me and Sky didn't talk on the trail to Henri's. For some reason, I was dead tired. Maybe I didn't sleep as good as I should 'a. There had been a lot 'a things goin' on that was holdin' my attention. A body needs rest from time to time. Settle with the happenin's of life. Like, my dad bein' murdered, Mary gettin' beat on, me havin' to get the farm back from Stuart and his bunch, or my friend near gettin' killed helpin' me and Mary. Then, of course, to take up what little mind I had left, there come Miriam. My newest worry was how Miriam had become a part of it all. *How come that to happen?* Should she be a part of it? Could I trust her? Seems like I wanted to. These were the kind 'a things that could trouble a man's soul. These was the things causin' me the most confusion, pain. Got the hurt I was holdin' to risin' whenever I allowed myself to think about Dad's killin'.

I could feel the hurt that was comin' fer me. A hurt I allowed just might near kill me, if I weren't careful in how I responded. I know'd it possible, 'cause 'a how hard I'd had to struggle to keep the sadness from my mind, from my heart, but I had to hold on for a while longer. If my spirit did give in, it would end all we was doin' for several days. I had to stay strong. But could I? My troubled thoughts was showin' through my person. The pain of death was near too strong fer me, tired and weak as I'd got. A body's gotta watch when they're tired and weak like I was, that's when ol' Lucifer attacks the hardest. Tries to catch you at your weakest. He hit Jesus at the end of the forty days. The battle is worse for spiritual folk.

Sky was feelin' fer me as I grow'd weaker in my spirit. I could sense her thoughts by how she looked at me. She let me know how she felt, the fear that was troublin' her, when we stopped to water at a small branch just west 'a Henri's place. We'd made good time. We was only a short trail out. The stallion turned out to be a good ridin' horse, strong. I was proud to have him. Proud Holy Spirit had gifted him to me. It'd been a pleasurable ride except for the uncomfortable saddle. My thoughts turned to the horse what'd been took from me. That was troublin' my mind. I'd get that horse, and the truck it was carryin' back soon, so I didn't let it trouble me much. Pestered me more'n anything. I just hoped the thieves had been takin' care of it all. Not sold my horse or the carbine or shot up all the cartridges. That would be bad for them, if any of that happened. I wanted that horse and gun. Considered it mine by the circumstance it was obtained.

The soft breeze, what run constant in the woods for those who could feel it or sense it, was holdin' the sweet scent of spring. Coverin' the strong, rich smell of the rotting mast what lay the forest floor. That helped my mind to calm 'fore I heard her start speakin'. Old Man Time was makin' the days grow longer. I was more than ready for the growin' season to make its way back, even though hard work would 'company it. The cold time had run long. It would seem longer for us since the takers had took all our stored vegetables. Meat is good, but a body has to have some plant food to balance out their eatin'. We kept cabbages, pumpkins, turnips, onions, taters, peppers, and other vegetables we'd grow through the season, in a pit center the woodshed. Kept it laid full 'a good, clean, sundried hay to keep our food from spoilin'.

We'd cover the bottom of the pit tight as we could with about four layers of sun-dried corn shucks, then lay a bed of the driest hay on top of that. Our stores was laid in and covered one from the other with what hay remained. A final cover of hay and some sawmill boards to hold it all in place, finished the pit for keepin' our stores of vegetables. The hay kept it all from rottening, or if one did rotten, the others wouldn't be hurt by it 'cause they weren't touchin'. It was always my job to go in and find the rotted vegetables once ever so often. I hated that job, but I liked the food, so I did it without complaint. That, and I didn't want any others in my family havin' to suffer the chore. Unfortunately, them takers had cleaned our vegetable pit out complete, 'cept for a few that was half rotted for Sky to eat, waitin' on Stuart to come back. We'd eat what we could 'a those for our supper night before. Weren't nothin' left.

"Warrior, Buach… Boo", I can feel the heart of your spirit. It is full of a hurt that needs to be tended to," she said, as we both sat gettin' a drink from the branch. Neither of us lookin' at the other. "I know you hold the pain inside that comes with the loss of a father. You are a mighty warrior, my new friend. Those of the Cherokee, or Mohawk, would do good to be as strong as you, but with respect, it is time to settle the pangs of your soul. You must take the days you need to mourn. Clear your mind. Heal your spirit. When we arrive at Henri's, say you will do this. I will stay with Mary. You must meet with Great Spirit. Talk to Him about the hurt in your life from the loss of your father. Through His spirit, you will find true comfort. You know this, Boo. I know you do. Ask Him to cleanse the evil that those around you have brought. I will fast and pray for you while you are away. I will pray your strength returns to you. You will be in my thoughts, my prayers, and my heart. I hurt, because I know you hurt. Tell me, warrior, tell me you will do this. I will believe your words. Speak from your spirit, filled one. I am listening." She raised her head some to look at me. My tired eyes met hers.

Sky was right in what she was sayin'. I could feel she was right as we looked at one another. It was time for my soul to settle with the loss it was holdin'. I would miss Dad more than I could ever be able to say in words. We'd been runnin' together all my natural remembered life. After Momma passed, he changed, but still made time fer me and Mary. My brothers gettin' killed in the war made it hard for him. He changed a sight with their passin'. Spent less and less time with me and Mary. Quit readin' the Bible to us of a night or in the mornin'. Stopped goin' huntin' with us any. Took to bein' alone most all the time he could. Got to keepin' his distance from the settlers around Swell Branch, and for some reason, I never know'd why, he stayed clear of all the Cherokee. Some days he never come from his sleepin' room. Stayed bedded down all day then on into the next night. No comin' out 'cept to use the privy and maybe eat a bite, then go back to sleepin'. I know'd he was sleepin'. I'd get worried over him bein' in there so long alone, so I'd go in and sit with him. For sure on those days he didn't come out none, fer privy or fer eatin'. It was near hauntin' to hear him durin' those times. He'd be in there sound asleep just talkin' away to Momma. Never wakin' none. I'd just sit, listen. Cry fer him on occasion. It was sad to hear at times, more pleasant durin' others.

It come to mind, after listenin' to a few 'a them conversations 'tween him and her, I couldn't blame him for stayin' asleep on them days. He was visiting with Momma, but on the other days, when he was awake and stayed quiet, that was troublesome fer us. Them's the days I worried over him most. It was like he draw'd into himself without leavin' room fer anybody else. Still, me and him was close 'til the day he died. He'd taught me much about bein' a man and doin' what was right. About faith and how it all works for the good. How to farm for keep and stock. How to treat people with respect, no matter if they was good folk or not. He was sound in his teachings. A good Father to me and my siblings. It was gonna take me a while, bein' alone with Holy Spirit, to find my true self again, once the full pain of his dyin' come on me. Just a mere thought of it made my legs near buckle, but I stayed strong. I owed it to Dad and his memory to do things correctly. Live a proper life. Settling one's soul is required to live true to one's nature. That does take time for a body to settle complete. Mourning would come, and it would be long for me, but I know'd it'd not be long enough. I'd never get over losin' my father.

I agreed to do as she thought best. I was comfortable with it. She'd be fine at Henri's for the time I'd be gone, however long that may be. Her and Mary could spend a few days in a much less hostile environment. That would give them a chance to learn more about each other. That would be a good thing for sure. Folks you could trust was important to them what lived in the wilderness. A body's survival could depend on those what know'd they could depend on you. I was starting to feel we could trust Miriam Sky Watcher, but I would hold that thinkin' for confidence 'til I was sure.

"I hear you, Sky Watcher… Miriam," I said calmly, almost sadly from the hurt that was commencin' to leak from my soul. "You learned much from your Mohawk family. Your wisdom is a blessing from Great Spirit. I believe he watches over you in special ways. A voice tells me this. I will go, when once we settle all at Henri's. I don't think I can hold off the hurt any longer. I grow weak, even now. I can feel it rise inside. This has been the worst fight, of all fights, I've ever had. The battle of keepin' the pain of death from my mind, while riddin' Long Shot of the varmint takers - no disrespect intended. I need to find my balance before movin' into life the way it will be lived from this time forward. I've thought about you… about you stayin' with us a while. Give you time to work out where your mother is. It would be good if you do as you have said. Live with us for a time. Help us through the growin' season, then stay on for harvest, if you wish. I can help look for your mother this coming cold time, if you want. It is for you to say. You are welcome as long as you need… or want. We can talk about it over a good smoke later, for now, let us move on to Henri's. I'm ready for some fresh fried ham meat, if the critters has seen fit to leave us any."

We both felt the need to walk a while, after we'd watered, so we walked what little trail there was left goin' to Henri's. I'd had my fill 'a that sorry U.S. Army issue saddle, anyhow. It was near to rubbin' blisters on the inside of my legs and across my backside. I'd got kind 'a tender in them places 'fore we stopped for a drink.

Sky took the lead, while I led the stallion behind. She'd have no problem followin' the trail to Henri's. It was kept clear for folks who was aimin' to come by. That way visitors would approach from the front, where Henri could see 'em 'fore they got to his place. He had his own comin' and goin' trails out from the back of the cave what served as part of his home.

It weren't right lookin' when his place finally come into view. It seemed to me, as we draw'd closer, that nobody was there. Weren't no smoke showin' from either chimney, main room or cook room, which there should 'a been at least some from one or the other, if folks was there. Weren't no lights showin' through the glass windows Henri had so carefully carted back from Market in Atlanta. I'd gone with him to help haul them back. It was a chore, but we'd made it home without a single pane in any of 'em crackin'. He'd only had gold for three.

I got to seein' house chickens scattered about in the woods as we draw'd closer to Henri's place. That meant they was havin' to scavenge for their own food. That meant nobody had fed 'em of late. I seen a couple up close sidin' the trail as we got closer in. I know'd for sure they was his. Them chickens bein' out there was a sign folks hadn't been home in a while. Most yard chickens tried to stay out from the woods. Too many meat eaters wanderin' the mountains for them to be safe roamin' wild. They know'd it, too. They was actin' more nervous than normal for chickens. Didn't like havin' to be out from the house and barn, but they had to eat, so they went to where the food was.

Then of a sudden, the most telling sign of all, which spoke many words to me - Gus was gone from the corral where Mary would 'a left him. The wood rail gate had been left open. What little barn Henri had laid to the north side of the corral. It had an overhangin' board roof coverin' one small three-sided room. The little barn's open side toward the corral. The north, west, and south sides was covered in white oak boards same as the roof. It was weather tight for needed cover of whatever stock was in there. The room was cozy for critters. Could maybe hold four common sized mules in the dry. It had no door. He'd simply left the east facin' side open. The actual side we was comin' down the trail on. Gus would 'a been in sight, as we eased into the barnyard, if he was there. He was not. That, along with no lights and no smoke from either chimney, meant Mary and Henri was most likely gone. That was prob'ly bad. I wondered for Henri, for Mary. I know'd his wound had commenced to festerin' 'fore I'd left to go back to Long Shot. He may 'a got worse?

I commenced to searchin' the ground between the corral and the house havin' little hope of findin' enough sign to tell what happened recent, because of the rain we'd had the last few days, but I did have hope. Fortunately, for whatever reason, there was just enough sign fer me to make out what'd happened. Judgin' from the edges of the faint tracks one could barely see, a trail of sign got to showin'. The middle of the tracks was washed away but the edges showed a path to the house from the corral. It seemed Gus had been led from the corral gate to the tall edge of the back porch. From there, movin' south, the edges actually had some depth. They was some easier to see. It was clear the mule had become heavier from the edge of the porch on. Only thing made reason of that, Gus was most likely carryin' Henri. I prayed he was alive.

The deeper tracks weren't hard to follow. They lined up straight south toward Tiny Creek. South to where the Cherokee lived. After findin' out for sure the house was empty, and seein' Gus had been led away heavy, only one thing stood to reason… for sure after we seen how the bed laid in the loft, Henri had got worse. Stains in his sheets still held the death stink what comes with a rotting wound. Come to mind, since they left goin' south, that Mary must 'a thought to take Henri to the Cherokee for healin'. That was wise on her part. The look in Sky's eyes told me she understood what she saw as well. She seemed good at bein' Indian, for as white as she was. Kind 'a like me. I wondered where her real folks had come from actual, her ancestry. I'd never met no women folk with her put together. It was hauntin' to me.

Miriam commenced to buildin' a fire in Henri's cookstove. I went for meat. We was ready for some recent killed fried ham meat cooked in fresh cut fatback grease. Me and Sky both know'd, from growin' up mostly Indian, and bein' taught to understand what the sign meant once looked at and read, that it could or could not be long enough for Mary to 'a got Henri back. They'd left 'fore the rain come. Prob'ly been four or five days since they'd gone. They could 'a been home when we come that afternoon. It all depended on how Henri healed. How long that took. I allowed they'd most likely be here 'fore too long. Maybe 'fore dark, even. Without a word said between us, we know'd the best thing to do was wait. Let 'em come home as they could. We know'd the Cherokee would look out fer 'em. Most likely see 'em home. I had no worries once I put it all together. Sky and I would make supper and wait. That would be nice.

    I was lookin' forward to the wait, even though my time of mourning was due. I found strength in her company. Adopted by Mohawk and raised accordingly, she was easy to be around fer a mountain man like me. Calm in the way she handled herself. She'd been taught to think things through 'fore speakin' or actin'. I learned that by conversin' with her on the porch all afternoon the day before. She was raised by older ones of the Mohawk, that gave her wisdom beyond her own years. She was smart. You could tell by the way she spoke. I liked havin' her near. We seemed to be of a like mind, prob'ly 'cause she was raised Indian near same as me, 'cept different than me, she lived Indian for many years 'fore meetin' up with Gideon and his wife. I only stayed with them a few moons at a time. One thing was certain, she weren't shy about herself. Most Indians weren't, though. Many went bare when the weather was warm. I could vouch for her, she didn't need to be shy over bein' seen by folks. She was beautiful in her natural body. Wrapped whole in the most drawin' pale skin a body would ever see. I was startin' to grow a deep fondness for this woman. I would needs be careful 'til my mind had become clear in its thinkin'. My heart emptied of its hurt. Me havin' strong feelings for a certain soul could be dangerous for them, and me, considerin' the times I was havin' to face up to.

    Trouble had got to roamin' the mountains of Southern Appalachia. South movin' people was causin' it. Many lookin' to prosper any way they could find, legal or illegal. Me and mine weren't gonna have 'em takin' from us. That was gonna make livin' my life more dangerous fer me. Sky would need to know this 'fore makin' a final decision to stay at our place. I didn't think danger was threatenin' to her, at least for the time. She meant to find her mother by the means it would take for the chore. That show'd courage. Findin' her mom would settle life in the world she wanted to live in. The want for that settling was touchin' her spirit.

    Rescuin' Mary and gettin' our place back was the first battle in what I seen as an ongoing, unspoken war. Fought by Southerners like me against the invaders comin' from the North fer profit. A war that would not be talked about in the open, 'cause the killin' weren't gonna be legal, as the law would see it. I did not doubt there would be more battles for me, and Henri. I wondered at what they might hold. The reasons they'd come to be. I prayed killin' weren't gonna be part of it all, but if it was necessary, and I sensed there would be times, I'd see to my duty. I had a lot 'a friends throughout the mountains, both settler and Indian, some others as well, and there was little to no law of any kind for protection. Only thing folks could do was look out fer one another. I know'd many had lost their men. Had no one to fight fer 'em. They'd put up a shallow showin' if armed takers come to call. We all depended on each other before the legal war, it was most important to hold to that thinkin' durin' the illegal one what'd come. We was gonna need each other a lot more now that trouble had found our little bit of the mountains.

    Bears, and maybe a coyote or two, was what found our meat. I smelled no cat stink, which was a blessing. Them critters what come had eat their share, but there was still a goodly amount left that we'd be able to smoke up for keep. Seemed there might be enough to get us through the rest of the cold time… maybe on into the time when some vegetables come ready early spring. I said a little prayer 'a thanks for what the critters had left us. Holy Spirit was watchin' out. The Bible said He would, if we trust Him to guide us. I'd seen His providin' many times in my life, other folks', too. It is the way.

    "I see the bears left meat for us. It is good they are willing to share," Sky said, as she slipped up behind me. That was twice she'd done that recent. She could move quiet as a fish swimmin'. I never know'd she was there 'til she spoke. 'Course, my mind was distracted.

    "Yep, we'll have to tell 'em thank ye when we see 'em 'cause they'll be back to visit 'fore long," I said, turning to look at her as I stood just outside the barn where I'd dropped the meat off Gus a few days earlier. It was just a big ol' pile 'a hog meat layin' east of our barn near the branch. I'd not been able to do anything with it 'fore Henri and me went for Mary, just relieved Gus of his load then turned him out to the corral.

"I believe they've only just found it recent. Their chewin' marks is still fresh. Must 'a been several of 'em to eat as much as they have in what little time they was here. It would be wise to keep your mind tight. Don't forget they been comin' around. It's not a question of if they will return for more, it's only a question of how soon. I was fixin' to come in and get you to help me. It is good you thought to come out. I believe it best to tie up and hang what meat there is left. We'll leave the little they've chewed on fer 'em to finish. If we hang it high enough, it will be out from their reach, but you will needs help me. It's something one cannot do alone without a mule, ox, or pullin' horse. It will take both our strengths to lift it high enough. Can you help me do this, Miriam?"

"Of course, Boo. I will be your mule, and you can be the ox. Together, we will lift this meat high where those of the woods can't go," she said, with a silly kind 'a giggle. She had a nice way about her. "You just tell me what you need me to do. I am here."

The Legend of Swell Branch

CHAPTER 15

Calvary, My Secret Place in the Woods

It was half a day's walk from Henri's place to the land where I would mourn my father's death. It lay closer to our place than Henri's. I'd made my mind to ride the stallion, bein' tired as I was from all the recent happenin's. That would save an hour or two, dependin'. Worked out good, me ridin' my new horse. I was needin' to learn more about him. The ride would help with that.

We was headed to a place deep in the mountains. Only a mile as the crow flies from where the Cherokee had finally been able to settle on Tiny Creek. It was my private place. It's where I said my prayers that I wanted no other ears to possibly hear. No soul had ever gone there with me, nor had I ever told anyone where it was, 'cept fer Dad. I'd told him, so if by chance he needed to know, he'd know. He never told, nor did he ever go there. He was wise that way.

I felt a settling whenever I made trail to my little place out in the woods. I'd go there when my life was out 'a balance, or if I needed time to calm my soul. I went there many times a year, so I had to be careful not to leave a trail folks could find. That was a chore 'cause of all the Indians what lived nearby. I'd come and go from different directions each time. Scout the trails leadin' in and out when comin' and goin', if I had the strength. I never saw another soul, nor any sign left by one, durin' all my times bein' there. It was a quiet place. Nothing but woods sounds and the poppin' of what warmin' fire I generally built. No branches or creeks nearby makin' runnin' water noise. I could feel alone with Holy Spirit when I went there, safe. It'd become an important piece 'a ground fer me, spiritually. I would mourn the passing of my father there same as I mourned for my brothers.

It had become my favorite place in all the mountains. A little oak covered hill sittin' about as far south as one could go 'fore runnin' into the big, steep ridges that surrounded Tiny Creek, Swell Branch, Long Shot Ridge, and the huge valley they was all a part of. The view out over that valley from the little top was long and wide. The land, where my private place lay, was know'd to mountain folk as Cherokee land. Close to where they'd settled on Tiny Creek after the removal. It'd be dangerous for most folk to be there, but not for me or mine.

I weren't feared 'a folks findin' my prayin' place, no, that weren't it. I kept little there that held value. Some rope, a small kindlin' axe, and a couple wore out knives was all a body might steal. I just wanted to keep it special by bein' the only person what went there. It was hard to find, even if you was lookin' fer it. I'd chose my ground well.

I'd about grow'd up around the Cherokee. Learned how to be respectful in their company. Know'd how to communicate to 'em when first meetin' that I was a brother, a fellow warrior. I was fortunate for the times. I got to know many Cherokee families durin' my growin' up years. Me, Dad, and Mary lived among 'em after Momma passed. Me and Dad for longer. Mary left while we was stayin' there to go live with Aunt Catherine in Atlanta, for a time. She liked it in Atlanta. I did not.

While me and Dad was stayin' at The Settlement, I grow'd enough to start huntin' with bucks my age, when they'd let me. Went to their dances, but only at their willin'. A body couldn't go near their inner workin's without their say. They was a most protectin' people, for sure, of their Settlement. I couldn't blame 'em for bein' like that, way they'd been treated.

The Cherokee stayed mostly to themselves on Tiny Creek. Draw'd no attention to where they was at any time I ever learned of. If you didn't know they was there, you'd have a chore findin' 'em. If a body did happen to wander in on their main Settlement, and the guards come across 'em, that body would most likely not be seen again. Dependin', of course, on who that person was.

I liked it when we lived among 'em. I liked bein' around 'em, most times. They could become a peculiar bunch when the spirits hit 'em, though, and they did get hit by 'em on occasion. Problem was, not all them spirits was good. You had to pay mind when travelin' in their world. Them evil things could latch on to a body. Make 'em do things they'd not normally do. I was makin' plans to be around 'em a sight, now that it was just me and Mary, at least for the time I felt it would be Mary and me, so I would needs be watchful at their doin's.

I figured Mary fer leavin' Long Shot 'fore long, same as she'd done followin' Momma's dyin'. I allowed she'd go to Aunt Catherine's in Atlanta. She liked Atlanta… I did not. I never could figure why folks'd wanna live like caged rats in the nasty stink of a city, when they could live free in the open air of the mountains. I reasoned it was ignorance of other ways, or maybe greed. There was money in the city. Maybe they just didn't know no better. Mary did, though. That's what made her goin' there to live so strange to me.

All the talk made 'tween me and Sky on the way to Henri's that morning, concernin' my needs, got to makin' sense while we commenced to waitin' on Mary and Henri to get back. After studyin' on it, while splittin' Henri some fresh kindlin' later that afternoon, it come to me that I was near useless to anybody anyhow, weak as I was feelin'. Would be for a time. I needed rest. My weakness was beatin' on me. Breakin' any hold I had over the hurt I'd been fightin' to keep hid from my mind for days. I felt I could not hold it down much longer. Thoughts and visions of the things me and Dad had done was chippin' away at my thinkin'. Like splittin' kindlin'. Me and him had done that together so many times. I was on the edge 'a breakin' down. I could feel it comin'. It was time for me to go away for a while. Get clear 'a folks. The way I seen it, I had no choice, so when the followin' morning come, I begged Miriam's pardon fer leavin', slung my possibles pouch and rifle sling over my shoulder, grabbed a couple quilts, then mounted the stallion, without the U.S. issued saddle, and took for the woods. I preferred sittin' those soft quilts to the uncomfortable saddle the Union issued its troops. It was time to properly mourn the death of my father. It was something that had to be done… and it had to be done soon.

I was not lookin' forward to the coming time alone. Bein' with folks made bearin' loss easier, but one could not come to an understanding without proper reflection. That's what mourning is. Spiritual peace from releasing all the hurt, hate, and anger that loss and killin' brings to one's soul. The release of his memory, from the place I could never have kept it without the power given me by Holy Spirit, was gonna hurt me to the depths of my bein'. I thanked God for the strength He'd give me to keep down the pain long as I had. I couldn't 'a settled with the takers had he not held me in His hand.

I missed my sister. I looked forward to seein' her when I'd rested, if I lived through the comin' time of sadness. As I rode the stallion east, I prayed my heart would not break, that my soul would stay whole, when once the full force of loss come on me. I prayed my soul would find peace, so my life could return full, or at least mostly full. I know'd in my heart - the real mourning for my father would never end. Some part of me would always miss him.

***

Henri led Gus as Mary rode. The trail to his place from the Cherokee Settlement on Tiny Creek was easy to travel. Mostly level all the way. Kind 'a downhill, even. It was a good trail to hunt. Wound its way through several stands of oak trees and gaps. Oak trees what drop a'kerns fer critters to eat. Henri's wound weren't gonna let him ride. He allowed the walk would be good for his healin'. Mary was tired, and agitated, so ridin' Gus was an answer to prayer for her. She silently thanked Great Spirit for the kindness. It'd been a long spell for her. Henri understood that. Talked to her about it on the way home.

"Miss Mary," Henri said, after they'd got down the trail a ways. He'd turn his head to one side, then the other, as he spoke, still keepin' his eyes on the trail ahead. That way he know'd she could hear him.

"I know that you are tired. It is good you get to ride. It is good for me to walk. The path is easy from Tiny Creek to my home. It will bring strength back to my body. I believe Gus could use the walk as well. He has been bound for many days while I healed. That was not fair to him. He is a pasture mule. He likes his freedom to move about, not with ropes around his feet keeping him in his place at all times. I can understand this. He is a good mule, and a good ride."

"Gus likes it when we go on trail together, Henri," Mary said, kind 'a short like. "We've been many miles in these woods, me and him. Most times with Boo leading. He certainly is a good ridin' mule. How about you, Henri? How are you feeling? How is your wound? Do you feel winded, weak or dizzy in any way, or maybe that you could lose your stomach? Do you feel like your wound is bothered by the walk we are on? Tell me straight, Henri. Don't try and hide any pain you might have. You know I can tell if you're not telling me straight. It will do you no good to waste the words. Now, me and Gus wanna know. How are you? Truth only please, or I'll have this ol' mule bite a chunk out 'a the other cheek on down the trail. Hear me, Henri?" smilin' as she finished.

"Now Mary, sister, no call for all that. I'll tell you straight. Hear, listen close," he said, as he stopped Gus and went around to the mule's right side. There he paused, still holdin' the lead in his left hand. He caught eyes with Mary while slowly turnin' his back toward where she sat Gus. Once his back was turned full, and with the quickness of a rattlemaker, he uncinched his britches, lettin' 'em fall to the ground around his feet. That move bared his naked backside, and his wound, toward Mary and Gus. No sooner had he done that, than he bent forward full from the waist. His head near touchin' the ground. That show'd Mary up close the condition of his wound, and his backside. It was a sight she had no notion she'd be lookin' at when she woke from her sleepin' that morning.

Without stoppin' to think much, he looked up from under his left shoulder hollerin' out kind 'a upside down-like with a laugh, "Here Miss Mary! Give it a look. You tell me how you see it to be.

It feels fine from where I stand. I ain't lyin', neither. How's it look to you, hey? How about you Mr. Gus?" He turned his backside more toward Gus. "How's it look to you my friend? Will it do?"

He laughed hard while flappin' his arms near scarin' Gus. He kept bent over for a short time 'til the veins in his neck commenced to poppin' out from all the blood runnin' down to his head from bein' bent over like he was. He was a sight.

Mary couldn't believe what she was lookin' at. Henri's backside shinin' right in her face. She didn't react too surprised, but show'd a little touch 'a shock as he looked up at her. She felt bad once she figured out why he'd done it. Henri was her friend, a lifelong friend. She should 'a not questioned whether or not he'd lie to her, and if he did, it was his choice after careful and cautious thought. Folks like Henri spoke their words with caution when dealin' with conversation. They'd not speak 'til thinkin' through what they was fixin' to say, and the consequences bound to the actual words they spoke. You had to be careful when speakin' to Indians. They could be a temperamental people. Said words from folks held meaning.

Henri had a right to embarrass Mary. She'd show'd him disrespect. Made him think that a part of her didn't trust what he would say when answerin' her questions. That kind 'a thing bothers Indians. It bothered Henri. Bothered him a sight, on the inside. Bothered him enough to strike back at a friend, a sister. It was his call, and he decided to teach Mary somethin'. He taught her, too. Learned her a most important lesson concernin' respect for your fellow person, far as Indians went... settler folk not so much. It was a lesson taught with humor. Meant to possibly save her life one day, if the circumstance ever arose. She could say that kind 'a thing to the wrong Indian in a different part of the mountains, and her life would end, quickly.

She come to understand the what-for of it all, after thinkin' a minute on Henri's reaction. There would be no need to talk about it further. Henri's point had been made clear as snow turnin' the ground white when it fell. He saw, as he straightened to look her in the eye while pullin' up his britches and retyin' 'em, that her spirit know'd his mind. She'd got it. He know'd she realized what she'd done. She would not do it again, to anyone. Both parties could move on. The disrespect had been accounted for and would stay in the past from then on. That's how Indians saw to things of a more personal nature between folks and friends. Get it settled and move on with life. When there was an issue in front of the council concernin' clan members, it was aired out and settled accordingly between both parties in the Council Lodge. Peace was easier to keep when differences between tribal members was settled and not allowed to fester. Trouble come when differences was allowed to grow over time, or if the offense was among clans and not just a couple tribe members. All peoples could learn from that way 'a thinkin'. It's the way the Good Book says to live.

Unfortunately for many Indians, as I always saw it, their laws concernin' honor, family, respect, heritage and resources was not founded from the Bible. Their way was just their way. Give to 'em by their ancestors. Best to leave 'em to it when their times come, 'cause in some matters, the settlin' among Indian folk could require a life, if problems was such that the council instructed 'em to fight it out for justice. Them kind 'a fights was most always the end for one of the two parties involved, possibly both. That was the Indian, and Cherokee style of solving serious differences what weren't common to settler law. Some things between clan members had to be atoned for in blood. Things involving family disrespect or killin'. Strong courage was an important thing to have, when dealin' or livin' among any tribe of Indians. It was their way.

"Why, yes, my friend. Your wound does look good," Mary responded. "Actually, almost unbelievable. I want to know how the healers of your tribe can heal so strongly the way they have healed your wound in these few days. You are a lucky man, Henri. Lucky that Blue Dove was staying at The Settlement when me and Gus got you there. I believe she saved you. Do you know that? I believe you were on a trail to meet the Death Angel. I could do nothing to help you. The infection was taking your life. I believe Great Spirit watches over you, Henri. I know the Cherokee do. You are fortunate in that, and yes, to answer your question, it looks to me like your wound has healed a sight. I think from how you're carrying yourself, that you probably feel rested. I also believe that you will be completely healed if you do as Blue Dove has told you. Remember, rest for the next four days. Take the mixes you promised her to take. Do not fail in this, Henri. That would be bad for you."

He had embarrassed her. Still, her smile was kind as she watched Henri move to lead Gus on down the trail. He was smilin', too. Their friendship had deepened and they both could feel it. Henri said later he'd felt a strange pull to his spirit after his talk with Mary that day. It seemed curious to me, when he spoke of it.

It was gettin' on toward dark as Mary and Henri come down the holler on the off trail what run to Henri's place. The off trail was Henri's home trail that connected the main back trail to his farm. That main back trail had become the native mountain folks' favored way to travel since all the trouble had got to comin' south, causin' problems for so many. It was safer.

The off trail was the last part of their walk home. As they got closer, they could see the windows to the side of Henri's house held light. They know'd somebody had to 'a lit the lamps inside. Also, with what little light there was left from the day, they could see a heavy smoke comin' from the main fireplace chimney, a smaller one from the cook room chimney. That was an unexpected blessing as Mary was considerin' it. A warm house to hopefully walk into, if those what built it was friendly. Henri allowed he know'd who it prob'ly was.

All the way to Henri's, Mary know'd they was gonna have to get a good fire goin' in the main room 'fore bein' able to get toasty warm like she was wishin' to be. That already bein' done was special to her, 'cause it'd got colder as evening had come on. A cold air that nobody expected, bein' that near to spring, followed the recent rain we'd had. In the mornings, you could see the freezing white that covered the ground as Old Man Sun rose to make it sparkle. The tops of the trees was covered over, too, so as the day warmed, and that cover started meltin', you could get soaked if you was under a big oak or poplar when it got to drippin' off fresh melted frost. It'd be a cold drip you'd not want runnin' down the back of your neck.

"You're thinking that's Boo in there with the fires goin', aren't you Henri?" Mary asked, as they stopped in the trail for a long minute to look the place over. It was always wise to make sure of one's surroundings 'fore just walkin' in on any unknowns. They was strangers about.

"I mean, doesn't it make sense that's who it would be?" She asked, kind 'a anxious. She wanted the warmth of the fires inside. Some hot food. She was ready to get Gus to the barn and get herself to the warm. She know'd Henri was cold. Reasoned he wanted to go in as much as she did. She was also comfortable with thinkin' it was her brother in the house, it should be safe, but that was careless thinkin'. Henri know'd to be more cautious. There was too many bad men wanderin' the mountains for a body to be disrespectful of the danger. We'd all met a few bad ones recent for proof. Henri reminded her of that.

"Sister, it was not all that long ago that you yourself were in a bad way because of the evil that is coming south. Do not forget the dangers we must all be aware of now. Yes, I believe that to be our brother in there, but until we know for sure, it is best to be cautious. We will tie Gus here, then both of us will go quietly to a window and look in. See with our eyes for sure who is there. Then we will know if it is safe or not. Does this agree to your thinkin', sister? You are cold. I am as well, but cold or not, we cannot be careless with things we do not know. Come, let us go and see. If it is safe, you can go on in. I will come back for Gus then see to him. I will lead. Let us go."

It was a cold walk back to get Gus for Henri. He didn't know who was in the house, but he could tell by the way Mary screamed and run in, she know'd who it was. Weren't nothin' to him, really, 'cept supper sure smelled good with what little scent he'd got as Mary slammed the door in his face. She was excited to see her friend. She know'd Henri'd be goin' back for Gus since all was safe inside. He understood her bein' like she was, but he wanted to go in, too. Warm by the fire and eat right then, after smellin' it, but Gus needed seein' to proper and he know'd best just how to do that. 'Sides, it was good for Mary to have a few minutes with the girl while he tended to the chore. He did learn enough from Mary, 'fore she run in, that they'd both been in the house with Stuart and his bunch while Mary was bein' held captive. It would be good for Mary to learn what'd happened to all the evil ones that had beat her so. Hear what her brother had done to get their place back.

Henri learned that Sky and Mary had become friends durin' Mary's captivity, once Sky figured out what was goin' on with Stuart and our place. She did not want to be a part of the taking. Her and Mary had become friends because of Sky's goodness and help. They'd bonded a bit in spirit. That would be a good thing for the coming future. Henri was ready for some fresh cookin'. Baked ham, it smelled like.

***

I felt a comfort as I walked the stallion into the heart of my special ground. I kept kindlin' there in the dry under a short rock overhang I used as a kind of altar for prayin'. I called the place I'd come to "Calvary." Same as where Jesus was sacrificed. It's where I went to shed my burdens to the Lord. I named it so after learnin' about it in the Bible. I never told nobody I called it that. They'd call me sack 'a religious, if they learned of it. Still, if you think on it, the real Calvary still holds the blood Jesus leaked out for us all. That's about as close to the body of the Savior as any will ever be 'til judgment. That made the name special to me, 'cause my little spot was as close to the Savior as I could get in my world. It's the place I went to surrender my burdens. Leave my troubles at the altar, just like He told us we could do, if we wanted. I worried little in my life, 'cause Jesus made it possible for me not to have to.

Worry, or the carryin' of worry, accordin' to the Word, is a sin. A believer in Christ can be concerned about certain things but can always have faith those things will work out for the best. They know God's Will is in control. All a body's gotta do is follow His Will and there is no need for worryin', but real worry ain't founded on that thinkin'. Worry what hurts us most don't go down that God trail.

Worry is against the comfort of Holy Spirit. It commits a body to bein' defeated 'fore ever gettin' in the fight good. Makes one see the end 'fore it ever comes to be, which ain't possible outside the spirit world.

    Worry didn't trouble me as I took on the troubles of life. There is power in the Blood of the Lamb. I relied on it. I lived knowin' I was watched over every day. I prayed each morning for guidance and protection, so whatever come, would come. Through Holy Spirit, and with my faith, I lived my life confrontin' it all. That's what give me my courage. That's what made me dangerous. I feared little, when my spirit was one with the Creator. Only sometimes, when justice was concerned, or the South was concerned, or my brother Cherokee was concerned, I might not 'a listened to Him as close as I should 'a, or maybe I did, dependin'. I held much hatred in my heart fer those comin' from the North that was bad. Many times I let my nature lead me. Them's the times, most often, when killin' happened. Unfortunately, as the North folk kept comin', my nature took over more often than my reason. Bad things happen when folks shove reason aside and react full on, instead 'a takin' time to think, then responding. I couldn't help it, when me or mine or innocents of any kind was hurt or threatened, my reason went to justice for all. I left that sin at Calvary many times over my whole put together.

The Legend of Swell Branch

CHAPTER 16

Mourning Comes

The stallion was trained to stay where I'd stood him. I didn't even bother tyin' him up or hobblin' him, just pulled his bridle over his ears, then dropped it to the ground as I made my way toward some sittin' places I'd fashioned a few seasons before. Them seats give me a long-range view that I would sit and look at for hours. They was whittled out 'a two old white pine log pieces me and Gus had drug up from a little gap what lay south 'a Calvary a short ways. We'd got 'em laid perfect for sittin' and lookin' out over the valley. The way I seen it, since I was the only one what should be sittin' 'em, I'd turn the longest piece up and down the hill. That way I could carve out my seat to have a headrest, a backrest, a seat, and a footrest. Made it where you could look up at the stars in comfort. Turned out to be most favorable. I'd fell asleep there many times while watchin' the stars for movement. A body couldn't sleep in it all night, though, wake up stiff and bent over like a broke stalk, but the view up to the stars was worth it if one did. When you sat there on dark winter nights, it looked like you could just reach out and grab a big ol' star for keeps. Seein' 'em fall while sittin' there was a treat for me. I'd watch the skies fer hours at a time seein' few, but then that big 'un would let go and all was made right. What a sight to see in the dark of an Appalachian night.

After riddin' myself of the bridle, I fell into the log seat to commence my mourning. The view was north. Old Man Sun was toward the west. The light across the valley let one see its depths. The shadows filled in the layers of ridges and hollers and tops that seemed to give the land life. Like it was breathing. It was spiritual sittin' there at them times. Made one feel they was sittin' with the Creator Himself. That's another reason I sat 'til after dark that evening. I waited to feel that closeness. My spirit needed time.

I sat lookin' out over the valley 'til night come on full, then I sat lookin' out over it some more. It was a dark night. Old Man Moon was sleepin', but I could see the valley in my mind's eye clear as if Old Man Sun was shinin' bright. Me and the stallion had made good time walkin' steady from Henri's. We'd got to Calvary not long after dinner, a few hours 'fore dark. All I wanted to do was sit. Just sit and not be, so that's what I did. Weren't no folks near. Weren't nothin' to worry over. All was quiet.

It was cool once dark come. I rose to gather the dried kindlin' I'd laid under the rock overhang, my altar, a couple moons back. It caught fast, bein' dry like it was, once I laid flint to steel to tender the flame. I'd stored a pile 'a big wood not more'n twenty paces off to the west. It was dry enough. Our last rain had been the day ol' Stuart died. Once the kindlin' lit hot, I pulled some of the smaller big pieces from the top of the pile to add to my fire. That got it goin' some. I added a few bigger pieces after a short time, which would lead to usin' the biggest of the pieces. These big pieces would make the bed of coals I needed, once they'd burned hot and settled to the bottom of the fire. My warmin' and cookin' fire, my hot coffee through the day, maybe my life, all would depend on that bed 'a coals for the rest of the time I was there.

A good bed 'a coals left from a spent fire from overnight was most important to a camp. It could save a body's life in times of extreme urgency. Keepin' a bed 'a coals allowed you to start a fire quick without havin' to tender more kindlin'. A body just simply laid on a few dry pieces and the coals would catch up a fire in no time. It was common practice for them who are camp savvy. They know'd to keep a bed 'a coals the whole time a campfire was needed. It's where you kept your coffee warm all day long. It's where you kept a kettle of fresh water ready to set the coals at a moment's notice, be it hot water for tea or an unexpected emergency. Happenings like wounds from a fight or a sudden need to cut out a lead ball or bullet or flint point. It's where you could heat the blade of your knife red hot, real quick, in case you was the one chosen to do the cuttin' when said bullet or ball or flint piece had to be removed. A red-hot blade could save a life if a cut happened in a bad place on a body. The hot blade could cauterize 'em quick to stop the bleedin' 'fore a body bled out and passed on. Simple to remember, really, a bed of coals could save your life if the worst of things come on ye. Made fixin' dinner and supper quicker, too, just havin' to lay dry wood on the coals to catch up quick for roastin' or fryin'. That was nice after workin' hard all day on whatever it was that'd brought you to your camp. Be it travelin, huntin', or a trail fer purpose. Yep, a good bed 'a campfire coals was most important for them that was campin' to live. Everybody what made a camp, good and bad, could settle on that.

  I'd got comfortable, squatted by my little warmin' fire. I weren't hungry none, so I was gonna wait a while to build it much bigger. I was tired, I was hungry, but I don't remember feelin' those pangs. Bigger hurts come to the front of my mind not long after I'd got there. The little fire I'd started had already given me a small bed 'a coals. The time it'd took to burn down seemed but a minute to me. I didn't even remember goin' for the bigger wood. My mind had become like an early morning fog what laid over a deep, calm beaver pond. Short sighted for sure, and cloudy. The world around me had come to a change in season. I could feel it as my eyes closed with a heavy pull… like they nearly found complete rest, but not quite. Why? The hurt of death had come. Its visit would be painful.

  The mourning I'd been needin' was finally on me. The release of thought was present. I understood clearly the time had come for me to deal with the killin' of my father, for my own sake. My body went from limp to knotted in a second, as my mind let in the flood of hurt I'd been holdin' deep inside.

  I commenced to prayin' hard, beggin' Holy Spirit to comfort my soul. Comfort me from the hurt of losin' someone I loved more than life itself. The loss I come to feel emptied my insides of all the darkness death can bring. I could sense my soul was cryin'. Rippin' at its seams. My spirit laid in anguish. The whole of me seemed to be exploding like heavy cannonfire from a ridge top. My voice, likened to that of a wolf's at the moon, laid long across the valley. It had to 'a sounded like torment to any what was hearin' it. My throat burned inside to out from the screams my body was makin', then it was calm. As I opened my eyes from the first wave of real pain I'd felt, the darkness seemed almost friendly.

I'd lit wood splinters from the heat of the coals to fire my pipe. I'd done had a couple bowls of Indian tobacco mixed with dried burley 'fore even realizin' it. That was my favorite smoke. My favorite flavor. It was Dad's favorite smoke, too. He'd learned it from the Cherokee. That memory comin' back was the final crack in the dam what held back the whole of my loss. The lake 'a hurt what'd been dammed up inside went through me like a river rushin' after a week's rain. The hurt I'd been holdin' in for so many days rolled through my body like a flood, touchin' every nerve it possibly could. Pain come on me so hard it lifted me from the ground in a second wave of shrieks and screams and howls. My throat commenced to burnin' again.

In my pain and anger, I'd reached fer my long knife without realizin' it, 'til I'd cut through my homespun top and deep into the upper part of my chest just below my left shoulder. The warmth of hot blood ran down my front. I cared none 'til my body convulsed from the sting of deep cut pain. It was like spirits was tossin' me around. I know'd the young watchin' out warriors in training from the Cherokee Settlement, over a mile away as the crow flies, had to 'a heard my screams as I emptied my soul of the hurt I'd been holdin' in for way too long.

It was a still night I was hollerin' into. Sound carried far on a night like I'd chose. Them watchers prob'ly wondered at first what kind 'a cat could make such a scream, but when that second wave of screams come, and the third, fourth, and others, they'd figure soon enough what it was… a spirit that was hurtin', be it human or critter, mattered not to them. They would respect it for what it was… for what they know'd it to be… only one thing could cause such a deep and painful release… a spirit what'd been holdin' in the hurt of death. Indians know'd it as the way.

***

"Miriam Sky Watcher, this is my friend, Henri," Mary said, as Henri eased through the back door into the cook room, comin' back from tendin' to Gus. He'd walked in on Sky and Mary catchin' up. "He is of the Cherokee tribe. A spirit warrior to those who know. One of the greatest you will ever meet. Trained by the last of the true, old time Cherokee elders. He is like a brother to me. I love him as such. I trust you will get to be friends with him. He is harmless to those he knows to be good, but his spirit is strong. If you are around him enough, and I believe you will be, his spirit will know you."

"Miss Miriam," Henri commenced to answerin' Mary's claims about him, "do not let the lack of wisdom from this one scare you. I am but a simple man, who tries to understand all. It's good to meet you as you are now. You are most welcome to be here. Yes, I am of the Cherokee, but I live here away from them. Being Mohawk, you would know to see this and ask why, but do you know to see who I am in life? Think, and you will remember, for I remember you. The one whose eyes are like the sky and whose spirit soars like the hawk. No one like me can forget a meeting with one such as you. I have come to know your father as a friend, while trading with him over these last few years. You are the daughter of Gideon, the trading man. The one who fears little and will trade with all who need along the North Trail, as long as they come respectful. I have traded with him many, many times. He traded with those in our tribe who wanted, members of my clan, and my mother. You know me as Cub. That is what Gideon always calls me. He says I am my mother's cub. Well, as he knows, I am her only cub. No more like me, thank the Creator," he paused with a grin 'fore commencin' on speakin' to Miriam.

"My mother and your mother are friends. We stayed in your camp a few times when trade was being made near Mule Camp, market, and other places. Your mother is Cherokee. That makes us of the same tribe, you and me, even though we look so different. You should not forget that. My clan will help you as one of our own. We would expect no less from you. Do you remember me from those times? It would've been before the war by a few years. I would've been much younger looking in those days, so many moons ago. Where is your father? It has been a time since last I've seen him. Is he here in this land? If not, he must be coming here? That will be a good thing. I have made some buckhorn and flint knives, Indian knives, recent. I'd like to trade him these Indian things for some new quilts. I know he always carries fine settler made quilts. Mine are becoming thin. What day do you think he might come? We will celebrate around the fire. I have a saved jug of my best hard cider for a time such as now. It's just waiting for him to uncork and try. I look so forward to this."

Henri finished with excitement in his voice, in his eyes, from hopin' to soon see his friend. Maybe make trade. Tradin' got a man's blood up. It was something to look forward to when it come near.

"Henri, hold to it there. Calm yourself. It's not like that. We don't expect Gideon," Mary explained, her eyes locked on his.

She grabbed his shoulders to hold his stare. She wanted to calm his excitement slowly. Henri was not gonna like hearin' Gideon was gone. She worried over how he'd take the news. Henri could be fearful, if his spirit become agitated or angry.

His look got cold, listenin' to her words. Feelin' her grab him. His stare got hard as any she'd ever had fixed on her. She could sense his anger was near. He had concerns about what she was fixin' to say. She understood him bein' anxious, understood his need to know. Still, she felt unsure of how he was gonna react when learnin' his friend had been murdered. Mary went on with her nervous explainin' as she released his shoulders.

"I'm afraid Gideon won't be trading this way for a time, Henri... I'm afraid Mr. Gideon won't be trading anywhere... for a time, Henri. To speak straight, he won't be trading anymore at all... Gideon has been killed. It happened on the trail back from Atlanta some time ago. Miriam has been left all alone from him being murdered. She has come south to search for her mother, the only family she has left. The man who brought her south told her he would help find where her mother had been taken, if she would travel with them to help with his family's needs. She agreed, but now he is dead. The rest of his bunch left her here to fend for herself. So far, she ain't doin' too bad... since she came across Boo, I mean. He helped her. She met me when I was being held captive. Tried to free me but we got caught. Both of us spent the night tied to front porch posts with little clothing to cover ourselves. Her on one side of the house, me on the other. It was cold that night, too, Henri. She has been left all alone in this world. Nowhere to call home. Boo has offered her a place to stay for as long as she needs. Now she's met you, and you're gonna become friends with her, I just know it. I think we might get to keep her for a time. I am looking forward to that."

"Oh, Miriam. I am sorry," Henri said with a soft voice, hiding his deep surprise. "It saddens my soul to hear your father, the one many of us trusted for our trade goods, a friend to all Indians, has been killed," Henri said, as he met eyes with Sky. His voice broken from the sadness he was feelin'. She could hear it in his words. Feel it from his look as he spoke more to her.

"He was a friend to our clan, when others would have nothing to do with us because of false claims. A friend to my mother, when my father never returned from a battle. A friend to me, when I needed help. This is bad. I want to know more of how this happened. Do you know who did this evil? When did it happen? Has justice been served for you? We will speak of this later, for now, we must eat. This new trouble has weakened me even more. I know his soul is across the river with the ancestors. I will let that give me comfort for a time. We will honor him around our fire tonight, as you tell me all you know about his death. That would be a proper time to decide what must be done next."

"I remember you as Cub, Henri," Sky answered, "but without you telling me, I would not have known you. I remember your mother. She was always nice to me. My father thought much of her. She and my mother spent many happy times when together on the trading trail. It would be good if they could come together once again. When I return with her, we will see to this, you and me."

Henri sat the table in silence. Mary sat with him while Sky laid the supper food on the Lazy Susan, then took a seat across from 'em both. They all commenced to servin' themselves, after Mary give thanks for the blessings they'd all come to know recent. The news of Gideon gettin' killed had struck Henri to the core, but he didn't let it show on the outside. He'd know'd the man as a friend. Hadn't seen him since near the end of the war, but figured to in time. His trade routes brought him to Tiny Creek often. It was exciting to the clan, to Henri, when they found out Gideon was on his way to visit. It was like Christmas Eve for settler folk. Learnin' of his killin' ripped a hole in Henri's spirit. Made his soul moan with hurt. He was fond of Gideon. Thought of him as a close friend. It made Henri sad knowin' he'd not see or trade with him again. It also made him mad that he'd been killed by evil folk. He was curious to know how it happened. He prayed his murder had been made right so Gideon's soul could rest.

 The food bein' set before him brought a scent to his nose that near made him pass out he was so hungry. Snatched his attention away from his deep thoughts. Findin' out the how of it all about Gideon would come soon enough. For the time, they all needed to eat. He'd had no settler food recent. Cherokee food was good, if you weren't used to other fixin's, but it didn't fill you up. I happen to favor gettin' fat on settler cookin'. I liked some 'a them Cherokee eats - grape dumplings and roast meat and such, but I preferred settler cooked food right from a store-bought oven. It took a lot 'a wood to keep our food cooked, but it was a slight chore for what we enjoyed from the effort.

 "I want to thank you for the use of your home last night, Henri, and thank you too, for making me feel welcome to stay with Mary while she is here," Sky continued. "It is good to be with her. Buach and I did not know you two were gone 'til we came yesterday. He believed by what sign we found in your house, and outside around the barn and corral, that Mary had taken you to the Cherokee for healing. He knew you might be returning soon. We stayed here last night waiting, or rather, I did. I don't know where Boo slept. Somewhere to the south. He was simply here when I woke this morning. Now he has gone. Left to go be alone for a time. He said he would be back soon. I told him I'd stay and wait for you and Mary. Keep the house until your return. I am glad you are home safe.

It is good that your wound is healing. I believe you had a close call the morning you and Boo came for Mary. I was there, you know, in the bed you landed the woman on. She fell on top of me when you knocked her out cold," Sky said with a smile as she landed a punch to the palm of her left hand from her right fist.

"That woman was big," Sky continued. "It took a minute for the others to remove her large self from off me. She came close to smothering me dead during that short time. That was scary. She is Stuart's younger sister. She deserved what you gave her. She's the meanest one of the whole family. I couldn't stand to be near her. She hurt me more than a few times. Beat Mary twice, that I saw. I was making plans to end our trouble with her. Get Mary free from their hold. I just hadn't had the opportunity because of all the eyes they have in their family. Mary was watched constantly. It made me feel a touch of vengeance when I saw you and Boo making for the woods with her that morning. See, and I don't know if you're aware, but they had plans to profit from her being captured. Never heard where they was gonna sell her, but I know they were thinking she'd bring a lot of gold. Also, if she was gone, she couldn't tell anybody Stuart had killed her father. I'm thinking they were planning on selling her to the foreign trade to get her gone. Those traders would've put her on a ship sailing west to be gone for good. God was watching out for her sending you and Boo the day He did. I'd overheard their plans to leave. Two more nights and they would've been gone with her. I was gonna try and stop it but thank God you two came first."

"Great Spirit watches out for us, if we believe," Henri spoke in return. "I have seen this many times in my life. It was Boo's mind to go that morning. I just followed him. I have known careless men. I have known fools. I have known ignorant men. Buach Whelan is none of those. Afraid of nothing. Wise beyond his years. Strong in spirit and in body. A dangerous man of deep faith. He is bold in his belief of right and wrong. He has a strong conviction for justice. He is my friend. I would do anything for him, and he would do like for me. Now, tell me about the killing of my friend, Gideon. I need to know if his soul is at rest. The news of his death has caused a wound to my heart. I want to know if all is square, as it should be. If it is, I will needs mourn the death of a friend. If it is not, I needs make it right accordingly. Now, come, let us rock by the fireplace. We will smoke, talk, and let our food settle. It is good we do this."

"There is little to tell, Henri," Sky began, after they'd all took a seat around Henri's big circle fireplace. Henri smoked his pipe. They all had coffee. "Gideon was camped with his helper, a young Cherokee boy from my clan, a few miles north of Atlanta. He'd gone there to pick up trade goods people had asked for on his routes. They were followed out of town. Killed during the night, stabbed while they slept. The Cherokee left straight away when they'd heard what happened from runners. Most of the sign had been walked over by the time they got there, but they found enough to know whoever killed them headed north. The trail ended west of Asheville. They began looking for any clues. By chance, as some of the Cherokee stood outside the town shops in Asheville watching for any goods they knew to be from Gideon, they saw a man with a Colt pistol they recognized for sure as one Gideon carried. It was his favorite of all the guns he owned. He carried it most everywhere he went. He'd owned it for a few years. You probably saw it. An ivory handled Colt .44 with gold inlays on both grips of an eagle's head. Late in the night, after the town had gone to sleep, two Cherokee warriors slipped into the lodgings of where the man who had the gun stayed. They talked to him about this gun. Took it from him to return to me. I have it hid at Boo and Mary's. After a time, and several muffled screams from the loss of both little fingers, they learned where he got it. A man named Soltor, Major Viktor Soltor, an ex-Union soldier, had sold it to him. I will never forget that name. An ex-Federal soldier turned outlaw moved south to set up trade.

The Cherokee looked for several moons trying to find him. They never found this man, nor anyone who knew of him. That is where it ends, as far as I know. It seems strange they could find not one soul who knew him. The Cherokee have been back to search several times, but nobody they talked to has ever heard of Viktor Soltor. He is the one who killed Gideon. Those Cherokee know this. My spirit knows this, but how is one to find out for sure, if he is not to be found? I pray Holy Spirit shows him to me one day. I would like to see this made right. I owe my father."

"Yes, Miss Miriam, I know of this gun. It was Gideon's favorite, one of his most treasured possessions. You are correct in saying that. It was custom-made for a judge who lived in Atlanta. He died from sickness. Gideon was offered charge to sell the man's estate. He accepted. Made a sack full 'a money for the deceased's family selling off the belongings none of the heirs wanted, all legal through the courts. He bought the gun as a gift to himself. None of the family wanted it. Can you believe that? It's an original. The only one of its making. Paid for legal by Gideon. It is wrong for this man Soltor to have taken it for profit. When once I'm fully healed, I will find this soldier. Talk to him about how he came to have Gideon's prized gun. I can meet with the Cherokee who trailed him north. Learn what they know. Using their knowledge, I will find this evil man, this murderer. I promise you. Be patient. I believe we will know more one day. Now, let's talk about Boo. I need catchin' up with all he's been doing, and it seems you two have been spending time together the last few days. I figure you will most likely know. So, tell me, how is our friend, and has he managed to take back his home? I would bet he has. I can't wait to hear what happened."

The Legend of Swell Branch

CHAPTER 17

My Mourning Time Ends

Days had passed since I'd got to Calvary. I weren't sure how many, but my stomach was sayin' several. I felt the sting of a couple more cuts to my person, as I woke late in the morning 'a top folded quilts layin' next to a cold fire pit. I'd been asleep so long even my bed of coals had burned out. It was good that I'd slept. I needed the rest, but I didn't remember layin' those quilts where I'd woke, or even layin' down on 'em to sleep. That was a strange feelin', not rememberin' simple chores such as those. Something else hit me hard after a minute 'a wakin'- thirst. It hit me right about the same time I realized I'd forgot to bring a water skin. That was a stupid thing to do. Me and the stallion could both suffer on account 'a me not thinkin' clear when packin' my truck for our trail.

Once I'd woke as much as I could, I rose, standin' from the quilts. It come to me that I weren't thinkin' clear at the time, neither. Couldn't stay focused on a straight line 'a thought. I figured to settle with it as my mind was most likely clear as it would be 'til I got water, and that was still gonna be a while.

I went searchin' for my possibles pouch. It held food, medicine. I remembered droppin' it somewhere after strippin' the bridle off the stallion. I found it there on the ground not far from where the bridle lay, just short 'a my pine log seats. It was clear I'd shed it quick, however long ago that was. I saw no sign of any visitors, as I walked from the fire out to the seats where I found the pouch layin'. I would search the grounds west and east 'fore leavin' out fer confidence nobody had found my secret place while I was sleepin'.

The horse was near. Not where I'd left him, of course, but close. He'd had to find water while I was in mourning. I wondered then, how far had he gone to get water, or had he even gone for any? He might be thirsty same as I was. Could be he was waitin' fer me to take him to get some, or maybe he was waitin' fer me to bring him some. Who could know? One thing was sure, I needed a long drink. I'd lost blood, and I hadn't thought to bring water. My mind was weak when I left to make trail for Calvary. I'd forgot a couple things I always toted with me, for sure whenever I went out on trail. Leather straps and homespun rags was a couple, a water skin. I'd thought about water, but there was plenty on the way to and from, so I put it out from my thinkin'. Not reasonin' there weren't no water streams up high where Calvary lay. That's why I usually brought a skin with me. Filled it up at the last branch 'fore startin' up the mountain. It weren't gonna be too big a burden for the trail I was on at present. I was leavin' to go back down into the valley where water streams was plentiful. I'd get a drink soon. Trouble was, my body was needin' water right then, more so than usual that morning. It was an uncomfortable feeling, but not something I'd fear death from, at least for a while. I'd find water on the trail back north. Start crossin' branches soon enough. If I'd needed to stay for whatever reason, I would 'a been without water or I'd 'a had to go fetch a pouch. I tried to not come back to Calvary for a time, when once I'd left from a visit. It was just careless what I did, or rather, what I didn't think to do, about fetchin' a water pouch to have with me. What little I, and maybe the stallion, was gonna suffer fer not havin' one was proof to that.

I was too weak to tender a new fire 'fore eatin', so I just sat cross-legged beside the cold rock ring like it was burnin' hot on the inside, ate what I had cold. Smoke dried bear jerky with sun dried apples and fox grapes. My gut cramped, askin' me to eat faster. The need for water commencin' to holler as I tried to swallow slowly. Hard to do when you're dry like I was. The long knife was back in its fur sheath. I slid it out to check the blade. None of my blood show'd on it. At some time or another I'd cleaned it off. I didn't remember that, neither. I could feel a sting on the side of my right leg a few inches above my knee, another on my left forearm up close to the inside of my elbow, but them two lay shallow compared to the one on my chest. That one caused the pain of loss to surface what'd been screamin' to get out 'a my person for days. In the end, it released the suffering of my spirit from the inside out. The cut was gonna require seein' to soon as I could, but I had salve in the pouch. Tried to never go on trail without it. Fortunately, I'd thought to bring it. Henri made the best salve. You could use it on your stock as well. That was handy.

    The true spiritual release of soulful pain, while mourning the death of a loved one, takes over one's mind, and most times, their bodies, when done with purpose and fasting. Cleans out the hurt at all three levels of a person's put together one at a time - soul, spirit, and body. Bein' raised as much a Cherokee as a settler, I'd learned how Indians dealt with the physical pain of soul deep sadness, just as I'd learned to cast my worries on Jesus, spiritually. Christian ways of settlin' hurt was more simple than the warrior style of mourning, when it come to spirit cleansin' through the heart. In the times I was livin' in, a body could get themselves kilt if an enemy caught you with your mind distracted by the loss of a loved one. Evil has no sympathy. Takin' time to get the hurt shed 'a your person in private, then findin' a way to move on, was important for a body's survival durin' dangerous times, for sure when you lived how me and mine did. Your mind had to stay clear. Your body rested. That's how come I'd done what I'd done over the last few days. I needed to empty out all the hurt I'd stored up from findin' out my dad had been murdered. It was important for me to leave it all at the rock overhang altar. With some rest, and a goodly amount of food and water, I'd get back to the land of the living in no time. I thanked Holy Spirit for His shared strength.

    My mourning time for Dad was over. It was all behind me when I come awake that morning. I would be sad about losin' him, and about how we lost him, for the rest of my life, but my soul and my spirit had settled with it. I was proud 'a that. Maybe it was the little talk Holy Spirit had with me through a vision He'd sent as a dream. A vision where we was sittin' the fire at Calvary, not Golgotha where Jesus was killed actual, no, He'd come to my special place, to sit with me. Weren't uncommon. I'd sat there and talked with him many times by my little fire pit, only this was the first time I'd ever seen him.

He'd made Himself to look like Uncle Silas, for the time, but I know'd who it was right off when first seein' Him. It was Holy Spirit come callin' to talk, but they weren't no conversation to it from me, really. I simply sat listenin' to His words, while enjoyin' a late evening pipe full 'a straight Indian tobacco. I could recall the vision when I woke, clear as any dream I'd ever had, even though I was weak. I was runnin' on spiritual strength given only by the Creator. I would study on what was said in my vision as my world kept creepin' back into focus over the next several days. The dried apples and grapes had made my mouth water, they tasted so good. That little bit 'a wet squirtin' out inside my mouth drained what water I had left in me. I was for sure dry then, at least I was able to swallow some food.

"Worry no more over your father, young Buach," Holy Spirit, as Uncle Silas, said. "Calm yourself and see to what you need to. I am your strength. You will know your due when the time is come. I see that your heart is angry. That you feel for your loved ones. Hold no hate for those who cause these afflictions, Boo. Hate will rot away your soul. I need you to stay your mind. I will show you needs that beg your attention. Be of courage, and favor mercy. I will not leave you. The coming battles you will face are known to Me. You are a refuge for those who will look for you because of Me. The strangers coming will cause much hate to fill the mountains. This will be your world. Walk in it carefully. Listen for my voice." He left same as he'd come after finishin' His visit with me. His message give me comfort.

My visit with Uncle Silas ended. I woke to a new life. I could sense my mind slowly comin' back to me as my body started feelin' real world feelings again. I didn't like it Dad was gone, but his killer was dead. Vengeance is the Lord's accordin' to the Word. I believe that scripture come to life with the death of Stuart. Yes, I would miss my father. I would miss him for all time, but I was at peace with his movin' on, even though it was evil what sent him on his trail.

Holy Spirit had seen fit to supply me spiritual comfort. Leavin' it to me for physical comfort by tendin' to the hurt in my flesh. I lay on a thick coverin' of fresh salve Henri had made up recent. I'd used his medicines often over the years. His mixes had serious healin' qualities. My body had been hurt durin' my spiritual reckoning. His salve would work to heal me. Them kind 'a hurts brought the most pain when one's spiritual experience had ended.

I left Calvary not long after wakin'. It was foolish of me not to fetch a water pouch 'fore leavin' out from Henri's, but I didn't have my normal travelin' truck with me. I weren't thinkin' clear, leavin' to go mourn on short rations and no water. I'd planned on taking some time for my trip to Calvary when once we'd returned from Henri's to our farm, but after listenin' to Sky on the trail, it got to makin' sense for me to go on ahead and see to it. I commenced to figurin' likewise. My mind was not right, thinkin' that. A body never left for a trail into the mountains without the things that could help 'em survive if circumstances turned bad. It paid one to be ready.

Water had mattered little to me when I first made trail for Calvary, but if I'd been in my right mind, a water skin pouch would 'a been the first thing I took care to pack. Maybe two empty skins for 'fillin' along the way, since I was takin' the stallion. Henri had several I could 'a used hangin' in his cave. I would not make that mistake again. I was dry from bein' careless. That was a bad thing to let happen. On a different kind 'a trail, forgettin' them things could be deadly.

Camp that night laid a short ways east of a steady runnin' branch of cool, clean headwaters, maybe a quarter mile off the main trail. I'd been to that branch and drunk my fill twice since me and the stallion first come to it. He drank big, same as me. That meant he'd never left my side to go get water while I slept. That was the sign of a good horse. I put a little extra feed in his bag that evening.

We'd walked slow, makin' no more'n a mile or maybe a bit more from Calvary 'fore I needed to stop for the night. I was beat. My legs was tired and crampin'. My chest hurt. I still needed more rest. I boiled some jerky for supper. Drank the juice for strength 'fore eatin' all the meat I'd used to make broth. I only had a few dried apple pieces to side my meat with, but that weren't gonna be a problem fer me. I'd be home 'fore dinner the next day.

Bein' back to our farm was gonna be nice, when once I'd got there. I figured Henri and Mary and Sky would be there, or maybe just Henri. Somebody had to take Uncle Silas some food. It would most likely be Henri. I was sure they was back. After studyin' on it a minute, I allowed the women folk would stay at Henri's waitin' for me. Unfortunately, I weren't headed there. I was goin' home to sleep a day or two. It would be nice if Sky was on Long Shot. I'd like to sit with her a while, talk some, but I doubted she would be there.

I finished all the jerky broth. Eat the last of the boiled meat what made the broth. That left me with one decent sized cut 'a jerky for the next day. That would have to do to get me home. I was only a little over a half day's walk out. One piece should be plenty for that. I'd make it last.

There was wild grass where we'd found to camp. After he finished his evening feed bag, I'd turned the stallion out to get some. He was havin' his fill as dark come on us. I went out and got him. Led him back to camp. Stood him where I needed him to be, so if things happened durin' the night that I needed to get away from, I could hit the trail runnin' with little effort. I had no idea for a need to do that, a body just had to be ready for trouble to come without expectation. The mountains had become dangerous with the comin' in of so many strangers. Required different thinkin' to protect one's person or property when out on trail or at home. I didn't like havin' to think like that. Like bad folks do. Made me wish the South would 'a won the war, then we'd not be havin' to deal with all the thievin' and killin' the North folks was bringing down on us.

The Confederates might 'a won, had it not been for that big fight what took place in Pennsylvania. From what we all heard around Swell Branch, that fight was the beginning of the end for Lee and the South. Thousands of Southern men died on foreign ground fightin' that foul war. Never to return home to their loved ones. That was foolishness as we all saw it. That war should 'a never happened. The North should 'a left us be in the South. Slavery was on its way out. Southern folks was growin' tired of the foulness of it all. President Lincoln's bunch should 'a stopped all the killin' 'fore it ever reached Sumter. He should 'a done everything he could to stop the evil that'd took over our country's thinkin'. He didn't. The South felt forced to join together and leave the Union. War come from that secession. Greedy politicians should not be elected to represent folks, wars happen when they are. President Lincoln was a humble man, a good man, but he did not belong in the mire of politics. Tryin' to do right got him killed.

I felt nearly whole when Old Man Sun woke me next morning. My senses had recovered to near full. The stallion stood close by. I know'd 'cause I could smell him. First time I'd noticed that stink since my mourning trail commenced. After wakin' good, I stood straight up from my sleepin' quilts. Stretched myself to the sky like I was reachin' for an apple hanging low on a tree, takin' care to not pull my wound apart. Turned to face east where the light was starting to show over the big ridge tops. Bent from my waist to put my right palm flat on the ground for a little bit. That stretched out my back and down the back of my legs. I enjoyed that peace for a short minute, 'fore havin' to go back to the branch for the first drink of the day.

The water was cold. Good for makin' blood. I become aware, after I'd got a good drink, that the air all around was cool, too. I liked feelin' that cold. Felt like life to me. As I drank, I searched my heart for the hard hurt one feels first thing in the morning after a loved one has passed. There was but a little. Nothing like it'd been for the last several days. The mornings are the worst about feelin' fresh loss. Takin' the hurt from your soul helps in easing that early morning pain of loss. I found my first morning after settling with Dad's killin' to be much less painful, 'cept for my cuts, than the ones of late. The inside hurt near all but gone. I said a little prayer of thanksgiving for the comfort. Holy Spirit had calmed my soul. The mourning of my dad was done.

The trail home took me right by where the takers had left the stallion a few days before. Left him there 'cause he was draggin' the dead, ol' Stu. Left him there, after stealin' my other horse and truck I'd got fair and square, including the carbine and what cartridges there was. The mad come back about them doin' that, when once I'd got on past where it happened. Had a minute to think on it durin' travel. I stopped the stallion, haltin' our walk. Stood him in the trail 'fore findin' a comfortable place to sit. I needed to rest a minute. I wanted to study on what I was considerin'… on what I needed to do concernin' the feelings I was havin' about my property. I did not like bein' took from. I was aimin' to get it all back 'fore long. It was startin' to make sense that sooner may be better than later, even though I was kind 'a wounded. I was close by where I believed them that took from me lived. My blood was gettin' up as I figured fer 'em. The ones what'd took the mare, the provisions, and the truck and possibles that once belonged to Billy, but now belonged to me. I'd shot Billy off her back while him and his partner was tryin' to kill me - to the victor go the spoils.

I smiled thinkin' about that shot. My Springfield .58 caliber rifle had blow'd the horse's saddle out clean, sendin' the thief and murderer what sat it to the ground, backside first. A hole near big as a man's fist through his middle. I wondered what that horse thought about that when it happened. It never flinched when I fired, that I seen.

Them what took my horse was mostly Cherokee. I know'd 'em from the sign I'd seen when recoverin' the stallion and Stuart a few days before. I recognized from their tracks who they was. There was seven all total. Only one of the bunch was a full grow'd adult, a Cherokee mix named Bear Hair Sandy. He did not like me. I did not like him. The others in his gang was young. Cherokee all, 'cept fer one. The sign told me certain who'd done the takin'. If I was right, and I was sure I was, then one of 'em I know'd was a freed colored boy. He would be the youngest of all of 'em, or was, last time I'd run in to their bunch. I hoped to talk some sense into his thinkin', if I saw him durin' my visit.

None yet had grow'd to manhood that I know'd of. A couple was gettin' close. They all followed Bear Hair. He was special to 'em, kind 'a like a father would be, 'cept this dad was teachin' his young'uns to be outlaws. They did what he told 'em includin' stealin', threatenin', beatin' of folks for money, and, if he wanted… killin'. Oh, this bunch weren't gonna like me comin' in on 'em. Bear Hair know'd me well. I smiled big on the inside, thinkin' how they was gonna react to seein' me there. I believe, if they'd know'd whose horse it was, they'd a left it be. Now they was gonna have to settle with me for the takin'. They weren't gonna want to, Bear Hair for sure weren't, but I would make them see reason. Teach 'em a lesson if I got the chance, kind 'a like an adopted dad. A lesson that might save their lives one day, if they continued to run with folks of bad influence like Bear Hair Sandy.

Seemed to me, after I'd built a small fire and lit my pipe a few times, that I might as well go on and see to this takin' of my property, even though my chest was fresh cut and hurtin'. Their hideout weren't too far away. I didn't figure to have to fight 'em, them bein' young uns and all, but the chance was there. They didn't know the horse was mine, but they know'd it belonged to somebody, bein' the two horses was together, and one draggin' a freshly dead body. It was stealin', plain and simple. They should 'a left 'em both be. I figured to teach 'em some manners when once I got to their camp, fer I know'd right where it was. It would add a day to my goin' and comin' home, and another night 'a campin', but I wanted the horse and gun back. I prayed about it as I smoked. Made my mind to go while finishin' a pipe bowl of some good settler tobacco. Home had just got to be a couple more days off. I would have to make do.

Turnin' my trail to go west next morning, toward where the gang hid out, I wondered about my food stores. To make this new trail, I would needs take some 'a their food when I left 'em or kill something fresh on the trail or just go hungry, knowin' I could eat when I got home, fer my jerky would be gone by the time I made their camp. I would worry over that later. Gettin' my horse back and truck had become a priority to me since I'd studied on it more. I was fixin' to have a peck 'a fun after havin' to suffer hurt for a time. I felt for the young ones, as I jumped the stallion commencin' to ride. I was eager to make some time. My showin' up in their camp was gonna put fear in 'em. They deserved it.

The Legend of Swell Branch

CHAPTER 18

The Bear Hair Sandy Gang

It was after dark when me and the stallion finally made it to the little valley the gang called home. I was weak, hungry. I started doubtin' my wisdom 'bout gettin' my truck back 'fore findin' my strength full. I needed the rest I was fixin' to take for the night. It was dangerous, me bein' so tired, but I'd figured for that when I made my mind to get my truck back.

It was a small valley, as some in the mountains can be. More like a big holler to me. The Indians called it "Frog Valley," 'cause it laid like a frog's mouth, shallow and wide. The gang had livin' quarters near the far west end, close to the only water one could find in the valley. A small runnin' branch that stayed wet year 'round. Their livin' quarters was dugouts. Cave-like rooms they actually lived in. I guess such is the circumstance of the outlaw life. I know'd some Cherokee that lived in caves. Henri built his house onto a cave. I never liked caves for stayin' in much. I'd rather camp in a big hollowed out Chestnut tree. Them was warm. You could build a small warmin' fire in 'em, too. The smoke would draft out whatever natural opening they was on higher up. They was dry, too. I know'd families that'd lived in the bigger ones for a while, 'til they'd got their homes built or such.

By chance, I'd been to the valley once. Trailed there with some Cherokee friends when I was younger. Never know'd what we wanted with the gang. The oldest of our bunch just sat and talked with 'em a bit, smoked a pipe of some Indian tobacco to show peace, then we left. Didn't even stay the night. The young'uns what lived there then didn't seem to be too bad a bunch, but I know'd by reputation that Bear Hair Sandy was, and he was there. The gang back then never killed nobody or preyed on local folks that I heard of. They preyed on strangers if'n they found 'em, though, same as the bunch had done to me. That made 'em outlaws and bandits to my way 'a thinkin', and I cared none about them kind 'a folks, 'cept for their souls. I'd not wish Hell on the worst of any enemy I ever met.

How outlaws make their keep is wrong. Uncle Silas would tell ya they was breakin' a couple of God's ten most important rules. Their kind 'a doin's got folks hurt, sometimes kilt. Thievin' weren't right. For sure when it happened to those what couldn't defend them and theirs. I figured ol' Bear Hair fer keepin' them boy outlaws busy, what with all the strangers roamin' the woods. Maybe that's why they was near Long Shot and Swell Branch. The Cherokee had been sayin' they was seein' more sign 'a folks movin' through. Maybe the gang had learned that. Decided to hunt the mountains around Swell Branch for folks from the North to deceive or steal from. I didn't care for the gang's company, but if they was takin' from them comin' south, I'd say let 'em take, if a body asked me. In my mind, sided with bein' abused by 'em recent, Southern folk was still at war with the bad and mean-spirited folks trailin' south. Some of the good ones, too, what often run with the bad ones.

Unfortunately, for the people of the mountains, of the South, the time followin' the war had become a time of great conflict and killin' between the good, what called the South home, the right and wrong, what trailed south lookin' to prosper respectfully or by force, and the bad, lookin' to increase at the cost of others' sufferin'. After a time, I come to see a small number of 'em, what come down durin' the post war invasion of the South, as friends. They was good people who held sympathy and good intentions for improving the beaten South, but unfortunately for me and mine, most what we run into in the backwoods weren't the good ones. The backwoods was where them not lookin' to get caught would settle. Majority of the ones what made it to our part of the mountains seemed only concerned fer makin' themselves more prosperous by force. Some by far weren't the good ones, outlaws and takers, gamblers, bankers, lawyers, and schemers, but worst of all, U.S. Government folk.

The outlaws and crooked government folks are the ones I mostly come to know, and would continue to have to know, while followin' my call to serve the folks I lived with around Swell Branch and the Cherokee I'd grow'd up with. Holy Spirit had outfitted my spirit and my person for the work He'd chose fer me. I had little fear of anything, that I know'd of. I was strong. A mite bigger than common sized folks, and I was handsome, or at least I'd been told I was. Didn't matter to me, one-way or the other.

My main thinkin' was to stay whole. Keep my person in one piece whether it looked good or not. That got me to wonderin' if Sky thought I was handsome. Maybe I would ask her. No, that didn't seem proper. One thing was certain, comin' to know a woman made a body think about strange things, like if one is handsome or not. I'd never thought about that in my life. I know'd she was handsome, all over.

In the South, followin' the war, it'd become a time when common folk needed help and protection. But, it was clear from when the Reconstruction commenced, at least to them that could see it, the new government controllin' the South weren't concerned over the troubles of whooped Southern folk. For sure them what'd lost their men. The people of the South had lost the War, the War of Northern Aggression, as they understood it. Why should the U.S. Government be worried over such as them? There was no law what come to help 'em. No hope for any, really.

I weren't lookin' forward to confrontin' Bear Hair and them young'uns he was runnin' with, weak as I was. I know'd they'd not wanna give up my horse, but after some explainin' from me, they would. I'd see to it, even weak as I was. I had an idea where my horse might be, so I made a plan that should keep things calm 'til I'd got what I come for. One learns, when bein' raised mountain, to use your mind as your best weapon, for sure, always, but double for sure when one finds themselves to be the weaker foe. Bein' smart could save your life.

I figured ol' Bear Hair might could handle me for the time, me bein' wounded and all, if I let him in close without some protection. I made sure my special knife was in place, even though my left arm was near useless, and my long knife as it should be for easy grabbin' if needed. I was goin' in alone. Nobody hidin' in the woods to cover my back. That would be dangerous fer me, would need consideration, if it weren't a pack 'a kids I'd be confrontin'.

I'd need to keep a cold camp durin' the night. I didn't want the gang to scent the smoke and realize I was near. Even mice can do damage small as they are. I might build a small warmin' fire come mornin', to heat my coffee. Keep the smoke small where they couldn't sense it. The morning airflow would keep my camp's scent movin' up the big ridges away from their hideout. I was lookin' to surprise the bunch of 'em. Know'd they was there, fer I'd caught the slightist scent of fresh barn stink on the evening breeze when I was layin' out my sleepin' quilts. I was gonna sleep on a nice pile 'a mast I'd scraped up from the forest floor. The rot weren't dry as I'd hoped, so I laid out two quilts doubled, one on top of the other. I shouldn't feel the wet or have my nose burnin' all night from the rich rotting scent. Most times I'd have a fire to dry the mast 'fore layin' out my sleepin' roll on top, but with a cold camp, life was uncomfortable for the most part. Fire is a great thing to have. I thanked the Creator many times for the gift.

I sat the ground cross-legged watchin' the camp. Old Man Sun's light was startin' to show some over the big ridges east. I'd left the stallion back where I'd camped overnight. I didn't need him with me makin' noises and wakin' the gang up 'fore I was ready to let 'em know I'd come fer a visit. I'd already checked their stock corral, and what they most likely called a barn, 'fore any of 'em ever stirred toward comin' awake. Fortunately, the mare was there in the corral. I opened the gate real quiet like. Slipped in layin' hold to the bridle she still wore, the one I'd cut the reins off of, then led her back to be with the stallion. I left the gate open for purpose. I wanted the rest 'a their stock to follow us out. I needed their horses gone in case I had to hit the trail on a run. I didn't figure for that too strong, but like I'd learned time and again, it paid a body to be ready.

I led the mare back to my camp standin' her with the stallion, then went back to sit and watch the gang's camp come to life as daylight got to breakin'. The horses wouldn't go nowhere. I'd seen that after shootin' Billy off the mare several days back. I swear, I think them horses was happy to see each other when once I'd got the mare back. They rubbed necks and the stallion jumped around like he was aimin' to breed, which made me glad I hadn't taken him along earlier, but the mare weren't interested in his advances. She weren't heatin', that was clear. Maybe she was gettin' close. That could make him act all stud like. I hoped she was. It would be good for me if she did foal. She looked to be a young horse. Could be her first carry. The firstborn to most farm critters was usually cull, but I would hope for the best. Could be it weren't her first. I didn't know enough about horses to figure it by lookin'. I know'd mules, but they couldn't foal.

Bear Hair was the first to rise, other than a couple young 'uns that'd went to the privy and back 'fore daylight. I watched as he walked, in a stretchin' your body out from sleepin' kind 'a way, stoppin' at the camp's main fire pit. He wore nothin' but his long underwear and boots. Only one button holdin' the back flap up. He crouched down and went to layin' kindlin' on the smolderin' coals, workin' to get their morning campfire goin'. That was a sight I know'd I'd have trouble gettin' shed of.

I'd been waitin' on somebody to show at the main fire pit to get it goin' for the day. I figured it'd be ol' Bear Hair. Young'uns like he run with slept late most days, without given reason to rise. Had it been one of the younger ones, I'd a waited for Bear Hair, I figure. Him comin' on first made things work for the best. I could kill him and not dread over it. He deserved killin', but them boys was young, I'd not hurt 'em too bad, if I could help it.

I moved up behind him real cat like, while his mind was on tendin' to the fire. I got in close slippin' my arm around the right side of his face, keepin' tight to his ear so he couldn't see movement from the corner of his eye. My right hand grippin' hard to the bone handle of my long knife. The sharp edge easin' under his chin to lay tight ag'n his throat. Stingin' him with my hello. That action stood him up straight from his crouch real slow like. My long knife stayin' steady under his chin.

I'd set the edge a might harder than I should 'a, maybe. I could feel it was hard enough to lay the hide open it was pushin' on. That would draw his blood. He never let on like it hurt, nor did I hear the slightest of grunts or moans. He was tough, mountain tough, and he weren't feared 'a me, or anybody else, really. He'd trained to be a warrior for a time, I know'd that, but failed in the effort. Mostly 'cause 'a who he was. What his heart was like. Who his spirit was. His ways weren't respectful like warriors are required to be. A warrior is expected to be square in his dealings with folks, for sure other warriors. Never is a warrior to be unsavory in their doin's or dishonest to anybody, friend or enemy. It was an honor among the tribe, and to the settlers who know'd 'em, to become Cherokee warriors. It was a disgrace when folks like Bear Hair tried to make warrior. I'd noticed them kind 'a warriors didn't live long, even if they did make it by the elders' watchful spirit. Bear Hair did not make it. They saw him for what he was, near from day one. They gave him a chance, as is the Cherokee nature, he just weren't wise enough to take it.

"Bear Hair Sandy," I said, kind' a slow like, while drawin' my long knife away from his throat and backin' up a couple paces. He turned his whole body to look at me. I'd kept the knife's handle strong in my right hand, switchin' my hold to keep the sharp edge up. The point holdin' steady only a short pace from his heart. My right arm locked stiff. It was ready and most willing to go to work.

He seen the predicament he'd walked into, as he finished turnin' square at me. He know'd not to move after recognizin' who it was holdin' the handle end of the knife he'd just met. We'd fought before. I should 'a ended him then but I didn't. I'd know better if there come a next time, and if it didn't end here, there would be a next time, no doubtin' that now. I come to see a small line 'a crimson runnin' down the right side of his throat. I know'd when I first put my blade to his person that I'd bled him. That made a fight for life or death 'tween me and him for sure at some point, now or later. Blood draw'd would require recompense. We both know'd it.

I watched close for him to try something aggressive as we stared each other eye to eye. He hated me. I could see it in his eyes. I cared none fer him. He could see that in my eyes. My spirit was screamin' to attack, as I'm sure his was, but I had to respect his ability to fight back, and mine as a wounded confronter. I was countin' on him respectin' me as a threat. I'd not let on that I was weak at all. I was hopin' he couldn't read that I'd just finished mournin' Dad, or he may 'a come to realize he could 'a kilt me right there. That was reckless on my part, but I tended to be a little reckless at times. Can't say that was a gift, with as much trouble as it caused me in my life.

As I commenced speakin', I made sure it was loud and clear. I wanted all there to hear every word. The young 'uns had rousted. I'd heard 'em movin' about behind me even though they was tryin' to be quiet. Could feel 'em watchin' me, but I weren't gonna let on I know'd they was there. Somehow, Bear Hair might 'a signaled 'em when I first raised him. It troubled me little. Them bein' near weren't somethin' I was gonna worry over. I just needed 'em to believe I had full strength in my body. I was fixin' to tell 'em just who they was workin' for. Bear Hair weren't gonna like what I had to say.

"You got yourself a nice piece of work goin' on here, Sandy, ol' boy, what with these young'uns 'a yours doin' all the hard and dangerous work for the least reward. You ought 'a be proud for their efforts, or are you just proud of the gold coin they make you? Yeah, I'd say that's more to the truth than you carin' fer 'em. What say ye, outlaw man?" I asked, as I bent my head some while wigglin' the end of my blade at him. I raised my head back to speak so's all could hear me good.

"You ain't had to 'do away' with any more of your gang lately, have ye, Mr. Bear Hair? Just so you know, and fer the ones you got now, I'd a laid 'em low every one, if'n I'd caught 'em when they was stealin' my U.S. Army issue horse and carbine from off the trail a few days back. Yep, that was my property. Y'all took my horse and truck. That's why I'm here, if you're wonderin', to get it all back. Savvy? You hearin' me Bear Hair?" I raised my knife to eye level. Wigglin' the tip in his face even harder.

"Buach Whelan, mock all you want. Yes, it is you. I thought I'd heard your voice correctly. How could I forget such an awful sound? I will remember it 'til I send you across the river, my friend. It is a voice I've longed to hear for many moons since that terrible night I last saw you. Yours is a voice I mean to silence when our time comes, "ol' boy". It will be my pleasure to send you to the ancestors when once our affairs are settled. To me, you are a heathen. Now, what is this about stealing that brings you to my camp? I wish you had not come. I don't have time for this. Go as soon as you are able. You are not welcome here by me, or any of us here. We don't have time to kill you right now. You are fortunate," he finished, while pointin' to the south.

I turned my head just a touch to look where his right arm was pointin'. There stood all six of his "boys." A couple had Springfield rifles slung over their shoulders. I would needs listen for one 'a them to cock while my attention went back to Bear Hair. I made sure to look 'em all in the eye 'fore lookin' back to Sandy. He was smilin' big as I sheathed my knife quick while takin' an even quicker step toward where he stood.

He never saw my right fist comin' as it smashed his nose flat to his face, layin' him out cold. It all happened so fast I didn't realize what I'd done, really, 'til it was done. My right arm lashed out like it was on somebody else. Faster than a rattle maker strikin'. My right fist landin' a blow to Bear Hair's face that surprised even me, sendin' him flat to his back on the ground, cold as a stump in winter. Blood sprayin' from the center of his face and out from under my clinched fingers. I squared back to the others quick. My long knife gripped tight in my right hand again. They stood froze. Prob'ly never seen their leader treated so, or the speed with which a true warrior can defend himself. My spirit was laughin' at 'em. I could see their fear. I'd forgot how much enjoyment one gets from makin' things right. I just hoped I didn't have to kill any of 'em 'fore gettin' out 'a there. I looked 'em square as I talked.

"Y'all took my horse, you thievin' little rats. You give me no choice but to come here and fetch it back. Let ye know it was me y'all stole from, and me ain't somebody y'all need to be messin' with at your age. I'll kill the bunch of ye if I take notion. I let y'all know that while explainin' things to your boss. I'm here to make things right. Give y'all one chance to put balance back into the world you're livin' in. Now, I figure you all know I want my mare. I want all she was carryin' when she was took, too. You can keep the saddle. I don't want it," I said calmly. Weren't no need to fire 'em up any more than they already was.

Even though I was showin' mercy, like Holy Spirit wanted, for the thievin', not one of 'em moved. I felt the need to keep explainin' things. It was obvious they really didn't realize the way life should be lived. I felt I was teachin' 'em something their folks should 'a taught 'em. Might save their lives one day. It would be a hard lesson learned, comin' from me.

"Listen, young ones, I know it was your gang what robbed me. The sign was clear around where I found y'all took my horse. I've come to get her back, or should I say, I've already took her back, so you got no say in that, but unfortunately for y'all, I do. Horse stealin' is a hangin' offense for them what committed it. Remember that as you make your next decision. What I want now is, the Spencer and its cartridges. Y'all know the one. It was in the saddle boot when you stole my horse. Army issue .52 caliber what holds loads through the back stock. I know y'all have it. Go and fetch it, go on now, one of ye go get my possibles."

I looked 'em hard and waited, but none was movin' again. I commenced on with some more explainin' about how life is lived in the mountains, and most everywhere else they'd travel in their time.

"Look, y'all, understand what this is. I'm giving one body here the chance to make amends with me. That will be important when once each of y'all become an adult, fer then, I will come back to settle this debt of theft as grow'd men. Oh yeah, don't think today is the end of our settlin' issues fer stealin' my horse. No, we can only settle this square when each of you come of age. Once that happens, and y'all are grow'd, we will settle this debt with honor. That will require a fight 'tween me and every one 'a y'all here. Count on that like the rain comin' each spring, my new young friends. Now, who will make amends? I am waiting."

"Why should we do as you say? You will be dead once we are all grown. We will kill you as I say it," the oldest of the bunch replied to my tellin' 'em what to do. I expected no less. He was one 'a them what had a Springfield. "You are not our people. We ain't scared of you. Yeah, we got your gun, your cartridges, but you got your horse back. That ought 'a be enough. We should be square, way I see it. Now leave us to tend to Mr. Sandy. Be gone on your way. You don't want us seein' to your leaving, "ol' boy."

I was glad it was the oldest one what spoke out. He looked to be near a man's age, but he weren't there yet. I understood he was just talkin' tough. Wanted his mates to see him stand against a full grow'd warrior that he know'd would not kill him because of his age. That gave him false courage. It cost him dearly, too.

I never paused. Walked straight at him once he threatened me. He seen my intentions. I made it to him just as he slung the Springfield from under his arm fer pointin' at me. I never slow'd as he cocked the hammer back. It was a good thing I didn't. I still had to do a quick step as he commenced to pullin' the trigger. I was able to bump the rifle and lodge my left thumb between the firin' cap and the hammer, keepin' the gun from goin' off. I was sure proud I did that. I'd thought for a short second I'd not moved in time. Feelin' the hammer break skin' at the top of my thumb told me I had.

The look on the boy's face was panic, when the truth come to him that he'd not killed me easy as he thought he was goin' to. I laid him out cold with a hard right fist what still gripped strong to the handle of my long knife. I almost felt fer him, hearin' the bones break in his face while landin' him flat his back same as Sandy, then watchin' as three front teeth rolled slowly down the outside of his face, blood layin' thick on 'em like honey, but I couldn't. He was gonna kill me if I hadn't stopped him. I grabbed the next boy in line by the front of his shirt with my left hand, which hurt my chest, while layin' the edge of my knife up to his throat drawin' a thin line of crimson. After lookin' him in the eye, I knocked him flat out cold as well. The next boy in line wet his pants. I smelled the stink. I laid him out cold with a left fist for that wrong. That caused a pain in my chest that could 'a give my weakness away if ol' Bear Hair had been watchin'. I didn't mind hittin' him. Did him a favor, really. I didn't want his friends to laugh at him once I was gone for losin' himself from fear.

None of the three left standin' said a word after seein' all I'd done to their mates. They'd just watched four of their number, the biggest three plus Bear Hair, get laid out on the ground cold by me. They felt no call to be disrespectful after witnessin' all that. The little colored boy went to fetch my truck. He brought it all back. Rifle, cartridges, and what provisions was left from their thievin'. He handed it all to me with tears in his eyes. My soul felt for him, but it was time for me to explain their wrongs. I used some 'a their rope to tie the hands of all the ones I'd knocked out, includin' Bear Hair, so they could wake and listen to me. I wanted 'em all to hear me clear. Weren't long 'til they come awake. I spoke kind 'a slow so their groggy minds could understand.

"You young'uns are fools to follow such as ol' Bear Hair here. This life y'all are leadin' will get you killed by somebody less understandin' of your age than I was this mornin'. Still, I would 'a kilt you all dead, had I caught you stealin' my property in the woods the day you took my horse. I'd 'a had every right to lay each one of you low. Know that as truth and it might save your life, when next a stranger comes callin'. Now, here it is. I've tied up your headman over here, ol' Bear Hair Sandy. I'm sure you know his history, or maybe y'all don't. He uses kids like y'all to make his money for a time, but wonder if you will, what happens when y'all get older and not as easy to control, or for some reason you might wanna leave the gang after a time? Go out on your own. You gotta ask yourself how he'd feel about that, or, better yet, ask Mr. Sandy himself how he'd feel about y'all leavin', knowin' every soul here could tell the law what he'd had y'all doin' while workin' fer him. Be sure you do, fer what y'all do is illegal, and he knows it. Now, I'm gonna leave y'all with him. You can untie him and carry on with his thievin' ways, or you can leave him tied and be on your way to a different life. I will judge you not, for whatever decision is made is yours. I am not without my misgivin's as well. I will go and take my truck. You are free to make your minds. Pray for wisdom. Choose wisely. Your choice could mean your life at some time. I wish y'all well, 'til we meet again as men."

With all that said, and it was a lot for me, I gathered my belongings, then left to go for my horses. I cared little what the thievin' pack did from then on, long as they left me and mine be. I'd got my truck. I was headed home. I'd show'd mercy. That's all I'd come to do.

I'd warned 'em as a gang to the consequences of the trail they was on 'fore leavin'. Show'd 'em I meant what I said. I could do no more. My thoughts turned to bein' with my own folks I know'd, trusted. As I'd thought it before, rest was gonna be nice. Only thing was, my dad was gone from Long Shot. He would not be back, but I was gonna be good with that. I was movin' on. I know'd I'd see him again with the ancestors one day. I silently thanked Jesus for His sacrifice. Him bein' the Way and all. My thoughts turned to Miriam. I wondered what she was doin'. Wondered if she was thinkin' about me. I hoped she was.

The Legend of Swell Branch

CHAPTER 19

Life Begins Without Dad

Gus was in the corral with Zion, Uncle Silas' stallion, when I breached the edge 'a the woods surrounding our farm. He was already lookin' my way 'fore he ever saw me. Prob'ly scented the horses or heard us comin' down the steep side 'a Rock Gap, the last gap on the east trail 'fore gettin' to Long Shot. Weren't no scoutin' trees on the east trail. A body had to be careful when comin' from that direction. You could see the farm from Rock Gap, when the leaves was off, but it was too far away to make out much. Zion bein' there meant Uncle Silas was still with us. I figured he would be. He was needin' more than a few days rest when last I'd seen him. He most always stayed a while when he come. That was common fer him. 'Sides, he was answerin' a new callin'. He had a church to build.

I didn't know who'd brought Gus back but I know'd somebody'd be bringin' meat to our place. Uncle Silas needed food, same as me and Mary was gonna need food, when once we all come back together to carry on with life. I'd been figurin' it for Henri as I trailed home, if'n he was healed.

Turns out I was right in my figurin'. He was healed, mostly, or it looked to be he was, walkin' without a limp from the back door of our log home and across the covered porch to the back steps, knowin' I'd be headin' for the barn. A slight smile showed at one edge of his mouth. I nodded my head at him, too tired to smile. I noticed he looked different as I led the horses past our back porch and on toward the barn. Tired, like.

I was for sure tired. I'd not be standin' 'fore too much longer. Been travelin' most all day, after havin' little food or rest over the last little while. I just wanted them horses out from under me, and behind me, and the trail to end. The barn was the end, and it was in sight. I'd made it.

Henri was done there. Standin' by the main door with his arms crossed, waitin' on me. It would be good to talk with him. We needed to catch up. I wanted to hear all he and Mary had been through. He'd wanna hear about the ones what shot him.

It was good to have Gus back, but he weren't payin' me no mind, bein' curious over the two horses what'd come fer a visit. I figured he might not be likin' their scent, since they weren't mules same as him. I didn't reason it was gonna be a problem. He'd get used to their bein' in with him 'fore long. Them horses was calm critters. Used to bein' around other stock. Even the stallion was calm around the more spirited Zion.

Me and Henri locked forearms hard 'fore I broke to commence seein' to the horses. No words was spoke. We just stared one another eye to eye for what seemed like half a minute, maybe more. That always made me uncomfortable, but he had that kind 'a pull on your person when first seein' him after not bein' near him for a time. I know'd what he was doin', starin' folks like he did when offerin' a greetin'. He was a spiritual man, as Cherokee go. He could feel the heart of a body's spirit when shakin' hands or starin' in their eyes. It was spooky when he done that to a body, even to me… traits of a true Spirit Warrior.

It was good to see him. I'd missed him. I'd needed him in the worst of ways when decidin' to move on the takers, but he could not be there. He would 'a been, if he could 'a. I know'd that, with no doubts in my heart, but he was hurt, and I know'd it. Got hurt helpin' me retrieve Mary. Near got himself kilt. That's how good a friend he was. I hated that happened to him. Made me mad thinkin' on it. We'd near got shed 'a them takers totin' Mary away 'fore that lead ball ever cut him. That's why I went ahead and moved on the thievin' varmints without waitin' on him. They deserved it fer what they'd done. That, and the fact I'd tolerated their means as far down the trail as I was gonna go. My thinkin' wouldn't let me wait. I couldn't wait. It'd come time to make things right, and Henri weren't able to do what he'd be wantin' to do. His fight turned out to be against his own death. It weren't fair fer me to expect a friend, hurt bad as he was, to stand for a fight without some time to heal proper. Fact is, it ain't respectful of a close friendship to even let that hurt one know you're headin' into danger. They'd wanna be there with ye, as a friend would. That could make one do something stupid to honor the friendship. Fightin' while bein' hurt gets folks kilt. My problem could not afford the time Henri needed to get his health back, or I'd 'a waited fer him out 'a respect. The fight I faced to get our farm back would only become more dangerous with time, for both me and the takers. I could not let that be. That weren't Henri's fault. I'd be holdin' nothin' ag'n him. He was my friend, as I was his.

Up close, I could see he'd been through a fight with something much stronger than he was. It'd whooped him, too. He was thin. His face, neck, hands, and fingers was thin, surprisingly thinner since last we'd spoke. We'd been close friends for many years, even young as I was, and that was the worse I'd ever seen him look. I'd seen him look awful rough, too. It worried me a sight.

I looked up to Henri. Looked to him like an older brother. Loved him like family, maybe more, rememberin' how some feel about their family. Not all family is good folks to all family, and to my way 'a thinkin', blood kin could be disrespected if they didn't treat blood family proper. Henri would never turn on family or friends. I respected him fer that.

"Henri, my brother, it is good to see you, and it is good to see you with both legs under you workin' proper. I worried, after leavin' you to go settle with the takers of our farm, that maybe they wouldn't be. Your wound had begun to fester. Sufferin' and confusion was commencin' a hold on your mind. Your body was heatin' from the fever that was on ye. I believe it got worse over the days. Mary took you to the Cherokee camp after I'd gone, if I read the sign right. That was a smart thing fer her to do. I am glad she did. I think that prob'ly saved your hide, Henri. Thank God she thought to take you. It would be strange not havin' you near. With the times we're facin', it is a handy thing you still live. I thank Great Spirit for your healin'. I thank Him that you did not die. Yes, it is good to see you again, my friend. Please, I'm askin' proper now, do not get yourself shot when next we go confrontin' heathen takers and outlaws, if ye can help it, then I will worry much less over you livin' or dyin'."

"My friend, Buach, your concern for me is a comfort hard to explain. I will do my best to stay whole when next you take us to a fight. No, my friend, you should know a simple fever could never take me across the river. The Creator of all things watches over me. It is true. I believe this, for he sent me a healing angel from the depths of the mountains to the north. A healer so powerful in spirit that her simple touch can make pain go from your body. I know this. I felt her take my pain away when she thought me asleep. She eased my hurt with a touch. Delivered me from fever with her medicines, her prayers. Without her spirit bein' there to cover my wound, these legs might not be where they should be, allowing me to walk normal and stand here with you. She is Blue Dove, the greatest of the Cherokee healers. She told me she had been led to stay in The Settlement the night Mary got me there. Yes, she told me this. I believe your Great Spirit guided her. Brought her to my need. I felt a presence I'd not been near before through her. I had a vision while the fever was breaking. I believe I spoke with the Peace Child. We should smoke on this. Talk about it more around the fire this evening." He stopped for a short minute to think before beginning his story again.

"I do not remember all that happened before my fever broke, Boo. Only bits and pieces from one thought to another from one time of being awake to another. As you say, my mind was confused. I was in and out of knowing. I remember little of the things that happened during my time with Blue Dove, but I do remember her from after the fever spirit was sent away. She is beautiful, Buach. I will make a trail to see her soon. If you would think on going with me, we could leave after planting. I want you to meet her. She is chosen in spirit. She is like me, in a way, raised to a spiritual calling as a healer. Mine as a spirit warrior. I needs sit with her for a time. Learn the things we both know. My spirit is restless for this. I will pray that you will go."

He stopped talkin' again. Looked down to the ground. I could see he had to. Weariness had come on him. It was obvious he weren't healed complete, or at least he hadn't got his strength back full. Prob'ly fought 'a struggle gettin' Gus and the meat to our farm, weak as he looked there with me. I found out later he was supposed to 'a been restin' at his place. He'd made it, though, cause he was Henri, and he know'd it best he made the trail with Gus and the meat. Left the women folk at his place to wait for me, but there was no doubt the trail had weakened him. He was movin' kind 'a slow while takin' a seat on one of the two benches to the side of the barn doors that me and Dad had made fer folks to sit on. I'd helped him with them two benches. We'd sat 'em by the doors when we was done 'cause that's kind 'a where folks would congregate when they come to visit Dad. They'd sit and talk and trade knives, tools, critters... or gossip 'bout whatnot. Sip hard cider most every time, away from the women folk.

Some comin' togethers by men weren't appropriate to worry the women folk over. There were things on occasion mountain men would come and meet with Dad about that weren't to be heard by the women or young'uns. Needed to be done outside their considerations. We put a bench to either side of the barn doors for all that kind 'a sittin'. Dad figured out a way to put a slanted back on them two. They was different than the rest of the ones he'd made. Six grow'd folks could fit on each one of 'em comfortable. Had to use a mule to move 'em from inside the barn where we built 'em, to outside the barn doors where we set 'em for keeps. We'd done it not long 'fore he got killed. They would not be moved from the spot me and him had left 'em, at least not in my time. I'd see to it. They was half a dozen other benches spread out around the barn and corral that could be moved, but them two by the barn doors was special. It was one of the last things me and him had done together. The coverin' sheds we built over 'em after gettin' 'em in place was the actual last work me and him had done 'fore he was made to go away. That was a special place to me. I would sit there often.

It's handy to have places to sit spread out around a homestead. A body never know'd when one might have need of a good seat, for one reason or another. Happened to me many times. Be workin' some chore or another and need to sit for a minute to rest or cool. They was nice for that. For sure the ones under the shade trees. Come in handy when one was close by, if you found yourself needin' a place to sit. We made the two beside the barn doors from sawmilled oak over two inches thick. It was tough augerin' out the leg holes and whittlin' down the ends to size, 'cause the stock had dried 'fore we'd got time to work it. Them benches was worth the effort when we got 'em slicked and finished, though. Comfortable as could be.

I could see plain why Henri needed to sit that bench. He was tired. Color was off. Kind 'a grey like the underside of a dead fish's belly. He'd most likely got lightheaded, weak as he was. We'd been standin' for a while, conversin'. It was warmin'. His gaze went up into the mountains east of our place as he sat, then he closed his eyes, leanin' his head back a mite. He lungs draw'd deep through his nose, fillin' his person with the cool, clean mountain air what surrounded us. I could tell by the way he was talkin' to me that his thoughts was rooted in some deep concern. I could sense a kind 'a sadness in his spirit that I'd never felt near him before. It made me edgy for some reason. He was weak, yes, but it was more like he was lonely, or missin' somebody. After thinkin' on it a minute, I was believin' this Blue Dove, the healer, had touched his soul durin' the time she'd been with him. I prayed she weren't a witch, 'cause she was a strong one if she was. By his look, I figured he might never be the same person he was 'fore he met her. That could be good or bad, dependin'. He turned his look back to me as he started explainin' again about Blue Dove. I finished tendin' to the horses while he spoke. Turnin' 'em out to pasture with Gus, after removin' my truck from the stallion. They'd need a rub down after I'd got some decent rest. That mule still weren't right about the new stock he was sharin' "his" corral with. I smiled as he raised his head high and perked his ears. The horses was some taller in the legs than he was.

"Not all can be near her," Henri began again. "Her clan won't have it. Warriors watch her day and night. Never is she alone. Her safety is that important to the tribe, but she will see us. Wanted me to bring you. She has said this to me. She also said we could bring the blue-eyed one. I did not know who she meant, at the time, but now

I believe she was speaking of the one called Miriam Sky Watcher, of the Mohawk. Would you be keen to the idea of asking her to take a trail with us? It is a long trail to where Blue Dove's clan lives. We will stay for a time. I would like you to stay the whole time I am there, but I understand you must leave if your spirit feels the call. You should ask Sky Watcher to go with us. Keep you company. A warm body can make the cool nights more comfortable when the cold tries to slip between the quilts, but you might not be interested in heat that close, or would you, my big friend?" He finished his words showin' a weak smile. He was there. His spirit was there, but he was weak in the flesh.

"I do not believe Miriam Sky Watcher would want to go with us on such a trail. She means to better her life. We are but common men, Henri. Beauty the likes of Miriam Sky Watcher is meant for those who will provide her comfort. Fancy female kind 'a things like you find in the city. Even though she was raised Indian, I don't believe she would desire the life we lead. We farm for our food. Hunt, catch, and raise our meat. We have to work hard to make keep. That's no way for a lady such as her to live. 'Sides, I take nothing from no man, and that brings trouble. With all the evil coming south, trouble will most likely become a constant companion for us here. Is it fair to ask her to live a life of danger? No, our trails are not meant for a woman of Sky's breeding. She should have the things of her heritage. The things of her ancestry - her true settler ancestry, not of the Indians that found her. I should take her to Atlanta to be with her kind. Leave her with Aunt Catherine. I feel Mary will be there 'fore long, anyhow. It would be best for her to be with Mary. There is a life in the city for women of her abilities. She would have a chance to become a woman of high resolve, marry wealth, but that won't happen here in the backwoods. Only if she moved to the city could she find those things. Yes, I believe I should take her to the city. Let Mary and Aunt Catherine introduce her to a life most feel is much easier than the life we live here in these woods. A life to 'company the quality of woman she was born to be. She deserves that for who she is. I will tell her soon. We will find her mother, then I will take them both to live in Atlanta. I feel that would be best for them. That bein' said, I would be honored to go with you to meet this healer. I will look forward to the trail."

"Ah!... What? Ha, ha, ha... ha, ha, ha, ha, ha... ha, ha, ha, ha, ha, ha, ha, ha, ha, ha, ha," Henri belly laughed out loud. My heart near stopped. I was bein' serious in my thoughts, and it made him laugh. I weren't likin' that.

"Boo! Forgive me for laughing, my friend, but listen to yourself, son. What are you thinking? It's Sky Watcher you're talking about. One raised by the Mohawk. That would be like taking a wild cat from the wilds of the wilderness and closing it up in a cave where it couldn't run free. You think it best to take a woman with the kind 'a spunk Sky Watcher has, a woman of the Mohawk, a woman of the forest, to live in the confines of a city, so she can learn to become womanly? Made to wear all them prissy and frilly dresses and cover herself with all that stink them women have to wear to get the odor of the city off their person? City folks smell bad. They have to wear the stink. Think about it. How can they bathe proper without fresh running water? You ain't right in the mind from your mourning, yet, Boo. Think, boy," Henri said, movin' closer to me. Lookin' me close up in the eye as any trace of a smile or laugh disappeared before my eyes. Near whisperin' when he spoke

"Think about what that would be like for her, Boo. She is a person of the forest. A person of freedom. Same as you and me. The city is no place for her. You will see. She will never agree to such. I believe she would rather go north on trail with us than move to the cold isolation of a life lived confined by roads and buildings. You must pray on what you are thinking. I find it to be contrary to the desires of her spirit, but you do as you feel led. Go ahead, ask her. I can tell you for certain what her answer will be. I know things you do not. Trust me on this one, my brother warrior. I have heard their overnight talk. She is a savvy one. You would do well to grow close to her. She is spiritual. Maybe even a seer. I know this. She speaks of you with favor. She knows things you have done. Things I don't believe you have had the time or concern to tell her. Forgive me if I am wrong. This is just my mind."

"Tell me, these things you heard, tell me what they are. I want to know. Why would their words change the way I feel about taking her to Atlanta to live with Aunt Catherine? It's only fair that I know what you know, then I will make my own mind as to what is fair."

"You ain't getting it, Boo. You ain't gonna tell her to do nothing. She is a woman with a heart and mind and soul all her own. She was raised to be that way. Free to think for herself and independent enough to act on those thoughts. She can take care of herself. I'm thinkin' you'd sooner stop the rain as get her to live in a city. I would think a visit there now and again would be to her liking, but living there, she will not see that as a choice. Don't breach your thoughts about all this to her for a while. Let her get comfortable being here when she comes with Mary from my place. Give her time. Feel her out. I think your mind will change when you've spent more time with her. Again, trust me as your friend, Boo. That's all I can say about this. Now, tell me about the takers. How many still live? We will hunt them down. Square this up complete. I hate I missed all the fun. It is good you have your home back. I did not want those thieves as neighbors. That would not do. I must go rest now. Blue Dove's orders. Forgive me."

THE LEGEND OF SWELL BRANCH

CHAPTER 20

A TRAIL NORTH BEGINS

Spring plantin' was done. Our lives had moved on. Uncle Silas stayed but a few days after we'd all congregated back at Long Shot. He went to live on the grounds he'd claimed as God's, just south 'a Swell Branch. He was stayin' there in a tent he'd used for camping while circuit ridin'. Same one he'd been usin' for years. It was a nice tent, as tents went, bigger than most. Had a woodstove inside for heatin' and cookin'. Just right for him, but you could sleep up to about eight fair sized people in it, if need be. He was livin' there to start the church house he claimed Holy Spirit had called him to build. I never allowed He'd not.

Folks from around Swell Branch was likin' the idea of havin' a church house. Most was bein' mighty generous in their givin' of time and what they could donate to help build it. They was cuttin' logs and hewin' timbers fast as a bunch could do. They wanted their church, and strangely enough, bein' as tight to the Gospel and the blood as he was, they'd come to want Uncle Silas, too. He'd been preachin' at 'em ever since he'd come off the outlaw circuit. Done baptized a bunch of 'em in Tiny Creek. They liked the way he preached with Holy Spirit teachin' through him. Pure, straight up gospel every sermon. I'd prob'ly not make it to all the Sunday meetin's. If Grandma Dew show'd up for worship, and the spirit got to movin', services could last all day and into the night, then on into the next day or two or more. Revival would sure enough break out on some occasions. Just depended on how much Jesus the folks attendin' needed.

Henri had healed complete after takin' the mixes Blue Dove give him. Rested his four days like he'd promised her. He'd not break a promise to Blue Dove. Miriam Sky Watcher was living with us. Her and Mary was growin' to be like sisters. It was nice to see 'em get along like they did. Mary needed that. I know'd she missed the woman talk her and Momma always had. We'd not talked about it, but I know'd it was true. I'd heard her cry of a night, even recent, same as she did back when Momma died years earlier. It was the pain of losin' a mother that Mary had never mourned proper. She never got shed 'a the deep pain of a mother dyin'. She was bad to hold strong feelings inside, but of all I understood, I could feel her pain. I'd cried myself a few times through the years, but Mary was older than me when Momma passed. She'd come to know her as a woman same as she did a mother. I only remembered her as my mother for a short time, bein' young when we lost her. Dad never got over her passin'.

Henri come fer a visit one morning, not long after we'd got all the plantin' chores done. He come just after Old Man Sun had woke, so I know'd it weren't a common visit, or he'd 'a come just 'fore supper time. He was needin' to talk. Looked to be he had something on his mind he needed to get shed of. I kind 'a know'd what was most likely troublin' him. Hard to get a woman out from your mind once she's laid a seed. I know'd that personal fer truth.

His face held much concern as I met him at the back door. We locked forearms in welcome, while he stared me hard like usual. That made me feel weird, like usual. You sensed he was lookin' into your soul when he did that. It was hauntin'. Mary and Sky had gone to help Uncle Silas with his church buildin' for a couple days, so it was just me and Henri there. I sensed his spirit was unsettled as he commenced our conversation. I felt for him.

"Buach, my friend. I hope you are well. Have the spirits seen fit to show you the corn we worked so carefully to plant this last moon? There should be little green signs of hope pushing through the skin of Mother Earth by now. I pray this is so."

"There is hope showin', Henri. We will have sustenance for our bellies if Holy Spirit sees fit for it all to make. I trust that He will.

It would be good if you prayed to Him, Henri. Ask him for a good, strong growin' season with plenty 'a rain, so our stores will be full the whole of this coming cold season. It would be a good thing for you to do. Holy Spirit is good for the soul."

"I will pray for our time of growing, Boo, to the Creator of all things. Same as you. My faith is strong, but I know the spirits will have their way. If it is to be, then we will have stores for the winter, as long as we do our work. It is good for our families to stay fed, so our crops must be tended to throughout the growing season. This stands to reason. That is why I have come to see you this day, Brother. We need to cross the big mountains to the north. It is time for me to go see Blue Dove. I cannot wait until after the harvest. My spirit is longing for her. I can control the pull of it no longer. It is something I have to do. I needs go there. Stay with her for a time. Learn who she is. Let her learn who I am. It is my hope, and don't think me crazy, that you will come with me on this trail. It would be good to have Sky Watcher along as well. Trails hold danger in many places with the North folk moving in on us constant. It is good to have one who is trail savvy to share travel with. What say ye, Boo? Do you think you can do this for me? Do you think Miriam will do this for me?"

"I won't do this now, Henri, and neither should you. As you have said, it is most important for us to be here and tend our crops through the growin' and harvest seasons. If we go, there will be no tending of our crops. Even if it all went perfect through the growin' time, there would still be the weeds nobody hoed to let the good plants grow through. No, Henri. It is a bad time for us right now. Can't you wait 'til we harvest and get our stores in to make this trail? That seems the proper time. Kind 'a like we talked about before, if I'm rememberin' correctly? I will gladly go then."

"I understand our responsibilities, Boo, and yes, you are remembering correctly, but, the same is true for me as it is for you. Our crops need tendin' to, and we need to do it, but what if we didn't need to? I mean, what if someone else saw to our crops through the growin' season, then we come back to harvest early in the time of falling leaves. Would you think about going then? If you knew for sure all would be fine with the growing of our food, would you go with me then, Brother? Please tell me you will."

"No, I could not. Too risky to our survival. We must have our food stores, or we will grow hungry before the cold time ends. You know this, Henri. How could you even ask that we go now? It is foolish talk we make. Let us be done with this. We will go after harvest like we spoke on before. I needs be here through the growing season. I must be responsible for Mary, and for Sky. Dad is no longer here to see fer us. I will not let them down."

"I am not asking you to turn your back on duty, my friend. I know you would not do this, but, what if I told you I have a way for us both to travel the whole of this growing season and still get our crops grown and stored? Listen to what I have to offer, Boo, I think you will like what I am thinking. For sure if you want some time out on trail. You know the Cherokee elders think of me as a spiritual connection from our tribe to Mother Earth and the Great Creator. They see me as a part of the tribe's spiritual being. I have come to accept that, as they did train me for that world.

I do for them many things, of which few know little or nothing about, other than the elders and myself. I do not share the tribal things with you, or any others, concerning my work there. Trust me, it is good you do not know these things. Bad spirits could pull the knowledge from your mind without you even knowing they are near. For your own safety, I know better than to tell you. So, my friend, because of my spiritual connection to the soul of the tribe, we will find freedom this growing season. I can ask anything from them that I need. They will honor my request. I have told them my spirit needs to be with Blue Dove for the time of growing, to the benefit of the tribe and to me. They also know Blue Dove has asked for you to come, and that I need for you to go. Because we will have to be away to the north while our food plants grow, my clan will tend to our growing needs same as they tend to their own. Buach, there are no better growers in the mountains than the women of my clan. They will do better with our crops than we could. I know this. You do as well. You have worked with them. You have seen their talents. They are to be trusted same as us. There will be no worry to keep us here.

Now, hearing what I have said, what say ye, Buach? Will you let my people tend to our crops so we can travel, or will you be disrespectful of their generosity? Be careful, my brother. This could be a trap set for you by a dear friend… but you know this, don't you, wise one of the forest?"

Henri finished speakin' to me with a slight grin that spoke many words. He was my friend, and I his. He was actin' as such. He needed me. He'd made a way that I could be with him. He know'd he didn't need to ask 'fore makin' them plans. They's a special bond 'tween certain folk, that one can act to the other like a true friend, when that friend is in need.

"You are crafty like the fox, Henri. I know no others as sly as you when the spiritual things in life need seein' to. Yes, I will go with you, as you know'd I would. I've met the growers of whom you speak. I will have no worries about our crops. Our food will be well taken care of. That is truth. As for Miriam, I will ask her tonight. She and Mary are coming back from Swell Branch around dark. You must stay. Share supper with us. Fresh poke sallet, peas, and ham is what we're havin'. That don't sound temptin' none, now does it?"

"Supper it is, my brother. I am in need of some fresh greens. Where did you find poke this early, Boo? I have looked many fields but have seen none. I am thankful the Creator has seen fit to give you some. It will be a treat for me, as I've had little greens this winter."

"I went south for a few days recent. I was lookin' for answers to questions about Sky's mother and her whereabouts. I come back with few answers, but I did find some fresh poke. I picked a few pounds in a field growin' full of knee-high plants. Filled my possibles pouch with all it would hold to bring back. These I'm cookin' now are the last of my harvest. You are lucky to get some. It is good that you are here, Henri. It is good to see you. Mary and Sky will be glad, too. Come, let us smoke. Make talk about our coming trail. I am ready for some time on a good, long trail, and I can think of none better than the trader's route north."

Henri had it all planned out 'fore he ever come to our place just after daylight that morning. His spirit was needin' to be with Blue Dove. I doubted he even know'd why for sure, he just know'd he needed to be near her. Spiritual things of this nature required time and understanding to know full. He would learn all she'd let him know after sittin' with her for a few days talkin', but he had to get there to do that. I figured our trail would commence on the quick. I could feel it was important to Henri that we get there sooner rather than later.

It was past the time I'd figured Mary and Miriam to get back from Uncle Silas'. Their moods quiet as they come in the house. Neither seemed to wanna speak much when sayin' their hellos. Near disrespectful to Henri, him bein' a visitor and all. They didn't seem angry, just quiet like something had happened between 'em. Mary went to her bedroom, closin' the door. Sky went to the loft without hardly even speakin'. Me and Henri looked at each other. We both recognized something weren't right, one to the other.

I'd learned while livin' with Mary all my years, you didn't wanna bother her when she was emotional. Sad could turn to mad real quick with her and she'd whoop them little knives 'a hers out on ye in about a second, if she come to mind about it. I'd felt a little sting from one of their sharp edges after tellin' Dad on her for something she'd done. I was little. I didn't know no better. She taught me to know better. Worked, too. I never told on another body, ever. I wished in a way she'd 'a not got them things back, 'cept she needed 'em fer her own protection. Sky stole 'em back fer Mary 'fore all the takers left Long Shot. Stole 'em back from Stuart's mean sister. The one what landed on her when Henri knocked her out cold. Mary was sure proud to get them sharp little devils back. She relied on havin' 'em when she went to the city. I was proud she had 'em when she went there. Atlanta could be a most dangerous place, for sure, if one found themselves where they shouldn't be. I learned that fer fact while findin' myself in them kind 'a places a couple different times.

I had no notion that Atlanta was the problem between the two women... my sister, and my friend. Both alike, but opposite as night and day about how to live a woman's life. I felt more comfortable seein' to the female in the loft, so I left Mary to Henri. I searched for my words as I stopped at the bottom step of the loft stairway to announce myself. I never heard a no, so I went on up. Sky was there.

Sittin' the bed with her hands folded in her lap. Her head hangin' down. A few tear drops layin' on the inside of her right forearm. She didn't seem to care, but I did. I wiped 'em off with my thumb, then sat the floor cross-legged in front of her real quiet like. She never raised her head 'til she heard my voice, and then only just a touch. I couldn't really see her face. I spoke softly. I was still learning this wonderful creature.

"Miriam," I near whispered. "My spirit knows you are troubled. I am here. Speak, if you wish, I will listen, or, we can just sit, or, I can go, if you needs be alone. I will leave it up to you." I reached up crookin' my forefinger under her chin, liftin' her head enough to see me. She smiled a mite, lowerin' her head as I removed my finger. I felt better. It was a minute 'fore she spoke back, though. That was worryin' fer me. Matters of the heart, I was learnin', could be most troublin'.

"No, Buach," she said, near as soft as I'd spoke. She looked me in the eye again. "Please, stay here with me for a bit. No need for you to leave," she finished, lookin' back down to her hands.

Something was hurtin' her deep, and I wanted to help, but I had to hear it from her first, so I just sat and waited, my head down as well. I figured she'd tell me in her time. Weren't long 'til she did.

"Oh, Buach. I am so sad and worried," she said as a few tears fell onto her forearm again. "I don't want to leave Long Shot. I want to live here with you and Mary, but that cannot happen now. You and I are not married. It would not be right for me to live here with just the two of us in the house, but I don't want to live in Atlanta. I want to stay here in the mountains. I want to be free to live my life the way I choose. Not bordered by the streets and stink of a city. I want to live here... with you... Boo," she raised her eyes back to mine, reachin' down to take my right hand in hers. "I want to live here in Swell Branch. I do not want to live in Atlanta. Not even for a time. Promise me, Buach," she said, as she pulled me up from the floor to settle on my knees. Our faces close. I could taste her scent. "Promise me I will not have to live in the city. I would rather be with the ancestors than live in such confines. I want to hear you promise me. Can you do that, Boo?"

Her forehead fell to my shoulder as she finished her words. I heard no sounds. I lowered my head to rest beside hers, my mouth close to her right ear. My words were again but a whisper as I answered her. "I promise, Sky Watcher. You will never needs live in a city 'cept by choice, if that is truly what you want."

It weren't clear to me exactly what'd happened 'tween my sister and Sky, but I would know when they wanted me to know. It weren't nothin' I was gonna worry over much. I didn't sense anger was a part of it. No, it seemed more like a change in their friendship had come, and from what Sky had said, I reasoned that Mary had caused it. Must be she was plannin' on goin' to Atlanta, maybe to live. That's the sense Sky's words made, after studyin' on 'em fer a quiet minute.

Sky sensed we'd be left livin' in our house together, with just the two of us. That meant Mary weren't gonna be there. That told me she was plannin' on goin' to Atlanta. All of us know'd she liked life in the city, even though that was contrary to the way Dad raised us. Since it must be that Mary was goin', Sky was figurin' she'd have to go with her. She'd have no other place to stay that was proper, at least for a time. Oh my, did I have a surprise for her. A trail north that would settle all her concerns for a season. I looked forward to asking her to go with us. I allowed she'd wanna go, or at least stay at our place while I was gone. Either way would help her in the predicament she'd found herself. I could hear Henri's words from earlier. They turned out to be true. Sky is a creature of the woods. There was now no doubtin' that. She was raised in the wilderness. That is where she wanted to live and most likely would be the place where she would die. Bein' raised in the woods same as her, I understood the comfort.

Holy Spirit controls our fate. Her fate was fixin' to be proven. I was proud for her. A strong lesson was headed her way. I hoped she caught it. I again chose my words carefully, while speakin' near soft as I could.

"Miriam," I said, as I draw'd my head away from hers while liftin' her head again, our eyes locked. "As I understand your worry, Mary must be thinkin' of movin' to Atlanta, at least for a time. You have so said. I know your need to live where you are most comfortable. I am of the same need. You will not have to live in a city, if you choose not to. Henri and I will see to that with our lives. Do not doubt our concern for you. Do not doubt my concern for you. It feels as though you are becoming family. You are welcome at Long Shot no matter who lives in our house. If Mary goes, and we are not married, I have a room in the barn where I can stay just fine. You do not have to go away or live where you do not wish to be. Does this help you find settlement for your fears?"

She sat there listenin' to me, but I couldn't tell if she'd heard me actual. Her face never once changed its look. She looked back to her lap as she finally found the words to whisper back at me. It was a struggle for her to talk. She spoke slowly.

"You are most kind, Buach. Your spirit is gentle deep inside. Your words have made my spirit soar like the eagle. My soul is dancing, but I must hold my feelings close, as I have known little joy for a time. I will stay with you, Boo. I would love to call Long Shot Ridge my home, but soon my mother will come, if Holy Spirit so wills it. You know I want her with me. Will this be a good thing with you, or will her being with me cause you to withdraw your offer of a home? This is something you will needs think on when the time comes. For now, I accept your kindness. It will be nice to be a part of a family again. Thank you for a life, Boo."

"Yes, we can speak on this later, but know your family is welcome at my fire. As for now, I want to ask you something that I hope you will be happy to hear. It is kind 'a confusing, so listen close.

"Henri is planning a trail north. He will be gone a few moons. He means to go visit the healer Blue Dove. She has asked that we, me and you... uh...yeah... me and you... uh... come with him... yeah . . uh... you and me. I am willing to take this trail. Maybe you would think on goin'... uh... with us... I mean... uh... yeah . . . with me then, see? We hope that you say yes... uh, I... hope you say yes, that is."

It was mumbled up speak again. *Why did bein' near her make me do that?* I had to speak on. I still hadn't asked her to go, really, where she could answer me proper.

"Okay... Miriam... uh...yeah,... uh, well, yeah, okay, okay, we will leave in two days, and yes, I know what your mind is askin'.

We will be gone durin' growin' season, but that will not be a problem. Henri's clan will tend our crops. I trust them as growers. They are the best. This is a spiritual journey fer Henri, Miriam. It will be a time of learning for me, and I figure, if you so desire, for you as well. The clan we are goin' to visit is the most private clan of all the Cherokee in the mountains. This is out of need to protect the tribe's greatest spiritual healer. As I have said, her name is Blue Dove, and Henri has taken to her. So, uh, Miriam, yeah… will you go… I mean, will you go with us? I know you are more than welcome, kind 'a more like expected, so to speak, by Blue Dove herself. She asked us all to come, you as well. She knows you. I hope you find it in your heart to answer yes. We need you… I need you, to go. What say ye, Sky Watcher? We have all the truck you could need."

"I will go with you to the land north, Buach," Miriam said, quick as she could with a grin across her face, excited at the news. "I know this Blue Dove. She was a friend to Gideon. He traded with her. She has a guard named Big Nose. I do not like him. He offered to buy me. Got mad when Gideon refused. Yes, it would be my treat to travel this trail with you and Henri. I know the North Trail better than either of you. Spent many nights camped along its creeks. Many of those that travel it are my friends. The one who killed Gideon travels it too, Boo. Could be, if we keep our ears open, ask the right people the right question the right way, we may hear word of where he could be found. That would be a good thing for me, for Gideon, for sure since you are with me. Yes, Buach, I will go. I look forward to spending time with you and Henri. It will be a good time for me to learn about you, and you, me. I look forward to that, my big friend. Yes, I look forward to that with a great curiosity. I am a creature of the woods, Boo, same as you. We will be happy, you and me, traveling this trail together. Now, let us go make ready. I am eager. My spirit is telling me our coming time will change our lives. I pray the Creator guides our way."

CHAPTER 21

A Need for Justice

Henri come to Long Shot 'fore daylight the third morning after we'd all decided to go north to Blue Dove's village. It was the three of us goin'. As planned, some women from his clan come with him to get their camp set for the growin' season. I would have no worries over our provisions once I seen all them makin' camp. More'n two dozen of 'em. They moved like a trained military command. Each one knowin' their jobs. It was impressive to watch how they set their camp, makin' ready for our food source growin'. You could see they planned on bein' there a while. They'd need to be.

Me and Henri both figured it best fer us to ride since we was plannin' to travel the North Trail. We took the stallion and mare for me and Sky; Gus to haul our campin' truck, possibles, and provisions. Henri had got his own mare recent. Gifted from the tribe for his trail to visit Blue Dove. I was proud we was takin' stock to ride. It was much better to be ridin' when travelin' such a trail as we was gonna be on for a few days. A body never know'd if they'd need to go fast or not, when bein' out among the kind 'a folks we'd most likely run a chance 'a meetin'. With outlaws and rogues huntin' the trail from both directions, that could be most possible fer us.

Since the War of Northern Aggression had officially ended, a couple years or more prior, open trade had become common among settlers along the North Trail. It was no longer as guarded a secret as it once was, when the Cherokee first created it years before. More folks comin' to know it from outside the Indian world made it more dangerous fer trade folk of all breeds. A body had to use caution when travelin' it fer trade purposes, more so than ever before. Greedy folk would lie in wait, and you never know'd where or how they'd be.

The business of the trail, the profits of the trail, same as the profits from cotton in the South before the war, would eventually come to the knowledge of the U.S. Government, once the aftershocks from all the killin' and destroyin' calmed down. That day would be the end of the trail as we all know'd it. Soldiers would be posted to patrol it, then lawmakers could commence to taxin' everybody who made trade on it. Them taxes would kill the profit what kept the trail alive. It'll die when the patrollin' starts, then the trail will become just that, a plain ol' trail. Its worth fer profit over, 'cept for common travel to and from. The outlaws would be forced to move on, which is a good thing, 'cause nobody would be left to trade no more, which was the bad side. Federal foolishness does that to good things folks create out 'a necessity. You'd think our leaders could see that.

We had other trails, but the Cherokee had started this one not long after the Indian Removal. The tribe patrolled it before the war. Kept trouble off and away from it. They started it with the intent of building an underground trade route north, mostly for Indians. They'd succeeded. It was a great trail fer many years for those who know'd to respect it, but the end of the war brought change. The new folks comin' south made travel on the trail more dangerous. The Indians had begun to draw away, findin' other ways to trade north that weren't know'd about by folks. We would needs keep our minds about us to stay safe while usin' it. We'd come back on the main road. That would add a half-day gettin' home, but it would be much safer. The North Trail had just become too risky fer folks to travel. Best to stay off of it, lessin' you got intentions like we did.

Villages had sprung up here and there along the trail. They'd been built by trade folk in an effort to make more money. Not have to travel as much. Stores, of a sense, if you thought about it. A body had to be as careful as they'd ever been when stoppin' anywhere along the trail. Bandits from the North, and some from the South, was bein' seen more and more. I expected trouble usin' it as long as we was gonna be trailin' on it. Blue Dove's village was four days steady walkin' from Swell Branch. That's a long way in mountain travel. No chance we'd not see some type 'a folk what liked to cause trouble. I prayed killin' of innocents weren't gonna be part of it. Settlin' with folks was tolerable to my way 'a thinkin', but killin' without cause weren't something I could come complete on. It bothered me a sight takin' that young'uns life accidental like when rescuin' Mary, but I cared little about the other two I'd killed. I'd come to find that deserved and required killin' come with little guilt fer me. That kind 'a settlin' never bothered me none. I guess it prob'ly should 'a.

Henri was leadin' our trail. He'd be the one to make the important decisions. We'd be on the North Trail for most of the time. The last half day's ride would be on the private trail to Blue Dove's village. You was watched the whole time you traveled that trail by warriors from Blue Dove's clan. That didn't bother me. We was know'd by the lot of 'em. They'd been told to be watchin' out fer us. I was sure 'a that.

I know'd the way to the village same as Henri. Traveled it a few times, but I'd 'a rather took the main road to get to the private trail. The main road was slower, yes, but safer. Henri wanted to take the North Trail fer time's sake. We'd save a half day, but I wondered if it was worth the risk, times bein' like they was and all. Maybe so. It seemed most urgent for Henri to get there.

Henri was in the lead. Sky close behind, trailin' Gus. I brought up the rear. It's where I preferred to be. Where I should 'a been. Several times durin' the day I'd drop back a quarter mile or more. Try and catch any followers that might pick up Henri's trail from a watch in the woods. It was a good thing I did that.

Camp the first night was kind 'a quiet. Not bein' used to ridin' constant, like we'd been doin' all day, made one stiff in the joints after gettin' settled in the evening. Of course, we all had things on our minds. The first day out on trail did that to a body. Ridin' all day without conversation gets one's mind to thinkin' on things of importance to their life. Them thoughts typically followed on into camp that first night. Kept folks thinkin' instead 'a talkin'. After a couple nights, talk would be made more steady.

Still, light conversation was always in the air when camping. Henri liked to talk. They weren't no keepin' him from makin' at least a slight conversation. I figured he'd be talkin' to me when he got goin', but he surprised me. Started askin' Miriam questions not long after we'd took seats on our quilts around the warmin' fire. She didn't seem to mind him askin'. She was sittin' my side 'a the fire. We was both kind 'a facin' him head on. She was close to me, but not too close. I wished she was closer. She was sittin' my side of the fire, though. That was another good sign she might be favorin' me... not over Henri, really, but over anybody else she might know or any buck what might be ruttin' after her.

"Miss Miriam, Sky Watcher," Henri commenced. "I am glad you came with us on this trail. It is nice to have other company when saddled with Buach Whelan for so many days. He can be a man of few words, but do not take it personal. His disrespect is only so deep."

Henri's smile bent the corners of his mouth as he finished his words, lookin' over to me. He seen my eye was on him, but I weren't really listenin'. Something was troublin' my spirit, and it weren't his funnin'. Felt like a warning of sorts. I would needs pay mind to our way.

"I am glad to be on this trail with you, Henri. Had you not invited me to come along, I would be without a place, or people, to stay with. It's a pleasure in the making, being out here with you and Buach. I don't think I know any other persons I'd rather be traveling with. I hope all stays safe... that we avoid danger. It would be dire if y'all had to take care of little ol' me, now, hey? Wouldn't that be bad, Boo?" She finished, turnin' to look at me. A slight smile showin'.

I was taken back by her askin' me something straight out direct like that. I weren't ready to make talk with her. I raised my head to catch eyes as she looked at me. What she'd just said made little to no sense. She was Indian, or close as you'd get without bein' one actual. She'd most likely been taught to defend herself. I had no doubts over that. What I did doubt, was how to answer her funnin' back. I had to think fer a short minute while we stared at each other. That was paralyzing. She had a pull to her that made it where I couldn't move good or think good or talk right when she got to lookin' at me. Mercy, that was aggervatin', but oh so wonderful at the same time. I figured it for love. An affliction it seemed, really, way it was feelin' to me.

"Miriam," I near hollered, as I rose from my seat to strike a grand pose. My left arm laid firm across my chest. My right arm straightened to the sky, fist clinched, head throw'd back so I could be loud. "Me and Henri will fight to the death of our lives for your safety. Have no fear. We are trained in the arts of war and battle. No better warriors have ever guarded such a wanted princess as you, my lady. Fear not. We will prevail against all manners of evil and hell what comes against us." I settled back to my seat while catchin' eyes with both of 'em. I couldn't help but hide my face while I commenced to quiet laughin'.

Oh, if you could 'a seen their looks when I got done sayin' all that, you'd a thought I'd grow'd horns right there in front of 'em. It took a minute fer 'em to get caught up with what I'd just done, 'cause it was so out 'a character fer me, but when they did, they commenced to belly laughin'. I mean laughin' loud. No sir, they never figured me fer talkin' or actin' that 'a way. Strange how bein' around a woman a body is carin' about could make one act. They was goin' on with funnin' me. Havin' a good time. I just figured to join in and fun on them some. Have me a good time, too. That's kind 'a what you do in camp on a long trail. You do things to enjoy your time, and we was doin' just that. They didn't need to know I'd seen Uncle Silas do something similar a few years earlier while actin' out a scene from a play he was tellin' me and Mary about seein'.

I caught Miriam lookin' at me on the sly a time or two after our conversation started back new. I know'd that was a good sign. I never caught her lookin' at Henri like that. It seemed to me I was the one drawin' her favor. Wouldn't 'a mattered if she'd had a feelin' for Henri. He was took by another in a strong way. It was clear to me, he was bein' held by deep feelings fer Blue Dove. Spiritually directed, even. Weren't no common woman gonna break that.

"What's wrong with y'all? Ain't y'all never seen actin' before? That was a piece I learned a long time back. A play, I believe, of some sort. I reckon y'all figure I ain't got no sense 'a humor or culture, like maybe y'all ain't never seen it. Well, I'm culturally founded when it comes to my city doin's. Aunt Catherine has seen to that, only problem is, I prefer the mountain ways," I said, as I of a sudden jumped up straight, slingin' my right arm at a huge white oak some ten paces to my left. My long knife gripped solid in my right hand as I released it toward the tree. Its point sinkin' dead center where a piece 'a bark was missin' about the size of a man's hand. Near same as where a man's heart would 'a been had a normal sized man been standin' there. My long knife would 'a ended his walk.

I was handy with my knives. Worked with 'em a lot to be that way, but the echo of my long knife hittin' that tree hadn't even died before another long knife hit the same barkless spot I'd hit. I know'd that knife soon as it stuck a little to the right 'a mine. Henri had taught me most of what I know'd about throwin' knives. Weren't none better than him. Still, no sooner had the echo of Henri's long knife strikin' next to mine faded, than a smaller bone handled blade stuck between the two of ours, only a mite lower. It figures Mary would 'a give Sky one 'a her little knives. It was obvious from where her throw hit that Sky could loose a knife as well as any. That was good to know, if or when a fight come on us.

"Oh my, Sky, that was perfectly done. I can see you are skilled in the ways of protectin' one's self. All funnin' aside, I believe you a worthy foe... for any that may breech our walls," I finished, with a little laugh. She grinned back while droppin' her head some. I was growin' fond of her smile.

"Gideon taught me, Buach," she said, raisin' her eyes back to mine. "He wanted to make sure I could protect myself, if he wasn't there when I needed protecting. He is not here now, and the murderer Victor Soltor still walks Mother Earth. This is a bad thing. I know my father's spirit seeks justice," she paused, her face turned to the fire as she stopped speakin'. The reflection of the flames show'd tears pondin' up inside the lids of her eyes. A good-sized one loosed itself down the front of her right cheek as she started back conversin'. She wiped it away with her fingers. I just sat quiet, listenin'.

"My Mohawk family taught me much about defending myself, as well. Throwing knives is a practiced talent, Boo. You know this, as I can see. I learned by doing, as I'm sure the same is true for you. Sadly, all my knives were stolen on our trail south, so I have little feel for a knife right now. I meant for my throw to hit between yours and Henri's knives. I was a little low, but this knife Mary gave me is not a good knife for throwing. It has no weight. Still, I thank Mary for gifting such a fine blade to me. It has become a favored possession of mine. Given to me by one I now consider a friend. I never found who took my knives. Never saw anybody in Stuart's bunch with 'em. I will have more like those one day. Made personal for my hand by a true craftsman. I feel alone without 'em, somehow. Like a friend that goes away who you know is not comin' back. Does that sound strange to you, Boo? Feelings for one's knives? Besides, I will need a long knife to settle with Victor."

Victor Soltor murdered Gideon. Sky know'd all about it. Know'd he'd not been squared with. That justice had not been seen to fer Gideon. That was a shame on all who know'd him or called him friend along the North Trail. He'd done a lot 'a good fer a lot 'a folks durin' his time, but they weren't no law to speak of in the mountains as yet. There was Federal law in the cities and around, but in the mountains, folks had to look our fer their own. The Indians weren't really doin' it no more.

Gideon's killin' needed to be looked after by folks concerned fer him and his. I was hopin' we might hear word on where the murderer might be stayin' as we made our way north. Could be he was on the trail someplace. That would be handy. You never know'd where Great Spirit would send folks when justice come to call. Few ever know'd they was bein' sent, just went 'cause it seemed right. I planned to ask different folks on the quiet for word on Victor, if I figured 'em safe in askin'. I also planned on askin' Holy Spirit to put him in our path. He'd do that sometimes. I'd heard stories.

"Not to my thinkin', Miriam. I feel for my blades every time I dress to go anywhere. I would be lost if they was took. Our lives are bein' lived durin' dangerous times, sister. You know this. We need protection for our persons. Knives hold importance in that. I feel much less safe when I am without my knives. I feel close in spirit to all my weapons, if that makes sense. My special knife was a gift from the wife of an old Cherokee warrior who was killed. She told me her husband always claimed it had a warrior's spirit what come to it while bein' forged. I believe it does from the things I've done with it. I treat my weapons with respect. It becomes spiritual at times, when havin' to use 'em. I look to my knives as the first source of protection when fightin' comes close. They've never let me down and I don't figure 'em to. So, no, as one who lives for survival each day in a land that has become so dangerous, I cannot be without my knives. It most certainly makes sense that you feel for your weapons same as me. It is good you have this heart. That's sign of a warrior's mind, thinkin' like you do. It is good you are with us on this trail. I feel much better knowin' a savvy third set 'a eyes is watchin' out while we ride, but I do not plan on havin' to protect you. I feel for the fool that under figures you, Sky Watcher. I believe that person will bleed."

"You will learn that no soul has to watch over me, Boo. No disrespect intended. We will need to watch each other's back if, or when, trouble comes to us on this trail, or in this life, but that is not watching over my life. There is a difference. I have lived the last few years under the watchful care of a man who traveled the trading routes unafraid. A man who had no worry over trading with whomever needed. I've met many unsavory kind traveling with him on those trails, but I never feared any of them. Gideon was always there to protect me, and he was skilled in the ways of defending one's person. He taught me much. I am good with a short gun, rifle or knife, as you've seen. I was not there to watch his back the day he was murdered. I feel his death is on me. If I had been there, and maybe I could 'a been, I feel death would not have taken him. I long to find Victor Soltor. I will see his heart gone from his chest one day, Buach. I promise you I will… and Boo, remember this, I never break a promise."

"It is not on you for Gideon's death, Miriam," I said back kind 'a soft like. "Evil men cause things to happen we can't do anything about. Oh, we can see things made right once a wrong has been committed. Find justice for those who've been killed or took from, but we can never guard our loved ones constant. I've lost family where the loss made me feel same as you. Guilty for not bein' with 'em when the killin' took place. I know your heart, Sky. In time, you will come to settle with the guilt you are putting on yourself. Trust me, Gideon's murder was just that, murder. It could not have been stopped, or it would 'a been stopped. You might have been killed as well had you been there. He would not have wanted that. Try not to blame yourself fer things you had, or have, no control over. I will pray your spirit finds peace from the acts of a coward like Victor Soltor, 'cause that's what killin' to steal is, an act of a lazy, no good coward. I, too, will see him pay for Gideon's death. I pray to the Peace Child that we find him soon. Maybe even on this trail. That would be good."

 We sat in the quiet by the fire after I'd finished my say. She never said nothin'. Our conversin' just kind 'a ended. Neither of us moved to leave or sit nowhere else. It was common to lay a quilt or blanket out when one sat the fire of a night in camp. I sat a quilt folded over and then folded in half twice. She had one 'a Henri's blankets. Henri and some of his Cherokee friends had filled Sky's need for clothes a day or two after we'd all got back to Long Shot. She had some fine lookin' things. Believe me when I say, she prob'ly never looked better. The Cherokee made some fine stuff, and when a body come to 'em in need, they'd give their best to the needy one. They know'd they could make more, and the one they was givin' to prob'ly couldn't. She had a fine bait 'a clothes for a woman of her recent history. Holy Spirit had provided her needs just like He said he would. That's biblically spiritual.

 Our fire was warm. It was nice just sittin' there with her. We shared a smoke later on. Talked a little more. Neither of us spoke much. Henri had gone to bed down not long after me and Sky had got to talkin'. I never really noticed him gone 'til I noticed him gone. I guess we kind 'a quit talkin' to him. That may 'a been rude, but my mind was distracted. Payin' her mind just felt like what I should 'a been doin' right then, and I couldn't think 'a nothin' else I'd rather been doin' right then.

We didn't have to talk. We looked at each other some. I was growin' fond of the looks she'd give me. Her voice broke the silence like the sweet sound of an angel singin' after a bit. Throughout my life, only a few words she ever spoke did I remember as clear as the ones she said to me on that first night's camp. What happened that night touched a place inside my soul nobody but her ever touched again. It was absolutely a life changing time for me. I welcomed it.

"Buach," she said as she stood. "I will needs sit your quilt while we wrap inside my blanket. I hope you will not mind. It has grown cold, and I am not yet ready to leave this warm fire to bed down."

She commenced to sittin' down beside me close, makin' sure she got her backside full on my quilt. That put us side by side tight. I could smell her scent. It was like sweet cake bakin' in the oven. My heart come near to stoppin'. I wanted more.

"Wrap this blanket around us, Boo," she whispered in my ear. "We will warm each other, as those who are more than friends can do," grinnin' slightly as she moved her eyes to meet my startled look. "It is good we are becoming friends," she finished sayin', starin' me hard the whole time. Her eyes hauntin'. It was makin' me weak.

I broke our stare to do as she wanted. Wrapped us close with her blanket. We sat there cross-legged with our sides touchin'. Our backs sidin' since our legs was crossed. The blanket around our shoulders coverin' us to the ground. Her warmth felt like sunshine. We sat like that for a while. How long didn't really matter to us, but it was a while.

Neither of us spoke a word as we sat there. Just stared into the dyin' flames of our warmin' fire, enjoyin' the closeness while our bodies relaxed against one another. We were both tired. Sleep was near. After a time, we let the flames burn down to orange and gray coals. It took Old Man Cold only a short time to move in and steal what little warmth our dyin' fire was tryin' to leave, so we stood to make for our own tents. I wrapped her in the blanket, tellin' her good night. She told me the same 'fore turnin' to go. I watched after her. It weren't far to her tent, but after a few steps in that direction, she stopped, turned slowly back toward me in her trail, then walked right square up to me. I allowed I was fixin' to be scolded fer something

I didn't know I should 'a done or hadn't done, but fortunately it weren't that.

Her eyes locked into mine as I felt her front press firm against my chest. Our faces near touchin'. Bein' taller than most women, it weren't hard fer her to reach me. I felt something in my center when she draw'd up close to me. I liked it. While never breakin' our stare, she slowly slipped her hands up my chest then in behind my head, pullin' my face to hers. Her blanket fell to the ground. I felt dizzy from her touch. Her hands was strong, warm. She pulled me closer, starin' deeper into my eyes. I could scent her breath as our faces was near touchin'. 'Fore I know'd what was happenin, I was feelin' the first ever real boy girl kiss I'd ever puckered up for in my life. I can't explain the explosion in my center that her kiss caused, but it was there. When we was done, and it was a while, she turned to leave. I seen she was smilin' like she was happy. I know'd I was.

I stood where I stood for a time, a long time, after our kissin' was done. I don't remember thinkin' on anything in particular, just stood there. She'd went away to her tent. I know'd that. How long I stood there alone don't really matter, but Old Man Sun was peakin' over the big ridges to the east when I finally realized what I was doin'. I'd stood after our kiss the rest of the night. It'd suddenly come time for us to make trail with me still standin' where we'd kissed like a silly schoolboy. I turned and left for my tent to pack up my truck and possibles. Something I should 'a done some five hours earlier.

I'd had no sleep, but it was strange, I weren't tired a bit. Bein' held by Sky had give me strength. I thanked Holy Spirit for bringing her into my life. I was beginnin' to feel I never wanted her to leave. I liked feelin' like that. It was good. I'd never know'd a feelin' as strong outside 'a family before then. Oh my, but fallin' in love was troublesome. My first ever kiss. I wanted another one.

THE LEGEND OF SWELL BRANCH

CHAPTER 22

Our Second Day on the North Trail

That worrisome warning feeling come back, not long after we'd made trail at daylight. I still didn't know what was causin' it. Near forgot about it comin' on me recent, 'til like a flash 'a storm lightning, it come to me again as we started back on trail. Old Man Sun was just breechin' the ridge tops east when it punched me in the gut no different than a hard fist. I'd got distracted, or rather, I'd let myself get distracted. Bein' such made me forget about havin' that same kind 'a feeling a day or so before. Call me careless. Call me stupid, but that was a dangerous slip up on my part. Foolishness like that could get a body killed in my world, if only fer bein' stupid. Bein' stupid had caused a lot 'a hurt and death in the mountains. I figured to pay better mind to our circumstance, since such a strong feeling had come fer a return visit.

A feeling like that comin' on a second time like it had, made me think my spirit was tryin' to get my body's attention. It was needin' to tell my person that it would be wise to keep a keen eye out for whatever danger it was might be comin'. I'd felt the warning. Could be something bad might 'a crossed our trail, no tellin'. I looked forward in our line toward Henri. Seemed he must 'a felt something, too. He was stoppin' us not a minute after I'd felt the return of the troublin' sensation, no more'n a mile out from our first night's camp. I figured his spirit was communicatin' with him as well. Maybe warnin' him same as me. We looked at each other serious like, as he turned his mare to stop and dismount. I could see his face held worry. That put me on edge.

"Buach, we are to have visitors, I believe. Rogues, if I understand correctly. It would be wise to meet them in a place of our choosing. We needs know their intentions, be they good or bad. With good fortune, they are simply traveling same as we. What say ye, warrior? Think on this thing while we rest a minute. They are drawing closer."

It always amazed me when spirt folk like Henri know'd things that was fixin' to happen, 'fore they ever happened. It weren't a constant kind 'a knowin'. Not sure it was a knowin' at all, really, more like a feeling with sight. They didn't know what was gonna happen all the time, but often they could feel future doin's near perfect, or close enough to make do. It weren't nothin' a body could depend on, but when it happened, it happened true, and most usually at a proper time fer needin' whatever it was the seer had come to know. It was spooky, even fer folks like me what was familiar with it, as testimonied by the look on Sky Watcher's face. I know'd that look. I'd seen it many times when Henri startled folks with his spirit doin's. It'd got to where seein' folks get surprised at him made me laugh out, on the inside of course. Amusing in its own way fer me. Most folks Henri met never know'd the depth of his spiritual connection to the world around him. I kept my inner thoughts to myself at times, because of that connection.

"How many?" I asked back at Henri plain and simple like, still sittin' the stallion. As our conversin' commenced, I looked to double check the load in my short gun, then unshouldered the sling of Stuart's carbine, makin' sure I had a full load locked in under its steel butt plate. They was both ready fer fightin'. I felt confident. Stuart's carbine had become my favorite. It was newer than the other two I'd collected. I meant to keep it as my personal choice. I aimed to give Sky her pick of the two. Henri would get the other. Didn't matter which one got which. Both guns was the same, solid. Looked to 'a been took care of proper by their previous owners.

They both needed them guns more'n I did. Henri was still totin' an old flintlock. Him gettin' a carbine would make it more safe when we was out on trail. I favored the one I carried, what few times I'd shot 'em all together. My aim with it was most comfortable. Stuart's was the only one that had a sling. Not all soldier rifles had 'em.

I felt for my knives next. They was secure. Right where they should be. Both handy fer grabbin'. I would introduce myself to those what followed, usin' my weapons to speak fer me, if I found 'em to be bad folk comin' with takin' intentions. I'd near had my fill 'a bein' confronted by folks with takin' intentions. Henri seemed to feel these might be a threat. I weren't gonna be threatened no more, neither, for sure with Miriam on trail with us. It come to me more'n usual with her bein' there, that it was my duty to end any threat to our travel. I had to pay mind, though. Could be, even with Henri sayin' they was possible fer rogues, our followers had nothing in mind fer us. We would see.

"There are five traveling by the warriors trot, Buach. Two in front, with three to follow. It would be good if they only saw me and Sky Watcher when they came. I would see it as wise if you left us for the freedom of the woods. I trust you will become our guardian angel, so to say, if you agree with my way of thinking. Be careful my friend, if you do. These are Seminole gone bad that possibly stalk us. I can feel their spirits crying out. That is how I know they come. Do not lay any trust to their true intentions. These are deceivers. What say ye, Brother? Is your heart with mine on how we should make ready for what could be an enemy? I know that in the woods you are best on your own. I will worry little for our lives, knowing you are watching out for us. Think quick, warrior, your time to move is now. They draw near."

It was a short look of understanding I give Henri. He know'd I was in agreement with his thinkin' 'fore he ever said a single one 'a them words he'd just talked out. I believe he wanted Sky to know clear what our minds was, more so than communicatin' with me. All he'd needs do on one of our common trails, after stoppin' of a sudden like he'd done, was motion with his head to the east for me to hit the woods, and I'd 'a been gone quick as a rabbit spookin'. Wouldn't 'a been no need for all that jibber jabber he'd just made. Wasted my time was all him talkin' done fer me. He know'd that, too. I allowed he figured we had time fer all his explainin', or he'd 'a kept his mind to himself. With a short glance and nod at Miriam, I turned the stallion east, makin' quick my leavin'. I wanted Old Man Sun's help. I needed him to shine in the rogues' eyes, if it come to me lettin' 'em know I was there.

Henri know'd best how to handle these that he figured might be followin' us. He wanted me hid as a watch ready to attack if their visit called fer it. He know'd my carbine would make it all square, if they didn't know I was close by watchin' out. I would consider them enemy, and act accordingly, if they made one move of aggression toward either of my friends. I didn't have many. Weren't aimin' to lose either of the two with me, neither. We'd see just how these rogues responded to our knowin' they was followin', if that come to be.

I rode the stallion a ways east, 'fore tyin' him there to go back and watch fer Henri and Sky. I tied him 'cause I didn't want him possibly followin' me. I'd be goin' out 'a sight from where he stood to hide from some dangerous folk. I couldn't risk him breakin' training and followin' me. They'd see him sure. That would not be good fer any of us, my stallion included.

I found a place to sit where I'd be unseen from the trail. It was in amongst one of those curious kind 'a places you sometimes found when out roamin' the mountains. This one place was a group of some good-sized boulders what sat suspiciously alone. They lay some fifty paces or less east from where I'd left Sky and Henri on the trail. You didn't commonly find boulders such as them out in the woods all by themselves. That's what made it feel strange. Most times, when you run into boulders out in the woods, they'd be a bunch 'a rock layin' all around with 'em, or even a rock face above where they could 'a fell from and rolled away, but that weren't the way with where these boulders lay. They weren't another rock on top 'a the ground fer as far as one could see in any direction. Made the place feel kind 'a spiritual. Like them rocks might 'a been put there by the hand of God Himself. I got chills on the back 'a my neck thinkin' that might be exactly how they'd got there. I thanked the Creator fer thinkin' of us when havin' them stones put down all handy like they laid fer me to hide in.

Weird as it felt, them big stones bein' there at all, made divine intervention seem reasonable. Weren't reasonable to think they just popped up out 'a the ground like a splinter jumpin' from your skin after it'd got all pussed up and you pinched it from the sides. That would 'a been a sight if you'd a been there when something like that might 'a happened. Nothing really goin' on around ye, 'til of a sudden more'n a half dozen huge boulders come explodin' out from the ground, then land in a kind 'a circle when they settled. No reason fer 'em jumpin' out. No earthquake or nothin'. They just come blowin' out 'a the ground without warning. Thinkin' how crazy that thought was, made it most unreal them rocks layin' where they was. Another mystery from the creation of Mother Earth. The creative hand of God is beyond our understanding, when seein' things like those boulders alone like they was out in the middle of the woods.

Henri had moved the horses west of the trail out 'a sight. Tied 'em there to separate trees to keep 'em from tanglin'. He'd moved 'em off trail 'cause he didn't want anybody knowin' they was there, or fer any stray bullets to strike 'em accidental if we got to shootin'. I hoped there weren't gonna be no killin', but it was feelin' like death was gettin' near. I fer sure know'd how that felt. Henri and Miriam stood some ten paces west of the trail, waitin'. It weren't long 'til their wait come to an end.

I swear I smelled them bucks 'fore I ever seen or heard 'em, with the air movin' from low to high like it did that time 'a day. Carried their scent straight to me, strange as that may be, but I know what I smelled, and it was them I was scentin'. All other smells I recognized, so the strange stink had to be from them. I would never forget that stink.

I watched close as they come to where Henri and Sky was now seated, leaned back against two different fair-sized oak trees. Their backsides sittin' the ground. Legs stretched out in front. One foot across the other. Arms crossed over their middles. Heads leaned back on the tree bark. Eyes closed. Henri closer to the trail than Miriam. His short gun layin' in his lap. They both looked plumb asleep.

You'd not know they weren't, even if you looked close. That was wise thinkin' from whichever one 'a them thought to do that. I figured it for Sky. We'd now see the true intentions of those comin' on behind us, or at least I would.

    I'd laid my possibles pouch on top of the center boulder, then made ready my carbine by levelin' it at the trail across the soft, thick hide of the pouch. I draw'd the strikin' hammer back as I let the gun lay balanced. I didn't wanna make that noise when the outlaws was near enough to possibly hear it. The pouch would help hold steady my aim, as fifty paces through the woods was a lengthy shot when one was on edge, like I was. If it come that I should need to shoot, I could not miss, 'cause if I was shootin', it was because I was bein' forced to protect Henri and Sky. They would be dependin' on me not to miss if a threat come to their life. I prayed I'd not let 'em down.

    I could see a long ways down the trail from where I'd chose to watch. Henri called it. His feelin' had been right. When they finally come in sight, over a hundred paces away, two was in front, then after a short minute, three followed, just like he'd said, 'cept they was all now walkin'.

    There was several paces separatin' the bunches. They moved like that so they'd have two sets of front watchin' eyes coverin' the same space at different times. If it worked right, and they was in a place where ambushers couldn't see as much of the trail as I could, the front two would pass on by, lurin' out any what might be waitin'. The ambushers would be suckered into thinkin' it was safe fer 'em to move once the front bunch passed. That would mean death for them foolish enough to fall fer that trail savvy trickery. Those followin' would be on to help in no time. Death to the hopeful takers would follow. It was a common way to travel among Indians. Settlers as well, if they was learned in Indian ways like me and mine.

    I'd never seen such Indians as these. They looked common 'til they'd got close enough to see personal. They was different than any I'd ever laid eyes on before, confusin' to my thinkin'. Their color was dark, deep dark, far as pure tribal folk went. Not dark like the colored folk, but Indian dark with more red than brown. They was common to a type you'd sometimes meet when out on trail. The kind you hoped to never meet again, once that first time meetin' 'em had ended. I'd seen their kind before, in passing, when travelin' with Dad, but he'd not stop fer 'em. That's how I know'd 'em when I seen 'em. Rogues!

No better example of rogue Indians traveled the mountains than them I was lookin' at. I know'd 'em right off as the first two come my way. Surprisingly, the second in line was a female, but I had to look close to know that. She wore buckskin leggings with a homespun top and knee-high footskins laced with braided cord from ankle to top, same as the male in front. Them kind 'a foot coverin's was made fer long travel, and the two looked like they'd been on trail for a time. Both was dirty top to bottom. Both carried their hair long, braided from the base of their skull to midway down their backs. They'd both shaved the sides of their heads, leavin' a streak 'a hair down the center to use for the braid. Both had story marks on their faces, necks, and hands. Warriors turned rogue for sure. Travelin' light, only the female had a rifle, and unfortunately, it was a carbine same as mine. Most likely took from an ex-Federal soldier, same as mine. Henri was right about 'em bein' rogues, but when I realized their breed, I draw'd a tight bead on the lead man. They weren't Seminole. Henri got that wrong. They was half-breeds, but strangely enough, they looked Seminole. Prob'ly been south livin' with 'em fer a time, bein' the travelers they looked to be.

The first one near lost his life as he stopped quick just shy 'a where he seen Henri and Sky layin' leaned up sleepin'. My carbine's bead was dead center his back, my trigger halfway pulled 'fore he ever settled in from his quick stop. I held off firin' by less than half a half second. He was lucky. Something had made me stop.

After a second or two 'a watchin', I seen he weren't in no hurry to assault the two sleepers. He didn't do nothin' right off that was appearin' threatenin', so I held my aim. For the time, he seemed more curious than dangerous. Doin' nothin' but lookin' close at the two tired travelers. I weren't gonna shoot him over bein' curious, so I waited to fire.

I lowered the rifle back to the soft leather of my possibles pouch as I seen him turn to the woman followin'. His face more curious than threatening. She looked back at him with a slight shakin' of her head. I think she was tellin' him to leave Miriam and Henri be. That was wise on her part, 'cause my .52 caliber would 'a slapped him face down to the forest floor had he moved toward my friends any.

I fixed the carbine back level same as it was before. Balanced across the boulder on my pouch, hammer back. I left it that way while they kept communicatin' with looks, but then of a sudden, I was forced to snatch it back to my shoulder for aimin'. My finger pullin' back near full again. The front warrior had took a quick step forward gettin' nearer to Sky but stoppin' again real quick like. Stoppin' like he did kept him from gettin' his killin'. That put him some closer to Sky, yes, but he still didn't seem threatenin', so I held off killin' him for the second time.

Still, he weren't done actin' strange. I near shot him again when he of a sudden bent from the waist after stoppin' complete, like he was tryin' to get his face closer to where she sat, then leanin' in hard to his left. He was actin' weird. Movin' like that made his head go out to the side. He looked to 'a lost his mind. Strange the way he was doin'.

I ciphered over that crazy Indian fer a minute or more. Again, lettin' off my trigger as I seen he weren't movin' aggressive toward Henri or Sky. He was just actin' weird. After leanin' left like he had, he simply raised his face toward where Sky lay. Like he was listenin' to a sound I couldn't hear. You'd a had to 'a seen it to understand it. Most strange to my thinkin'.

After watchin' him fer a bit, it come to me what he was doin'. I near pulled my trigger again, realizin' his intentions. I'd seen critters and bulls do the same thing in their natural surroundings, when their females come in heat. That scoundrel was at it same as them. No different than any critter durin' their matin' season… he was scentin' Miriam for breedin'. Same as a buck deer when he's seekin' does followin' the rut. I should 'a shot him for the thoughts he was holdin' in his head pure and simple, but I know'd he couldn't help it, bein' the animal he'd become.

I could find no call to shoot him fer actin' on his natural calling. He'd done nothin' wrong, as yet. I understood his kind. Dad had explained their existence to me. They was near same as any animal of the woods in their livin', purely by instinct. I would respect that, for the time. Treat this 'un as such, but one day, soon, we would settle over him scentin' my girl.

My blood got hot thinkin' on what that buck was doin'. He stayed at it fer a minute 'til he'd scented all he could and got his answers. I had to calm myself in the warrior way or I was gonna shoot him dead fer spite. I needed my focus back to the time at hand or somebody might get hurt from my bein' careless. Oh, I did not like him doin' that to Miriam. It seemed so personal to her, to us both. It was a feelin' what come just a little too close fer me. We weren't animals. We didn't live that way. I would not have folks treatin' us as such, for sure some rogue outlaw. I didn't know their clan, but I'd come to figure their breed. They was from the west as I was beginning to understand. I recognized the footskins they was wearin'. Made from the western Buffalo. I'd seen traders what had 'em.

The near killin' come to an end as the first two rogues finished their visit with no actions more aggressive than lookin' and scentin'. The followin' three seemed to never even notice Henri and Sky as they walked on by, at least they made it seem they never noticed. I figured they did. Most warriors with any skill would 'a, and I could tell these was skilled warriors. All five was the same after seein' the back three in closer. Their faces, necks, and hands held story marks and fightin' wounds same as the first two. Sure signs of battle hardened warriors. We would needs be careful. Life most likely meant little to these.

I thanked Holy Spirit for the warning He'd give us prior. I hoped any possible trouble had passed as I watched the back three walk on out 'a sight. But havin' rogues such as these nearby meant havin' to watch our camp close at night. One could not be careful enough when evil ones was travelin' the same trail, and these rogues brought me and Henri strong concern. We talked it over later that evening around the fire. Could be we weren't done with the travelin' warriors, but one could hope.

"What say ye of these that have passed us by today, Henri?" I asked, as we all three sat the fire for a smoke after supper. "You was right knowin' they was followin', but to me the sense I had before they come was more one of warning. It might be wise to not put these out from our mind too quickly. We should make watch tonight. Remember they are near. I believe we'd be ahead to not forget their kind are an evil kind."

"I know what I felt was a warning, of sorts," Henri replied after a minute. "I know these may not be the ones our warning was about, but I believe they could be. I saw them clear as anything in my mind. Yes, it will be most wise to not forget they are near as we should start a watch tonight. I feel we have not seen the last of these followers as yet. Now, tell me how you both feel about watch. My thoughts are that you take the first watch and I take the second. Miriam will stay the camp to guard our truck and stock. What say ye, Buach? Is this reasonable to you, or do you see it another way? I trust your mind."

"No, Henri, this is not what we will do. Yes, I agree Sky Watcher should guard our camp, protect our truck and stock, but you will not take the second watch. That watch will be for me. We both know that is the time these rogues will most likely choose to come, if they choose to come. You are due to Blue Dove. It is for the good of the tribe that I stand the second watch. If they come, I will do away with them before our morning meal. You will not lose sleep. Now, I'll have no more talk. This is how I see it. This is how it will be." I finished with two fingers pointin' at my eyes. In our way of conversin', that meant talk was done. Miriam didn't know that rule, yet, but her response was as it should 'a been.

"I am thankful to Great Spirit for bein' on this trail with the two of you, my friends," Sky finally spoke. "I will do what I am needed to do. I will stay and guard this camp. You both can depend on me, but if a fight comes, you should know I can fight. I will not need you two risking your lives rushing to my rescue because I'm a woman, unless, of course, they are more in number than me, then I would appreciate all the help you can spare. Is this agreeable to you both? I know my rights as camp guard. You do not have to die being careless for me."

"Your rights?" I asked quick. "There are no such rules for camp guard. You are good with your words, Sky Watcher, and I believe you can defend yourself with little issue. You are strong, yes. A good warrior, yes, but these are battle tested rogues we are worryin' over. I am not sure you've fought up close to such as these before. You might 'a met some similar, when out on the trader's trail with Gideon, but I doubt it. These kind are hard. They live in the shadows. I believe the ones we saw today could be as evil as any rogue warrior that has ever turned. It feels as though the evil one guides their path. If his is the way they have chosen, their demons will be strong. I pray Holy Spirit watches over us, then we can be stronger. We should all pray for this." Nobody said any more words.

With all our talk done, Henri accepted that I'd not be swayed in him takin' the first watch. We both know'd the evil ones we seen earlier would most likely not come 'til a couple hours 'fore daylight. I would be on watch if they come at that time. It was my life that would be most at risk, but I understood that is how it should be. In human thinkin', Henri was more important to the world, to the tribe, than I was. Sky Watcher was important, too. I would give my life for either, but I prayed it wouldn't come to that. I wanted to spend more time gettin' to know Miriam Sky Watcher. She'd got rooted in me somehow. Maybe she was a witch castin' spells, but her stayin' safe had become a big worry fer me. I was proud she'd agreed to stay in camp as guard. It really was an important responsibility. Our stock had to be healthy, ready, and standin' where we needed 'em. Henri seemed to trust her to the task. He wouldn't give her charge over something so important, if he'd had any doubts she couldn't do what was needed when trouble come. We could hide our truck and possibles, but our stock had to stay safe. That meant they needed to be guarded. He obviously felt Sky Watcher was warrior enough for the chore. I'd agreed with him... when we talked it over 'fore ever leavin' Long Shot.

The Legend of Swell Branch

CHAPTER 23

Rogues Come to Call

Henri took first watch. We'd brought my spare carbines and a few extra cartridges fer purpose. Knowin' what the North Trail could throw at a body, we'd packed a little heavier on the fightin' truck 'fore leavin' Long Shot. Henri toted one of the carbines with him. Sky had the other. She could shoot with it, too. I'd seen it the day before we left.

I sat in camp with her for a time, after Henri'd headed out for watch. Sittin' the fire in Sky's company seemed a most pleasant way to spend the evening, at least to my way 'a thinkin'. Some hot coffee, a poke of air-dried Indian tobacco, a hot fire, the company of a woods savvy woman whom I was feelin' close to, all was good as could be fer me at that moment in time. I felt for Henri havin' to be out on watch without any camp comforts, but my concern was only so deep. At least he had a full belly.

I was glad he weren't around, really. Give me and Sky some together time. 'Sides, I didn't wanna bed down, leavin' her all alone to the night, even though it would 'a been wise fer me to go ahead and get as much rest as I could 'fore my watch time come, expectin' a fight like we was. I looked up through the leafless treetops to check Old Man Moon while takin' a deep, cool, clean breath of pure mountain air through my nose. The fresh scents of spring strong. He weren't sheddin' much light, so seein' to move quiet would be risky. Unfortunately, havin' to move in the dark would not stop the rogues. If they had it in mind to come on us durin' the night, then come on us they would. Their spirits held little concern for anything other than their own greed.

The coffee was fresh, the fire comforting, our second night in camp, but she and I sat without finding anything to talk about, once I'd finished my pipe. It seemed uncomfortable between us fer some reason. I couldn't think 'a nothin' I'd done wrong, or nothin' I hadn't done, but things didn't seem proper 'tween her and me. I figured it to 'a been more comfortable, with just the two of us in camp, but I weren't feelin' comfortable. She didn't seem to be, either. Something was makin' us feel most uncomfortable. I was confused. I had no understandin' of the circumstance we was in, then it come to me, after studyin' on it a quiet minute. I weren't seein' things as she was most likely seein' things. She was sittin' all alone, which was not what she was prob'ly expectin'. I'd took a seat opposite the fire, whilst bein' distracted by the thoughts of my upcoming watch. I weren't thinkin' clear when I'd come to the fire fer an after-supper smoke.

She'd sat first after we'd all eat, it was my night to clean up. Henri had left for his watch, leavin' us alone, and I'd not sat by her when comin' to the fire after gettin' done cleanin'. I believe she figured I would, and I didn't, hence the problem I come to believe was between us. We'd show'd each other affection the night before, so me not sittin' next to her would for sure cause her to wonder about my intentions. We'd sat close together then, so bein' alone in camp like we was, she'd be figurin' it natural that we sat close again. I could see it clear in my thinkin', once my mind got focused like hers. I felt disrespectful not sittin' next to her. We caught eyes after I'd figured out what was wrong. I could see her confusion. I moved to her side of the fire, standin' while I made talk, the night air cool. She looked up at me kind 'a sad like.

"I am cold, Sky Watcher. Would you be open to lettin' me sit your blanket, so we can warm beside each other 'til time to bed down? I have my quilt. We can wrap up like we did before. Warm each other. What say ye, Miriam? It would feel good to share our warmth. The night air is freshenin'."

"Suit yourself, warrior, but build up the fire some, first," she said, while turnin' her face back to the fire. "I want to see flames. I want to see your face in their light. Make sure you're speaking truth when you speak," she looked back up at me, grinnin' a bit, then back to the fire. "I am feeling the cold. It would be nice to have a quilt about my shoulders, and if it requires you be in it for me to get it, then I guess you sharing my blanket will be of a purpose, won't it, Buach?"

She looked back up at me still grinning, then her grin faded. Breakin' our stare, she slid her backside to the left part of the folded blanket then patted the right side, showin' me where I was to sit. Her eyes locked into mine.

"Come, you are welcome to sit here, warrior. I will share my blanket with you, and you can share your quilt with me. I was beginning to wonder where your person went. Your seat across the fire was a long way away."

She smiled again after finishin' them last words. It didn't pass me by that she enjoyed life. I hoped she would enjoy life with me, but I weren't for sure that life together would work for us or not. As I took a seat where she'd patted, I tried to explain my rudeness. Her scent was strong as I wrapped us tight in my quilt. Her sweetness made it hard to breathe.

"I am sorry, Miriam, if I show'd you disrespect by not comin' to sit your side of the fire after supper. I have a lot on my mind," apologizin' to her fer bein' rude. Our eyes come together. "If you please, you will needs be patient with one such as me. I am not used to mixin' with a woman of your independence. I am learning to be near you as we go, so I hope you will not take personal my ignorance of proper courtin' customs. It is difficult for me to be near you. Your world… how you think… who you are, what you are made for… how you make me feel… is different than the world I've been used to durin' my time on Mother Earth. You feel, in your soul, and that is a good thing. Your spirit is wise. My spirit senses this. Your thoughts… my thoughts… are alike. I feel… when you are near. I feel… you… when you are near. I hope I am not sounding foolish with what I'm saying, but my heart has been touched by you. I can't help what I feel, or how I feel, when thinkin' of you."

I finished them words kind 'a quiet like, then sat silent as a mouse hidin'. I wanted to hear her feelings to what I'd just said, but I heard nothin'. She didn't respond any. Just sat there with a dry look on her face, starin' at me. Why didn't she say somethin'? I sat, starin' back. Wonderin' on what she was thinkin'. I could only know what I was thinkin', and what I was thinkin' was, I wanted another one 'a them kisses she'd give me night before. I set my mind to get me one, but I was gonna need to plan out my attack 'fore any kissin' would take place, way she was starin'.

I didn't allow she was gonna oblige me this time. Do all the work it takes to make kissin', like she'd done for our first comin' together. I allowed she was feelin' it was my turn to take the risk. I come to realize, that if I wanted to feel her closeness again, and I did, I would needs take that risk, and fer me, it was a serious risk.

After thinkin' on how to do a kiss fer a short minute, I come to understand I'd never figure no good way to plan somethin' like that. It weren't no chore a body had to get done, it was somethin' your person just felt and did. I wanted to kiss her. Show her how I felt the same as she'd show'd me. I somehow know'd it was important for our movin' forward that she know that. I thought back to how she'd done it, and I did the same. Crazy part was, it weren't but a second after thinkin' it that we was lip locked in the sweetest tastin' kiss I'd ever had, 'course I'd only had one other, both from her, but oh, they tasted so sweet.

We broke apart after a long minute. I had to. My neck got to crampin' somethin' fierce. It weren't used to long time kissin'. Near knotted up on me 'fore I ever come to feel the pain what sides with crampin'. I had to stop my part 'a the kissin'. I never let her know our partin' was 'cause 'a my neck crampin'. I was wantin' to keep on with it, but I'd 'a started convulsin' if we had. Didn't seem I was gonna have to make any excuses fer stoppin', though. All worked out natural as could be, at least I thought it did, but her look weren't confirmin' my thinkin'. I got to feelin' uneasy.

She turned her face away from mine to stare the fire, after we draw'd apart. Never lookin' at me. I studied the side of her face for any sign she approved of what we'd just done, nothing. She had no emotion showin'. She weren't smilin'. She weren't frownin'. She didn't seem mad. No, nothin', just starin' into the flames like she was thinkin' deep. What had I done? I'd hurt her somehow. No, I allowed maybe I'd cut her air off and she was passin' out, but then she blinked her eyes. Her mouth was open. Had been since we'd stopped our kissin'. I figured with that she could breathe all right. All was normal lookin', so I just kind 'a settled back comfortable and watched. She finally turned her head toward me. That was a good sign. Her body was movin' proper.

I wanted to kiss her again, so I commenced my effort. Movin' my right hand to the left side of her face, I gently started pullin' her close. I got a shock when I done that. She jumped quick as a rattle maker. Near smothered me mouth to mouth after feelin' my fingers touch her. Without ever breakin' our lips apart, she jumped her backside from the blanket to my lap, while wrappin' her arms about my neck, settlin' square face on to me in my lap. Her chest tight to my chest. Her knees resting to the side of each of my hips. Still locked in a most amazing kiss. She squeezed my neck so hard I saw a bright light come on after a short time. I weren't gettin' no air. She must 'a felt my sufferin', 'cause she let off squeezin' 'fore I passed plumb out.

Her kiss was like that of a thirsty woman suckin' in good, cool water after bein' dry fer a time. I liked it all somethin' fierce. I never know'd kissin' could be done like she was doin' it to me. Oh, but oh my, was I enjoyin' her kind 'a kissin'. I couldn't wait to try it back on her later. My heart near stopped 'fore she got done, though. It took a lot 'a effort to kiss the way we'd just finished kissin'.

She leaned back a bit once we finished our comin' together. We never spoke fer a minute, just laid our foreheads against each other's and breathed in and out kind 'a hard. Her warm hands still locked around the back of my neck. I could not have been more at peace. This love thing was becomin' to me. Miriam was makin' it that way.

Our conversation continued, once we'd rested a bit. My heart full as I listened to her voice. It wouldn't 'a mattered what she talked about. Her words was pleasant to my ear. Our foreheads come apart after a time. She looked me in the eye while still sittin' my lap as she finally spoke. Her hands moved to the top of my shoulders.

"You are one who feels deeply your inner most thoughts, Buach. You feel deeply. I've just experienced it, same as I did the first night out on this trail. How do I feel to you now?" she asked back, while lookin' deep into my soul. "I know you have strong feelings. I have known this since first meeting you in the rain on your back porch. The way you feel with your spirit is one of the best parts of you. I have seen it. I have felt it. I am drawn to it." She brought her face closer to mine 'fore commencin' on to speak.

"Do not let what I am saying throw you, Boo. We are alike, you and me. The things we've spoken to each other, the things you've seen, these have come easy for me. Since first hearing your voice, you spirit has brought a comfort to me. Now hear me. Listen with your heart, warrior. Feel what my heart is saying… believe what you hear… my soul is being drawn to you like a flower to Old Man Sun. I do not think many like you have been made. You are special to all, but none more so than me. I see you in my dreams. You are becoming a part of me. The Creator has blessed you with who you have become, and who you will be. I have seen it. You are something difficult for one like me to explain. I can't wait to learn all there is to know about you. Thank you, Holy Spirit, for this man. I want him to be mine." I could not speak, after listenin' to her words. My soul had been touched.

Her eyes never left mine, as she draw'd me close for the most heartfelt kiss to date. It weren't like the others. This 'un had meaning. It was soft and feeling. A special comin' together after some serious words had been spoke. It was pulled from our innermost parts. Pulled with spiritual power.

I could feel the difference after that kiss. My heart had just realized something I feared might happen. I'd give in. Crossed over. True love had come to wrap me in her chains. I couldn't stop her visit, even if I'd 'a wanted to. It hit me like a tree limb swattin' you in the face when walkin' a trail behind somebody without trail savvy or respect. I could not believe it, but I know'd it true… I'd grow'd to love this woman from my insides out. Weren't a doubt in my bein'. I now had a love for her that was deeper than I'd ever felt for any other person I'd met in my life. I loved my family, but family love was different than attraction love. I could feel that for sure.

I felt I needed her life to be a part of mine, now, and I wanted it to be so for the rest of our time on Mother Earth. I prayed she wanted to be with me the same. That she would desire to be my wife one day, the mother of our children, if she said yes. I hoped she would. I believed she would, 'cause I felt Holy Spirit had guided our meetin'. I would honor Him in my love for her, if a marryin' day fer us ever come. She was a creature like none I'd ever met. I almost feared my feelings for her but didn't. I'd never felt real fear, outside the spirit world, that I know'd of, 'cept for God. I feared God in both worlds. Any wise man should, and I considered myself somewhat of a wise man. Time would tell as my life walked this newfound trail.

"Buach," Henri's voice outside my tent was soft as he woke me for my time of watch. Miriam and I had gone to our tents late in the night. I'd not got much sleep, but I come awake full as I answered his call.

"Henri, one minute," I responded in a whisper while slippin' on my knee-high footskins lacin' 'em up quick, then throwin' on my belt what held my long knife. Strapped on my special knife to the center of my back, then grabbed my Spencer and hat. The gun was fully loaded. I'd made ready for my watch 'fore beddin' down to sleep a bit. Had all my possibles laid out to grab in the dark. I was standin' outside the tent in front of him wide-awake in less than a minute. All my fightin' truck in its place. No matter I'd not got much sleep. I'd slept enough. A warrior's way is to overcome tired, when there was need to protect life and property. We had that need.

"Henri, how was your watch? Did you stay awake, my friend?" I finished with a humble grin.

"My watch held nothing worth wasting our time speaking over. Two bears scented our camp. Came in close. I near shot the smallest one for meat. Had our trail been longer, I believe we would have fresh bear tenderloin for our morning meal, if I could 'a picked up on the carbine's bead. It's dark out there. No shadows to show those that move. Little sense of light. I didn't see the bears 'til they was ten paces out. Never heard 'em, neither. It's spider quiet in the woods this night, Brother. Be careful. Watch close. There is a strangeness near."

We locked eyes after he said them last words. Callin' me by my whole first name had meaning to me. His words had a point to 'em. A warning of such. Maybe he felt more than just some passin' bears as his watch draw'd to an end.

"I will," I replied. "See you at daylight for some fry meat and coffee, good Lord willin'."

I turned to leave, trailin' them last words out as I headed east. Same direction Henri had gone to start his watch earlier in the night. The sling of my Spencer slung over my head, layin' a top my left shoulder, the rifle's butt settlin' just above my right hip. My knives laced into my braided mid-belt proper, as they should be. My special knife slung low in my back. Out 'a the way of my carbine, but perfect for quick drawin'.

With all my fightin' truck in place, I was a dangerous foe. I set my mind fer a fight, as I neared the place where I would start the second watch. I set my mind fer possible killin'. That got my spirit busy. It commenced to leadin' my thoughts as I found a place to start the late watch I'd demanded takin'.

The nighttime breeze was movin' in from the west as I moved silent through the woods. Havin' to feel every step close, so not to snap twigs and sticks, got my back up. That would help me with keepin' a sharp eye out for them with evil intentions what might come to call durin' the night. It would be best for them to stay their camp, leave us be, but I know'd sure as I was thinkin' on the wisdom in that thought for them, they'd not. I felt fer 'em. None needed to die this night. I said a short, silent prayer for their souls. It was the best I could do for the time.

I walked east fer a few slow minutes 'fore turnin' north maybe a hundred paces out from camp. The night breeze was comin' steady, cool. I found a little island of ivy not more'n twenty paces around that I crawled up into. It was a good place to start my watch. I could see the east side of our camp, what little to none I could see. Could watch it with my eyes and ears somewhat. I could not see the west side. I'd have to scent the folks movin' in from that side by trustin' the little breeze what was movin' toward me to carry that scent. I know'd these rogues' scent, too. I'd never forget the foul odor what got trapped in my nose from it. The smell of evil. There is a demon stench what covers folks like them. A stench that could only be scented by spirit folks like me, Henri, and Sky Watcher.

Henri had come in from the east after his watch time was done. His thinkin' was same as mine about protectin' the west side. I figured our trouble would come from the east, but it was hard to call. I know'd Indians to have better sense than to move on an enemy while slippin' in downwind. Movement like that let a body's scent reach a place before their person did. That give warning to folks lookin' out fer ye. That weren't smart.

Henri was sure right about one thing, it was hard to see out into the woods, from anywhere. A body could stand watch in the wide open and I don't believe he'd be seen, but that weren't my way. I tried to stay the cover when facin' danger. Didn't make no sense to me bein' out in the open unless it was fer purpose. I'd been bait fer catchin' outlaw Cherokee before, havin' to stay in the open fer purpose when Henri needed me to, but they weren't much threat 'a bein' killed when we done that before. A body on watch like I was would be killed if found out by the rogues on their way in. I had in mind to prevent that from happenin'. I had somebody to live for now. Somebody that would miss me if my killin' come. I didn't wanna hurt her, or be disrespectful to her again, by dyin'.

I'd changed watch places five times durin' the night, as the night breeze kept shiftin' to the south. I ended up on the north side 'a camp, watchin, scentin', same as I had when first startin' out on the east side. I'd not seen, heard, nor scented no nighttime creature of any kind. That was a bad sign. Critters know'd when bad weather was fixin' to hit 'em. They'd lay up in dry places out 'a the wind. Woods spots they know'd to go to when they sensed foul weather comin'. Not move much 'til it passed. Dependin' on how long it lasted, of course. They had to eat after a time, rain or no rain.

The nighttime breeze had shifted full on from the south. You could feel the warm in it. That told me what the critters was hidin' from. Warm air from the south meant rain, and it felt like it was gonna be a good 'un. I dreaded trailin' in it. I hoped it weren't gonna be a long, hard, constant, two-day kind 'a rain, but my bones was tellin' me it might be a good spring soaker. I dreaded it. Nighttime camp weren't comfortable when the rain fell of a night. One had to stay in the tents to keep dry, or as dry as one could. Seems you still got wet, even bein' in the tent. I figured it to move in around midday, slowly. Didn't seem to be a fast movin' rain. Them kind usually dropped some serious water. I prayed for the best.

It got even harder to see as the night grow'd long toward morning. Old Man Moon had went completely away 'bout halfway through my watch, leavin' me and mine in total darkness. No light, none, nowhere. Stayed that way 'til just 'fore daylight. It'd been a safe night. No rogues had come to call, at least none that I could see or hear or scent.

I stood to leave my watch, meanin' to head back toward camp. Old Man Sun was just crackin' a sharp, yellow edge over the outline of the big ridges to the east. I was gonna stand the few minutes that was left for seein' light to come. I should 'a stayed where I was squatted. The slightest snap of a dry twig sent me right back to my knees. My carbine unshouldered and firm in my hands ready fer firin'. I know'd that sound. Only a handful 'a bodies could a broke that precious little stick causin' it to make that certain kind 'a smothered crackin' noise. Bein' from the woods, I know'd the critter movin' out there in the dark was most likely human, and unless Sky or Henri had come out to call, I had company. I thanked Holy Spirit fer the warning.

THE LEGEND OF SWELL BRANCH

CHAPTER 24

TO FEEL DEATH CLOSE

I reckon anybody I ever know'd understood the sayin, "stuck between a rock and a hard place." Well, I was livin' it, pure and simple. I was in a bad way. The stick breakin' sound was close. Due east from me. Had to be close fer me to 'a heard it good as I did. I couldn't see to move none, weren't gonna risk slippin' toward it, but whoever it was out there couldn't risk movin', neither, after makin' such a careless noise. We was in a standoff, 'til one could see. If they was woods savvy, they'd stay right where they was after causin' a sound like that on such a quiet night. Not move no more 'til light come on to see a bit. That's what I aimed to do. Stay down right where I'd took a knee when first hearin' the breakin' noise. Listen for more sticks to break, while waitin' fer whatever it was broke the stick to move first, or daylight, then maybe I could find 'em.

I stayed kneeled, figurin' they hadn't seen me, and I'd not made a sound that could be heard by folks. Whoever it was couldn't know I was near. That give me confidence to check the air. I raised my head some. Scented the breeze that was now coming from the west. Caught the slightest smell of rogue stink just like I figured I would. That told me they was some 'a their bunch to the other side of our camp. I would needs wake Henri and Sky fer warning. If the rogues come in on 'em, and them asleep, I could do nothing, they'd be able to do nothing. Death would be on 'em. I needed to get their attention. I weren't gonna be shy in doin' it, neither. I just had to wait a minute more for enough light to see by. It wouldn't take much. A smidgen would do. It come faster than I sensed it would. I commenced my warning.

"Yeeeeeee-Haaaaawwwww," I let out at the top of my lungs, soon as I could see enough to move, runnin' quick toward camp with all the speed I could muster. Dodging trees much as I could see. "Yeeeeeee-Haaaaawwwww," I let out again on the run 'fore divin' in behind a big oak not twenty paces from where Miriam's tent was staked. I could see Henri leavin' his tent in a crouch. The carbine leadin' in front. I'd need to watch fer him. Not shoot him by mistake. He'd do likewise.

"Henri, Sky, they are here," I hollered in my normal voice. I wanted the rogues to hear as well. "West, south, and east. Sky, do you hear? Go to the stock. Shoot any that come near except me and Henri. Be careful. Be wise. We will find these varmints. Send 'em to their ancestors. Go, our horses must be kept."

"I hear, Boo, and I am going," I heard her whisperin' close in behind me. I turned to see her squatted not ten paces away, smiling 'cause she'd slipped up on me, again. "I will wait for you and Henri with the stock. You be careful. We have many things to talk about, when once these evil ones are gone. Worry none for me, warrior. I will be fine. Watch yourself. Do not be careless with your life. I want it."

I watched her leave for the makeshift corral we'd made some fifty yards away from our main camp to the north. It was in amongst a stand of huge oak trees. Them big trees was great for hidin' in. She'd be safe there 'til we went for her. I was sure 'a that.

I looked around to find Henri. He was crouched on one knee at the far edge of camp opposite me. He pointed two fingers out in front with his left hand, then headed due east. That told me he was gonna find any that he could in that direction. He left, bent from the waist. His carbine out front, tight in both hands. With him workin' east, I'd figure him to turn south 'fore too long. Thinkin' that, I made my mind to work east then north. If we had any luck at all, we'd only have to face one at a time. We was outnumbered, but I weren't gonna worry over that. I'd take 'em as they come.

Same as Henri, I slipped off east, bent from the waist to keep my person as a target low. My carbine in front held tight by both my hands. My thumb on the hammer. I stayed that way 'til I scented my first rogue. I had no idea which one was nearest me, but I could fer sure smell 'em. I took to followin' the foul scent, quiet as a snake huntin'. Watchin' close and scentin' hard. I moved slow and cautious 'til I finally seen his outline. Fortunately, I didn't think he'd seen me as yet. He was crouched watchin', squatted next to a good-sized oak. The breeze was in my favor, so I eased on in to get closer.

By chance, I recognized him. It was the lead warrior of the first two we'd seen earlier in the day. The one I'd near shot a couple times. It seemed he had no thought I was in the world. He was lookin' straight opposite from the direction I was comin' in on him from. That was a bad mistake on his part. I slipped to within a couple paces of where he was crouched from his watch, but then a chillin' cold thought come to me. Gettin' in that close to a warrior on watch had been too easy. That weren't right. Thinkin' that of a sudden caused me concern on the quick. That concern put me on edge. I suspected treachery. That concern fer treachery suddenly saved my life, cause without me realizin' he know'd I was there, he jumped straight up, spinnin' his whole person clockwise at me. The blade of his long knife followin' sharp edge first from around behind his shoulders, missin' my nose by no more'n an inch. Had my spirit not heard the warning, I'd 'a not made it past this warrior. He had me 'cause I was inexperienced, 'cept fer Holy Spirit lookin' out fer me, I'd a been gone.

God put me on edge when I needed to be on edge. That was spiritual intervention to my way 'a thinkin'. Saved my life, most likely, for sure saved me from serious hurt. Saved my hide many times while livin' out my trials on Mother Earth. All I had do was pay mind fer His voice. That give me comfort.

The shock on his face, to the knowledge that he'd failed to strike first, was my call to respond. After missin' me clean with his surprise attack, he was off balance. As he tried to come back on me with his long knife, he seen his reaction was gonna be too late. I'll never forget the look on his face just before the butt of my Spencer shattered the whole right side of his head from the ear forward. The walnut stock takin' out most of his teeth from the bottom right jaw sendin' the lower left jawbone through the meat parts on that side. It killed him I was sure, but he was aimin' to end me, so I considered it watchin' out fer my person.

I hadn't meant to hit him that hard, but concern for my life added to my strength when the fight come, it happened. Weren't good fer him that the butt stock of a Spencer Carbine is hard like steel. If he weren't dead, and he might not be, he'd never be the same as before he met me. I'd seen men hurt worse and live, but his head looked a lot different than it did when I first seen him. If by his fortune he weren't dead, he'd wanna be, after wakin' up with the pain he was gonna experience for many days.

It bothered me little that he was gonna feel terrible pain, or that he might be dead, now that I know'd the rogue bunch's true intentions. Him tryin' to kill me was testimony to their efforts. I let out a screech owl call. That was a signal me and Henri used to let one another know if danger come near. He'd know by hearin' it that the rogues had come to raid us. Most likely intended to steal Sky, then kill me and Henri fer our possibles, if they got the chance. They weren't none he met while goin' east gonna get that chance, now that their surprise had been busted. Neither was the one I seen slippin' in from the south, comin' straight toward me. He must 'a heard me take out his friend. Might 'a scented the blood. They was a right smart of it comin' from the oulaw's head. I figured he was trailin' to where I stood by that scent. I squatted and waited. I meant to have a word with this 'un. Let him know he had a choice. I spoke to him as he got close to where I was hid. He stopped dead in his tracks when I broke the silence of his world. He had a bow and a quiver of arrows. I would take those from him 'fore he got shed 'a me. I liked them things. Had a fair hand with 'em.

Old Man Sun had rose a bit more while my new friend had eased up the hill lookin' fer me. I could see this rogue more clearly. It was one of the big ones. Totin' full battle truck. I thought to go ahead and shoot him when I recognized him, but I didn't. I was hopin' he'd choose life.

It was for sure one of the back three that'd come on behind the first two. All three 'a them was big. Looked to be seasoned warriors as they went by on the trail earlier in the day. He was big. Might 'a been wise to 'a shot him when first seein' him, but I weren't the ambushin' kind, lessin' I was outnumbered and bein' hunted.

"Warrior," I said, kind 'a loud. I wanted him to hear me. "Why is it you and your friends stalk my camp? I know you fer what you are, but there is no need for you to die this mornin'. Be on your way. Take nothing you don't own personal, 'cept your friend here. I don't think he will be makin' it out on his own. Now come, I will let you pass, if you will leave us be. What say ye, friend? My carbine is center your chest and my time is growin' short concernin' you. Be gone with yourself, or I will see to your leavin' one-way or the other. You and your kind, you heathens, will never take from me again. I've had the last 'a bein' took from by outlaws such as yourself. Be gone, now. I grow tired of your stink. I want to shoot you."

"Pull your trigger, coward," the rogue answered me back. "I fear nothing from you. If you have to hide yourself behind a tree to confront me, then you are no warrior. My death will hold no honor, so don't speak to me as an equal. You hide behind the trees with your rifle like a scared woman. Yes, shoot me, boy, I do not fear death, but I see that you do by the way that you hide. If you do not fear the trueness of death, then come out from your hiding place. Face me like warriors do. I fear none. What say ye, foolish one? I am the warrior Gray Moon. I have never been beaten in a fight. Come to me, you who seem so brave, but leave your gun. Let us fight like warriors. I fear no man."

Leanin' my carbine against the oak, I dropped my possibles pouch beside its butt and stepped out straight away to answer his call. He needed to know I weren't scared none to confront him. I weren't fond 'a bein' called one of the fearful kind, or for sure a woman, so I would put him in his place fer namin' me that. Fightin' like warriors meant knives. I had no equal when knife fightin', even Henri believed this. He said the Creator had give me a talent fer handlin' knives. I know I liked 'em. My brothers had show'd me everything there was to know about usin' 'em for protection and killin'. Elder Cherokee warriors had taught them. I'd been taught everything they know'd, and I learned even more from Henri, who was the best I ever saw. I searched my soul for how I felt about this fight. I found no sympathy for this evil man. I would carry on as such.

We faced each other square, after I'd come from the trees. Some twenty paces or so between us. He held his long knife in his right hand, sharp edge up fer killin'. I filled my right hand with my long knife as well. Made mind as to how I wanted to work my left hand to reach my special knife when needed. I got that clear in my mind. That simple chore of figurin' could save my life.

His day was fixin' to get bad fer him, if he didn't back away. I'd been trained to know the ways of the best knife fighters what ever lived in the mountains, and I could perform 'em all. I felt a call to warn him. I know'd it wouldn't matter, he'd not listen, but it would make me honorable before my God. He's ag'n killin'. Got mad at me several times over my life fer it.

"Gray Moon is it, hey? I will remember this name when I tell my warrior friends of how I sent you to be with the ancestors this day. I am no coward, warrior, nor am I a woman. I fear no man. Never have. For sure coward outlaws. Don't believe I ever will. Leave this place, I tell you again, and never come back. If you do not, then your greed has ended your life. I have no equal with a knife, warrior. Consider this a warning if you push on. When you die after me tellin' you this, you can die with honor, and to answer your question before you go, no, warrior, I do not fear death. I welcome it. Now, tell me how it is to be, but be careful, it will mean your life, if you choose wrong."

The stare he gave me after I finished my words, did not hold a look of surrender by Gray Moon. It was more the opposite. I could see in his face we was fixin' to get tangled up. He was a big man. Most likely strong. I would use that to my advantage as he started his charge toward me.

Once I recognized him comin' and our fight startin', I dug in my toes to the soft forest floor pushin' off hard as I could to charge him back. Our bodies collidin' near square on. Both of us tryin' to rip the other apart. He missed in his effort to draw blood from me with his long knife. I did not. We stopped a few paces apart. I turned to him quick. My knife hand empty. He was facin' straight away from me after our comin' together. Standin' without movin', with this arms hangin' down to his sides. The long knife slipping from his right hand, fallin' to the ground. The point stickin' straight up beside his right foot. Slowly, and fer purpose, he commenced to turnin' toward me. Not too fast, no, fer my long knife was hinderin' his movement. I could see it was sunk hilt deep in his chest as he finished his turnin'. A small trickle of blood leakin' from the hole down his front. He would die soon. My blade had done its work. I had warned him, to be fair.

One of the more important things my brothers taught me was how to kill with a knife durin' a charge. Indians like to fight that way. Gray Moon did just as any other fighter does, they raise their front arm to try and block the body of the one chargin' at 'em, then work their stabbin' effort under their lead arm. With somebody like me, who knows how to defend against such a charge, that will make you dead right away. You see, once that front arm raises, the chest is open. A trained warrior will stab on contact first, then block with his front arm second. I had my long knife in his chest way before he ever made a move to stab me with his own blade. I felt his effort after our comin' together, it was weak at best. I simply pushed his stabbin' arm away with my front arm, which never moved from my body 'til after I'd set the blade of my long knife in his chest. It was kind 'a sad to see his look when he figured out what'd happened. I bid him farewell as I pulled my knife from his chest. The blood poured out when I opened up that hole. He sank to his knees. His head hangin' low. Arms limp to his sides.

"Warrior Gray Moon. You are to be with the ancestors soon. I will let you say your last prayer, if you can. I warned you to leave me be, but you did not listen. I spoke truth when I told you to leave this place, or I would end you. Now I will sit with you as you die, then see to killin' your friends. Know this before you go, the evil in your life has seen to your end. I will pray for your trip across the Great River."

He raised his head what he could, after I finished speakin' at him. Blood leakin' full from where my knife had been stuck. His raised his eyes to look at me. His arms still hangin' limp. His mouth moved to but a whisper. His final words was even evil.

"Name... warrior. Tell... me... name," he finished, while gaspin' hard for air. My long knife had prob'ly done some damage to his left lung, maybe both. I know'd his heart was cut. I'd felt that when the blade went in. I was kind 'a shocked he was still alive. The hate in his spirit was strong.

"Buach," I answered back. "Buach Whelan, from the Irish clans of old. I know the Cherokee. Lived with 'em a while. My family lived there, too. My brothers taught me knife fightin'. How do you think they did, Gray Moon, huh?"

"Whe-lan... I... curse you. . . Whe-lan. Your death... pain... ful... as is..." He never finished his cursin' me, but his last glance to my left, as his head sagged in death, saved my life.

No sooner had I seen that look did I hear the gentle whoosh of an arrow comin' fast. A last second move saved my life but did not save me from pain. The burnin' fire that shot out from my right side was proof to that. I'd been hit by the arrow under my right arm. The flint point showin' through my front just to the side of my chest. Oh, the pain was awful, but I forced it from my mind as the need to survive come to my thinkin'. I had to move, or whoever it was tryin' to kill me might get lucky.

I grabbed the arrowhead by its shaft in my left hand, then took off on a run for my carbine. Another whoosh went over the top of my right shoulder, only a few inches from the back of my head. I was fortunate that one didn't hit me square. It was close.

I made my carbine just in time, as I could hear the footfalls comin' hard, gettin' closer by the second. My carbine was just where I'd left it. I'd no sooner turned, shoulderin' my rifle with only my left arm, than the footfalls ceased. He... or she, since they was a woman with 'em, must 'a seen I had my rifle in hand and it was pointed at 'em. They would not be in such a big hurry to come on closer with me havin' it ready to fire. Holdin' the arrow while runnin' kept it from doin' any more damage to my person. The pain I was feelin' told me it'd done enough.

I stood behind the big oak where my carbine was leaned, peekin' out from both sides as best I could. It was hard to move with an arrow pierced through your side. Fortunately fer me, the flint had made its way on through my back and kind 'a out my side. It'd found no vitals on its pass through. A few inches left would 'a been a completly different ending.

I said a silent prayer as I watched my surroundings, thankin' Holy Spirit for lookin' out fer me. I could see no movement. Could hear no noise. It was creepy silent. I wanted to scream out to Henri, but I know'd not to. He was somewhere, and they was three outlaws left, unless he'd had some luck. It seemed best to stay quiet.

I was growin' weak for some reason. My mouth was gettin' dry. I hoped to see Henri or Sky soon, but I was startin' to think the arrow's point had done more hurt to my person than I was figurin' it had. Obviously, my hearin' was goin'. I'd not heard the rogue warrior as he slipped up close to me. I'd not remembered layin' down, neither, but there I lay, lookin' up at him helpless as a new baby, not able to move, other than breathin'. It was another one of the big ones. I believed death had found me. I felt done.

"Boo-ock," he looked at me and sneered. "I will remember your name same as you were to remember my brother's name. Gray Moon will be waiting on the other side for you. Your fight is not done, warrior. I will send you there now."

My heart sank as he raised his arm to end my life, and even though I was close to passin' out, I still sensed how it felt to feel death comin'. I'd often wondered what knowin' you was gonna die would feel like, now I know'd. He was fixin' to show me literal, too, as his arm started down to stab my heart. The ones I loved come to mind, as I felt him start his killin' move. Miriam first, then Mary. It all didn't seem real. Everything was happenin' in slow motion, and I was thinkin' of the things I could do to stop it, but I couldn't move to do any of it, but then, of a sudden, his killin' strike went away. I had no more worries 'cause he'd went away. He weren't standin' over me to kill no more. My life hadn't ended. The loud boom I'd heard, just as he disappeared, punched a hole through his center that broke his body in half, sendin' him face first to the ground. Blood and folk meat covered my front as he fell forward over my legs. His weight slammin' down on me, the last thing I remember 'fore total dark come to my eyes. I never know'd who saved me, 'til I woke next morning, thirsty as I'd ever been.

The Legend of Swell Branch

CHAPTER 25

A Cherokee Doctorin' Hospital

It was difficult to see, or think clear, when I first woke. I believed it to be pushin' midday, judgin' from how bright my world was around me. I wondered why I was still bedded down at such a late time of morning, and why I was so thirsty, then my thoughts went to why I was there at all. Them thoughts troubled me fierce.

As I lay there wakin', my mind clearin' a bit, I got to rememberin' parts and pieces of what'd happened recent, 'fore I woke where I was. Seemed we'd had trouble with some rogues. I'd got hurt, blacked out, now I was bein' looked after by strangers. I wanted to know what happened to me, to Henri, to Sky, and why was there a terrible hurt under my right arm? My head weren't right, neither. It pained me somethin' terrible, and that made me feel sick. I wondered what'd caused all the damage to my person. I was feelin' kind 'a like I'd woke late in the day after havin' too much 'a Dad's hard cider of a night previous. I felt bad, and I was weak. It was hard to breathe.

The inside of the skin covered long house I was wakin' in didn't come to mind as any place I'd ever been or seen before, but my mind weren't workin' proper, neither. The underneath of the oak board roof looked like the work of a hand I might recognize, but I know'd I couldn't trust my thinkin' full on 'til I'd rousted up a bit more. The scent in the air around me was bitter, kind 'a smoky. Strong to the eyes and nose. I figured it fer sage burnin'. That meant Indian healin'. Knowin' that made things even more curious.

They was folks about. I could hear 'em movin', inside and out. I wanted to know who, so I raised my head what I could, lookin' to my right, then over to my left. I was alone, 'cept fer all the other sick or hurt folk layin' in the long house with me. Must 'a been a dozen or more. Indian womenfolk tendin' to 'em. Looked to be room for a couple dozen more from all the cot lookin' beds what lay empty. It come to me where I was when I seen all that. I was in the Cherokee version of a hospital. A Cherokee doctorin' hospital they'd built years earlier to keep the sick and diseased away from the rest of the tribe. I'd heard they had one, but I'd never seen it. Bein' there meant somethin' bad had happened to me. I needed answers to the questions concernin' all I'd been through. First and most pressin', what'd happened to my friends?

The skin bed I'd been laid on was similar to an Army cot, but these beds was made by stretchin' deer and bear skins across a hickory frame. Surprisingly comfortable, really. Somebody had been sittin' with me. There was a couple cane backed chairs to the side of my bed. I figured whoever it was had answers to the questions I was askin' myself. I simply needed to get up and go find 'em. That didn't seem too hard, 'til I commenced to makin' the effort.

Slidin' my feet to the ground beside my bed, I pushed off the frame with my right arm meanin' to sit upright. That was a mistake, fer I couldn't stop the sittin' up part at the sittin' upright place, after I'd started with the effort of sittin' up. My person just kept on goin' to my left, rollin' me curled up right out in the walkway what passed by the end of my bed. It was the walkin' lane that separated my side of the long house from the other. It didn't hurt none, me rollin' out 'a bed, but I couldn't move well enough to get back in the bed. Therein lay the problem, 'cause fer some reason, I was bare bottom naked like the day I was born. My clothes was gone from my body complete. They weren't a stich 'a homespun 'er sewed skin coverin' my hide. I hadn't realized I was naked when tryin' to sit up, but I full on know'd it now, layin' there in front 'a folks.

Weren't 'til some young maiden caretakers come to help me that I was able to get back in my bed. I was embarrassed, but thankful fer 'em bein' there to help. I was weak, and they handled me, through their peeks and giggles, most gently and caringly. I appreciated that. The one what come a bit later, after they'd got me back in my bed and settled, who I could tell was in charge by the way she handled herself, weren't real happy with me. I could see it in her face. Feel it in my spirit. She hadn't liked me tryin' to get up, but she was still kind in her doin's toward me, even though I'd made her ill. It was a shock when it come to me who she must be. I allowed she'd know what happened to me better'n anybody. I would ask her, if she failed to tell me.

I'd never seen Blue Dove, but I'd heard enough about her from Henri to know I was lookin' at her. The skins she wore told me more. Her rank among the tribe was as high as any I'd ever been near, 'cept Henri. I could feel her presence, too. Like warm air. She brought peace. Her eyes most comforting when once she locked 'em on ye. There was a power in her touch. I felt it as she checked my forehead, eyes, shoulders, arms, and hands. She squeezed the back of my neck, then checked each finger, base to tip while holdin' my wrist firm. She spoke as she finished her once over of my person. I waited on every word.

"Buach, warrior, friend of my friend, Henri. I am Blue Dove. A healer for the Cherokee nation. Welcome to my home, or rather, where I spend most of my time. I regret you have come with such a burden, but by the grace of the Great Creator, you are still with us. Your battle has been a struggle with evil blood spirits. A poison, like none I've ever known, covered the arrow point you were shot with. It caused you to be without life but still live. Henri thought you dead when he brought you here, but you were not dead, only sleeping in spirit. You are thirsty. That comes from leaving your blood behind. Your body will make more, over time, but it will require several moons. You must give your healing what it requires, or you will suffer for not. Henri thinks it best if you stay here to heal. I think his mind is wise. Sky Watcher feels the same. The arrow made you bleed out heavy. It passed through, hitting no life parts on the inside, but

I believe it sliced a main blood run. That cut saved your life, Buach. It forced most of the poison out from your body when the blood left you. It is good fortune you were shot through and the arrow point did not stay inside. It is good fortune as well, that you were close to our Healing Lodge when your wound came. Henri and Sky Watcher brought you here during the night. It was almost too late for you, warrior. Had our lodge been any further away, you would not have lived long enough to have made it to us. I had trouble getting the blood to stop flowing, but you fought hard, so now you still live. You came near to crossing over, young Buach, but I am glad you are with us. I believe the Great Creator looks out for you. Later, when you have healed, I will tell you the things you said to me during your struggle. You will find your words interesting, as did I, but obviously, they were meant for another."

Turns out, the "Healing Lodge," as the Cherokee caretakers called it, was a day's ride or more south from Blue Dove's actual village. That put it a day or more closer to Swell Branch; less than a half-day to the main Cherokee Settlement on Tiny Creek. It weren't far from the North Trail, neither. Had we not been but a couple miles of where it lay when I got stuck, I'd a not made it. The poison would 'a got me. I thanked Holy Spirit for lookin' out fer me, again.

The lodge was built where it was 'cause of all the sickness and disease the settlers had brought to the Cherokee. Tendin' to their sick, dying, and hurt there, kept sickness away from their main living quarters. That helped keep any bad sickness from spreading. Kept the sick folk away from the tribe and kept the tribal folk away from the sick ones. Worked out good for the clan overall, and they was a bait of 'em what lived in and around Blue Dove's village.

Henri told me the elders built it where it was 'cause it weren't near no other homesteaded folk or Indians, and it had a good source of fresh water from a small creek what flowed close by. Blue Dove had made several improvements to the conditions of the house. Surprisingly, I come to find out, this great Cherokee healer, Blue Dove, had actually studied medicine with a travelin' missionary who was a trained doctor. She spent a season under his teachings. The tribe welcomed her to go and train with him after he'd offered to take her for a time, then bring her back. The elders understood that settler doctorin' had some good to it. Studyin' with the missionary give her knowledge of both worlds of medicine, but she didn't favor the "white man's doctorin'" in the end, choosin' her native healing over the missionary's ways. Always claimed the Cherokee way better, 'cause it healed with natural healing plants and their roots, give to the people by Mother Earth every spring. To the Cherokee mind, those plants was growin' out in the wild just for their intended purpose of healin' folks. I had no doubt there was truth to their thinkin'.

"Poison?" I asked back, after findin' enough voice to speak. "Paralyzed me? Couldn't move? Why? Henri, is he hurt? Sky? Where is she? Is she hurt? Either one 'a them passed on? Tell me won't you, how they are? Tell me what happened after I blacked out. I've recalled a good bit of what happened before the rogue warrior was shot, but I know nothing of what went on after. Help me to understand this poison. What has it done to me? I feel like two people in one. I can't focus. I try to get up and I fall, as you saw, I'm sure, and… why do I have no clothes coverin' my person? I would like to have my homespun and skins back if I could. Oh, I feel bad."

"Calm yourself, warrior. I am here with you. I will answer your questions. Your friends, who have been sitting with you for the time you have been here, are resting. Sky Watcher will be sad she was not here when you woke. She has rarely left your side for three days. She had to sleep today, and she wanted to bathe. I told them I would watch you for a time.

The poison is not known to me," Blue Dove kept on. "I have never known this mix. Its scent is strange. Henri caught one of the rogues, a woman, she will tell me what I need to know. Then I can tell you what has made you weak. I do know it stopped your movement. You could move little when you first got here. Only to breathe, and that was a struggle. As I believe it, the bleeding you had probably saved your life. The blood flow washed out a lot of the poison the arrow's point had left as it passed through you. Had the point stayed in your person and not passed through, much more of the poison would have made it to your heart. You would have stopped being able to breathe. Your heart would have quit. You would be gone across the river to feast with the ancestors instead of laying here hurting with me. I am sorry, warrior, that you suffer.

The reason you find yourself bare is because your clothes had gotten soiled as you laid here in your torment. The maidens that helped you back into bed have washed them, and yourself, just this morning. You have not been bare except for the last little while. You can dress when you find the strength.

Now, you are most likely curious as to what has become of the trail bandits. That is something I am not fully certain of but have learned a bit by listening to Henri and Sky talk about it. Tell me what you know. I will share what I know once I hear what you remember. Take your time, warrior. We have nowhere to be."

Three days? I'd been layin' where I was for three days. That was some mighty dangerous poison them rogues had shot me with. If they was still alive, I'd settle with 'em soon as I could, but as I was rememberin' what all I did, I believed most settlin' had been done. I commenced to tellin' her what I know'd. She listened. "I remember two rogues I fought with."

"Both of those are across the Great River," she replied kind 'a quick. "I know this for truth."

"Another was standin' over me, fixin' to end my life, when of a sudden he was shot dead. He landed on me. I never know'd who shot him, but I was sure proud they did."

"I know who shot him," Blue Dove declared to me. "If I tell you, I need your word you won't admit to Sky Watcher the knowledge came from me, but I think it important you know, and I don't think Henri will tell you. It was Sky Watcher. Her spirit told her to disobey your order to go watch the stock. She checked on them, yes, but finding all okay, she returned to help you and Henri. She understood that you sent her to guard the stock to remove her from danger. She respects that, but she is Mohawk, and she was raised Indian. She is a fighter, same as I understand you are. She only just found you as the rogue was ready to kill. She is a good shot. Saved your life. If you think on these things, you will see many different ways your life was saved these last few days. You will need to thank the Great Spirit for His care. He must have a purpose for your life. Live it with His guidance."

I was shocked when I heard her say, "thank the Great Spirit for His care." She was referrin' to the one true God Christians believe in by sayin' that. The Christian God, not the Cherokee gods or Mother Earth. It was interesting that she spoke that way. I would learn later why. The Three in One is most powerful.

"I promise to you, Blue Dove, never will I say a word of this to Miriam. Thank you for trusting me," I barely spoke, even though I was tryin' hard to speak. The words just wouldn't come from my mouth like I meant fer 'em to.

"You will heal, Buach. I want you to know I did little. I stopped the blood from leaving your body, but your life is your own. I had no medicines to kill the poison you took in. It is your strength, your spirit, that caused you to survive. I only prayed, as did many here in this house. I will see you soon. Your friends come."

She got up and left straight away, after alertin' me to Henri and Sky comin' to visit. I raised my head what I could, again, lookin' left and right but saw neither. Blue Dove was gone as well. My, but she could slip around fast. Weren't but a few minutes later they did come. How Blue Dove know'd that is one of the wonders I always had about her and Henri and their kind. They just know'd things. Know'd 'em 'fore they ever happened, too. I never had that gift.

Miriam was the first to sit. She pulled the straight-backed chair up as close to where I lay as she could. I could smell her scent. She'd washed recent. Oh, I loved her scent. I can only describe it as bein' near to sweet bread bakin'. Yeah, that's close, and when she come near, I wanted to just eat her up. I got to wantin' one 'a her kisses after a minute, but I figured I weren't real kissable at the present. My mouth and face weren't workin' right. The poison still beatin' on me some.

She couldn't talk after sittin'. I could sense that. They was tears come to her eyes as she looked at me. Her face held hard worry. Them signs told me I'd concerned her a sight with my bein' near death a couple days prior. I said a short prayer 'a thanks for my survivin' what must 'a been something awful, accordin' to the way she looked at me when first gettin' there to visit. Like she was surprised I was still livin'. I commenced our conversation to oblige her, knowin' she was strugglin'. I had to speak low and slow I felt so bad.

"Miriam Sky Watcher, you are here," I said slowly, almost in a whisper. "Thank you for being here. It makes me feel better seeing your face. How are you, how is Henri... how am I? Tell me true. I trust you for the truth." She wiped her eyes 'fore she answered me.

"I am good, Boo. Henri is good... but you have not been good," she said, shakin' her head as the tears come back to her eyes. I felt for her. I reached for her hand. I was able to take hold. She gripped back and smiled when I did that. She kept on answerin' me.

"You have nearly died many times over the last few days, Buach! It's been most difficult to watch you suffer through all the convulsing your body has been doing. Blue Dove says it's from your muscles fighting with the poison you were shot with. Henri thinks he knows what the arrow was dipped in, but that doesn't matter to me. You're alive, that's what matters to me. Blue Dove disagrees with him. She believes it comes from somewhere else far away. She believes it to be a white man's poison, uncommon to the mountains where we are. Like I said, I only care that you beat it. You are a strong man, warrior."

That's right! We had confessed strong feelings toward one another. Rememberin' that give me strength I'd not had just minutes earlier. I sat straight upright no problem. Looked her shocked face eye to eye. My words still hard to speak, but I said 'em to her true. She wiped more tears away as I commenced speakin'.

"Oh, Sky Watcher," usin' her Indian name to show her I was good with all she was. "Those are words that lift my spirit from this muck I'm bein' struck to. You have touched me deep by helpin' me remember on this day how special you are to me," I muttered, as I fell back into my bed. I couldn't sit up no longer. My strength was gone.

Love is strong, there is truth in that, but that poison I'd took was stronger, against my body, anyhow. It was hard on my person. Her words had power when I first heard 'em, but the poison killed any comfort or strength she'd brought to me. I come near to passin' out 'fore ever finishin' what I wanted to say to her. Blue Dove weren't leadin' me wrong when she said it'd be a while with my healin'. I understood to be good with that.

The Legend of Swell Branch

CHAPTER 26

We Leave for Home, fer a Time

Two days after first wakin' in the Healing Lodge, I was mostly back on my feet. I weren't near strong enough to do much, bein' low on blood, and weak like I was, but I could get around a bit. Sit and talk with folks. Visit here and there with healin' ones and their visitors. We'd sit around the outside of the skin lodge. They weren't no big trees fer fifty paces or more in any direction on the outside. The healers know'd Old Man Sun was good fer folks. Blue Dove said the direct heat on my person was good fer helpin' me make new blood. The walkin' about was good fer me, too. I could feel that. Sky helped me get around when I got weak from walkin'. I got weak a right smart, too, seein' how it caused her to come in close to hold me up. Them was nice times.

She helped me wash. That didn't feel as strange as I thought it would when first realizin' I needed help. I hoped, after seein' me in the full raw, that she felt me as handsome as I felt her beautiful, without our clothes on. That would be important as our love moved on down the trail of life. I caught her stealin' looks at me more'n once or twice. I took that as a sign she liked what she saw. I know I did, when lookin' at her after she'd shed them wet clothes on my back porch that afternoon we'd first met.

All I was experiencin' helped with my healin', but the best happenin' what helped me was, I got to do it all with Miriam Sky

Watcher. The whole of it. She was with me durin' all my time at the Healin' Lodge. That was a gift from Holy Spirit, way I seen it. After a few days with her bein' so near, I kind 'a started thinkin' it was a good thing I'd got shot with that poisoned arrow, 'cept for the near dyin' part. Give me and Sky some quality days together while takin' my healin' out to the woods for some adventurin'. The fresh air and movement helped me. We had times that could fill most folks' life span in just the season we was there. Small notions to us both of the times we had to come. I was longin' to make her my wife. I wanted to know her complete. Our marryin' day was gonna be somethin' special. Spiritual for sure.

    She stayed with me everywhere I went for the whole four moons or more we ended up camped at the Healin' Lodge. Our tents was right next to each other's so she could "watch out for him during the night while he heals," as she claimed. The Cherokee wanted her to stay with the maidens, bein' she had no man, but they felt it might be all right 'cause we was white. They seen it as our way.

    Camping close, we got to share one campfire durin' our whole stay. Fix and eat our evening meals together every night. Woke each morning to share hot coffee and conversation. Eatin' with her at the fire was most enjoyable. That was a good thing, 'cause we spent almost all our wakin' time together. I had no issues with none 'a what we was doin'. I enjoyed it all. Truth was, bein' happy like she made me helped with my healin'. She was good fer me.

    I'd come to love her. I wanted her close. She give me strength. Sided me near perfect. Love is a strong medicine when it comes to healin', and her's was the best. 'Sides, Henri was spendin' all his time with Blue Dove. I hardly saw him the whole time we was there. I'd not blame him fer that, 'cause I weren't missin' him 'er nothin'. I was enjoyin' my time with Sky. I would 'a done the same thing he was doin', circumstances bein' what they was, them bein' who they was, natural.

    He was there to visit so they could learn from one another. What else would he be doin', but spendin' time with her? Weren't no tellin' what'n all spiritual doin's they was in to, knowin' Henri like I did. I looked forward to hearin' what bits Henri would feel like sharin', when finally he would talk about what'n all they'd done. Could make for some good conversation on the trail home, but that would be up to him. Blue Dove was not someone I'd breech conversation with Henri about. He'd tell me what he wanted me to know, when he wanted me to know it, concernin' her.

Our time to return home had come. I was near healed. Henri had spent the time he'd needed with Blue Dove. Our trail was due. Leaving Blue Dove was hard on my friend. He said nothin' in words 'til we was way on down the main road headin' back home. Henri made no complaints about us going home on the main road instead of travelin' the North Trail. I thought he would, but he never did. Didn't seem he cared when I told him we should go that way, neither. He just loaded up and went on.

Sky and me jibber jabbered some about nothin' serious as we headed south. Just talked to ease the burden we all felt. Me and Sky fer Henri. Henri from his longing for Blue Dove. They'd got close whilst we stayed there. I could sense it pained him to be apart from her, that was obvious.

I felt fer him, same as Sky, but what can friends do when one's heart is broken? Ain't but one person could make it right fer Henri, and we was walkin' straight away from her. For Henri, the pain prob'ly felt like the separation death causes after losin' a loved one. I could understand that.

Our camp that first night was on the bank of a small, still flowin' creek. Sky made a gig from a maple saplin' grow'd perfect for the task. She cut the big end off near the ground, leavin' it a bit longer than I was tall to the little end. She cut off all the limbs, leavin' two small ones on either side of the small end. She cut those short, then sharpened their tips a certain way. Didn't take her but a little while and she'd snagged four eatin' size brookies for supper. We cooked 'em on a spit over a hot bed 'a coals. Seasoned 'em with some salt and dried pepper the Indians had give us for our return trip. We'd built us some stores for our trail back durin' our stay, but the Cherokee are a generous bunch. The ones we'd come to know gifted us plenty 'fore we left. It was just their way.

I had no issues takin' their gifts. They was a generous bunch. They wanted to help folks. It was a blessing to 'em, and no obligation was expected for acceptin'. One gift was a full rump bear shank. Seasoned, smoked, and ready to eat. What fool wouldn't take that? It was good, too. Gus didn't like the roasted meat smell bein' strapped up on top of the truck he was totin', but we sure enjoyed it. Mostly ate it for our midday meal. That way we'd not have to stop and make a fire to cook dinner, we just cut off a few chunks to eat cold whenever we stopped to water, then went on our way. That saved us a lot 'a time on our return trip. We had concern from bein' away so long. I felt a need to be home.

"My friend, you're mighty quiet fer your typical self this evenin'. Maybe you are tired," I said to Henri in an askin' kind 'a way, as we sat havin' a pipe by our campfire after supper. Sky had gone to her tent to bed down not long after we'd eat. The long ride of the day had made her weary.

"I will leave you be, if you need some time, but Henri, know that your mind needs to be here with us. You will have watch tonight same as me. I'll give you your druthers, I'll take the other. If you can't pull the one, I'll do both. It's your call. So you'll know, Sky is worried fer ye. You might needs talk to her. Let her know you're all right. I can feel your spirit is lonely, Brother. Mine would be, too. Tell me, so I can pray for you."

"Boo, dear friend, I will tell you why I am quiet. Yes, I am tired, as we all are, but that is not my affliction. Blue Dove and I spent many hours together these last few moons. We taught each other about how we each see this world. I came to understand from her, that my place in the tribe needs to be more important to me. She brought me to see that my spiritual responsibilities to the elders is being put aside for want. That my talents are more important to the tribe's overall well-being and eventual survival than I would let myself believe. She opened my mind to this, but I opened her's as well. Love one another as we may, Buach, we both know we can never be one. Our duties will prevent our finding true happiness together here on Mother Earth. Yes, my friend, my spirit is lonely, and hurt. I love this woman, but I can never have her as my companion because of who we are. There lays my sadness. I feel my life's will needs to change, yes, but my heart will long only for her, constant. Please friend, I welcome a prayer from you to your God. I hurt deeply, Buach, but as a loyal warrior and friend, I am here. I will take my watch. My spirit will keep me strong as a warrior."

He chose first watch. That was good. I took the later. Nothing happened on either of our watches. Fact was, nothing happened durin' any of our first two nights' watches. It weren't 'til our third night's camp, did we get to feelin' any concern.

A full-time trader, complete with a full team 'a mules, six in all, and a covered wagon fer haulin' trade goods, similar to what Gideon had used but much bigger, come callin' durin' the evening to share our supper fire. He was taking the main road east, makin' a run to Atlanta for tradin' stock. He had two Cherokee warriors with him that was obviously his guards. They both packed full battle truck. Guns and knives and such, but none more noticeable than the lever action .44 caliber Henry rifles they had slung over their shoulders. I'd seen that kind 'a gun before. A minority of Federal soldiers carried 'em in the war. I wanted one 'a them to partner my Spencers. I would look to trade with one of the Cherokee, if I got the chance.

He'd brought news, this trader, only he didn't know it as news, but it come to us as news. Simple conversation to him, really. Just repeatin' the goin' on's of his trail life.

We all just sat the fire havin' an after-supper smoke, while he made conversation about his recent journeys. His guards nowhere in sight. He talked about how far north he'd traded, who'n all he'd been tradin' with, where he was headed, what he'd seen. He allowed he'd been meetin' mostly Northerners along the trail, eager to trade as they made their way south. He'd met several families of settlers lookin' for trade at a few different stops. He'd spent a night's camp with a bait 'a free colored folk headin' north. They somehow had gold coin to trade with. Sat and tried to talk trade with some German folk what just arrived to their new home in "A-mur-i-ka," as they said. It was near the only English word any of 'em know'd, 'cept fer George Washington. Still, he managed to work a few trades fer some Indian pipes and blankets.

The worst ones he'd run into was rogues, and freed slaves what'd turned rogue. Some of the slaves had gone ahead and took their freedom without it yet bein' legal. They was mostly bad folk. Most slaves waited out the legal means that freed 'em all without question. Folks of all kinds 'a backgrounds would come to the trail to trade from all different places. Weren't no figurin' the rogues. Mean, with a grudge, lookin' to take as debt, most of 'em.

Come to find out, he'd been tradin' on the North Trail for over a year. Had mostly good times, but he'd had some bad spells as well. The worst was only two days prior from a pack 'a outlaws come down from the North. Outlaws led by an ex-Federal soldier named Viktor. The trader said he was a funny talkin' man who claimed to be from across the great water to the east. Went by the given name of Soltor. Fought for the Union. His words made us take notice.

The trader had watched him kill a man with his bare hands in a fair fight for justice a few weeks before they come on him, only problem was, it was the dead man's justice what was bein' sought after. Viktor and his bunch had robbed and killed the man's folks somewhere up North. Later on, Viktor and his gang tried to take from the trader late one evening while he was makin' camp, but the Cherokee guards stopped that foolishness. They was warriors. Viktor's men weren't no match for their warrior skills. They killed a couple of the outlaws. Got the trader and his truck clear from the evil ones' efforts to steal it all. They said ol' Victor got plumb agitated about them breakin' up their thievin' by killin' his men, but him and the rest 'a his bunch rode off and left their dead just the same. 'Course, not without cleanin' their pockets of whatever gold or valuables they had when killed, then helpin' themselves to their personals. That's just the way it was, when livin' a life with outlaws.

Viktor Soltor. We not only took notice, but we all sat upright after hearin' that name. Viktor Soltor had been seen on the North Trail recent. This knowledge brought a whole new direction fer us. Justice for Gideon was suddenly within reach. I know'd Sky would think 'a nothin' else, now that she know'd the killer of her father was near. After hearin' that Victor had been seen, Henri questioned our visitor as he was makin' his way to leave our camp shortly after dark. He'd only stopped to share our fire to heat his food. He'd make camp somewhere else with his guard, where he could protect his wagon and tradin' truck from nighttime bandits. Stoppin' in to share an evening fire was a common practice among trail travelers. Folks accommodated one another. Bein' on trail was work enough. Sharin' a fire saved a lot 'a effort of a evening, when you're most tired from trail travel.

"Viktor Soltor?" Henri said as a question. "You are sure the man who tried to rob you was called by this name? We know this name. Tell us where you saw him last. We are curious to go and ask him about a friend of ours. Father to this woman here," Henri finished, pointing at Miriam.

As I looked to Sky, my heart knotted. Her eyes held tears. The murderer's name had touched her deep.

"I am sure, my friend," returned the trader in answer to Henri's question. He climbed into the seat of his wagon, makin' to depart 'fore sayin' any more. His guards was with him.

"He and his kind near had me, but my warrior friends came to my rescue. I will never forget that name. If ever I see him again, I will not be so kind as to simply leave with my truck and get safe - no, I will engage him for attempting to steal my belongings. People along this trade route depend on me to bring them good, quality items. I put forth my own money to purchase these trade goods. I intend to keep them in my possession, at the highest cost, if necessary. My warrior friends have proven that several times, unfortunately. As to where you can find this man, go back to the North Trail. Travel a few miles north. You will encounter a traveling trading post staying there for the season. Along with it travels a tent tavern. There you will find this Viktor and his men.

He left with a slap of leather reins to his mules' rumps. His warriors leavin' his side for the woods. He had three now. I'd only seen the two before. Made me wonder how many more he had out and about, hidin' and watchin'.

He was an important man among those what lived in the mountains, includin' the Indians. His wagon held treasures most common folk wouldn't recognize as treasures. Simple tools for cookin' over a fire could change the lives of new come settlers raisin' a family in the backwoods of the mountain wilderness, or black powder fer their old flintlock huntin' rifles. That produced meat. Folks would camp fer days beside the North Trail after learnin' the trader man was comin', just so they could get a few simple things that would make life better for them and theirs. Cloth and sewin' truck was one of the most treasured wants from the trader man. Many what lived in the mountains never got to make trips to market in Atlanta or other towns. Them folks just couldn't go or chose not to for whatever reason. Had to make everything they had. These traders held their only connection to outside merchandise. What few goods they could get was most appreciated.

It was always a pleasure when trustworthy tradin' folk come 'round. Most I ever met was good, dependable, business folk who worked hard for their pay, but they was some that weren't so straight. Outlaws like Viktor caused all them that depended on the traders to suffer when they stole the trader's goods. Fortunately for us all, the traders come to realize they needed protection to continue their tradin' business. Not all protected themselves with Indians, but they all had protection. Couldn't survive without it.

"Buach," Miriam said, kind 'a soft like, lookin' me in the eye from across the fire. Her stare cold. Her face without expression.

Henri had gone to his tent to sleep some 'fore he took first watch. I sensed his heart was troubled over Gideon's killer bein' near. That, mixed with missin' Blue Dove, made him need some time with his thoughts, his spirit. I respected that. It is the way.

"Is there time to go and find this man, Victor Soltor?" she continued, after a short minute. Her cold stare not changin'. "I would like to find him if there is, but I know you are worried about the winter stores. We must eat, I understand this, but what is, will be now, right? If all is good now, then all will be good later. If all is bad now, all will be bad later. Us being there will not change that this close to harvest. Buach, I've not told anyone this. My spirit bid me to keep quiet, but Gideon screams out to me in visions when I sleep. His soul seems lost on this side because the murderer Viktor Soltor walks Mother Earth and he does not. He went before he felt it was his time. Tell me we can go and speak with this man, Buach. Tell me we can go and help send this evil servant of the devil down to meet his god. I want to see him hang for killing my father. Why has Great Spirit allowed this evil to come south? The reasons could be many, but he has delivered him into our hands, we should deliver him to justice."

"Gideon know'd the risk of bein' a trader man, Miriam. Know'd evil thievin' folk tended to look out fer his kind. His courage rooted deep, keepin' to his trade the way he did. Knowin' it could be most dangerous to his person. I respect the fact that he understood settlers depended on him in ways only he could deliver. He was the kind to not wanna let 'em down. That's who he was, an important man to many. A friend to me and mine. As I live, I believe his blood would be on our hands if we did not pay a call to this murderer. See to his killin' of our friend and father. This one who talks funny from across the great waters. Yes, Sky Watcher, Gideon will have his justice. He will get his freedom. We do have time to go north. We do have time to see to this. Our stores are fine. I trust Henri. He has said his bunch will tend to our winter food, so I have no concern they won't. When Old Man Sun comes in the morning, we will be ready to leave. We must tell Henri of this new trail. He will needs make his own mind as it seems he has taken on responsibilities to the tribe that before he ignored, but I believe he will want… no, need to go. He know'd Gideon as a friend, too. When I wake him for his watch, I will explain our minds fer turnin' north. He will agree. Makin' things right for a friend holds meaning to our kind. It seems true for you, too, Miriam. Your heart is pure."

"Well said, warrior." Henri's voice got louder as he walked from his tent back to the fire, totin' full battle truck, carbine included, ready to take his watch. "I will be packed and ready at daylight to take this new trail. Gideon was my friend," he said, while turnin' to look at Sky. "Viktor Soltor will no longer walk this rock, when once our talk with him is done. Tell Gideon this when next he visits you, then he will know to leave you be. Yes, Sky Watcher, you are correct in seeing he is stuck. I have felt this as well. Soon, we will set him free. I leave for my watch now. I will see you soon for yours, Boo. Look for me to the east."

With all that said, he left camp quiet and swift as a mountain cat on the hunt. I would relieve him in a few hours. We would talk more then. Me and Sky both just kind 'a sat there, starin' into the fire after he'd gone. His words confirmin' how we all felt. Gideon's soul was longing for Viktor Soltor to be settled with. Knowin' Henri held favor with our trail's purpose, and all he now represented with the tribe, Viktor Soltor would be seen to. No doubt in my mind over that.

The Legend of Swell Branch

CHAPTER 27

THE NORTH TRAIL TAVERN

Daylight was slow comin' fer me. I'd had to sit my watch knowin' nothin' was gonna be stirrin' or threatenin'. We was travelin' this new trail north over dark nights. Old Man Moon had gone for more light a couple nights back, which was of a benefit fer us. Bein' they weren't no light to see by limited nighttime raidin' by outlaws. Their kind would hit ye on a dark night, if they know'd where you'd made camp, and they was of a purpose, but we'd kept a close eye out for travelers of any kind, and we'd seen nothin' to worry over. We seemed to be alone in our travels for the time.

"Buach, it is Miriam," the voice but a whisper. Close enough that I should 'a heard her movin' 'fore she spoke, 'cept I was near asleep.

"I am here," I answered with a louder whisper from the big white oak I was sittin' leaned back on. I felt safe conversin', if even usin' normal voices, but that would be careless, considerin'. I moved over to where she was squatted in the dark, settlin' on one knee directly facin' her. Oh, but she was beautiful in what little light they was.

"I am come to tell you that Henri is ready to go. He has packed your things and readied our horses, even though there is no light from Old Man Sun. He is acting different than I've ever known him to be. It may be common to you for him not to speak, but I know little of his real person. It seems terribly rude, or terribly troubling,

I can't decide which. That is why I have come to fetch you. I do not know what to say to him."

"Ah, Miriam, yes. That would seem strange to you wouldn't it? I believe from what you say that his spirit may have taken over his person. Might be that way fer a time. To be clear, his mind is wanderin' the spirit world, while his body does what it needs done here. Most times he comes from this world without hurt, sometimes not. It may take a while to know. We will wait to see. It's okay, though, he goes there from time to time, for sure when facin' something like we aim to see done. Don't think it personal ag'n you, nor consider it disrespect from him, he treats me the same way when the call comes fer him. He can't help it. His spirit takes him over. It comes to figure it's best to visit whenever it senses Henri needs direction in his walk… or at least that's how he explains it to me.

He may not speak to us for a time, but he'll do what we tell him, dependin'. We are close in our souls, him and me. His spirit trusts me. I have been with him many times as his whole being has become a tool of spiritual workin'. It can get plumb scary if you fear it. I ain't had to ever fear it. I fear little from where his spirit goes. I know the place. Henri tells me what it means, when he feels it best I know. It's his world, Miriam, not mine. I don't understand it all. He don't tell me all. That makes me cautious when he comes back.

Enough said over that, I reckon," I kept on after a minute of quiet thinkin' between us. "Henri is just Henri, strange as that is. I'll go talk to him. You should be there as well. Hear what it sounds like if he speaks from where his mind has gone. Only way you'll know what it is if ever you hear it and I'm not around. Don't fear the voice, Sky, if you can help it. That will help get his spirit to welcome you. It senses fear, his spirit, believe it or not, if fear is near. That tells it something ain't right, so don't feel fear. You can do this, Mohawk."

We both smiled after I said that. I turned to lead us back to camp. She followed, walkin' so quiet I never heard her foot set down once. Walked as quiet as smoke floatin'. I'd never met a body so easy footed.

Yep, he was gone. His mind was travelin'. Noticed it right off when walkin' into camp. He was standin' with his back to the fire warmin', watchin' me as I come in from the east. His arms crossed in back. His eyes far away. His spirit makin' whisper words. He weren't sayin' nothin' a body could understand, barely could hear him, if at all, but his lips was movin' constant from a soft whisper. Words was bein' said, but he was talkin' to somebody else, or something else, somewhere else. I walked right up to his face. Stared him eye to eye so he'd know it was me, then turned and pointed to his horse, tellin' him to mount and lead us north. With the smoothness of a mountain cat, once it come to him what I was sayin', his backside found saddle leather and he commenced to walkin' his mare up the North Trail whisperin' right along. Never sayin' a word common folk would understand, if they could 'a heard it any at all, but whisperin' all the same.

    Miriam's mare fell in behind Henri and the lead mare. She had Gus' lead tied to the back of her saddle. She give me a curious look as the trail took her away followin' Henri. I brought up the rear, tendin' to our back trail same as we'd been travelin' the whole rest of our journey, only this time we was all quiet out 'a respect for where Henri had gone.

    Our words was few as we rode, 'til way up in the morning. That's when Henri got to whisperin' a little louder, and then a little louder, and then a little louder, progressin' as we kept movin'. Workin' his way up to a full, normal voice after about an hour of it – speakin' in spirit the whole time. Couldn't understand a word. At least Sky got to hear how it sounded.

    It was spooky when you first heard it. Sounded like a cross between a boar hog gruntin' and an old woman strugglin' to talk from lack 'a air. Near scary at times, but that voice meant his mind was comin' out from the spirit world. His normal voice would be speakin' within a short time, if things went as they did usual. He let us know his thoughts as we stopped for a break mid-morning. We all needed rest. He needed to talk. His look was no longer far away, fer he laid eyes on me hard as he walked by, headin' for the woods. I figured to answer nature's call. Sky had a small fire ready 'fore he ever come back. Could be he took some time to pray, as well.

We all sat fer a smoke after we'd finished supper. It was a while 'fore anybody spoke. Me and Sky shared my quilt. I'd folded it up short, that way she'd have to sit in close to me. She liked I'd done that. I seen her smilin' as she moved to sit with me. She laid the inside of her forearm over the inside of my thigh as we settled cross-legged next to the fire. Henri looked at us kind 'a strange fer a second, then smiled as he must 'a remembered we was courtin', so to speak.

It seemed his mind was back. I was proud 'a that. I wanted to hear his common words so I could understand his thoughts correctly. A clear mind was needed when Henri got to talkin' about things he'd come to know in the spirit world. It give a body chills sometimes with the things he'd tell ya. Sky was feelin' it, too. Her eyes was huge. She seemed most curious as Henri commenced talkin'.

"As you have seen, I was in the 'other place' for a time." That's what Henri called where his mind went when it trailed thru the spirit world. "I met with the ancestors. Shared a pipe of some sweet, air-dried tobacco while we talked. They showed me all that had gone on before us. The reasons for the troubles that have come to our home. The things that Viktor Soltor and his gang have done, and will do, if not stopped. I saw the people he has hurt, those he's took from, and the ones they have killed. It was made known to me… that the children…" he lowered his head to finish his words, "that the children weren't always spared on their raids."

He said that last part through gritted teeth. He kept his head hung fer a short minute. I could feel his anger. His voice was back to normal as he raised up to finish tellin' us what'd happened on his visit with the ancestors. I felt for my friend. Hurtin' little ones touched him deep.

"Francis was there among the ancestors, Boo, but Sky Watcher, I have come to know your visions are true. I did not see Gideon. I am sorry. He has not crossed over. He still sits with the Peace Child. He prays for you. Many on the other side are angry that his soul cannot be with them. Because of this, they have brought us the murderer Viktor Soltor. He is close. In two camps, we will cross trails with him not long after Old Man Sun shows full in the east. We are to bring him and his to justice. The old ones believe this should have been done moons ago, as I know we all agree. Your father's time for vengeance draws near, Sky Watcher. We will hang this man Soltor for killing him, then Gideon's soul will find peace. I have seen this. It will be done. There is no getting by that. They are a mean lot, these outlaws. We needs move on them with all our skills. They are dangerous, but the ancestors are with us. Pray to your God, Buach Whelan. Thank Him for his will."

To understand what Henri was sayin' about bringin' Soltor and his bunch to justice, was to understand the laws we all lived by in the mountains, for sure followin' the war. This message to Henri demanding settlement fer Gideon had come from the spiritual side of our lives, as lived in the Cherokee world. The command to us fell under their law. There'd be no turnin' away from the duty of this newfound responsibility. No matter the effort, or if it be in blood. Henri bein' with the ancestors like he had recent, made it clear to him they would settle fer nothin' less. They held a lot against Viktor and his bunch fer reasons known and unknown to us. It stood to reason his gang had hurt a lot of people. What Henri told us, was what the ancestors wanted. Their desire was that there'd be no Viktor Soltor left on Mother Earth, nor any of his bunch, after we finished our settlin' chore. They required that justice be death to the lot of 'em, once the work of our duty was complete. I explained that to Sky in camp after Henri had gone out for first watch. She was quiet while sittin' the fire. I could sense her mind. She had questions concernin' our intentions she needed to ask but thought better of for the time. I answered what I could, without her havin' to ask.

"Yes, Miriam, I know your mind. I do trust him, and settlin' with this bunch full is exactly what we aim to do. You are correct in your heart for Gideon, none will live when once we are finished with our call. These are the worst of the worst, this bunch. I can tell by the way Henri speaks that he's touched deep about what he senses is the right path concernin' their future. For sure, when considerin' all those who travel the North Trail and the danger forced on 'em whenever these outlaws come 'round. As Henri is seein' it, we've been called to right the wrongs, and stop more wrongs to innocents, from the evil these bring with 'em. I believe this will answer most, if not all, the questions you have concernin' what's fixin' to happen 'tween us and them. We will be fine, Miriam. Do not fear what is ahead. Me and Henri know what to do. Let us pray to Holy Spirit for protection and wisdom and good judgment, then leave it all with Him when the time fer settlin' comes. We will have enough to worry over just tryin' not to get killed."

"You are wise in the way, Boo. I love that about you. Yes, my spirit knows the truth to what Henri has said concerning the wrongs that have been committed by these and their kind. I stand in agreement. We need to send a message to other thieves and murderers who come to this trail to steal from good people, that it will not be tolerated. I look forward to confronting these evil ones. We will end their threat against the innocents they would do harm to in the coming moons. I am with you in this effort, as I personally know the pain these kind can cause. It will be a burden lifted to know they will hurt no others like they hurt me and my family, and I will find pleasure in helping release the soul of my father to be with those he loves across the river. He deserves this, for he was a kind and good man who feared none but the Lord Himself. Thank you for doing this, Buach, my friend. I want you to know I am grateful."

Finishing those words, she rose to stand on her knees, facin' me as I sat cross-legged. She reached with both hands to pull my face to hers. The kiss she give me was from somewhere deep inside her being. I could feel her arms quiverin', her heart pounding, as she pulled us together with a pull I know'd was hard as she could do. Still on her knees, she moved herself to my front puttin' her legs on the quilt one to each side of my hips. I wrapped my arms around her middle after she'd pushed her frontside up ag'in mine lettin' her backside settle to the inside of my thighs, our kiss never breakin'. Our fronts pressed firm to one another, our lips mashed together hard, her pull strong. That give me thought while we stayed locked in that most passionate comin' together. My heart told me this woman was gonna be a perfect wife and mother one day. Her heart was pure as any I'd ever met. I thanked God for her, as I silently longed for the day He would join us as one. I loved her deeply. She caused me to stir in a place I'd never felt stirrin' before. I prayed in the silent she'd not get killed in the upcoming fight. I made mind to watch out for her even though it could be distracting fer me, which was dangerous.

I weren't used to women folk bein' in a fight. I would needs think of how best to use her talents when once the time for our settling with Viktor come to hand. She was not strong like men warriors, but she was a deadly foe just the same. I know'd better than to have her in close fightin' by hand. These we would be facin' was used to fightin' and dyin' up close. I would pray about that, as well.

Our trail for the next two days seemed long. The North Trail itself was easy, but the burden we carried made it hard. I found myself praying almost constant. At times fer lack 'a anything to keep my mind off the blood I know'd was fixin' to be draw'd. I prayed it didn't come from one of us. I hated it fer the outlaws, their death comin', but not much. Theirs was a trail caught up to, caught up to 'cause 'a the demons they'd been followin' the whole of their miserable outlaw lives. We was doin' 'em a favor, really, settin' 'em free. Gettin' 'em shed 'a them bad spirits what held 'em, sendin' 'em to be with the ancestors. I doubted the elders would have 'em, when once they'd crossed over, but we was gonna send 'em. Most we was trailin' toward know'd only one master, greed - and greed come from the devil. We'd need to watch for the evil leavin' their carcasses after Old Man Death found 'em. Didn't wanna tangle with no mad demons what know'd ol' Lucifer would be lookin' fer 'em once the killin' was over.

Camp our final morning, 'fore meetin' up with Viktor Soltor, was surprisingly calm, and to be honest, comfortable. We all talked for what seemed like an hour while eatin' the morning meal. We even sat for a cup 'a coffee by the fire after we eat, while me and Henri smoked a pipe of some a Dad's air-dried burley tobacco. The last he'd ever cure on Mother Earth. That was special, an honor to Gideon in a way. He and Dad was friends.

We broke camp and left out north a little while after daylight. Trailin' most all morning with no sightings of any travelers. I was plumb settled into our ride for the day when Henri come to a quick stop just shy of a short curve in the trail. The curve fronted what looked to be a long straight run. His stare through the woods a sign that something lay ahead. When I looked, I seen it right off, we'd come to the trading post and tavern. Nothing but big tents fastened together, really, all they was to 'em. I looked to Old Man Sun. He'd just broke full from the southern ridges. Henri's vision had been right.

Seems the trader man was tellin' the truth. I'd kind 'a got to wonderin' after a while of bein' back on the trail north, if his information had been based in truth. We was way past the trail what went to Blue Dove's village. Henri's vision was all that was keepin' my confidence up most of that second day of travel, but finally, the third morning, just like Henri said, there it was, the trading post. with all its muck and filth. The tavern hooked on the back, just like the trader had said. It was less than a hundred paces ahead of us at the end of a straight. Another curve to the left just shy of the tents took the trail on north away from the tradin' place. Folks goin' in and out couldn't see us from where Henri had stopped, but we could see them. They was a bait 'a folks visiting fer the day. Lots of 'em, at least they was a lot 'a horses, buggies, and wagons tied up outside. I figured it must be "come to the tradin' post day" fer most of 'em, seein' how many rides they was around the place.

Henri backtracked us near a quarter mile 'fore haltin' and dismountin'. We did likewise. I know'd it was time to figure the way of our proceedin'. Justice was soon to be had fer Gideon, if the gang was still there. I allowed with all the patrons visiting, they would be. Easy time fer outlaws to discover ways to take from folks when they was a crowd. Profit bein' their motivation. Yes, them outlaws was there. I know'd it. I could feel 'em. A quiver went up my back from the need to get this done. Henri saw my anger rise. He spoke with calm in his voice. I know'd that was fer me.

"We have found the place our new trader friend was telling us about. He was speaking truth. That will mean the evil ones are here or have been here recent. It seems we have come on a most busy day. I think it wise that one of us go in and scout out what is happening. See if the men we seek are there. I believe they will be. There are a lot of visitors to attract them to the trading post this day. What say ye, Boo? I think a look about would be wise."

"Well, I wouldn't wanna walk in amongst all them folks with settlin' on my mind without knowin' what they was doin'. Could be we need to use caution. You are wise, my friend. I will go at once to see what it is they do. Hold my horse, Sky. I will be back soon."

"No, warrior. I will go," Henri said, as he kind 'a grabbed my elbow, stoppin' me from leavin'. "They will fear you. They will notice you. You will be questioned when they confront you. I think it wise you wait here and let me go in. I will be less threatening to them than you. This is how I see it."

He put his hand up to his face with two fingers pointin' at his eyes. That meant he was done talkin'. The decision of who should go had been made in his mind. I stopped that hand 'fore he ever draw'd it clear of his face, which was a most disrespectful gesture to my friend. He shot me a cold look when I did that. Backin' off a step, I seen his right hand find the bone handle of his long knife. Our eyes locked as my right hand found the handle of my long knife as well. We both froze, starin' each other cold. We'd never fought since knowin' one another, but we had wrestled a few problems out between ourselves. This would not be one of those times. He would try and kill me if we got to knife fightin' over what I did, or at least he'd try. I know'd him. No question he was mad enough, but fortunately for us both, he got control 'fore he pulled on me.

He didn't push it no farther once he calmed himself. It prob'ly helped when he seen the look on my face. That look told him he most likely wouldn't make it if he tried, so say no more. I'd have none of it. I was the one goin' in 'cause I was the one who had to go in. He understood, simply, that sometimes size does matter, if one is willing to use it, in a sense. In this decision, he understood I would stand my ground. He backed off.

I left him and Sky there without another word. Sky holdin' the reins of my stallion. There was no arguing with me sometimes, and Henri know'd it. He could feel this was one of those times. Shouldn't take long to find out what we needed to know, if it could be found out. He said no more to me about it as I made to leave.

I left my carbine in its boot on my horse but kept my short gun stuck solid in the braided belt I wore at my waist. It was a Colt .36

caliber revolver my dad carried. I'd took to carryin' it some since he was gone. I didn't figure to need it, hardly ever used it, but I'd feel naked without it amongst the kind I was headed toward. A body never know'd, when bein' around outlaws, how things could work out.

A last look to Sky told me she held worry. She was starin' at me with a serious kind 'a stare. I winked at her and smiled as I commenced to walkin' north, away from her and Henri.

I know'd Sky understood it best that I go to find out about Viktor. Henri would find nothin' but trouble around the bunch that was gatherin' at the tradin' post this day. He was a half-breed. Lots 'a folks in the mountains still held hard feelings ag'in the Indians. Thirty years removed from the last fightin', really, but some pain roots deep when losin' loved ones is concerned. Some around that tavern would not like Henri bein' near. They weren't the kind to tolerate Indians of any kind. That's just the way it was when bein' around settler folks. Henri never realized it, even when it was laid out in front of him. Didn't believe it when we would explain it to him. He couldn't understand it. That's why he was so mad when I stopped him goin'. He wanted to do the scoutin' but know'd he couldn't. That was one of the reasons he'd got away from the tribe, too. Bein' half French and half Cherokee could be good, or bad, dependin'.

I was took by a strange feelin' as I walked on north. It bothered me to leave Sky Watcher. I got to thinkin' if something happened unplanned that I might not be comin' back. It was possible I'd never see her again. A feelin' punched me in the gut when I realized I'd not said goodbye. Didn't think to, really. I weren't used to havin' to say goodbye to nobody. I never said goodbye to Henri, ever, but it seemed in my heart that I should 'a said goodbye to her. I fought the urge to turn and go back, but I dared not, after confrontin' Henri the way I had.

Love was so confusin'. It was troublesome and worryful. It was gonna get me killed if I didn't learn how to deal with its ways. It come to me that I had to catch my mind back. The warrior in me understood the danger of a mind distracted when a fight come. Weren't but a long second after them thoughts even come to me, that

I forced myself to shuck 'em from my mind. I didn't want to hurt Miriam by not comin' back, but I didn't wanna get killed worse, so I got my back up and cleared my mind as I draw'd closer to the tradin' post. I remembered Henri sayin' we'd need all our skills on this trail.

I made my mind 'fore finally gettin' to the tavern, weren't nobody gonna hurt me. I'd not let that happen no matter what I had to do. I'd keep the risk low for the time, since I was alone. Try and not let my anger get to sparkin' from my sense of right and wrong. This was just a scoutin' trip. I was simply lookin' fer somebody on the quiet. Weren't plannin' on talkin' to folks much, just listen mostly. Then it come to me, I'd never seen this man Viktor Soltor. I didn't know what he looked like. I said a short prayer 'fore reachin' the place askin' Holy Spirit to show him to me without doubt. Argue all you want 'tween believin' folk and others, but the Good Lord has a sense 'a humor. I believe that with all my bein'. He'd proved it to me many times.

I stopped and checked both knives 'fore entering the place. Felt like my spirit was givin' me warning. I was heedin' that warning. Wisdom I'd gained from experience. Both knives was as they should be, if by chance I come to need 'em. They'd never let me down before. I know'd if I used 'em to their proper call, they'd not let me down again.

It was a travelin' tavern, what hooked to the back of a travelin' general store kind 'a tradin' post lookin' thing, or what folks might call a store, that I walked into first. Two big tents stretched tight was all it was. Kind 'a brown in color. I couldn't tell if the brown was the color of the canvas, or if they was just stained and dirty as I walked up to 'em, but as I got closer, I could see it was mostly stain. The place was filthy all around the outside. Looked to be the tents had been where they sat fer a time. I expected no less. The patrons had tied their horses up close, so the common horse stink added to the nasty of it all. I did not want to enter such a place, but for my friend, Gideon, and my hopefully future wife, his daughter, I would without regard.

The floors in both places weren't nothin' but mud a few inches deep. The place stunk of cheap beer and sweat, spilt rotgut whiskey mixed with the stinkin' mud of the floor, and smoke. Pipe smoke, cigar smoke, and stove smoke near smothered me as I breeched the flap door of what must 'a been the back of the tavern. Most of the folks was standin', a few was seated on makeshift benches around small tables what sat near the main center pole - the very main pole what held up the tavern tent. A locust, eight inches across and near twenty feet tall. Must 'a been forty to fifty folks inside. They was big tents.

Everybody was facin' away from me as I come in. Most seemed foreign in their dress to what the local mountain folks looked like... what I looked like. I recognized that. Henri was right. I stood out among these men.

It come to me that most there looked to be from the North. That got my back up hard. The stink makin' me have no hankerin' fer a taste of their sour mash, even though a taste might 'a been nice right then. My need was to find out about the ones I was lookin' for, get some knowledge of them and their numbers, then leave when I got it all collected to report back to Henri and Sky Watcher. At least, that was what I come to do. Unfortunately, things rarely work out to plan when dealin' with evil men.

My run in with Viktor Soltor had to 'a been sent by the Great Spirit. I give credit to his sense of humor. I could 'a never dreamed the goin' on's He had planned fer me in that tavern. The half-covered Cherokee maiden, with a long, muddy rope tied about her neck, bein' made to serve the evil ones their drink while bein' groped by their nasty hands, was His first call fer my attention. She was pitiful. The loud, strange talkin' man standin' at the sawmill slab bar, that most all in there was focused on, was His second. I was thinkin' I might 'a just found Viktor Soltor, or at least some of his bunch, 'cause they was men with the speaker dressed same as he was. I would bide my time 'til I found out fer sure, but I had a feelin' I was close to findin' the murderer and his bunch.

I'd have to worry over that in a bit. My first order of duty had changed upon entering the nasty tavern. My new first chore was to tend to the maiden... and whoever put that rope around her neck.

The Legend of Swell Branch

CHAPTER 28

To Set a Maiden Free, the Rope

I was thinkin' the maiden couldn't be no older than twelve, maybe thirteen. She was dirty, barefooted, muddy from the knees down, soiled. The rope had worn raw places around her neck. A few was bleedin'. The homespun dress she wore barely hung from one shoulder. The other side was tore through and hangin', exposin' her half bare bosom to all in the tent. The bottom of the dress had been split up both the back and the front near to the tops of her legs. That helped with walkin' and carryin' drinks, 'cause her feet sunk in the mud with each step she took, but them slits was bad 'cause they exposed her even more. My heart broke as she and I locked eyes. She looked like a scared fawn.

　　I motioned with my hand for her to come to where I stood just inside the tavern's back door. The rope drawin' tighter the closer she got to me. It was obvious it weren't long enough to reach the outside, neither was it long enough to allow her fresh air from through the back door. *What kind 'a person would do such evil to a young'un like her?* I know'd the answer to my question soon as I thought it. Evil ones with greed as their conscience. The young Cherokee had most likely been stole, then sold. Those who did the stealin' and sellin' is the ones I wanted words with. I figured it possible fer Viktor Soltor and some, or all, of his bunch.

The rope come up taut as she got to within' a pace of where I stood. I moved up to where she'd had to stop, kneelin' on one knee in the mud. That put my eyes down level with hers. Most everybody was watchin' and listenin' to the man up front. I allowed they weren't nobody payin' us no mind. I spoke Cherokee so none near would know what I was sayin', if by chance or intention they heard me speakin'. I had to talk normal and not whisper. The noise in the place was a kind 'a constant buzz topped by the funny voiced man shoutin' over everybody. She was scared, trembling shakin' her whole person. I could see fear as we looked each other in the eye. I spoke kind words in her language. Looked to be that give her comfort.

"Maiden, I will not hurt you. I will help you, but I must ask you some questions," I said, in what should 'a been her local native tongue, starin' her eye to eye. Both her eyes swollen from bein' slapped. She nodded understandin'. That was good. I weren't sure she'd been taught her own language, young as she was.

"Do you mean to be here working in this place?" She shook her head no. I nodded to tell her I understood. "Are you here for obligation to anyone, as property to be owned for debt? Are you pledged in any way to those who own these tents?" She shook her head no. "Have you recently been taken against your will and sold?" She nodded yes. I nodded again to let her know I understood.

I raised my head to take a quick look around 'fore I asked her my last question. I had to make sure she weren't bound by contract, and surprisingly, if she would leave if I gave her the opportunity. It could be dangerous to her family if she left without bein' bought. I had to know these things. I could feel the cold wet from the floor's mud had soaked through my skin britches where my knee was settled. I needed to hurry. The stink that close to the floor near made me lose my stomach. I wondered how such a child could be doin' what she was doin'.

I come to realize of a sudden, that my anger was commencin' to rise as I locked eyes with her again. I weren't doin' too good at holdin' it down inside after seein' that child had been beat. I could feel it workin' up my spine as she listened for my last question. It was obvious to me that this girl was livin' in misery. I took her by the shoulders to voice the last of my questions that needed answerin', then hopefully lettin' her go.

"If you could, and your family not be harmed, would you free yourself of this place? Go to be with those who could care for you, never having to return?" Her face brightened after I said those simple words in Cherokee. She nodded yes, as tears filled her eyes. "Okay then, hold still and don't run off, yet."

I slid my long knife from its leather home with my right hand, cuttin' the muddy rope off from around her neck with one easy pull. I held the cut end in my left hand as I wiped the mud from my blade onto my skin britches. Once clean, I put the razor-sharp knife back in its home. Takin' her by the shoulder with my right hand, my left still holding the rope, I spoke direct to her face on. I needed her to hear me straight without confusion.

"Now, when I turn you loose, you need to run from here. Take the North Trail south about a half mile. You will see a man and a woman with three horses and a mule waitin' the trail. Tell them I set you free. Tell them to come quickly. Go now, maiden. Run fast, my life will depend on you finding my friends."

She nodded her head in understanding. Her eyes still bright. As I released her shoulders to set her free, she hugged my neck tight, then wasted no time gettin' shed 'a that evil tavern. I watched as she headed out through the back door. I could see she was runnin' south fer all she was worth as the door closed behind her, just as I'd told her to do. My life really was fixin' to be in her hands, after I finished up with whoever it was had commenced to jerkin' on the rope. I know'd they weren't gonna be happy with what I'd done, settin' their property free.

I followed bein' pulled by the rope from the back toward the front without resisting. The outlaws didn't like me bumpin' into 'em from behind, disturbing their drink. Most was ready to fight 'til they seen what was happenin', then they got interested. I allowed they was figurin' trouble for the one pullin' on the other end after sizin' me up, for sure if they saw the mad on my face.

Havin' that young girl tied with a rope was more'n I could stand. I didn't care who was doin' it, they was gonna pay. I even got to thinkin' hard thoughts against them that was congregated there. Standin' around lettin' that girl serve 'em in her condition was just pure coward on their part. They should 'a not allowed it. I aimed to have words with 'em 'fore I got gone, too. Tell 'em to their faces what kind 'a cowards, or "ean-kees" in the Cherokee, I seen 'em as.

I'd not been as mad as I was right then in a long time. It seemed all there sensed it as I let the rope pull me forward through the gatherin'. The place got to gettin' real quiet with me passin' through their ranks. The outlaws started payin' mind to me and the rope instead of the funny soundin' man. He'd had to stop yellin' over folks. Nobody was listenin'.

Weren't but a little bit 'til I broke free from the crowd, steppin' right out in front of the makeshift bar not but a few paces from where the orator had been oratin'. I could see the one doin' the pullin', it was the barkeep, but the funny talkin' man was gone. He weren't there and he should 'a been. Had been just the minute before. I thought that strange.

The rope puller's face show'd shock as I suddenly appeared from the crowd, holdin' the other end. He quit pullin' when he seen that. Mad went full on his face, takin' the place of his sudden surprise. I weren't the little Indian girl he was expectin'. That spooked him. His look give that away. Had I not been so mad, I would 'a laughed in his face. He weren't spooked after a few seconds, though. His face went back to plain mad. I felt the same.

I throw'd the rope aside fer it to lay in the mud but followed on toward the barkeep like I was still bein' pulled. He dropped his end as well. The whole of the place went graveyard quiet when they saw that. Most of 'em prob'ly figurin' I was crazy. Maybe I was, 'cause I didn't stop 'til I got close to him, right up in his face close, but only as close as I could with a two-foot wide oak slab bar between us.

We stared eye to eye fer a bit. Neither of us sayin' nothin'. His stare weakenin' some, but less than I would 'a hoped for. He didn't seem too shocked, bein' that mine was not the body he was intent on pullin' to the front for another order of drinks.

I allowed he was the owner, or at least know'd the owner, since he was behind the slab bein' used for their bar. He had an apron on that was stained black in front with a homespun rag laid over his shoulder what looked to be grow'd there. Bein' back of the bar servin' folks meant he was the one takin' in money. That's how come I figured him fer the owner. That, and not many in their right minds would want to own such an awful establishment as he run.

He was an older man, gray headed, heavy, filth coverin' his person. He chewed a half eat, half burnt cigar as he studied me. It was the blackest cigar I'd ever seen. He held it with what few rotten teeth they was still in his mouth. A long, matted, filthy beard grow'd to the center of his chest bound in the middle with a slim piece 'a homespun rag. I vow I saw some tiny critters crawlin' around in it as I looked him over on the sly. Very little hair covered the top of his head but plenty grow'd thick along the sides. All gray as well. He pulled that back into a tail bound with braided leather cord. His hair was slick lookin', like it'd been dipped in lamp oil. He stunk like the dirty human he was, too. A body could smell his stink up close like I was, smell it over all the other foulness in the place. His breath was rank like ruint cabbage as he commenced to hollerin' at me. I should 'a shot him when I first seen him pullin' the rope, just fer bein' so nasty.

"Just who in Satan's Hell do you think you are, white Indian man? Just what do you think you're doin' holdin' my rope, you fool?" He hollered, from what had to be the top of his lungs, tryin' to raise me. Everybody in the place stayed silent. I remained calm. Kept my eyes locked with his. My senses sharp to them around me.

"Where is my Indian girl what used to be tied to the end of this rope, hey? You got any notion, boy? Maybe you seen the one what cut her loose? Say boy, hey! Maybe you be him. Maybe you be the one what cut her loose then, huh? Is that right? Tell me true, stranger. Where is my Indian and how is it that she's not tied to my rope no more?"

I stared him without flinchin' for a long minute once he quit talkin'. I could sense folks was movin' about in the room. I paid mind to who and where, so if a fight come, I'd know who to take out first. Workers of his most likely. It come to me that I'd do good to settle and get out. I know'd they was several hard to kill men watchin' me at that moment. I would needs think 'fore actin' for the next little bit.

"So then, old man, dirty one, you admittin' to be the one who claims that little Cherokee girl what was tied on the end of that rope you was pullin', yes? You tellin' me that, are ye? Do you own this filthy place as well? Say if you do, but I warn ye straight, say with courage, 'cause I will settle for her if this is true. I see no reason to let you do what you do, 'cause I bet she ain't been the only one workin' fer ye of recent, is she, huh? You hearin' me, hawg face? You've had more like her in your employment recent ain't ye? Where they be now, then, huh? Tell us true, evil one, so we'll all know."

"My business works is no business of yours, mountain man. You best be careful gettin' curious over me. You're the one what set my girl free then, huh? Well, that is a small problem fer me. Yes, I do own this tavern, and I know many in the business. I'll find another girl like her before tomorrow is out. Maybe with this next one, I won't have to keep her tied to the bar from fear of her runnin' off," he said with a big grin. Chewin' his cigar some more 'fore finishin' his say to me. "Now, boy, you've upset my business. I will needs you settle your debt to me for losses, since you've made my business your business."

"What?" I kind 'a growled back in his face through near gritted teeth. "Settle with you? I have no business with you, outlaw. What contract could you possibly figure we have? Who in their right mind would make business with you, anyhow?"

"Gold, my friend. I want gold. I demand you pay me for the slave you let go," he growled back at me. Near bitin' the butt of his cigar in two. "You same as stole her by settin' her free. I want a twenty dollar gold piece, same as I paid Viktor. Hear me, boy? Give it to me and be gone. I don't even want you drinkin' here."

Viktor, huh? There it was, then. My feelin' was correct. He'd paid Viktor twenty dollars gold for the girl. I would not let that go. Somehow, through all the settling comin' his way, I would make it understood to Viktor that judgment for the girl was part of it.

"As you say, barkeep, and I believe your words, you will find another girl for your business here. Won't take much effort. That will be a simple chore for the likes of you and yours," I said loud for all in there to hear. "I am sorry for that truth, fer what you do here with them is a bad thing. Slavery is over, hawg slop. Ended in 1865 after your Federals won the war. This is 1868. Slave ownin' is now illegal, even if it is Indians you claim to own. We ought 'a hang you with that rope you had the maiden tied with, but I'm gonna figure you're among friends here and you gettin' hung ain't gonna happen with them watchin' out. Still, you'll not get off that easy fer all the hurt you've caused folks. I'm gonna see to it personal. You ain't gettin' no gold coin from me to buy more slaves with. Fact is, you won't be gettin' no more slaves again at all, evil man. That ain't gonna happen no more. You're done here with abusin' the young ones. I will see that becomes truth however you choose. You understand my words, hawg breath? Your time of usin' slave girls is now over."

The place was quiet as could be after I'd finished speakin' at the owner. Me and him just kind 'a kept holdin' our stare. Thinkin' on what was happening, what I'd just said. Most in the place was drunk on old beer or out 'a their heads on soured whiskey or opium. Them that was there for pleasure weren't payin' no serious mind to my concerns, 'cept they seen they'd lost their little Indian girl. Them that was there to hear the funny talkin' man I'd heard when first entering the place seemed to be payin' mind. Some 'a them most likely had stock in what was goin' on 'tween me and the barkeep. Them was the ones I had to watch out for when tryin' to get gone from the place. Their purpose there was dangerous fer me. I never did hear what was so important that they was all there to hear.

I held my stare with the tavern owner but straightened up a bit as the look on his face changed from confusion to plain ol' mad. I figured it would. He weren't real smart when makin' his choice to settle our feud or back off. His response to my challenge was all wrong on his part, it cost him.

"You call her maiden, do you, white Indian man? Well, she ain't been that fer a long time, friend. I've seen to that personal, as you say. Heeheeheehee… hahahaha," his laughter growin' too loud. Others around him laughed with him. I took that personal.

Near slow as I'd ever seen a body move in a fight, he went for his short gun what laid inside his apron while still laughing. I know'd it was there. I'd seen the handle stickin' out when first confrontin' him, after the rope pullin'. Reachin' for that gun was his last mistake on Mother Earth. My reaction was just that, a reaction to instinct, while never breakin' our stare. The blade of my long knife, whipped from its leather home by my right hand, sank hilt deep into his chest. Happened 'fore I ever realized what I was doin', slicin' his heart into two halves just like I'd been trained to do. He was dead 'fore he ever got his pistol's barrel pointed square at me; however, in his death grip, he pulled the gun's trigger, firin' a .44 caliber lead ball into the locust pole what held up the middle of the tent. Fortunately, the pistol weren't pointed at nobody. I didn't hesitate to take the weapon from the man's hand with my left hand, my right sill holdin' the handle of my long knife, which was sunk in his chest. I slid the short gun into my mid-belt fer keeps. I'd been wantin' a .44 caliber and his was a good one. A Colt made revolver. I seen they was other bullet holes in that pole when I looked to where his ball hit, the lead balls still visible.

We held to starin' full at one another while he passed. I watched the life go from his eyes. The cigar fall from his mouth. His eyes go dull. I heard and smelled the foul air of his last breath go from his lungs as Old Man Death come fer him. I felt his body go limp, same as I'd felt with Walter, back when I'd put him in the privy for the takers of our farm to find. All the killin' I'd committed lately seemed the same to me. I cared little, really. I felt justified because of all the evil they'd put upon folks over their time, and no law to provide fer 'em. Now I'd just ended the life of another evil outlaw man. He deserved it as well to most folks' thinkin', but it was still death, and no man is God.

Judgment would now be on him, and I'd sent him there for it. That thinkin' troubled my soul fer a short second, then it bothered me little. When them guilty feelings come, then and later on over a smoke that night, all I had do was remember the look on that young Cherokee maiden's face when I first walked into the tavern. That made it all right fer me, and to most folks, but unfortunately, not for all that was there. I figured Holy Spirit would have words with me when I give Him His time later on.

I quickly slid my long knife out from the dead one's heart, once I'd felt him go limp. Wipin' the blood off on the barkeeps back. His upper body slumped across the bar as my arm come free from under his weight. His life's blood puddlin' up and drippin' off both sides of the oak slab. I turned to see all those there lookin' on in disbelief. I took the quiet I'd caused as an opportunity to say my piece. I know'd I'd have the tent's attention for a bit, so I figured to make the best of my time. I was sure in my thinkin'… I'd just made some deadly enemies killin' that barkeep. It come to me, bein' where I was and who I was among, my life was on a short lead that I was only leadin' fer what could be a short time. I slid my long knife back in its leather home, then went to talkin' to them that was payin' mind. Tellin' my side of what'd just happened to the ears of all fer confidence. I would try and make 'em all agree to the purpose of the killin', so maybe the man's real friends would stay at a distance. That would give me a chance to get out and gone.

"I killed this man to protect my person. He was intent on killin' me. You all saw it," I said to 'em as I looked around the tent. "I freed his Indian. He didn't like it. Went for his short gun to get vengeance on me. I defended myself, as any here would 'a," I said, pausin' fer a short second to make sure they was listenin'. "Anybody see different? Speak now or leave me be. I have business to tend to. 'Sides, y'all should 'a done something about him holdin' that girl 'fore I ever got here. The whole lot 'a ye should be ashamed. Drinkin' and funnin' while that girl was muckin' around here in misery. Well I'll not be ashamed. I'll not tolerate such in my company. No, I, Buach Whelan, of Swell Branch and the Cherokee, will not stand fer such as this bein' done to a young maiden in my presence. It ain't right. The war is over. The Union won. Slave holdin' is now illegal, even if it is Indian, and I'm thinkin' some 'a y'all believes keepin' Indians is acceptable. Well it ain't, and I'm here to declare it fer 'em. Now, I'll say it again fer them what didn't hear. Anybody got a grievance with me killin' this man to protect my own hide? If so, say it now or from now on leave me be. I will listen as I leave this place. Do not make me defend myself again. I am good at it, as you have seen. That kind 'a killin' follows my training as a warrior. It bothers me little."

None there said a word, as I stood my ground waitin' fer a word to be said. I watched as many shook their heads in agreement. Others just stared at me. Some just stared. I felt no threat from any near, so I started for the back, makin' to leave. I weren't fortunate enough to make it all the way out 'fore somebody had to say something. The funny soundin' voice, that I'd heard when first enterin', spoke up. I was only two paces from steppin' through the flap what made the back door, too. It weren't Viktor, but it was the next best thing. I never did find out what he was talkin' about fer all them men to be gathered listenin', but I allowed it must 'a been important fer 'em to be bunched up the way they was.

Seein' the girl sufferin' got me out 'a sorts in my thinkin'. The only doin's I paid mind to after that was settin' her free. I forgot my purpose when once I set my mind to what'd been done to her. My spirit took me over. All other thoughts had left my mind. Havin' that girl there was such a terrible wrong, I felt it had to be made right sooner rather than later. I allowed it needed to be sooner. Justice for Gideon was important, yes, but gettin' that maiden gone from her living hell jumped to the front of my thinkin', when once I'd laid eyes on the rope holdin' her there. The trails of blood runnin' down her neck from under that rope drove it home to me. None as innocent as her deserved that. I'd not have it.

"You there, Way-lan," the strange voice hollered. I hadn't seen him the whole time I'd been busy with the barkeep. I figured him fer hidin' behind his men like a coward. "You'd done made your grave, foolish one. You have killed friend to me. Friend to my bruw-ther, Vik-tor. I am Boris. I will tell him you have caused this murder. He not will like how you did. The maiden made owe to this place. Bought with gold on barrel as you do it here in A-mar-e-ka. Why have you made it bad for yourself with us? We do not even know who you are. Say what it is you are come for."

"You may not know me, heathen, but you know'd my friend. He was a trader here on the North Trail. A friend to all who wanted," hollerin' back at him as I stomped my way through the crowd, makin' toward where his voice trailed from like a mad man. I kept walkin' right on toward him 'til one of his men blocked my way. He seen I was gettin' too close. Seen I weren't stoppin', neither, 'til I got to ol' Boris. Me and the guard locked eyes hard. I saw nothin' but fear down deep. I respected him little after that. I hollered from where he'd stopped me, not takin' my eyes off his. "Gideon, the trader, is who I mean." A groan went out from all that was there. I figured most must 'a know'd him to react like that. "I know you and yours are owed for his killin'. I have come to settle that debt and settle it I will. You be damned fer the effort."

That was the wrong thing fer me to 'a said, reckless and dangerous for sure, but I couldn't help it. I meant it. Still, right or wrong, no sooner had I finished speakin', than I felt at least six other men start my way, not countin' the one in front of me, which I seen was makin' his move as well. He weren't near fast enough gettin' at his knife to trouble me. I grabbed his reachin' arm with my left hand, stoppin' his grabbin' effort, then laid him out cold with a hard right fist to the left side of his head. I had no doubt I hit him hard enough to break several bones, most likely a few teeth. I was gettin' used to feelin' how that felt. I'd had to hit so many folks over the last several moons that it was becomin' commonplace. Rooted in all the evil comin' down from the North.

He was a weasel of a man, small. No different than I'd figured him for when first hearin' him speakin'. He was judged to be guilty by the ancestors, same as the others he run with fer all the evil they'd done. He'd just made sure 'a that to my way 'a thinkin', but I had to survive for the next little bit to see it through.

I had no defense against those movin' my way, so I just went on the attack like a trapped boar hog penned by dogs. Another step forward, after ending his man, put me face-to-face with ol' Boris. He seen he was had, then. I smiled at him.

I grabbed his goodly amount 'a hair while shovin' the barrel of my Colt into his mouth and partway down his throat. That move broke out his front teeth, top and bottom. I turned to face all them that was gonna do me in from behind while holdin' Boris' head steady in my left hand by the hair. My right holdin' the Colt stickin' out from Boris' mouth. Blood leakin' out through his lips. His throat gurglin' something awful. Makin' terrible noises from my gun barrel bein' in his throat, but I let it be. I could hold him up with one arm no problem, he was so small, so I just kept on.

They all stopped soon as they seen I had their leader hooked like a fish with the barrel of my short gun. None said nothin', nor made a noise, for fear I'd pull the trigger accidental. This man held weight among these I was defendin' myself against. I'd not know'd how much 'til I seen 'em whoa up like they did after seein' my gun in his mouth. Them holdin' back was a good sign fer me.

The cocking of a Colt revolver gets any man's attention what hears it. I cocked mine hard, after makin' sure all there had seen where I'd stuck the pistol's barrel. Not a soul moved once they seen that. Ol' Boris wet himself right there in front 'a everybody he was so scared. I come close to feelin' fer him after he done that, but I didn't.

None there tried to stop me as I eased toward the side door, draggin' Boris along with me. My pistol's barrel still stuck in his mouth and partway down his throat. He was still makin' strangling noises something fierce. His head turned at a most uncomfortable angle to try and draw air. His face turnin' blue from my effort, but I cared none. I only needed him to stay alive long enough fer me to get outside and down the trail a ways. I know'd Henri and Sky would be close by now, or even outside waitin', if the girl I'd freed had done what I asked. Fortunately, she had.

Once on the outside, I grabbed on even tighter to ol' Boris' mane, takin' off south on a dead run fast as I could go. I took the gun from his mouth so I could run faster droppin' it back in my belt. I was mostly draggin' Boris by his hair as the crowd busted through the side door behind us. Them loyal to Boris leadin' the way. A double volley of carbine fire was a recognizable sound to the mostly ex-soldier bunch what was followin' me. They all turned quick, headin' back to the tavern. Boris' men know'd to respect that sound from the range it come from, and it was obvious the others would rather drink as get shot. Them carbines saved my hide I believe, them and the friends firin' 'em. I said a short prayer 'a thanks when all that come to mind.

Boris was havin' a tough time, what with me steppin' on him, even stompin' on him at times, as we headed south down the trail on a run. I was sure at least one of his ankles was broke by the time I come to a stop over a half mile south of the tavern and trading post. I wanted to keep goin' with him, tried to keep goin', but I could go no more while havin' to drag him like I was. I looked hard behind. I saw nor heard no followers. Boris evidently didn't mean that much to the patrons of the tavern, only to the men what worked for him. I know'd that bunch would be to us come morning. Rescuin' Boris in their minds, vengeance as well. I figured Viktor to be with 'em. We would confront him then.

The soft steps I suddenly got to hearin' was the one set I wanted to hear most. Sky Watcher was at my side near soon as I recognized whose steps I was hearin'. She moved quiet as a soft breeze. Henri close on her heels. Boris was moanin', which meant he was still alive. That was good fer us.

I had a lot to tell Henri and Sky about what happened at the tavern. They'd have several questions about who and why Boris was with me, but one thing was sure, we now had a way to get at Viktor Soltor. Our effort to find justice for our friend and father, Gideon, was startin' to bear fruit.

The Legend of Swell Branch

CHAPTER 29

Justice for Gideon Swift and Sure

Sky Watcher was up early as the morning come on us. Old Man Sun was still hid when I seen her stokin' the morning fire, movin' the coffee pot to hotter coals fer warmin'. I was just comin' in from the late watch, maybe a little early, but we was most likely gonna have an eventful morning, as Henri figured it. I wanted to make ready with time to spare.

It weren't right, her bein' up. She'd never got up 'fore me and Henri the whole time we'd been out on trail, that I know'd of. Henri was still bedded down in his tent. It was a bit early to rise even fer him and me. We'd tied Boris to a poplar tree for overnight, not ten paces from where our tents was staked. He was moanin' when I'd left out for my watch. Moanin' when I come back that morning. Been moanin' all night, most likely. That was good. Told me he'd made it through alive. We could still hang him with Viktor come evening.

I understood what it was botherin' her. Know'd how she was thinkin' over what we'd be facin' 'fore long. I'd felt it many times in my young life. The unknown of goin' on's a body ain't used to. It's worrisome. Your person could only get comfortable with that feelin' after facin' it a few times. I thought little about it anymore I'd experienced it so much of late. I used to let it make me rise early, same as she'd done. Couldn't help it. Your body had to. It weren't from gettin' good rest, no, it was from tossin' about all night and growin' tired 'a bein' bedded down. Your fear was that you'd be asleep when the fight come. That would mean death for the one left asleep. It's a troublesome worry when one can't sleep fer thinkin' on them things. Caused me to learn how to wake early regardless, then you had no trouble sleepin', 'cause you had confidence you'd wake with time to spare.

The chore was simple, really. All you had do was empty yourself out 'fore headin' to bed down for the night, then drink half 'a tin of water. You'd wake in about six hours to answer the call of nature. If a body went down at a proper time, they'd have plenty 'a dark left 'fore Old Man Sun commenced to showin' next morning. That give you confidence to sleep, if you could sleep. Sometimes sleep just didn't come regardless, even for warriors. You had to be careful, though. A body couldn't drink a half tin of coffee, no, fer some reason that would keep you awake. It had to be a half tin of water, or you'd get no rest at all. Worked for me every time. The call of nature is a powerful force.

"You're feared of the unknown, Sky Watcher. I tell you, Mohawk, as warriors. Do not fear whatever that unknown may be, it will be," speakin' to her as I breeched the firelight returning from my watch. "I know what you feel, Miriam. I feel it, too. It's what all true warriors feel before the enemy comes. It's the unknown of how the fight will go that worries the soul, to be sure, but trust me, that troublin' you feel, that's what gives your spirit the edge it needs to stay calm when the fight comes. Trust your instincts, Miriam. Use that warning of danger to protect yourself when the enemy is on you. Keep your head up and your eyes open for anything movin' toward your person from any direction. It's what we all do… simple as that. These are bad men, but we will have them when they find us. They will not harm me or you or Henri as long as things go the way we plan, but I will tell you now, consider yourself warned, most times they do not."

"I am feared of the unknown, Boo, yes," she replied quietly from across the fire as we stood warming, "but not the unknown of this morning so much, although them coming concerns me greatly. The worry I'm struggling with most, is for you, and what will happen to you when Viktor comes, or any other bad man in the coming times. I am longing for a life together. I am longing for my mother and a family. I fear you will go away, same as Mr. Stuart did. I am aware that such feelings are selfish on my part. It makes me ashamed, but I can't help it. I've grown to love you, Buach, not that I would change my feelings if I could."

She stopped speakin' when finishin' them words. We both stood frozen. Her stare through the building smoke of our warmin' fire was one of question, concern. Had she said the words that would end our special feelings for each other? Had she just run me off like a feared little boy of his own shadow? No, she had not. I hoped she know'd that. She'd made it where I couldn't breathe, though. Her words had stopped my life fer a minute. I had to catch my mind as it began to wonder. I longed to be back on our back porch with the spring rain comin' down, only this time… we'd both be sheddin' our clothes… and not from the wet of the rain.

"If you get killed in this, or any other fight, Boo, I will be left alone in my heart. That is the unknown I fear most, of all the fear I have. These men coming scare me. I do not deny that. Not for me so much, but for you. I don't want their weapons to be the ones that take you away. You have come into my life, now I want to live it beside you… hopefully… if Great Spirit wills it… and you desire it… as your wife… if that is our fate, and then, Buach… as the mother of your children." She searched my eyes after finishin' her say. She saw the truth.

Wife! Mother! Had she said wife, then mother? She did, I was sure. My heart jumped so hard inside my chest I felt it skip a beat. My eyes never left hers as we stared deep into each other's soul. Her words fresh. I could say nothing for the time. I would have to talk about it with her later.

"You worry for nothing, Miss Miriam," Henri's soft voice said, breakin' the silence of our moment. "Lone Eagle will be fine. No warrior can best him in battle. We will all be fine. I have seen it." Henri kind 'a half said as he come to the fire for a tin of coffee. "It's time to make ready for our soon to be visitors, Boo. We left them a good trail to follow. They should be here shortly. I would think not long after Old Man Sun shows in the east. That is my feeling." I agreed with him as he walked away to gather his possibles.

"Buach, I am curious," Sky said, askin'. "How is it that you and Henri are so sure these outlaws will be on us this morning? I need to understand the things that make you believe this. It would seem to me they would've come during the night."

"Yeah, I can see that way 'a thinkin', and they might 'a, sure, but no, they'd wait 'til this morning," I answered kind 'a quiet like, not wantin' to offend.

I moved to her side of the fire to pour myself a tin of coffee, that's where the coffee pot sat the coals, crouching beside where she stood to do so. I stayed squatted there fer purpose, as I wanted to catch the warmth of the building flames she'd got goin', and I wanted to be close to her.

The morning air was cool. Her morning scent strong. The warmness of hot coffee mixed with her scent and the building flames was most comforting. She squatted next to me, close, pourin' herself a tin of coffee as well. Our eyes come together as she grinned at me. Them words she'd spoke earlier come back to my mind. My heart stoppin' again as the side of her body come tight to mine. I could feel her warmth. Her smile was spiritual. The beauty of her standin' on my porch that rainy afternoon come floodin' back through my memory. I had to break our stare at the thought of her nakedness, her natural beauty. Lookin' back to the fire, I answered her with explanation.

"They'd have no reason to follow us 'til they could see good. They'd know havin' to travel with Boris would slow us down considerable. Too dangerous fer 'em followin' of a night, too, in case we decided to ambush 'em in the dark. 'Sides, they'd need time to make ready for a possible long trail to find Boris, but that won't happen. A long trail is not good for us. That's why we camped close to the tavern for the night and didn't travel farther south. We wanna let 'em come on in, then make our intentions known. A trap, you could say. It is wise when outnumbered to be cautious, it is also wise to attack with surprise. Remember, these will want us dead if they find us first. We will protect ourselves accordingly if they do. We only needs hang Viktor. The rest we will leave to fate. Do not let them stand or sit their horse if Henri's command comes. Leave them on the ground for the worms and night critters. It is important to take each chance we get to end this fight, 'cause they will mean to end us. Don't forget that. These are dangerous souls we will be facin'."

After my explainin', we sat fer a minute finishin' our coffee. Thinkin' about what'n all we'd just talked over… the coming fight worryin' us on the inside. That couldn't be helped. It's human nature to wanna protect one's person against harm, but the warrior in us kept our thoughts on the need at hand. We also had another in camp that was a concern. The maiden I'd freed had stayed the night with us. I allowed once free of her obligation to me, she would go back to her home. She had not. I was kind 'a glad, considerin'.

Weren't but a little bit 'til Henri come back to the fire. It was time he told us how he thought we should do concernin' Viktor comin' for Boris. Most every time in happenin's like we was in, his plan was always best. He was most wise when important things needed tending to. This time, though, I know'd what his plan would be. I still let him tell us. It would 'a been disrespectful not to.

"We camped in a good place here. It is open out beside the trail. This will help in giving us clear vision from the woods. We will put Boris there. Sky Watcher, I feel it is best for you to go and hide some distance back in the trees. There you will wait for Viktor and his men with a carbine. Find the proper place to hide, so if I need to give the order to fire, you will have a clear shot. Boo, Lone Eagle, you are best in the woods alone with your skills. You need not be seen as the evil ones approach. Maiden, you will stay in camp and care for our stock and all our truck. This is a big responsibility, so watch close. Soon, we will take Boris out to the trail, tie him to a tree, then Boo can go into the woods to make ready for our visitors. I will find a place to wait close by to where we tie him. Near enough to speak with the outlaws once they stop but hid enough to not be seen. Listen close now, both of you. We will give the gang a chance to leave Viktor and go. Don't shoot any until we don't have a choice, or if they move to fire on us. Do you hear, Sky Watcher? No shooting until we have to. You will know by listening to me, if or when, that time comes. I want to make it known to Viktor why we are here before his gang goes away and we capture him for hanging. Once I've made it clear and give him his options, we will defend ourselves by how they proceed. Sky Watcher, if it comes to killing, shoot any and all that you can, but spare Viktor for the noose. Do not miss, my sister. Our lives could be in your hands if a fight comes. This is how I believe it should be. Speak now if either of you can see a better way." He paused. We said nothing.

"One final thing," Henri brought to mind. "The ancestors want us to settle with the whole of the gang. I have thought on this. Not to be disrespectful of their needs, but our main purpose is to avenge the death of our friend and father, Gideon. That is our main concern. If the Great Spirit sees fit to end the others, then so it will be. We will leave it in His hands as to the fate of Viktor's followers. This is how I believe it should be. Now, let us prepare. They will come soon." After sayin' that he rose, leavin' us on the quick.

Henri had took a bold step commandin' that to us. One in which he included Great Spirit. I wondered fer that. The vision he'd had from the ancestors was to punish the whole lot of 'em. I was more than willing to make 'em all pay, as just Viktor, but mercy had its place. I did not know if I could honor that notion of Henri's to spare the heathens. I'd just have to see when the time come.

Me and Sky looked at each other without a word spoke. From there, we went to make ready. It was an effort movin' Boris from the poplar we'd tied him to durin' the night, to the oak we tied him to next to the trail. His right ankle was broke no doubt, his left might 'a been. Both so swollen he couldn't walk none. His mouth was hurt. Broke apart from me shovin' my gun barrel down his throat. He was havin' trouble breathin' from all the swelling inside his mouth.

Because of all that, we had to carry him from our camp, sittin' him on the ground at the base of a small white oak only a couple paces off the trail to the east. We tied him solid from there, puttin' a rag over his eyes and stuffin' one in his mouth. He weren't doin' too good. I'd hurt him more'n I'd thought gettin' out from the tavern. The rag in his mouth botherin' his breathin', but we didn't want him warnin' his brother. Viktor couldn't help but see him tied where he was once he got there.

Old Man Sun was just peakin' over the eastern ridges as we all headed our own way into the woods. We'd seen to Boris and now it was time to wait. Our aim bein' to hide, question, and assault. Miriam moved some thirty paces away, climbin' a white pine about twenty feet up. She would have a good aim at the outlaws when they come. The main trunk of the tree would be between her and where Boris was tied. That was smart of her. I lost a bit of worry when I saw that.

I found a place to watch from not too far away, kind 'a off to the side of where Boris was tied. It was a boulder tall enough for me to hide behind while waitin', listenin' for the evil to come. I would move on the outlaws as I saw fit from there, but I would needs be patient.

I got to wonderin', while I had time on my hands, about why Henri had called me Lone Eagle, twice. He'd called me by that name like I owned it. I heard him say it both times clear as a rooster crowin' at daylight. I didn't study on it then, but I got to thinkin' on it as I stood waitin'… what reason would he have to call me that? I couldn't figure the why of it all. It was true, as a warrior, I fought best alone when fightin' in the woods, that made sense to me. Still, most warriors did, unless it was a settled target they was after. I found the name most interesting.

The target we was after was not settled. We'd have to wait and watch to know our next move. It all depended on what the gang did when once they figured out they was caught. We'd tied Boris to the far side of a sharp curve in the trail from the direction the gang would be comin'. Viktor would be right up on top of his brother 'fore he ever realized he was there. That made the trap we was settin' most deadly to the outlaws.

I would needs worry over my new name later. My spirit had of a sudden commenced to warnin' me, and I know'd to pay heed. Something in my senses had picked up travelers. I prob'ly heard something I didn't realize I'd heard, maybe, but I know'd for sure, somebody was comin'. No question. I kept sensing. Trying to confirm if it was Viktor or not.

My spirit held true. Our wait was short. I strained to find it, but then it come to me on the breeze. A bunch was near on us. I figured it for Viktor and his gang. I'd caught the slightest sound of horses movin' quiet. That show'd caution from the ones travelin' toward us. I jumped from the ground to a squat on top of the boulder in one easy motion. My carbine tight in my hands. My eyes sharp like that of a hawk huntin' supper. I tilted my head back, scentin' for the slightest smell of horse. It was there. Time to warn my friends. I cupped my hands and made a soft dove call to Henri. He answered back. Then, without expectin' it, a soft dove call answered from the white pine. Surprised a bit that she had the knowledge, I called back to her. We was ready. That was good.

The horse scent got stronger on the breeze 'fore I ever heard more noise. They was movin' quiet to be as many as they was. Weren't long 'til I seen 'em. I counted six followin', and one lone figure out front by a couple horse lengths. Weren't no doubtin' who that would be. Our confrontin' Viktor Soltor was fixin' to commence. My blood got up. I checked my special knife for the third time. I had a feelin' it might be needed to save my life soon, if the fight got to be up close. It was ready. I was ready. I said a silent prayer as I felt fate comin' to call.

"Hold," I heard Viktor call to his men when first seein' his brother tied and gagged to a tree. He stayed his horse, lookin' close at Boris, 'fore liftin' his head to search out the woods around him, seein' nothin'. He dropped his head back down to look at his brother. He'd not see none of us 'til we was ready. He know'd that.

I wanted to shoot him from his saddle where he sat. Same as I'd done Billy what was helpin' Stuart take my home. I could put a .52 caliber bullet through the side of his head from where I was squatted 'a top the boulder, but we wanted to hang him legal-like fer justice's sake. Henri's voice boomed without warning after a couple minutes of Viktor just sittin' his horse, lookin' at Boris. He know'd we'd talk to him after a bit. He didn't needs talk 'til we did, but why hadn't he said something to his brother? He just sat there on his horse lookin' at him, not sayin' nothin'.

"I should shoot you where you sit, Viktor," Henri proclaimed, breakin' the silence. "You've been judged for murder by the daughter of the one you killed. The ancestors have found you guilty of the same. Their judgment is for justice. Like for like. Life for life. We've caught you, Viktor Soltor. Like a fly in a spider's web. Do you realize yet, how it is for you? You're surrounded. You can have your say, but we mean to hang you for murder, slave tradin', and a whole host of other law breaking acts, or shoot you, it matters not to us. Depends on you. Our friend, Gideon, the one you killed, deserves you get your just reward for his murder. Your bunch is guilty, too. Decide for them when you decide for yourself. What will it be, murderer? Rope or lead?"

On the sly, I saw two of Viktor's men back their horses up real slow and dismount a few yards back of where they'd first stopped. Henri couldn't see 'em way in the back from where he'd found to wait. They figured to get away clean, circle in behind where Henri was hidin', capture or kill him, and they'd be flanking in about a minute. I moved in a crouch to cover his nearest blind side. I went quick, like a life depended on it. I figured it did.

I know'd for sure them rogues was movin' on Henri, but they didn't know how many of us they was. They'd have to pay mind movin' through the woods. Take their time, makin' sure they didn't get their killin' from somebody they didn't know was there. I know'd exactly how many 'a them they was. I just had the two I had to look out for, and unfortunate for them, I know'd where they was goin'. I liked my chances. My only worry was movin' quiet enough to get to them 'fore they got to Henri. They'd never see me unless they heard me. I'd remove their threat 'fore they ever got near Henri, as long as they didn't hear me. I just had to find 'em.

"You are not true," Viktor finally answered. "Why do you hide like coward you are? You name me murderer. How so you call me? I kill no one. You know that but lie. I am not kind for killing. Tell me this, hiding one. Who is Gideon I am killed, huh? I must know name to make defend for my life from such as you."

I happened upon the first of Viktor's men. He was close 'fore I ever seen him. He was workin' his way in behind Henri. Easin' along best he could, watchin'. I took notice that his mind was only on Henri. That was a mistake. A true warrior would never make that mistake. He weren't slippin' quick looks to no place else fer caution. Eyes straight ahead to Henri meant he was missin' danger like me slippin' up on him. His nose weren't even workin' the breeze. He sensed nothin' about me bein' near in the woods. I caught him full unaware, as I eased the blade of my long knife under his chin from behind, puttin' the palm of my left hand to the center of his back. He froze when he felt that. I couldn't blame him. I backed him up by pullin' on the blade at this throat. I did that hard enough to bring blood fer meanness. I felt him flinch from the sting. That was good, fer I wanted him to know I was serious. My words was spoke in his right ear, after I'd stopped backin' him up. He did not like me doin' that.

"You run with a murderer, coward," I whispered, real quiet like. My knife still at his throat as I slipped out from behind him to his front. The point of my knife now pressin' on the meat near his jugular. I stared him in the eye. "He's a killer of women and kids, as I hear it. Him and his bunch are a judged lot. I figure you done your part as well, hey, since you are of his bunch. Same for the rest of you travelin' with him too, huh? Now tell me straight, that true? What I hear. Y'all abuse women, kids? Huh?" I mashed the edge of my knife into his throat a little harder, backin' him up ag'n a huge poplar tree. The point of my long knife still at his throat. He could go no farther back. He was cornered. A solid line of blood leakin' down his neck from the slice I'd give him while backin' him up earlier. Another flowin' from under the point of my knife.

"I can see the fear in your eyes, strange one," I kept on. "Fear tells on a body. You done your part, didn't ye, killin' my friend? Had your way with them women and girls I heard about too, I bet. You should fess up, fool. You could be meetin' your maker soon. Chances are good, considerin'. Tell ol' Boo, hear? Y'all did all that evil to them innocents didn't ye? Nod yes if it's true. I don't wanna hear your evil voice so I ain't removin' my knife, but if you shake your head yes, you can consider yourself admittin' before God for forgiveness. I'll be sure to pass it on fer ye to make sure He knows. You know, confessin' before the Good Lord like that could make me consider savin' your sorry hide. They say the judge in Atlanta is fair about givin' guilty folk time to serve in prison instead 'a hangin'. You confess and you might make it out in a few years with your life. What say ye, outlaw? You gonna make it right 'fore God while you still can? Do some time then live some more? Future's up to you." I said, while smilin' at him.

It was my experience through life that outlaws and trail bandits was not the smartest folks I would ever deal with. Some, like Viktor, were thinkers of a sort, but even then their evil ways made 'em stupid. This 'un shook his head, meanin' yes to all I'd ask him. I couldn't believe it. He had no mind fer concern, tellin' me for sure him and his had done them evil things I'd told him I know'd about. That was just a stupid thing fer him to 'a done. I had no call to lay justice to him without knowin' positive he'd done such, but when he shook his head yes, I know'd for sure he was guilty.

My look changed. He seen it change. He know'd he'd been judged. His face sunk as I slowly began pushin' the blade of my long knife deeper into his throat. He reached with both hands to try and stop me. That was a useless effort, only gettin' his fingers sliced. He tried screamin', but that weren't gonna happen, neither. My long knife had sliced his voice works clean in two 'fore he ever felt it. His life on Mother Earth was ending. I watched his eyes to know when his thinkin' figured it all out. That death had come to call. I had to hold him against the poplar with my left palm, as blood started shootin' out from his throat coverin' the handle of my long knife, my right hand, and up my arm a ways stoppin' shy of my shoulder. It was warm and thick. I could smell it. The flow stopped as death made the man's heart quit beatin'. The first of the bunch was settled with. Number two, I'd suddenly realized, weren't far away.

It was faint, but I heard him slippin' up behind me as his partner's eyes dulled in death. Near so quiet I didn't hear him, but I did. I turned quick as a rattle maker strikin', spottin' his head first thing, of all things, not ten paces away. His right hand looked full of a U.S. issued Colt revolver, the barrel raisin' to shoot me as he cocked it.

Slingin' my arm, blood and all, toward where he was crouched, I loosed my long knife as he kept raisin' his short gun. It was all slow movin' to me. *Was my knife gonna make the shooter 'fore he pulled the trigger on me? Which of us was to strike first? Which of us was to die?*

Fortunately for me, the long knife won by a short second. The point of my blade hit him solid right between the eyes, sinkin' to the hilt from how hard I throw'd it. He never got the gun level fer shootin' 'fore Old Man Death found him. Why did I aim at his head? It was the first thing I seen when I spun around to face him, so that was what got aimed at. I hit it too, hard. He fell backwards with a solid thump.

No sooner had Viktor's men heard that landin' thump than they swung their horses in that direction while bringin' their carbines up level to fire a volley toward where the noise come from. One ball spinnin' way too close to me fer comfort. No other noise was heard. The outlaws stood their ground lookin' for targets. Their carbines readied for another volley. Only then, did they all see their back two men was gone. I was raisin' my Spencer to end at least one more, when Henri's voice boomed again. Not sure how he know'd, but he know'd. I figured Sky maybe signaled him.

"You've lost two already, Viktor. Lone Eagle has met them in battle just now. They walk with the ancestors, as will you, if you don't surrender your weapons and turn yourself over to us. You other four, leave now or settle for meetin' your maker as well. You won't get another round off at us. You got ten seconds to decide, Viktor, then we're gonna clean them saddles of your sorry hides fer shootin' at us. Make your minds, evil ones. The last few seconds of your pitiful lives is now being spent. Don't waste it. Ten, nine, eight . . ."

I leveled my carbine at the back one nearest me. I figured Sky fer the one beside him and Henri for one in the front. I figured he'd shoot the one to the left so I could shoot the one on the right with my second round. I felt comfortable in that thinkin'. Time would tell.

"Hold on, A-mar-e-kans! Hold fire for us. We will talk. Let us sit for time. Talk of settlement. I am innocent of this crime. My men, they are like me, innocent. Look what you have did to bruw-ther. Why you did this?" he asked, near soundin' like he was crying.

Suddenly, without warning, he raised his head toward where Henri had been talkin. Standin' his saddle, he pointed right where Henri had chose to wait. "Now men! Fire! Kill!" he commanded, as he sat back in his saddle. His arms braced against his saddle horn. Four guns fired all at once, straight to where Viktor was pointin'. Henri wouldn't be there. He was smart enough to move after speakin' them first words. His words come quick, and we had to react quick, as the sound from the outlaws guns died down. It was unexpected at first, but me and Sky know'd to be listenin'. Time to strike back had come.

"Five, four, three, two, one... boom... boom, boom... boom... boom." Henri had warned 'em, but none heeded it. I know'd they wouldn't. All of us know'd they wouldn't.

We was there to serve justice for a murder the law would never hear of, never look into, and never care about, so that's just what we'd done. These would never again hurt folks. All the gang Viktor had with him, when he come to rescue his brother, was layin' dead in the woods around him, but he never moved from his horse. Just sat back in his saddle where he'd stopped original to stand and call the kill order to his men. Weren't 'til all the smoke had settled that we seen him, for sure, still sittin' there tall on his horse. I commenced to drawin' a bead on the side of his head again, wonderin' at his doin's, then I seen it. Blood spurtin' out from his front, landin' on the saddle horn, the base of the horse's neck and mane, his hands, what was crossed over the saddle horn holdin' on. The leak had to be jumpin' from a hole near big around as a grow'd man's fist, judgin' from the amount that was leavin' him every heartbeat, but he just sat there, dyin'.

I know'd a hole that big was most likely made by a lead ball or bullet leavin' a person's body all of a sudden like. It come to me what'd happend soon as I seen that blood leavin' him toward the front. I was lookin' at a shot man. I know'd them kind when I seen 'em. I'd seen a few when the war come close to our home.

Him bein' shot was bad. That meant somebody close enough to shoot him had not been able to wait for proper justice. I was kind 'a glad they didn't wait, but it was bad they hadn't, worse. The only one I know'd, that was south of where we was, that had a cause in this fight, was Miriam. But, there could 'a been a follower from the tavern what come on behind 'em lookin' fer justice, too, so, would we ever know? I studied on that as Viktor finally fell from his horse with a sick thudding splatter. Dead 'fore he hit the ground, of course. Dead, really, while still sittin' the saddle, starin' at his brother. We come from hidin' when once we seen weren't none of 'em movin'.

Boris was the only one left that we thought alive, and he weren't like we'd left him. We hadn't know'd it when conversin' with Viktor, but Boris had passed while waitin' for his rescue. I know'd after we found him dead, that's why Viktor had just kind 'a stood his ground where he stopped. Lookin', castin' eyes about, then askin' why we did what he was lookin' at to his brother. His strange doin's made sense once I know'd what he was lookin' at. A dead brother, not a hurt one, while sittin' his horse there in the trail. That'd give anybody a shock.

Justice for our friend, father, and trader man, Gideon, had been swift, sure, and final, once the outlaws got caught in our trap. Springin' it was easy, just a simple shootin' in defense, if one could tolerate it. Seemed fightin' and killin' was a chore I was becoming most familiar with in this new South. The new South I was bein' forced to survive in. Having to fight against some of the worst a body could pray to keep away.

The South had become a most dangerous place for its native peoples, whatever their breed. I longed for my old way of living. I wanted no more than to be at peace the way it was before the war and killin' come. Before the horde of business and outlaw folk come bringin' their dreams of livin' high off the hog by takin' what the whooped Southern folk had. Most without payin'. Leavin' precious little for the native mountain folk to survive on. I'd not have it fer my friends and folks. Fight fer 'em I would. Fight fer 'em I did.

The Legend of Swell Branch

CHAPTER 30

Home to Long Shot

Comin' home to Long Shot after all we'd been through the last few moons was a welcome relief. Just as Henri had promised, our stores had been seen to. Grow'd, raised, harvested, and stored just as he said they'd be. I praised Holy Spirit for it. Still, even with all that done, they was left the usual chores of a farm. Most hadn't been tended to what had no part in the growin' season. The woodshed was near empty. We'd need a store of firewood and kindlin' 'fore the cold time come on us. That would keep me busy for a time. The vegetables from the house garden had been harvested, but the Cherokee women didn't know what to do with 'em, so they left 'em piled in the front part 'a the barn fer us. We'd need to get 'em packed into the dugout pit we'd made for our store 'fore they took to turnin'. We'd put it right in the center of our woodshed. That was the driest ground we could think of. The shed was built so air would flow over and around our wood, keepin' it dry fer burnin'. That airflow kept our vegetables from turnin' as well.

Corn had to be hauled to the mill in Swell Branch to be ground. Providin' meal for both us and the stock. Fer some reason, we had more chickens than we'd had late spring at the time of our leavin'. Not sure how that happened. The Indians never told us. Had to come from them, though, I figured. They know'd them what tried to take our farm had eat most of our layin' hens. It was good we'd got them chickens, too, there was another mouth to feed. The little maiden I'd rescued took to Miriam like a chick follown' the mother hen. I'd never seen such. It was almost like they know'd each other. Close in spirit, if truth be told.

We'd been back near a moon when Mary give us her news… her bad news. She'd made her mind to go live in Atlanta fer good, leavin' the mountains as her principal home. She was gonna stay with Aunt Catherine. Work in the hospital as a nurse. Learn to be a doctor. Seems there might 'a been another reason what spurred her on as well. She'd met a suitor while staying with Aunt Catherine the season before. A suitor she'd not told us about, or at least she hadn't told me about. Sky prob'ly know'd. Women tell each other them sort 'a things when they won't tell their men. I'd learned that for sure. She was gone within the week.

Her future husband to be was a storekeep by trade, but not the common type 'a storekeep. No, his store was big. I don't mean any ol' big. His was big, big. Had three full floors with stairs you could walk up on the inside of the building. Took a fast runner ten seconds to go from end to end on the outside. Boys would race down the length of it while folks would congregate and bet on 'em. They'd time the boys when the bets was fallin', to be sure which of the runners won. Took near ten seconds for the fastest ones to run from the back end of the store to the front end, fast as they could go. They'd hold the races rain or shine. The boys, and some girls, would race. The crowd what gathered to watch placed their bets tryin' to win a little bit of money, then if they won, most often they'd go into the store and spend it. I promise you they did. I even seen church deacons at it with all the rest. It come to be a big doin's every fourth Saturday of each month, that the weather was fit. They'd start about nine o'clock morning time. Food and spirits and other forms of gambling was spread about the grounds. It was a big happening during its time. Draw'd a lot 'a folks. I went to it some, when I went to visit Mary. Won money racin' folks my age and size. The younger, smaller guys beat me most every time. I got to where I'd not wager them.

They weren't nothin' you could hardly imagine needin', that Mary's beau didn't have in that store. He called it a General Store. Said it worked best by carryin' a little bit of everything folks might need. Me and him got along after a time, even though he was from the North. Like I said, a lot of 'em what migrated south after the war was good folk. I respected their efforts, what with leavin' a home most had lived in all their lives. Packin' up to move their families, their businesses, their ways, their hopes, to a land they know'd little about, to search out a means to better their lives. I couldn't blame 'em for wantin' to do better. Couldn't blame 'em fer movin' south. I just wish the bad ones would 'a stayed north of the line. I never cared for outlaws what preyed on innocents. Be they from the North or from the South. I met both in my put together.

With Mary leavin' for Atlanta, it would 'a been improper for Miriam and me to live in the same house without weddin'. Our problem was, we weren't ready for marryin' just yet… desired it heavily, but weren't quite ready for the full call of it between us. Fortunately, it all worked out. The Cherokee maiden had no place to call home after gettin' her freedom. I figured she would 'a, but if there was a home out there for her, she couldn't remember it. She couldn't remember her name, neither. That was strange. Made me wonder why.

Bein' that her and Miriam had become close, and with Mary's decision to leave, I asked her to come live with us at Long Shot. It was a few days after we got settled back in. She accepted, wantin' to stay with us for a time to sort things out in her life. Maybe her memory would come back. We hoped it would. I felt she was sincere. I explained she'd have to work and hold up her end of our survival efforts for her keep, same as the rest of us. She agreed, and she did. I never had a problem with her in all the years she stayed with us. She worked same as me and Miriam. She was a handy addition to our lives, to my life. I thanked Great Spirit for her. Grow'd to love her like a daughter, and since she had no name that she could remember, Sky gave her one, two actually, after a time. She brought it to mind a few days after we got back, as she and I hunted wild ginseng on the north side of Long Shot late one evening.

"It's difficult that our new friend has no name to call her by, Boo. I've been considering this. I believe, after some prayer and searching, I have the name that fits her spirit and a Christian name that we can all know her by. I will tell you tonight as we sit the porch after supper, while we rock. It is a name you will like. It is a name she will be proud of. Buach, I grow to love her, even like a daughter. Is this a bad thing? What if she is not who we are coming to think she is? That she hides her intentions inside her spirit? I have seen nothing to make me believe she is any other than we have come to know, but I am leery. I feel she is one who speaks truth, but these are strange times and my sense of trust is most guarded. Is this bad, Boo?"

"No, Miriam, no. I too, see it as you, nor will I make my mind for sure until after a time of being with her. She is a stranger to us still, so it would be wise to not give her full confidence until we are sure of our concerns. I am coming to be close to her as well. I'm starting to feel that she belongs here, almost as one we claim as family, but I aim to hold caution. I have seen too many during these times that are wolves hiding in sheep's clothing. She seems most innocent, yes, and my spirit seems to say we can trust her, yes, but my mind says we will know in time. That is how I see it."

We spoke no more about her name 'til after supper. I had a few chores to finish 'fore we eat. I seen to 'em, then stopped by the well to wash up 'fore goin' on in fer supper. Miriam was there, preparin' our meal… the maiden helping. That'd been the way for the whole time she'd been with us. She was a good hand. I believed all would be well.

It was nice to sit down to meals again. I'd seen a change in Miriam since we got back. She no longer seemed to be carryin' a burden for her father. His soul was across the river with the rest of our ancestors. Henri had sensed it. That was a blessing to Miriam, a relief of sorts. I felt she held guilt, to some measure, over shootin' Viktor like she had, or may have. Oh, she'd not admitted it, and we'd not asked her, but we all know'd she most likely did it. If she did, it would be her secret to live with. Me and Henri weren't gonna pester her over it. We left her be. Justice had been served, wilderness fashion. That give us resolve.

Supper had been all vegetables and no meat of any kind. I didn't like not havin' meat with my evening meal, but on occasion it was okay. We had a bait of fresh vegetables. It was that time of year. My favorite time 'a year for eatin.' Miriam, with the maiden's help, had laid a fine spread includin' sweet cake for afterwards. I was home and livin' my new life without my father, my brothers, or my sister. I missed 'em, for sure, but I was likin' the new way as I grow'd more familiar with it.

Miriam would be my missus 'fore long. She would run our home by her standards. I would learn to love her standards no matter. She wanted children. I wanted children. Ones we'd make after our time of becoming one had passed. I was near to being ready for that time. I would ask her soon.

The sweet, dried Indian tobacco we shared after supper was some of the best I'd ever had. We'd brought it back from Blue Dove's. She'd give us a good-sized poke. Her guard, Big Nose, had cured it. It was clear he had a fine hand. He rolled cigars, too. Give us a few 'fore we left, like we was kind 'a friends, so it surprised us greatly when Henri's trouble with him come a time later. Big Nose didn't like Henri, 'cause Blue Dove liked Henri. Jealousy can be a dangerous thing, for sure when held by those who are dangerous.

"So, Miriam. We are sittin', rockin', enjoyin' some good burley. Will you now tell me what it is we can commence to callin' our new young friend here?" I asked, while winking at the maiden. She smiled.

She sat a rocker with us as we finished our pipes. She hadn't learned the spiritual side of sharing tobacco with those close to you, nor had she learned to use tobacco in her prayers. I would teach her these things and much more. So would Henri, but slowly, so she'd not get frustrated.

"I will, yes, Boo, but first, I must tell you why. Young one, when you first met us you were scared for your life. Living in filth. You had been treated poorly. Abused by those looking to profit from your suffering, instead of caring for you proper. Boo set you free. Gave you this new life. You have shown much courage in your will to become one who should be here. The Great Spirit shines on you. You walk in His favor, or you would still be in that evil place. The Holy One is your watcher… Buach, His tool. I believe you're chosen. So, knowing these things, and learning how you think from our talks, I believe your Indian name should be "Fawn Runs Free." I believe your Christian name should be "Hope," for you now have true hope. This is how I see it, because that is how I see you. A young one set free who runs with the wind. A creature of the forest. What say ye, either of you. How do your spirits speak?"

"I love it, Sky Watcher," the maiden responded quick, jumpin' up to hug her neck hard. Tears flowin' from her eyes. "I thank you for it. It honors your man's courage in freeing me and it fits me perfect, just as you say. I am Fawn Runs Free. I did run to find you for Buach. I do have hope, since meeting all of you. The name fits who I am. I will honor it with my life. Thank you so much. I really love it." She bowed her head to wipe her eyes.

I smiled and nodded to Hope as she looked back up at me. Not really worryin' about likin' her new name or not, fer it didn't matter to me. Even I know'd when two women agree on a fact, they ain't no man gonna change it. Didn't matter if it was fact or not, to them, it be fact. Best left alone. I know'd just to agree and go on as Fawn left us to go inside. She was touched by her new name, but I'd not let 'em know 'til later that I liked it. Miriam had thought it through. The names did fit perfect.

I figured she'd gone up to the loft to have some alone time. She and Miriam had took to sleepin' up there while I stayed in my father's old room. That was hard for the first few nights, but I'd got used to it. I missed him something awful, always would, but I'd moved on, painful as it was. My life had changed since his death. I would never be the same. Mine and Mary's home on Long Shot his final gift to us.

To say my life had changed, was to say all our lives had changed. Henri had found his callin' with the tribe, as he needed to. Blue Dove had helped with that. Miriam had found herself a home… fortunately or unfortunately, it come with a man. Me bein' that man. She settled for me. Fawn had found a life, a home, and prob'ly a family, if she wanted, for as long as she wanted, if she cared enough to do her part to be a member of our family. I'd found myself almost suddenly the master of a decent sized farm that provided all we'd need, as long as we'd need, given we kept the ability to work it, store our wares. We'd provide for others as we went. Them what couldn't fend for themselves like they was used to. We paid mind to those concerns in the mountains where I lived.

I thought different on how I should lead my life, after coming to understand my life mattered to folks around me now that Dad was gone. The things I did, the decisions I made, affected those concerned, dependin' on what those decisions was over. My future wife, my sister, my friends, my new live in kind 'a daughter person, all depended on the decisions I made for our lives to exist on Long Shot. That was a demanding responsibility for one of my raisin'. A responsibility I never took lightly.

My life with Miriam, our life together, was out in front of us for the coming future. No telling what that future might hold once we joined as one. I would needs continue takin' care to watch for the evil that was comin' south from those with takin' and killin' kind 'a minds. I figured havin' to contend with the bad ones from the North was gonna be a constant problem, at least for several seasons. I would take those things as they come, and they would come often, as trouble was bustin' out in the mountains of Southern Appalachia. The Cherokee runner that'd just breeched the edge of the woods surrounding our farm, who was running for all he was worth, most likely held a message of need I'd feel responsible to oblige. I'd volunteer Henri as well, most likely.

I didn't know what the message was, be it good, bad, or other, but I know'd it would likely call up some duty I'd feel the need to face. Be it fer me or others. That was a life I'd come to accept - the life of a warrior who watches over his own. It was a life I come to suspect I was born for, after livin' it for a time, but, was it a life Miriam Sky Watcher could live with? That was a question only time would answer. It seemed she was aware, and felt a need to see for herself, so we would find out. I know'd my call. She'd seen clear how my life would be 'til the evil what'd come to the South went away or was confronted. I felt she understood what I offered from the things she'd told me earlier. I had faith in her words.

I rose from my rocker, beatin' the ash from my pipe on the locust post what held up the porch roof. Watched as it slowly fell to the ground like black snow floatin'. The runner come through the front gate hardly slowin'. He wore only his breechcloth and footskins. He was covered in sweat with trail dirt mixed in, streaks runnin' down his body. No weapons of any sort. He'd stripped himself like he had to make time. Travelin' light to make time was a bad sign.

I recognized him when he draw'd close to our front porch. He was son to a Cherokee warrior I'd called friend for years. Knowin' he'd sent his son to fetch me was another bad sign. That told me the word prob'ly weren't good. No warrior would send for folks in such a hurry if they weren't needs to be seen about.

A quick look to Miriam, as I descended the porch steps to meet the runner, told her my thoughts, and me hers. She could see my look held concern. She could see I'd becomed troubled. It was a look I figured she'd needs get used to as my wife. I'd made it clear to those who'd listen, I'd not run from my calling. She'd heard me, fer she cared enough to listen. Folks in the backwoods needed help, and me and Henri and a few like us was about all they was around Swell Branch they could depend on. Maybe Uncle Silas some, now and again. It's just the way our world had worked out since the war ended. That concerned her.

I saw the feisty little grin what stretched the corners of her mouth as her eyes locked on mine. It seemed she was showing a bit of excitement at the prospect of us bein' called to a new trail, whatever that may hold. An adventure, if you will. A time to be together. I liked her bein' of that nature. Common to mine. I understood the excitement of the unexpected and unknown she was feeling. What a treasure she was becoming. I hoped she felt the same about me. The voice from my spirit made me believe that all would be right and proper, when once we resolved ourselves to become one. I'd learned through experience to listen close to that voice, then be patient. I would do accordingly with us.

I paused my mind to silently thank the Great Creator for the gift of Miriam Sky Watcher, again. As I thought of our coming life together, our future family, I come to realize my home on Long Shot would never be the same... and that would be a good thing... 'cept fer Mary not bein' there . . . I was gonna miss her.

The End... for a time...

Made in the USA
Columbia, SC
01 November 2021